Luca Veste is a writer of Italian and Scouse heritage, married with two young daughters. He studied psychology and criminology at university in Liverpool, and he is the author of seven novels: *Dead Gone*, *The Dying Place*, *Bloodstream* and *Then She Was Gone* are all part of the Murphy and Rossi series. His other novels, *The Bone Keeper*, *The Six* and *The Game*, are standalones. He is also the co-creator of the acclaimed podcast Two Crime Writers and a Microphone, which he records with fellow crime author Steve Cavanagh.

Find out more at www.LucaVeste.com or follow @LucaVeste on Twitter and Facebook.

THE
GAME

LUCA VESTE

SIMON &
SCHUSTER

London · New York · Sydney · Toronto · New Delhi

First published in Great Britain by Simon & Schuster UK Ltd, 2020

Copyright © Luca Veste 2020

The right of Luca Veste to be identified as author
of this work has been asserted in accordance with
the Copyright, Designs and Patents Act, 1988.

1 3 5 7 9 10 8 6 4 2

Simon & Schuster UK Ltd
1st Floor
222 Gray's Inn Road
London WC1X 8HB

Simon & Schuster Australia, Sydney
Simon & Schuster India, New Delhi

www.simonandschuster.co.uk
www.simonandschuster.com.au
www.simonandschuster.co.in

A CIP catalogue record for this book
is available from the British Library

Paperback ISBN: 978-1-4711-6818-5
eBook ISBN: 978-1-4711-6817-8

Typeset in Sabon by M Rules

Printed and bound by CPI Group (UK) Ltd, Croydon, CR0 4YY

MIX
Paper from
responsible sources
FSC® C020471

*For my fellow Fun Lovin' Crime Writers –
Mark, Chris, Doug, Val and Stuart. Can't wait
to get back on stage with you all – as long as
it's big enough for me to fit on.*

NOW

One

The First Interview

Tuesday 30th October
Interview Room One
Lancaster Police Station – sixty miles from Liverpool City Centre

He settled in the plastic chair, feeling an itch grow under the cuff of the prison-issue jumper on his wrist. He could sense the fabric against his skin, its coarseness grating against the indentations left by the handcuffs which had been removed a few hours earlier. They'd taken his clothes as soon as they'd reached the station. Bagging them up carefully, as if they might bite.

'This interview is being recorded both visually and audibly. Investigating officers are Detective Inspector Patrick Hicks and Detective Sergeant Victoria Lee.'

He didn't look up at them, staring at the marks and stains on the table in front of him. Making patterns in the random smears.

He knew he looked uninterested to the cameras pointed

in his direction. As if he did this every day, a normal occurrence in his life.

Inside, his heart was beating hard against his chest. Outside, he remained cool. Aloof. Calm.

They asked for his name again. They had been doing that regularly since he'd arrived. He'd shaken his head and declined to answer. That way, they would spend more time trying to work that out than questioning anything else. And without a name, they wouldn't get very far.

All part of the plan. What there was of it, anyway.

He wasn't going to give them anything easily. He was there for one reason and one reason only.

When they'd offered a solicitor, he'd shrugged his shoulders. They'd taken that as an acceptance. The solicitor was now sitting close to him, tensing up with every word he said that wasn't 'no comment', a folder full of notes balanced on his knees. A weedy little thing, who looked like a strong wind would blow him over. He wouldn't be required.

He was ready to tell them what he wanted them to know.

'You have been arrested on suspicion of the murder . . .' the DI said to him, the words coming through a fog of coffee-scented breath that made him wrinkle his nose in disgust. The guy kept talking, but he wasn't listening anymore. Simply waiting for his turn to talk.

'I did it. I killed them all.'

A shared look between the detectives. A shuffle of papers and a throat-clearing from the solicitor. Trying to get his attention. Stop him talking. Do as he had been told. Say the things that would give him a chance of a defence when they got to court.

There was no chance of that happening.

'All?'

'I'm the one.'

'You're the one what?' DI Hicks said, a crease forming across his forehead, as his eyes scanned his notes and then shot back to him.

'I'm the man you've been looking for. Eight people dead. I killed them all.'

He could feel the atmosphere between them shift a little, as the detectives slowly began to understand what he'd said.

'You're saying you've killed eight people?'

'Yes.'

'Who are the eight people?'

'What do you need to hear?' he said, wondering how his voice would sound on the recording. Whether it would resonate with someone listening back later. Whether they would read into what he was saying and make assumptions. Psychoanalyse him in sensationalised documentaries. They would call him evil. A psychopath. Wicked and immoral. Mad or bad. As if those two words were interchangeable.

That wasn't the truth. He was just like everyone else in that room.

He was just human.

'Why don't you tell us about the woman you were found with,' DI Hicks said finally, locking eyes with him. He knew it was an attempt to regain control, but it would fail. He'd had them on the back foot from the start. That had been the plan. The game. 'The young woman. What was her name?'

'She's not important right now. If I'm going to tell you everything, I need to start at the beginning.'

'And when was that?'

He saw the names of the victims as if they were folders

in a filing cabinet. Each one filled with facts and figures. 'Steven Hallet,' he repeated, thinking of the young man who had been killed first. He closed his eyes, remembering the facts. 'Twenty-two years old. I killed him at a service station on the M6 in the middle of the night, not far from here actually. I made him play. He was doing ... bad things. I killed him because he lost. He was my first.'

There was another shared look between the detectives. He glanced at the solicitor, who was furiously making notes, his handwriting becoming more scrawled the further down the page it went. His hand was shaking every time the pen left the page.

'You're saying you killed Steven Hallet?'

It took a few moments, but he could see the pair starting to regain their composure. Making quick decisions without even talking to each other. He knew this could have been a tricky part. That they might have ended the interview there and then and gone outside to regroup. Perhaps pull in other detectives who knew the case better. Instead, they'd obviously decided while he was talking that it was best not to stop him.

That was the first hurdle cleared.

He knew there were bigger hurdles than this one. That they would need to try to explain his very existence. He wasn't there for that. He hoped it wouldn't happen.

'You assert you killed Steven Hallet and ... what was it ... seven further victims?'

'Well, yes. Eight is the right number. All told.'

'And the girl you were found with was number eight?'

He thought for a second, then nodded. 'Yes, but I need to talk about Steven first.'

'We'll get to that.'

He watched DI Hicks clench his jaw, saw the thoughts running through his mind. His need, his *desire,* to reach across the table and lay his hands on him. The anger danced across the detective's eyes for a moment, before he remembered his place.

'The woman you were found with ... what was her name?' More aggressive in tone now.

He wanted to lie on the table. Close his eyes and sleep, but he knew it would be a long time until he would be able to rest. Perhaps he never would again, now he was unburdening himself. The solicitor beside him had gone still, seemingly wanting to hear the rest of the story himself. When he'd met him earlier, he had been advised to say nothing. To answer 'no comment' to all of their questions, while they came up with a statement for the situation which would be put before him. He hadn't engaged the lawyer in much conversation.

He'd been too busy preparing.

Remembering.

'I'll tell you what you need to know, in the order I want to tell you, or I don't say another word. I know you want to keep control of this *interview,* but that's not how this will go. Understand?'

He would have enjoyed the look of wounded pride that flashed across Hicks's face in any other environment, but for now, he could only try to keep the little food he'd eaten that morning from making a reappearance. No room for error. No room to show nerves.

Another moment passed and then Hicks asked him to continue at his own pace.

'I killed Stacey Green after Steven Hallet. Found her a different way. She was trying to be found, I think. This time I didn't make the same mistakes I did with Steven. It was *cleaner*. I did it differently, but you know the story, or you'll find out soon enough. In fact, you'll know how I killed all eight of them if you look properly. That's if you want to know. I can tell you about them all. How they failed. After Stacey, there was Andrew Hill. Then, Melissa Carmichael . . .'

'We want to hear about all of them, but first, we do need to talk about the woman you were found with,' DS Victoria Lee said, the younger of the pair speaking for the first time since the recording had begun. 'We want to hear your story.'

'There is no story,' he replied, leaning back in the plastic chair, wondering if the detectives had ever sat opposite a serial killer before. Whether they would be able to tell a difference between him or anyone else. 'Just a list of names. People who have lost. You know, it's amazing what people will believe when they have nothing else. If your life is empty, you're easy to . . . manipulate.'

A frown, a pause. A look of incredulity from the detective who had probably never interviewed someone like him. It passed quickly.

'Okay, let's move forward a little. You were found in the early hours of today, in a lock-up garage. Can you tell us what you were doing there?'

He almost laughed. Almost. It was ridiculous. The entire line of questioning. He hadn't expected it to be like this. Not at all. They kept returning to safe ground. They couldn't handle what he was telling them. He'd just told them he'd killed eight people, yet they seemed to want to ignore that and keep going back to who he had been found with. Safer, more pertinent, he guessed.

He would have done it differently if someone like him was sitting there. Waiting. He would ask better questions. Maybe that's why he wasn't sitting where DI Hicks was. Or DS Lee. Maybe that's why he was sitting on the other side of the table instead. Just because he'd been brought there.

Chosen to be.

'You found me next to a dead body. Why do you think I was there?'

'Who was she?'

'I suppose it doesn't matter all that much, now I think about it. She was just another player.'

'And what happened to her?'

He scratched at his left wrist finally, ignoring the bite of pain which responded to his touch. Glanced up at the camera once again.

'Why don't you tell us,' DI Hicks said, unable to keep the irritation out of his tone, 'what happened to her?'

He almost laughed at the utter absurdity of it all. There was only one answer he could give them. He cleared his throat and looked DI Hicks in the eye for the first time. 'It's simple. She played The Game and lost.'

BEFORE

Two

Status: Live
Likes: Eighteen
POST TITLE – NEW GAME

These are the new players.
Remember the names.
Let's watch them play.
If you have any ideas for levels,
please post them below.
This is going to be *fun*!
REMEMBER THE RULES
Only two players at one time.
They are never referred to by name – they
are always Player One and Player Two.
No one talks about this place.
No one talks about what we decide here.
The Game is all that matters.

PLAYER ONE

She wasn't the first.

The voice on the phone had told her so.

The way it had said her name. *Joanna.*

At first, she had wanted to ignore it. Pretend it wasn't happening. That she hadn't been found out.

How did they find out?

One more level.

That's all she had to complete. Then it would be all over. She could get back to her life and try to make it somewhat normal.

No one would know what she had done.

No one would know what she'd had to do to hide it. Protect herself.

'I didn't mean to do it,' she had pleaded to the voice on her phone, the first time they had called. 'I wasn't thinking, I'm sorry.'

She had to carry out tasks. Like levels in a video game, the voice had explained. She had to complete a level, then she would move on to the next. She couldn't skip past, she had to keep going until she reached the end.

Once it was completed, this would all be over. That was the promise. She could go back to her normal life, with no further contact. Everything would be erased and she could forget about it all.

If she didn't play, then she would be exposed. It was as simple as that.

She had felt a lump grow at the back of her throat as she'd begged.

She hadn't wanted to hurt anyone. This was the wake-up

call she'd needed. Now, she could do as she was told and not look back.

She was on Level Five. Level One had been easy. Level Three had been difficult, but Level Five seemed easy enough. Just weird. Remembering a specific pattern of numbers, movements.

She was standing outside the lift, her back against the wall that bordered the small room where she had lived for over a year now. Waiting. Excitement building as she thought about the finality of it.

The final level.

'You play to the end and it's all over. They'll never know what you've done,' the voice had said, then the line was dead. Joanna looked at her phone now, for the last time, then chucked it through the open door onto her bed, and closed the door.

She entered the lift. A grimace played across her lips, as she imagined someone watching this all back. Up in the corner of the lift, a familiar black globe looked down on her, recording her every moment. The bottle of cheap white wine she'd drunk to quieten her nerves swished and swirled around her stomach. She leaned over and whispered numbers to herself, pressing buttons on the control pad. As the lift ascended, her tummy lurched, as if she were in a car going over a hill at speed. She blinked and steadied herself with one hand once the lift stopped, then spoke the numbers louder. The second time, her body was ready and the nausea wasn't as bad.

Ten minutes later, she was walking down the corridor. Her head was still spinning a little from the ride up and down the building, the sound of her shoes on the hard floor echoing around her.

So close to finishing now.

No second thoughts.

There was no other way. They knew everything.

She had to play and that was it.

As the lift ascended and descended, as she stepped in and out, struggling to remember each step properly, she didn't yet sense the shift of weight around her.

Didn't sense anyone watching.

As she stepped out for the final time, she didn't notice anything other than ...

A noise made her pause.

A shift of weight, of breath that wasn't hers.

She turned, expecting to see someone from one of the other apartments – the students who never spoke to her, never made any effort – finally coming to invite her to one of the parties she always heard. Or to tell her that everyone had grown tired of ignoring her and she was now the centre of attention. Would never be alone again.

But the passageway was empty behind her.

Only a few more steps remained between her and the turn in the hallway ahead, where she would find the access door to the roof. The final part of the journey in The Game.

She cocked her head, waiting to hear the noise again. Silence surrounded her, almost suffocating in its weight.

There was something about being alone that made you believe in the impossible, with thoughts your only companion. She could lose hours alone, even when mildly pissed and wandering through the halls of the fancy block of flats they passed off as *Luxury Student Accommodation*.

Alone.

On your own.

As she always had been, when it came down to it.

The lights above her seemed to dim as she continued to walk.

Determined now to see it through. To move on from all that her past held. To forget. To erase.

It didn't stop the feeling, though, that something was in the increasingly small, short, constricting hallway with her. The lift far behind her now. The turn towards the roof door now only a couple of feet away.

She straightened up and turned the corner without thinking. There was a moment when she caught herself flinching, expecting something to be there waiting for her. Instead, it was a short walk and a grey metal door that led to the stairs up to the roof.

All she had to do now was walk towards the door, try to open it, then find out if this was going to work.

And it had to work.

It had to be enough for them.

She couldn't go back now. She had to make it to the roof and perform the last act.

The feeling of being watched was still there. The feeling of not being entirely alone.

She wasn't going to give up.

The last few yards stretched out in front of her, yet she crossed them in seconds.

The door opened.

She almost fell forward, flat to the ground in surprise. Behind the door was darkness, but she could feel the cold from outside. A stone step was the only visible thing in front of her.

She stepped over the threshold as the light slowly

dimmed behind her. She almost slipped as the door slammed shut and plunged her into total darkness.

She was blind.

Light rushed into her eyes, blinding her and shifting the world around her. The noise and anger and love, all coming towards her at once, overwhelming her.

How could this happen? When she had done everything right. She had played his Game to save herself.

But playing hadn't made any difference.

She saw it now. The Game wasn't a way out.

It was an end.

PLAYER TWO

A game is supposed to be fun.

Something that you do to pass the time, laugh and be merry. A chance to be silly and foolish maybe.

Depends on the game you're playing, of course.

The evening had become night had become early morning. All in the blink of a thought. She shivered at the cold wind as it whipped from the river hiding behind the buildings and swirled around her. Pulled her coat tighter around her body.

The yard she had reached seemed empty. She couldn't see much in the black, but she listened for any noise. Any sign she wasn't alone there.

All she could hear was her own laboured breathing.

This was a way to stop it all.

Play along and it'll all be okay.

A way out.

A way to unfurl the knot that had grown in her stomach for months.

Years.

It had started with a phone call.

A low voice on the other end of the line. Almost a whisper. She had hung up on the private number four times in ten minutes, but answered the fifth call.

'Don't hang up. I need you to listen. For your own good.'

So she had, hearing the soft and soothing tone of it, intoxicating, even as it dripped with venom and horror.

'We know what you've done. We're going to play a game. You win, no one finds out what you did. You lose... and that's it for you.'

They knew everything. Everyone she had hurt. Every lie she had told.

The voice gave her only one way out.

This night.

The Game.

She was standing with her back against a wall, waiting.

The traffic on the main road a few hundred yards away quietened momentarily. The black silence that followed began to smother her, amplifying her thoughts as they raced through her head.

Shadows began to take shape around her, dancing into being.

She was alone. Finally.

A noise made her pause.

A shift of weight, of breath that wasn't hers.

She turned, expecting to see someone emerge from the shadows. For the reality of what she was doing to be revealed. She cocked her head, waiting to hear the noise again. Silence surrounded her, almost claustrophobic in its weight.

There was something about being alone that made you

believe in the impossible. Your mind can play tricks on you. Make you believe in something you know not to be real.

This was one of those times.

She needed this to be over. This was the only way. Then she could move on, without the knowledge that she could be exposed. That was the deal.

Still.

She knew she was being watched.

Someone was following her every move.

She wasn't sure where that thought came from, but now it was in her head, it was all she could think about. Unseen eyes, tracking her feet with each step she took. They had to be watching, she guessed, so they knew she was doing it right. Watching, as she stepped away from the wall and removed the knife she had taken from its block in the kitchen. Her mum would wonder where it had gone in days to come, but would never think it was her who had removed it. She shivered again as the temperature seemed to drop further.

She could feel her heart begin to crash against her chest. 'Hello?'

Her voice sounded alien, as if it belonged to someone else. She wanted to laugh, nervously, at the sound of it as it hit the air and died there.

There was no answer.

It didn't stop the feeling. That something was in the increasingly small, constricting, disused yard.

The feeling of being examined.

Another shift behind her, but she was only dimly aware of it now. The suffocating silence, trying to recall the correct patterns, feeling the tears well up, believing that she was going to fail.

Believing she was going to lose.

In the darkness and silence, her heart beating madly against her chest, her breath shortening, a sudden sound snapped into it all.

A ringing noise, coming from behind her. A few feet away. She held her breath as she turned, seeing a dull illumination on the ground. She stepped towards it, bending down to pick up the mobile phone, turning it over in her hand and staring at the screen. She knew the voice would be there as soon as she answered. Comforting and chilling in equal measure.

She answered.

'It's the end,' the voice said. 'You lose.'

Then, she could hear the breath behind her. On her exposed neck, as she dropped the phone to the ground. She opened her mouth to scream, but no sound escaped.

No sound *could* escape.

Game over.

Three

Mark flicked through the BBC Sport app on his phone as he waited for Natasha to get dressed, leaning against the bedroom door while she scanned the room looking for something.

'Do you need a hand?' Mark said, glancing over at her, wishing they didn't have jobs to go to. That they could just stay there all day – watching TV and eating food that would be classed as 'bad for them'.

'No, it's okay,' Natasha replied, her tone betraying nothing. 'It's here somewhere.'

Mark nodded, even as her head disappeared fully.

Natasha. He really liked that name. It had been a couple of months now, but he still enjoyed saying it out loud. They'd met through Tinder, of all places. After a few one-night stands and fizzled-out-after-a-week-or-less relationships, he'd almost given up on it.

He'd prepared a meal the previous night, but he needn't have bothered. Roast chicken and sweet potato mash. By the time they'd emerged from his bedroom, the chicken was black and the potatoes had ruined his good pan.

They'd ordered takeaway and eaten greasy pizza and garlic bread in the living room instead.

That had happened a fair few times. A couple of months of dates, nights spent together here and there.

He wasn't sure if she was as serious as he was, but he hoped so. It was yet another thing they hadn't really discussed.

'I'm busy later, by the way,' Natasha said, grabbing her remaining shoe and slipping it on. 'But I'll let you know if I can get round after. Never mind if you don't want to,' she said, standing up, a mobile phone disappearing into the side pocket of a small backpack. 'Just thought why spend days apart at this point? It's not like we're having a bad time together, right?'

'Of course,' Mark said, a little too quickly. He took a breath before it slipped away. 'I mean, you're welcome to come round any time you like.'

Natasha smiled at him and he suddenly felt his stomach lurch a little.

'I bet you say that to all the girls.'

'No ... I mean, there isn't ... no.'

'Of course not,' she replied, but she rolled her eyes at him and shook her head. She looked away and he stepped back as she slipped past him. He followed her downstairs, trying to think of a good closing line, but was distracted by an insistent buzzing from the phone in his pocket.

'I'll call you,' Mark said, holding the front door open for her, as she stopped and waited there.

'You best had,' Natasha replied, then kissed him for a fleeting few seconds before skipping away up the path. She didn't turn round to wave. He watched her walk away until she was out of sight.

His phone buzzed again as he closed the door finally. He took it out, checking the screen and swearing silently under his breath. 'Mark Flynn,' he answered.

'Mark, got something for you. Have you got a pen?'

His shoulders slumped a little, as reality came back inch by inch.

The job.

'Go ahead,' he said, already placing his feet into the polished brown shoes left by the door the night before. A clean jacket was hanging close by and he slipped it over his shirt and tie, even as Detective Inspector Angela Bennett continued to talk into his ear.

'Blood discovered.'

'What?' he replied, wishing he hadn't answered the phone. That he'd missed the call again and she could have handed it to someone else. Like that would have made a difference. 'I'm not following you.'

'This missing teenager. Everything points to a death, but we have no body yet. Only thing we have is her blood. And not much of that.'

'The Emily Burns case,' Mark replied, remembering it from the briefing the previous day. It had been a minor annoyance then – something that uniforms were handling. The blood hadn't been mentioned. 'Was wondering what was going on with that one.'

'Yeah, well, nothing good, that much I can tell you. We've got everything but a body at this point and we're hoping that's not too far away. Or, you know, that she turns up safe and sound.'

'Blood, you say?'

'Found by uniforms earlier on. One of the abandoned work yards down on the front, past the docks. They tracked the girl there on CCTV and went to check it out. Found a pool of blood. That's it.'

'What's the story on the family?'

'The usual for the estate they're from,' Bennett said. Mark closed his eyes briefly, wishing he could just go back to bed.

'Hoping one of them doesn't go rogue and tell the media we're sitting on our backsides doing nothing,' Bennett continued, a curl of annoyance in her tone. 'Emily has been missing two days now.'

'Not that long really . . .'

'Apparently it's massively out of character, blah, blah, blah. Now with this, well, starts to look suspicious, you know? So, it's no longer for uniforms to deal with. DCI has asked Major Crimes to look into it, with this discovery. So, it's now on you.'

'What's the address?' Mark said, locating his car keys and looking back into the house, trying to think of anything else he might need.

'Sefton Street, by the trampoline and Go Karts place. There's a big patch of land just behind it that hasn't been built on yet. You know what it's like around there. Seems strange that the only place with nothing on it is the last place she's seen.'

'Not that strange; probably intentional. It's not like CCTV is well hidden in this city. If someone wants to try and avoid it, they only have to look around for the best places.'

'Of course, ace detective,' DI Bennett said, a playfulness to her voice now. He could almost picture the knowing smile playing across her face. 'Good to know you're not a total imbecile.'

'That was up for debate?'

Bennett didn't respond and Mark realised it probably was.

Four

Things changed so quickly. An hour earlier, in bed with Natasha and her laughter, her eyes. The way he had become lost in them so often, as if he were staring at waves crashing onto the shore. Now, he was plain old Detective Constable Mark Flynn, loitering near a pool of blood.

It was the quiet moments he looked forward to now. None of the horror of his job.

It hadn't taken him long to find the place, a short drive along the city's waterfront, down The Strand and past the old buildings which made the skyline iconic. He barely registered them now, even though when he'd been a kid, he'd stood in awe of the giant structures. The Liver Birds had been his favourite part of the whole lot.

Now, they were just normal. Nothing special. Just part of everyday life.

A couple of uniformed officers had obviously been awaiting his arrival – elbowing each other as he stepped closer to the scene. Mark slowed as they approached from the other side of the yard, taking everything in. There were a few people in the distance, stopping for a quick look at what was happening and then moving on when they didn't see anything of interest. He didn't think it would be long before the *Liverpool Echo* had rolling news coverage on their website.

It was quieter here, far away from the bustling to and fro of the more touristy parts of the Albert Dock and town. Only a few minutes further from there, towards the south, there was less foot traffic. Only the main A road which ran along to Otterspool and up to Aigburth and beyond. Here it was still technically the city centre, he supposed, but it was stuck in the beginnings of transformation. The area, once forgotten, was now seeing new developments daily. The yard he was standing in was one of the last to be looked at, he thought. Surrounded by giant warehouses, now housing trampoline parks and go-kart circuits. More places for tired parents to entertain bored children. Behind him, further down the waterfront, new houses and a tall building overlooked him – new student accommodation, which seemed to be what every new tower block was for now.

'Sir?' one of the uniforms said, bringing his attention back to the scene. 'You our DC?'

'Yes, Mark Flynn,' he replied, almost reaching out a hand and then thinking better of it. 'What's the situation?'

'PCs Robertson and Banks,' the female uniform said. She was young, brown hair tied back in a tight ponytail. Dark lines hung under her eyes, but they still contained a little life. 'Forensics are just finishing up now.'

'What are we looking at then?'

'We received a call from a Julie Burns, a few days ago,' PC Robertson said, both hands finding her hips as she began talking. She was shorter than him by a few inches, but broad with it. Stocky didn't seem the right word, but it was the only one that came to mind. 'Her daughter – Emily– was last seen late Saturday night. Nineteen years old, no history of taking off or anything like that. She didn't say where she was going and nothing was missing from her bedroom, apart from her mobile phone. It seems she got on a bus into town, then walked from the London Road area to here. We had a look at CCTV yesterday and this morning, tracking her along The Strand to here. Wasn't exactly difficult, but that's where the trail finished.'

'No cameras in here then?' Mark said, looking around for any familiar technology on the walls but seeing only bare brick.

'Nothing here or on the promenade over there,' PC Robertson replied, gesturing towards the end of the yard in the distance. 'We came down just for a look while we were quiet. Found what looked like blood spots leading to a bigger pool. Dried up now, but unmistakeable if you've seen it before, like. Thankfully it hasn't rained since then, otherwise we'd probably have missed it.'

'Take me over.'

Mark followed the two uniforms to where a forensic tech officer was on his haunches packing up kit. He stopped a few feet away, cocking his head and taking it in. 'Not a huge amount.'

'Enough to be worrying,' PC Robertson said, crossing her arms across her chest. 'We've looked around the place to see if we could find anything else, but there's nothing to suggest any violence of any kind. Apart from the blood, of course.'

Mark followed her eyes to the steel railings that bordered the end of the yard from the waterfront, understanding what she might be thinking. 'If it is blood, maybe she tried to do something here and eventually ended up in the river?'

'That'd be my guess,' PC Robertson replied, her voice softer now as she looked out across the water. 'Someone's gone to see the family again. I guess that's your job now though. They haven't mentioned suffering from depression, but doesn't mean she wasn't and they just didn't realise it. Only thing is, we can see most of the waterfront from a camera further down. Nothing clear enough to be sure, but there was nothing that looked like a body going into the river.'

'Late at night though, so not the best light. Could have happened in a split second for all we know.'

'Maybe,' PC Robertson replied, but Mark could tell by her tone she didn't quite buy into his theory. 'The family say Emily showed no signs of being in distress, mentally or physically; it was a normal evening by all accounts. No outward signs that she might harm herself, or that she was worried about something. She just disappeared overnight. No note, no nothing. Everything points to something else going on. Not just a . . . you know.'

Mark could see she didn't want to say the word *suicide*, which meant she'd probably had a bad one recently. He was beginning to recognise these small signs, which made him feel better about himself. Like he wasn't wasting his time with the career choice he'd made. Like he might even be good at it. 'At the moment though, we have no evidence that anything has happened to her from an outside force.'

'I suppose not,' PC Robertson replied, barely above a whisper now. 'Nothing ruling that out either, though.'

'Hmm,' Mark said, nodding to himself as he walked around the pool of blood, which had coagulated and stained the concrete. He'd seen stains like this before, so was pretty sure it wasn't just an oil patch or the like. The CSI gave him the nod, just to confirm his suspicion.

Blood. But that wasn't enough to start making assumptions, he reminded himself.

They were a good twenty feet away from the nearest wall, not exactly near the centre of the yard, but far enough away for it to tell Mark a few things. 'If she was doing something to herself, I don't think this would be the place. What, slit her wrists and then jump in the river? Or cut herself? Without her back against the wall or anything? It doesn't seem right.'

Mark followed the few spots of blood that led away from the larger pool, watching as they grew smaller and eventually vanished. 'They're not leading to the water anyway,' he said, turning back to the uniformed officers. 'Over to that side, which doesn't show a way out.'

PC Robertson hesitated, while the mute uniform standing next to her gave Mark a lazy shrug. 'It might not even be her blood for all we know,' he said finally, making a few notes to himself in his notebook. 'At the moment, we need to concentrate on the fact she's missing and that'll have to do for now.'

'You're the detective,' PC Robertson said, then turned away from him, following the path back out of the yard.

Mark stood for a few minutes, taking the scene in again, wondering what the hell he'd stumbled into here. Probably nothing, he thought. Yet, there he was – looking at a stain on the ground and wondering where a nineteen-year-old girl had disappeared to.

He felt the familiar nervousness in his stomach build, wiped a hand across his brow and moved away. Tried to ignore the feeling that he didn't belong in the suit he was wearing and reminded himself that he wanted this.

Five

When Mark had read the family's address, he'd winced. Searching for a friendly face in this vicinity would be difficult. A residential area that turned more industrial-looking towards the top.

He took his time making his way over to the front door. He scanned the surroundings as he did so, trying to spot anything out of the ordinary, but it couldn't have looked more normal if it had tried. White double-glazed bay windows at the bottom, a double-pane above them. Dirty brown bricks and a patch of grass that needed mowing, but wasn't exactly overgrown. It was difficult to discern any difference from any of the houses on its row, apart from the decorative numbering on the pane of frosted glass at the top of the entrance. What cars were parked up on the road were all in various states of disrepair, with only a smattering of newer vehicles further down the road. The houses behind them looked even worse. The money being spent in the city centre rarely made its way further out towards the estates.

He tried to prepare himself for what was to come; the questions he'd be forced to answer, the information he couldn't yet give them. He turned the file over in his hand, the sparseness of the details provided to him even more annoying than usual.

A uniformed officer was loitering outside the house, which at least gave him respite before entering.

Mark pulled his coat tighter around him as he crossed the road and pushed open the gate.

'PC Olsen, right?' Mark said, recognising the officer blowing into her hands as she stood outside the front door. 'How's it going?'

'Can't complain, sir,' Olsen replied.

'What's the score then?'

'I was asked to come and keep an eye on the family until you arrived,' Olsen replied, her hands now resting at her sides. 'They're still in a bit of a state. Came out here for a break. The mum is pretty messed up.'

'Who else is in there?'

'The mum's brother, and two kids. Well, I say kids. Both teenagers.'

Mark took another look behind him at the street, wondering what type of family he was about to encounter. His days in uniform hadn't been exactly fun when dealing with anyone who lived within a mile or so of this address.

'Well, I'd best go in and speak to them,' Mark said, taking a deep breath and raising his eyebrows at Olsen. She gave him a tight smile and stepped to one side.

Mark moved past her and pushed open the front door, which she'd helpfully left open for him. A flight of stairs led almost directly from the front door with a short hallway behind it, which led towards the back of the house. He could hear the voices from what he presumed was the living room to his right. Quiet murmurs for now, which relieved him a little.

'Hello, I'm Detective Constable Mark Flynn,' he said as he entered the room. Announcing his presence. Taking control of the situation, just as he'd been taught. He scanned around quickly, marking out the missing girl's mother and addressing her directly. 'I've taken over the investigation into your daughter's disappearance. Did PC Olsen tell you I was coming?'

The mother looked him over and then towards the mountainous man currently leaning against the mantel-piece. He stepped forward towards Mark, hands thrust into his jeans' pockets. 'Have you found her yet or what?'

Mark glanced at the man, deciding against offering him a handshake. Instead, he turned back to the mother and shook his head. 'Not yet, but I want to reassure you everything is being done to find your daughter. I've only just taken over the case, but I can tell you we're doing everything we can for Emily.'

'Well, that's not been much so far,' the man-mountain muttered under his breath. He shaped to say something, but the mother stopped him with a raised hand.

'It's okay, Rich, no need for that right now. I'm Julie, Emily's mum,' she said, standing up slowly from the sofa and extending a hand towards Mark. He took it in his, closing the other hand over the top of it and smiling thinly at her.

'I wish we were meeting in better circumstances,' Mark said, waiting for her to break the hold. 'Tell me, is there anything you need right now?'

'Just Emily,' Julie Burns said, letting go of Mark's hand and dropping back down onto the sofa. Mark had read as much as he possibly could before driving over. He would have guessed at her being older than forty-six, but then the past two days had probably aged her a few years. The vertical lines on her upperlip were more pronounced than they might have been the previous week. More cigarettes being smoked, the wearing away at her skin taking hold. Her dark brown hair was looking limp, lifeless. Grey roots beginning to show on top. He used the pause in the conversation to pass a comforting look to the two other people in the room as he moved nearer to Julie – one boy, one woman. The boy looked to be in his mid-teens, the other around the same age as Emily.

Her twin, according to the notes, but having glanced at the photographs of the missing Emily, there wasn't much resemblance.

'What do we call you then?' the man in the room said, his voice now slightly softer, but with the edge of someone who was used to dealing with police and not used to being ignored. His shaven head revealed old scars, a tattoo crawling up the back of his neck and around to the front. A faded, black tribal design. 'Shouldn't you be out there looking for our Emily anyway?'

'Call me Mark, if you like. I can promise you there's uniformed officers looking for her as we speak. I'm here to get as much information as possible to assist that search. And to make sure you're all informed as much as possible.'

He gave a grunt as a reply, but the man didn't move. Still trying to stare him down, even though Mark wasn't even looking in his direction.

'Is there any news at all?'

Mark turned towards Emily's twin sister as she spoke, his mind conjuring up the name he had learned only minutes earlier. 'You must be Stephanie.'

'Yes, well done for remembering my name,' she

replied, rolling her eyes theatrically. 'Can you answer my question now?'

There was a brief moment when Mark wanted to let the disarming smile he wore slip from his face. He didn't blink, taking a seat in the only available spot, next to the mother.

'We made a small discovery of interest this morning,' Mark said, leaning forward and talking to the twin now. He swivelled a little to face the mother, too. 'Now, it's not her, but it could be the beginning of finding her, okay?'

He told them what had been found, expecting to receive more reaction than he did. He ploughed on, choosing his words carefully as he did so. As he finished into silence, he cleared his throat and gave them his final platitude. 'We're doing all we can to make sure Emily is found safe and well.'

'It's been too long for that,' the other sibling said, quietly. Charlie, Mark thought. The younger sibling. From the look on his face, he was smack bang in the throes of adolescence and all that went with it. His face wore a well-rehearsed scowl, which Mark imagined was a permanent feature. He remembered that age well. Sometimes, it didn't feel like all that long had passed since he was angry at the world and all it contained. Not knowing it would pass soon enough. The lad didn't look like the popular type. He remembered being like that once, too.

He'd soon learn, Mark thought.

'Don't say things like that,' Julie replied, almost spitting the words out. 'It's only been a couple of days.'

'Yeah, well, we all know it's not looking good, right? She wouldn't just go off on her own for days. You can barely get her out of the house at the best of times. Plus, the fact that she dropped out of college and didn't even tell us.'

'Let's not get ahead of ourselves,' Mark said, sensing

he was losing control of the conversation before it had
even really begun. He hadn't read all the report – what
there was of it – but had read about Emily dropping out
and not telling her family. 'It's best we all remain calm
and see what we can find out in the meantime. I've gone
over the notes so far, but the more things you can tell me,
the better.'

He was greeted by near silence, only broken by the mum
chewing on the end of her wool jumper like a small child.

This would be his life until the missing girl was found,
Mark thought. This family. This dodgy estate. This misery.

He made a decision to split them up, talk to them indi-
vidually, rather than letting them continue to snipe at each
other. It was probably in a handbook somewhere that it is
better to do it that way, but he allowed himself a mental
pat on the back for thinking of it now.

'I'll put the kettle on,' Mark said, breaking the growing
discontent brewing in the small living room. 'Stephanie,
do you want to show me where things are in the kitchen?'

He waited for her to stand up and make her way out of
the room before following close behind her.

Mark followed the twin into the kitchen, leaning against
the doorway as she busied herself filling a kettle. He'd only
seen a picture of Emily Burns, but he could see major differences between the pair. Differing hair colours – Emily
a brunette, Stephanie blonde, albeit from a bottle, he
guessed. Life looked like it had been kinder to Stephanie,
it seemed. Which made him think of the nineteen-year-old
Emily, possibly living in her twin's shadow.

'Sugar?'

'Two please,' Mark replied, watching as she removed
cups from a cupboard on the wall. 'Should I be worried

about the rather large bloke in the living room? He looks ready to take my head off at any moment.'

'Uncle Rich is harmless really,' Stephanie replied, still facing away from him. 'His bark is worse than his bite.'

'Good to know. Although I don't think I want to test that theory.'

Mark turned away from her and looked at the small kitchen. There was a patch of darker paint in three corners of the room, damp or mould patches that had been painted over, he guessed. It was a perpetual problem for houses in the area, where landlords were more interested in the money appearing in their bank accounts every month than the state of the houses they were letting out. Other than that, the place was much cleaner than he imagined others in the road would be. A small fridge-freezer was closest to the door, silver and covered in various paintings and drawings. All done by the children when they'd been younger, he suspected.

'Do you think you'll find her alive?'

Mark didn't speak for a moment, working out the best way to answer a question he'd been asked countless times before. Stephanie finally turned to face him, hands braced against the counter behind her.

'We never give up hope until there's evidence otherwise,' Mark said, hoping it would be enough. 'People go missing every day. Hundreds of thousands a year. Most of them turn up within days – that's why you don't hear about it more.'

'But some don't turn up at all, do they?'

'Very rarely. Emily might be found at any moment. Don't give up on her just yet.'

Stephanie smiled thinly at him, then turned back to

where the kettle was boiling away. 'I hadn't given up, not at all. Not until you said about the blood. I'm just preparing myself for the worst. That's all.'

Mark had been waiting for one of the family to say the 'B' word. He had been careful not to use it himself, but it was quite obvious what he'd meant. The fact they hadn't been able to positively identify the blood as belonging to Emily yet meant he could still pretend it wasn't hers. 'We don't know anything for sure right now, other than that it's blood.'

'That copper that was here before you,' Stephanie said, her voice betraying none of the worry or hurt Mark knew she'd be carrying inside her. 'She said they'd tracked her on CCTV then you tell us that blood was found there. Would be some coincidence if it wasn't hers.'

Mark's phone buzzed in his pocket, as if it had been waiting for the perfect time to interrupt. He excused himself and checked it. A text message, with a simple and short meaning.

Same blood type.

He tried not to react, but felt his stomach drop as he placed his phone away. DNA results wouldn't be back for another day or so, but Mark didn't think they'd turn up anything shocking.

It would be Emily's blood.

Then, they would continue looking for a body. Probably wait for the river to hopefully wash it back to shore. If it was suicide.

A thought jumped into his mind, which he quickly tried to forget.

Please be a suicide. I don't want it to be a murder.

'I've seen people come back,' Mark said finally, watching as Stephanie lifted the kettle and began pouring. 'I've dealt with many families over the years who think there's no hope. There's always hope. Nothing is over until it's over.'

'And then the real battle starts,' Stephanie replied, handing him a mug that had probably been new when he was starting out in the police service. He swivelled it in his hand so the chipped rim faced away from his mouth. Tried not to think of what the inside of it looked like before the liquid was added.

'So, you're just going to be asking us more questions then?' Stephanie said, stirring milk into the rest of the cups on the counter. 'Seeing if any of us slip up and tell you she's in the attic. I've seen these stories before. You always think it's the family . . . if she hasn't done something to herself.'

'I'm only going to be trying to find Emily,' Mark replied, enjoying the warmth of the cup in his hand. 'No one is under suspicion at the moment. If you need to tell me anything, that's what I'm here for. I'll listen to everything you've got to say – any worries, or if you have your own theories. And to learn about Emily.'

'Sounds like a hiding to nothing to me. No offence.'

'None taken,' Mark said, waving his hand away at the remark. 'I know what you mean. It might seem small, but that's often the thing that provides the answers. It's my job to recognise that tiny bit of information.'

'And what if she's never found?'

'That's something we don't need to think about now.'

And he hoped they never would.

Six

Mark asked Stephanie questions he was sure had already been asked. He guessed she would be used to going over the same thing over and over by now, but it made it no less awkward.

'I don't know much of anything,' Stephanie said, as he made notes while she spoke. 'Nothing that would be of any help, anyway. I've been away the last few months. Second year at uni. First one in the family to go.'

'Emily didn't go?'

Stephanie shook her head. 'Don't think she was ever interested in going to university.'

'Did no one suspect she had dropped out?'

'No, my mum was as shocked as anyone. Mum works now – she must be a better liar than we thought. I didn't really talk to her about it anyway, so I had no idea. Charlie . . . well, he does his own thing.'

'What are you studying?'

'Sociology and criminology,' Stephanie replied, then caught the look on his face and rolled her eyes. 'Don't worry, I'm not going to start eulogising on the criminal mind to you. I don't know enough to start doing that yet.'

'Feel free to tell me anything you like. I'm happy to listen.'

'You're quite young to be a detective,' Stephanie said, looking away after a few seconds of staring into his eyes. 'I was expecting someone older. More weathered.'

'Give it a couple of years and you won't recognise me.'

'Let's hope you find Emily before then.'

Mark lowered his head, trying to think of something to say to that. Failed. Stephanie eyed him for a second or two more, then picked up two cups and walked past him into the hallway. He waited a moment, then picked up the other cup on the counter and followed her through, mentally logging all the questions he hadn't asked yet. He paused at the photographs on the wall, seeing Julie's three children in various stages of their lives. It seemed that the twins had been dressed and groomed identically through-out their early childhood, but diverged once they became teenagers. As he moved past the pictures, crossing each year of their existence as he did so, he could see the obvious similarities between the sisters fade, as they took different paths. Emily, putting on weight and looking darker-eyed with each school year, Stephanie going the opposite way.

The other child – Charlie – seemed to stay much the same over the years. Never smiling. Always a sullen look on his face, much like the one he was wearing in the living room now. As if it was a burden to be anywhere.

Mark stopped at the final picture of the entire family. Julie Burns and her three children, snapped at a table in a restaurant, he guessed. All dolled up, an evening out for some special occasion. There was a balloon on the table, but it was too blurred to read the writing on it. They were all turned towards the camera, varying degrees of happiness spread across their faces.

'That was taken two months ago,' Julie Burns said, appearing beside Mark without warning. He shifted his body round a little, looking down at her as she stared at the photograph. 'My birthday. They took me for a meal in town. It was a lovely night.'

'Who took the photo?'

'I think it was the waiter. It was just us. Me and my three kids.'

'I'm guessing it's been that way for a while.' Mark couldn't remember reading anything about the father being around in the scant notes he'd been given, but thought it was a good bet he hadn't been involved for a long time. He made a mental note to check on his whereabouts.

'We split up about fifteen years ago,' Julie replied, confirming his guess. 'He was useless anyway. They didn't miss out on father of the year, you know? He buggered off as soon as he could, the lazy sod. Got sick and tired of me nagging him to get a proper job, rather than doing the odd foreigner for his builder mates.'

Mark tried to remember the last time he'd heard of a job taken off the books as a 'foreigner' and decided it was probably twenty years earlier, back on the estate he'd grown up on. 'Did he keep in touch with them? Visitation, that sort of thing?'

'The first few years or so, he was around a lot. Mainly trying to worm his way back into the house, you know? Didn't work though. I wasn't having any of it. We were better off without him. The kids definitely were. He started coming round less and less once he'd found a new soft lass to take care of him. Don't think that one lasted long either. Probably spends his days in the pub or the bookies these days.'

'How long has it been since they've seen their dad?'

Julie took a moment to think. It never failed to surprise Mark, the ease with which some people could turn their backs on their own flesh and blood. The way it can be forgotten that you have family you never see. Children you choose not to watch grow up and become adults.

'Years,' Julie said finally, shrugging her shoulders. 'Must be at least eight or so by now – 2011, maybe? I think it was when Charlie was still at primary school. Emily and Stephanie would have been in first year at high school, I think. Old enough to start making the decision whether they wanted to see him or not, I suppose. He just stopped making the effort, not that he ever really made one to begin with.'

'Have they spoken to him in the years since then at least? Is it possible Emily tried to find him or something?'

'She wouldn't even know where to start,' Julie said, shaking her head. 'No idea where he is these days, but I passed his name and details to your lot anyway. I'm not sure Emily would meet up with him. He made his mind up years ago that he wasn't interested in them. Good riddance, if you ask me. They've done better without him in their lives.'

Mark needed to find the father, but something told him that might be difficult. Nothing suggested it was a case of a teenage girl deciding to find an estranged family member. Especially not with the blood. The images of her disappearing round that corner and never being seen again. At three in the morning.

'She was doing so well recently,' Julie continued, now seemingly lost in her thoughts as she stared at the photographs on the wall. 'She's always been withdrawn, a bit different from the other two. Less outgoing. Lately, she seemed to be happier. Like she had something to look forward to for once.'

'Has she struggled before now then?'

'Probably no more than any other teenage girl,' Julie replied, lifting a hand and then moving the frame on one of the photographs a fraction one way. Correcting a crookedness only she could see. 'Maybe it was more pronounced because of Stephanie – she flew through high school. Always had friends to go out with, did well in her exams. Emily seemed to struggle in her shadow a little. They separated them, but only because Emily wasn't as good in school as Stephanie was. She started eating more. Always in secret and that. Which only made things worse with the other kids at school. You know how cruel kids can be. I never treat them differently though. Or Charlie. They all get the same attention and discipline. It isn't easy – just me being here for them. And living round here doesn't help.'

I can imagine, Mark thought. They were on the outskirts of it, but the notoriety of nearby Norris Green overshadowed them still, he guessed. 'I'm sure you did your absolute best for them all.'

'I tried. That's the best you can do. And now ... and now she's gone.' Julie turned to him, tears forming in already reddened eyes. She blinked them away, swiping a hand across her cheeks. 'I feel like I should be out there. Looking for her. That's what I should be doing, right?'

Mark shook his head. 'You're better here, waiting in case she calls or comes back. There's nothing more you could do out there, other than driving around aimlessly. There's people searching for her right now.'

'I just don't understand what could have happened to her,' Julie said, blinking rapidly as a few tears escaped down her cheeks. She made no effort now to brush them away. 'She seemed so much happier recently. She had made friends. Over the internet, but still. And she was meeting some of them over the last few months. She'd really turned a corner.'

Mark hesitated before he spoke. He hated this part. Choosing the words carefully, not putting himself in a position where he promised something he could never deliver. 'Everyone is working hard to bring her home, Julie. I promise you that much.'

'Yeah, that's what they all keep saying to me,' Julie said, leaving him in the hallway and returning to the living room.

The photographs of a happy family stared down at him from the wall.

He wondered what kind of friends Emily had made online. That seemed like a good place to check, he thought. He drained the last of the tea, shuddering at the aftertaste, and wondered how many more cups he'd have to drink before he admitted he didn't even like the stuff. It seemed wrong to refuse though. He stared at the photographs a little longer, then made his way back to the kitchen.

As Mark put his cup in the sink, he glanced up to see the big fella outside, through the window. Pacing the small yard, rolling a cigarette as he did so.

He made a decision.

Mark breathed in deeply and started walking.

Seven

Mark stepped out into the back yard, thrust his hands in his pockets and walked across the limited space, looking towards Rich, wondering if he'd grown since the last time he'd seen him.

He could feel the clouds above them threatening rain.

'Any news?' Rich said, patting his pockets looking for a lighter for the rolled-up cigarette dangling from his lips.

'Not at the moment, no,' Mark replied. *Not since you last asked, five minutes ago,* he decided not to add. He realised he was now at the other end of the yard, with no other way back into the house, except past Rich. He considered taking a running jump at the fence and going next door, but thought it might be an overreaction. Besides, he'd walked out here to talk to him. 'That's not to say we're not getting anywhere. There's a number of possible routes in this investigation to go through yet. And there'll be a more detailed search of the area soon.'

'It's not far from the water. If someone has put her in there ... could be a long time until we find her.'

'Let's hope that's not the case,' Mark said, still trying

to look for any signs of something being hidden. 'It's early days. We haven't exhausted all the possibilities yet.'

'The first coppers that turned up couldn't find her phone,' Rich replied, taking a drag on the cigarette and blowing a large plume of smoke in Mark's direction. 'Means she took it with her. I thought you could trace the last place someone was from that alone.'

'That's true, unless the phone has been destroyed, or the SIM card has been removed, things like that. It doesn't mean anything though. She could've just lost her phone . . .'

'Anything could have happened,' Rich cut in. Mark snapped his mouth closed, happy to allow the bigger man to talk. 'She was a good girl, you know. Quiet, didn't have many friends, but was never any trouble for our Julie. The other two, they've had their ups and downs, but Emily . . . Emily was always the good one. Kept her head down, let her twin do the talking. Not that they were close really.'

'No?' Mark said, wondering how well the man knew the family. And why he was already referring to Emily in the past tense? As if he knew that when people go missing for any length of time, they didn't usually come home.

'I thought twins were usually quite close?' Mark said, when the quiet between them grew too much to bear. 'That's what I've always thought anyway. Not that I've known too many.'

'Not those two. They're far too different. Weird how that can happen. They were identical growing up, but then they just grew apart when they got older. Even though nothing changed really. Both brought up the same. One goes one way, the other . . . Well, we don't know yet, I suppose. I'll tell you something though. If anything has happened to her – if anyone has *done* something to her – I'm going to be doing time. A long time.'

Mark was standing about ten foot away, but suddenly felt very close to Rich. A vein bulged in his neck as he took a last drag from his cigarette and flicked it towards the fence on his right-hand side. He exhaled one last breath filled with smoke as his face crumpled and then he turned away, his body shaking.

'Are you okay?' Mark said, knowing it was a stupid question even as it fell from his lips. He tried to keep the surprise from his voice at the show of emotion from the man.

'I'm fine,' Rich replied, raising a hand to wipe away his tears. He was still standing with his back towards Mark, but even without seeing his face, Mark felt it was genuine emotion.

He just wasn't sure if it was fear or regret he was witnessing.

'This is just going to tear our Julie apart,' Rich continued, turning back to Mark now. 'She's always done her best for them kids. On her own as well. They wanted for nothing. She deserves a bloody medal. Not … not something like this to happen.'

'Do you spend much time with them?'

'As much as I can, but I have my own stuff to sort out, you know? It wasn't like they needed a father figure or anything. Julie was enough for the kids. She's a diamond, our Julie. Worked hard all her life.'

Mark nodded, but still didn't step closer to the man. He could see that wouldn't help. Rich wouldn't want a comforting hand on his shoulder.

Still, Mark didn't know if he was talking to a grieving

uncle, or someone who potentially had something to do with his niece's disappearance. And there lay the dichotomy he had to live with as a detective. One part of him providing comfort and resolution to a family; the other, constantly on guard. Looking for inconsistencies in stories. Viewing every word spoken with suspicion.

'I'm sorry for the way I spoke to you when you turned up,' Rich said, catching Mark's eyes and holding them.

'It's okay—' Mark began, but stopped as Rich moved forward a couple of steps.

'No, I mean it. I know you're only doing your job. And that you're all doing the best you can. It's just I'm not used to being this side of it. Usually when I speak to your lot, it's defending something or other I've got myself mixed up in.'

Mark smiled thinly, but didn't reply.

'Just bring her back home,' Rich said, turning away. 'Not for me, because I don't expect you to do anything for me. For her. For Julie. She doesn't deserve this. Any of this.'

'We'll do everything we can,' Mark replied, watching Rich nod his head but not turn back. Then, the older man opened the back door and went inside, leaving Mark alone, wondering whether he'd just been played.

Eight

Leaving the house as soon as he'd finished the third cup of tea he hadn't really wanted, Mark made his way back to the station. The family hadn't been exactly what he'd been expecting. He was too used to barely constrained anger from the occupants of that sort of estate. The family had seemed more lost than anything else, the only exception being the big fella.

Good ol' Uncle Rich. Keeping stereotypes in business.

He wasn't expecting much to have happened in the time since he'd turned up at the house, but he guessed his boss would be interested in an update of some sort. Especially as he'd been away from his desk for a few hours now.

He knew the score. Someone goes missing, usually they either have problems they want to escape, or someone close to them wouldn't allow them to get away from problems they had created for them. He also knew that finding blood at the scene meant the second option was going to be the most likely scenario. Whether it was by her own hand, or if she had come to some harm by someone else, it would be up to him to find out. All that would be up for discussion now; he would have to look into every aspect of this family's life – the way they interacted with each other, the way in which problems were solved when they came up. Whether any of them had any secrets.

It could get messy, he thought, as he pushed open the door into the offices. A few heads turned his way briefly, but no one welcomed him back. That was a standard greeting for him. He'd been there a year, but still felt like an outsider. Moving from a quiet station outside the city centre, suddenly being thrust into a major crimes unit as a detective . . . It was a change he was still getting used to.

Mark approached one of the DCs who worked near his desk. 'Is the boss in?'

The bloke held up a finger to him and continued to type on his keyboard. Mark waited patiently, wondering why he didn't even deserve a polite *just a minute*. Manners cost nothing, but for some people that was still too expensive.

Eventually, the DC turned to him and leaned back in his chair. 'What do you want?'

'Just wondering if the boss was in?'

'Why don't you go over and check yourself?' the DC replied, then turned back to his computer without saying anything else. Mark shook his head as he made his way over to DI Bennett's office. Knocked and then went inside when he heard her voice from within.

'Mark, how are you getting on?' Bennett said as Mark went in and hovered by the empty chair on the other side of her desk.

'Not much to report so far,' Mark replied, resting a hand on the back of the chair, waiting to be invited to sit down. DI Angela Bennett didn't move. She was as pale-faced as a full moon, all cheekbones and dark mascara. 'The blood is being tested as we speak. The family seem willing to talk, but I haven't formed any early impressions yet. A mention of making friends recently, but online, rather than in real life.'

'Nineteen-year-old going missing usually isn't a major event for us. Not been long enough really. I've got a bad feeling about it, though. I'm sure you have as well.'

'Yeah, can't argue with that,' Mark replied, noticing one of his fingernails was a little long and resisting the urge to bite into it. He wanted to chew it off in the silence and spit it out onto the floor. He thought about the ridiculousness of basing things on *bad feelings*. Wondered if his DI realised how pointless an exercise that would be. 'I've asked uniforms to go over the CCTV again, but I could do with some help from the tech team on that.'

A long sigh greeted his request. 'You know we're busy at the moment, but I'll try and get someone on it.'

'We need to work out what happens after she enters that yard. There's a few exits but not all of them are covered by CCTV. She doesn't show up again. We're going over all the previous footage, but if no one goes in there ahead of her, I don't know what we can know for certain without a body.'

'Could be that there is no other footage. That she left via one of the exits that isn't covered by CCTV.'

'Yeah, that's what I'm worried about,' Mark said, then gritted his teeth at the thought. This was the type of case every detective dreaded now. With the wealth of cameras covering the city, it was almost impossible to enter any area without being monitored. It had made their jobs easier, but also meant that when a case came along that didn't have easy answers, it was all the more difficult.

'How about her movements?' Mark heard DI Bennett asking, tuning himself back into the conversation. He looked up towards her and saw she wasn't even looking at him. Her computer screen seemed to contain something more interesting than their discussion.

'They've put a request in to track her phone's last location, which should tell us if it was ditched anywhere,' Mark said, ploughing on regardless. 'Info should be with us soon. According to uniforms, it seems like she walked a long way to get to that yard, which is unusual. Means she was going to a specific place. If it was just to the river, then she had plenty of options before reaching that yard. Speaking to the family, it doesn't seem like she had many friends, or a boyfriend, who lived close by. Not sure she spoke to anyone at all, other than over the internet.'

'A social media trail it is then, Mark. I know you'll love that.'

'I'm living the dream,' Mark replied, going for cold indifference rather than the excitement he actually felt. He knew the way most detectives reacted when social media was mentioned. Everyone lived online, it seemed. Every aspect of their lives posted for all to see. Even those who believed they kept things under wraps would usually have a Facebook or Twitter account. There, with personal photos for all to see.

Privacy had ceased to really exist.

For Mark, that was the kind of thing he enjoyed. Seeing what people were hiding behind the public facade. Behind the posts, the pictures. When you began to delve into the private messages and emails, that's when you learned the truth.

'Was the uncle there?'

'Yeah. Wouldn't have minded a bit of warning about him. He's a big fella with an even bigger temper.'

'He's got a record as long as one of his arms,' DI Bennett replied, a smirk behind her tone. Mark didn't exactly share the joviality she was feeling. She didn't have to spend time with him. 'Some of it is a bit too close to be ignored.'

'What do you mean?'

'I thought you said you'd read the file?'

Mark paused, wondering if she was going to get annoyed with him for not reading every last sentence she'd handed over to him. 'I read most of it.'

'I suppose you didn't have much time to familiarise yourself with the case,' DI Bennett replied, seeming to let this one go for now.

'Sorry,' Mark said, hoping the oversight would be ignored. He made a mental note to read everything before barrelling forwards. Hoped he'd remember to do that in the future. 'Forget it. Anyway, he's got some previous,' DI Bennett said, sighing loudly and turning back towards him now. 'Domestic violence, accusation of rape, which didn't make it to court. CPS refused to take it on. Matrix think he's into drugs now as well. Has some connections to some known dealers. An ex-girlfriend had a restraining order against him for a while, too. He doesn't seem to have been in trouble for a few years now, apart from the odd disorder on a Saturday night. Nothing major. Guy has a temper and doesn't seem to stick to targeting one gender either.'

It was Mark's turn to sigh, as he tried to put a list of all the things they didn't know against the little they did. And why this was even his job anyway. 'I'm guessing you want me to find out what his relationship was like with Emily specifically, then?'

'In one,' DI Bennett replied, the sound of paper shuffling

accompanying her words, as she began moving things around her desk. A sure sign he was about to be ushered out. 'It's usually someone close to the victim, after all. If we find a body, it'll make things easier, but for now, unless anything else comes to light . . .'

'He fits,' Mark finished for her. 'Especially with a record like that. Not such a stretch that there's been abuse and she's threatened to out him. Or this was the first time and she fought back. Or something to do with the drugs angle. Lot of possibilities for me to work on. So far, he doesn't seem anything other than pissed off with us for not doing more to find her. And he seemed to be genuinely upset earlier. Could be an act, I suppose, but if it is, it's a convincing one.'

'It's not like we haven't seen some damn good actors over the years. He could be hiding something.'

'You might be right,' Mark replied, the thought of going back to question the man-mountain filling him with dread. 'I'll get working on things. See if there's anything more to it. I'll check in with you again later.'

Mark went straight out of the office and went to the bathroom. Looking himself over in the mirror, he tried to see if anything was out of place, anything that would suggest he wasn't up to this. He looked as he always did. He walked into a stall and relieved himself before reaching for the flush. His finger paused as the door opened outside and he heard two deep laughs.

'Has he gone back there then?' A voice he recognised. Dale Williams. He was a detective constable from another office, who was a few years older than him.

'Yeah, think so,' a higher voice replied. The DC from earlier, who had so casually dismissed him. 'I don't know why he's annoying, but every time he speaks, I just want to lamp him.'

'I know what you mean. Some people are just like that.'

'Wonder how long it'll take for him to finally realise this isn't for him.'

'Thought the penny would have dropped by now, to be honest.'

'He's just a pain in the arse. Hopefully getting something like a missing teen will be the end of it. She turns up dead and he's screwed if he's missed something, which he probably will. He's not exactly the brightest bulb in the box. Press will crucify him if he gets something wrong.'

'I'm just glad he's not on my team now. I had to work with him on something a while ago and almost tore my own hair out at the endless questions.'

Mark listened in silence, then flushed the toilet and walked out of the stall. Didn't make eye contact with either man as they looked over their shoulders at him from the urinals and he washed his hands. He thought he saw something approaching guilt pass between them, but couldn't be sure. It was more likely defiance – he couldn't imagine they'd be that bothered by him hearing them talk about him behind his back.

He tried to think of a response, something witty and cutting, but failed.

Instead, he dried his hands and left the bathroom without saying a single word.

It had been this way since he'd joined the team. Only from a certain group, but still, it was enough to know there were people out there watching his every move, waiting for him to make a mistake. They thought he was too young, too inquisitive. Not willing to just shut up and do the job the way they did.

Mark was standing in the corridor outside the bathroom, trying to forget the words from his co-workers. Eventually, he put his head down and made his way back into the main office.

Hearing that had made him feel determined to prove that he belonged there. He would keep going, keep doing the job.

Show them that they were wrong about him.

And he would start by finding out what happened to Emily Burns.

Nine

The rest of the work day disappeared in a blink of a few hours. Requests for more information about Emily's social media, trying to track down her father. It had been time to leave before Mark knew it.

Now, sitting in his car, mobile phone in hand, his finger was hovering over the call button of Natasha's contact details. The screen dimmed, then finally turned to black, as he hesitated. The sky outside was darkening and his stomach rumbled, as he tried to decide whether to call her. Or eat first. Or grow a backbone instead.

He brought the phone back to life and swiped his pass-code over the screen. Stared at the contact name a little longer, then shook his head. He was about to place it back in his pocket, wondering what he'd eat, when a knock at his window nearly gave him a heart attack.

'Are you coming out or what?'

Natasha's voice was muffled by the window, but her smile wasn't. He placed a hand across his chest and then opened the car door. 'Scared the life out of me.'

'I was getting bored of waiting for you to decide to call

me,' Natasha replied, walking away from him and towards his house. 'That's what you were going to do, right?'

Mark didn't answer as he caught up to her and opened the front door.

They didn't exchange much further conversation once the door closed behind them.

Later, scrolling through a food delivery app trying to find something that looked appetising, Mark felt the inevitable slide from personal life back to thinking about the missing girl. Wondering if while he was smiling, satisfied, she was out there waiting for him to be interested in her again.

This was happening more often. It had once been easy to close his door and forget about the job as soon as he was at home. Lately, that had become more difficult. The more horror he witnessed – even in those short periods of time the job wasn't mind-numbingly boring – the more difficult it became to forget. The things people did to each other . . . It was enough to make him wonder how the human race had made it this far.

'I want something quick and greasy,' Natasha said, shaking him out of his thoughts. She was already getting dressed and sitting beside where he lay. 'I'm starving.'

'I don't think you'll have to worry about the greasy part,' Mark replied, settling on a takeaway place with the third-highest rating. 'Here you go.'

He watched her as she chose something on the menu and handed the phone back to him. Mark went for something similar and paid for it quickly. 'I best get dressed.'

'So, were you deciding whether or not to call me?'

Mark paused, boxers on but trousers still halfway down his legs. 'What do you mean?'

'Outside, when you were sitting in the car for five minutes. Was that what you were trying to decide?'

'No ... well ... yeah, I guess you caught me. Only because I didn't know if I should, you know?'

He managed to get his trousers up but couldn't see his socks anywhere. Probably balled up at the end of his bed. Or on the landing. He couldn't remember taking them off now. He was just glad that he had.

'That's okay, I know we've been moving a bit more quickly lately. I just wondered if the line you gave me at the start was real or not.'

'What line?'

'The whole shy thing,' Natasha said, waving it off as she spoke, as if it didn't matter. 'I suppose I just wasn't sure if you were telling the truth or not.'

Mark grimaced, his teeth coming together and grinding against each other. 'It wasn't a line. And things aren't moving *too* quick. I would have called. Eventually. It just takes me a bit of time. Courage and that.'

'It's fine, honestly, I get it. I'm just used to men who look the way you do being overly confident. Arrogant, even. It's not often you see someone who has everything together but doesn't realise it.'

'Now you're just trying to make me blush.'

Natasha laughed and it filled the room. 'Maybe so. Doesn't mean I'm not right though.'

'You're ... you're really good-looking too, you know.'

Mark waited for Natasha to respond, but she didn't say anything. Instead, she smiled at him then left him to put on more clothes. He heard her going downstairs.

That time, he was sure he'd said the right thing.

He found her sitting in his living room, legs tucked

underneath her on the sofa. He stood in the doorway, unsure what to do next. Would she want to cuddle? They hadn't really done much of that but he'd like to. He wanted to know if they were boyfriend and girlfriend in her mind, as they were in his. He hated that there was no way of knowing these things without asking.

'Stop hovering and sit down,' Natasha said, making the decision for him. Mark made his way into the room proper and perched on the edge of the sofa next to her.

They fell into a comfortable conversation – small talk, which made Mark feel on safer ground – until the food arrived. Natasha attacked it like she hadn't eaten in days, while he tried to take his time and not spill sauce down his chin.

'So, when you told me you were a detective, I thought you might solve murders and stuff like that,' Natasha said after a few minutes demolishing a burger. She was already reaching for a slice of garlic bread, before closing the Styrofoam lid on the container. 'Like on the telly.'

'Well, we don't get all that many in Liverpool, but I am with Major Crimes, so I guess it's only a matter of time. Honestly, it's not as glamorous as it sounds. Especially at my level.'

'Yeah, I'm sure you think that, but to an outsider, it definitely sounds more interesting than stacking shelves at Tesco or something like that.'

Mark let out a short laugh. 'Okay, I'll give you that. But your work sounds way better. More rewarding.'

'Then you've not met enough people in social work.'

That wasn't true, but Mark let it go. Working in the police service meant he'd dealt with all levels of social workers. Some more enamoured to their jobs than others, but commendable the vast majority of the time.

Probably the closest he could find to matching the police, to be fair.

'And anyway,' Natasha continued, sitting back into the sofa, seemingly finished with eating for now. 'I haven't been doing it long enough to have the really interesting cases that the older lot get. That's probably the same for you, I suppose.'

'I've been in the police for almost a decade. When I moved over from uniform to being a DC a couple of years ago, I thought it'd be something else. Turns out there's still the same problems, I just don't have to wear a uniform when they come up.'

'Or those ridiculous helmets,' Natasha replied, then laughed again, the sound of it echoing off the walls.

'You'd be glad of one of them when you're working in Concert Square on a Saturday night, I can tell you.'

Natasha stopped laughing and stared at him. Mark held her gaze for a few moments, then looked down at his half-eaten burger. He closed the lid, leaned forward and placed it on the coffee table. He was aware she was still staring at him as he brushed a few crumbs from his top lip.

'What are you working on at the moment then?'

Mark sat back on the sofa and shook his head. 'Nothing much. A missing teenager. Only been gone a few days, but they're not hopeful. I'm trying to be.'

'Happens all the time. I'm sure you know the score on that one. Quarter of a million a year? Usually back within a day or two. Only a tiny proportion disappear forever or end up . . . you know.'

'Dead,' Mark finished for her. 'There's something about this one I can't quite put my finger on. A part of the story I'm not seeing yet. I've only been on it a day though, so I'm sure it'll all come out. And I'm probably just pretending I have some kind of intuition, like all those old detectives seem to have.'

'Would it help if I started calling you Poirot?'

'As long as I don't have to grow the moustache.'

Natasha started to laugh, which set Mark off. When it subsided, he sighed and scratched the back of his head. 'Honestly, I thought it would be ... not easier, but something like that. Like I'd know what I was doing as soon as I was actually doing it. It's been eighteen months and I still feel clueless.'

There was a slight shift of weight from his shoulders as he spoke. A release. A momentary feeling of relief to share this with someone.

'I get that,' Natasha replied, moving a strand of hair back behind her ear. 'I'm sure it'll get easier. And that you're doing fine anyway.'

'I haven't made any massive screw-ups yet, thankfully.'

'How old is she?'

'Nineteen.'

'An adult ...'

'Exactly. Yet, the way her family talk about her – not outright, but it's implied by what they say – they act like she's far younger. Like she couldn't be trusted to look after herself. It doesn't seem like she was very popular. No friends in real life, only online.'

Natasha sighed and tucked her legs beneath her once more. 'Hopefully she'll turn up. I'm seeing a lot of that sort of thing at the moment. Teenage girls, dealing with social media and all of that crap. The bullying that's going on is rife. My colleagues who have been doing the job a lot longer reckon it's never been as bad as it is now.'

Mark nodded, unable to disagree. They sat in amiable silence for a little longer, tiredness suddenly washing over him. He thought about Emily Burns, the house where she'd last been seen and the family who'd been left behind.

He wanted Natasha to be right, for Emily to be found soon.

But something told him not to get his hopes up.

Ten

He was a minute's walk from the yard where the blood was found when the call had come in. Mark imagined there would have been little discussion before DI Bennett had taken over and called him in.

The scene was a hive of activity; uniforms swarming from all over the city. Young students being led from the fifteen-storey building overlooking the scene and questioned by uniformed police. Asked what they had seen, what they knew.

All of these people there for one reason.

The body of a young female had been found lying in a crumpled heap at the base of the building. In an alleyway, which was hidden from view at the front. Found that morning by an unlucky refuse collector. Dead after falling from the top of the building, which seemed taller every time Mark looked up. A long drop down.

He tried not to think of the condition she was in now as he worried about what he was going to say to Emily's family. The proximity of the scene where her blood had possibly been discovered suggested she had now been found. Possibly. Mark wasn't feeling the usual sense that something was about to end.

He could see the buildings around the yard in the distance, the walk from there to where he was now standing being cordoned off and checked.

'We're pulling CCTV at the moment,' a voice said beside him. Mark turned and saw a familiar face among a crowd of strangers. Detective Sergeant Stuart Cavanagh, a kind-eyed bloke who was only a few years older than him. They'd barely shared more than a few words of conversation over the past year and a half, but it had always been cordial. He hadn't shunned him or talked behind his back like the rest seemed to. Mark guessed he'd been told to make sure the new guy didn't mess anything up.

'Going to be difficult to pinpoint a time of death quickly,' Mark said, stepping back as another forensic officer turned up. 'Have you seen her?'

'You don't want to know.'

Mark nodded, but knew he would eventually have to see the body. If only to make sure it was Emily.

If that was possible.

'We're pretty sure it's her,' DS Cavanagh said, as if he was reading his thoughts. 'Same age, same build, same hair colour. Her face is ... well, not in the best condition. Hopefully they can sort that out before the family need to identify her.'

'No chance it's someone else? It's strange that no one has found her if she was there for a few days.'

'I see your point, but it would be some coincidence. From what I've been told, no one from the apartments has said anyone is missing. We asked a fair few of them if someone hadn't come out. Tough with these students, though. Don't know their arse from their elbow. I'm sure this has already got its own WhatsApp group. If anyone was missing from inside, we'd have been told by now. We have a young woman, possibly suicidal, nineteen years old, who was last seen on CCTV a few yards down the road. Now, a dead woman of the same age and build, lying at the bottom of a tall building. Doesn't take much to put it all together.'

'We don't know anything about Emily being suicidal, though, do we?'

'I'm just guessing. You know what these teenagers are like these days. Not a day goes by when we're not dealing with some form of bullying on social media, or mental health issues. Everyone pretending that they're kind people, until someone does something they don't agree with. And we're left to pick up the pieces.'

'Suppose so,' Mark said, wishing he could make this giant leap with DS Cavanagh. They didn't know for sure that Emily was suicidal. No one did. 'Take me over.'

DS Cavanagh gave him a look, but didn't say anything. He led the way, the sea of various forensic and uniforms parting in waves. They couldn't go too close without donning white suits, so they kept their distance but he could see into the hastily erected tent from where he was standing.

Mark could only see flashes of her. A flay of hair here, a twisted foot there. And a lot of blood. More than he'd probably ever seen. It fanned out around the body, like a painting by an artist he couldn't remember the name of. He didn't want to think too much of the impact from a height such as it was, but he could see the body hadn't broken up. That was what he'd been worried about most, he realised. That it would be unrecognisable to anyone. Instead, it looked like she had simply dropped to the floor and stopped being.

That's if you ignored everything around her, of course. It certainly looked like the young woman he'd been looking for. It was difficult to be sure, though, and it didn't help that he'd never met her in person.

There was only one way to be sure. The family would have to identify her.

He was suddenly glad he hadn't eaten that morning. Wondered for a second if he ever would again. It never became any easier for him, it seemed. Even when the others carried on as if this was just a fact of life, he still felt that queasiness in his stomach.

The faces behind the masks of those working in the tent looked blank and uncompromising. He knew that's the way they had to be, but not for the first time, he wondered if a career in welding or topiary would be more his thing.

'You've looked at her picture more than we have,' DS Cavanagh said, bringing Mark back to the real world. 'Does it look like her?'

Mark made a show of leaning forward for a closer look, but didn't really take much in. 'It does. Damn. I was hoping this was going to be one of those rare times we had good news for one family, at least.'

'Have you got very far in tracing her movements?'

'Not really,' Mark replied, taking the opportunity to turn his back and make a show of looking around the rest of the area. 'It was three nights ago that she left the house and was seen further up the road. Makes you wonder where she was the rest of the time. But the CCTV didn't show her leaving the yard where the blood was found.'

'You think this happened last night?'

'That'd be my guess. What about you?'

Cavanagh scratched the thick beard covering half his

face. 'I don't know. It's not an easily accessed area. She could have been sitting on that roof for a couple of days, I suppose. Working up the courage, maybe? We've worked stranger cases.'

'Yeah, I guess,' Mark said, but didn't feel confident. 'I hoped this wasn't going to be where I ended up with this one.'

There was a moment when he thought Cavanagh was going to lay a comforting hand on his shoulder, but he seemed to think better of it.

'That's how it goes sometimes,' Cavanagh said instead, placing his hands in his trouser pockets slowly. 'There'll be other cases for you, though. Ones with a better ending. You couldn't help this girl. Doesn't mean there won't be others out there you can help.'

Mark nodded without conviction, thinking of the family Emily had left behind. The faces he would soon have to visit and deliver the news to.

'Maybe it's not her,' Mark said, but even he didn't believe it now. Cavanagh gave him a grimace and walked away to talk to someone else on the scene, leaving Mark alone. He thought of Emily's mother, the way she was already struggling to face reality. The sullen younger brother, Charlie, who would retreat even further into himself now, he guessed.

He thought of Stephanie. Hoped this wouldn't break her. Knew it probably would. He could feel the weight of responsibility weighing him down, but also knew his role in all of this would soon be over. There'd be an inquest, where he'd have to explain his actions, but it would be a formality, he hoped.

He couldn't get it out of his mind, though. The fact that

something could have stopped this. If he had stayed at his desk all night until he'd found a secret – a key to finding her at the top of that building, waiting to be saved.

Mark tried to put that away – putting it in the little box in his mind he'd been told to construct when he first joined the police. In there, you place all the cases, the people, the victims, the perpetrators ... all the faces you try so hard to forget. You place them in the box and forget it exists.

He'd never been able to close the damn thing.

Eleven

Him

This was the part he hated the most.

Hearing them downstairs, moving around as if only a few feet above their heads, their son's life meant nothing.

Acting like all he needed was a job or a college course, rather than being left alone. Sitting him down at the dining-room table periodically to ask him what he was doing with his life. What he *wanted* to do with his life, as if they had all the answers.

Concerned eyes and the ability to make you feel both loved and like a disappointment at the same time.

Affecting interest. Strong hands, tapping against the table, as he explained what needed to happen.

Worried about him, wondering if there was anything they could do to help.

He could feel their eyes on him still, even now when he was alone. The look of desperation, as they attempted to work him out. To *understand* him. His wants, his needs, his *desires*.

There was nothing they could do now. It was too late.

They had missed the opportunity to make a difference. Lost in a haze which they had believed was a normal, everyday, family life. He'd felt ignored because they'd never listened. They'd let him drift away without ever realising he'd become unmoored. They'd been involved in his life every single minute, but never in an attempt to know him.

He felt hatred for them all.

He lifted the lid on his laptop and clicked in the address bar. He had the website memorised now, but it had taken a long time to remember the string of digits which had been thought up a long time before. When the site had been set up, privacy had been key.

He needed to be in this group. They were the people he needed to speak to most. And it couldn't be taken away from him.That's how it seemed to him now.

His fingers trembled over the keys as he finished typing, a black screen appearing and shuddering as he moved his cursor across the monitor. In the upper right-hand of the screen, he clicked a few times to find the hidden link, then pressed down.

The screen changed, a simple username and password box revealing itself. He logged into the forum, his password an endless, indecipherable series of letters, numbers and punctuation. Something he'd learned from all the time he'd spent lying on his bed, his laptop perched on him, reading and absorbing everything he could. Living a life he could never do outside that room. He tried to breathe normally, but he was beyond normality now. He pressed enter on his keyboard, waiting for the site to load and the posts to begin appearing. His breathing slowed as his safe space appeared. The place where he could find solace and freedom. He clicked on the only thread.

THE GAME

New comments were towards the bottom of the thread, the rules posted at the top. The beginning of the thread a series of questions – to the point, no messing around.

He could see new messages to be read, almost coaxing him to go there first. To read what other people had sent him. To see what stories had been shared, what people were saying.

Instead, he navigated to the last page. The newest comments left on the thread.

> **Deadbehindtheeyes** – *Advanced Member –*
> *3 hours ago*
> > Does anyone have any pictures of her yet?

> **Artasdeath** – *Forum Junkie – 3 hours ago*
> > Bit early yet. Got to make sure they
> > weren't caught. Could be she just chucked
> > herself into the river. Wouldn't surprise me.
> > She was messed up by the sounds of it.
>
> > NEED ANSWERS!

> **WestsideBlackSheep** – *Noob Member –*
> *2 hours ago*
> > OP – Where are you?

> **Deadbehindtheeyes** – *Advanced Member –*
> *2 hours ago*
> > @JaLoNeNoMoReYou need to come back
> > NOW! We need to know!

He rubbed sweaty palms against each other, clicked on the reply box, then hovered his fingers over the keys.

The Game had been a saviour to him. This forum, these people, they had saved his life. Gave him a purpose he didn't realise he needed. Didn't realise existed. They were more of a family to him than the strangers he shared a house with.

He didn't know if the people on here even realised it was real. That people were dying because of them. The power they had.

The Game gave him what he'd been looking for all those long, lonely years spent alone with only his thoughts for company. The dark, hidden secrets he kept inside.

If she had just loved him, things would have been different. If she had just given him the time of day, listened to him, accepted him ... maybe this wouldn't have happened.

She had been a nobody. A girl with no other options than the one he'd given to her. He had offered her salvation and she had rejected him. She could have been someone with him. But if she'd simply given in to him, he wouldn't have found this place. Wouldn't have found all those who had the same story as him, all looking for the answer The Game had given them.

There was a sound from somewhere, crunching and gravelly. He was aware of it, the noise making his fists clench, sweat break out on his brow.

He realised it was coming from him.

His teeth grinding together, as he thought of her face. The look she'd given him. Sympathy, sadness. The way she'd hummed and hawed, trying to find the right words.

Not the *right* words. The right words would have been very different to the ones she'd chosen. She would have welcomed him in. Touched his arm, smiled and reciprocated.

Instead, she'd stuttered and stammered and looked at him with nothing but pity. As if he'd just announced a beloved family pet had died, or he hadn't got a job he'd really wanted.

He never wanted to see that look.

Not from her. Ever again.

Now, he hunched over his screen as he imagined a different look on her face.

Like the look on Emily's face.

He needed a new player.

And he knew just who it should be.

She shouldn't have let slip what she'd been doing to people. Trusted him with her secret.

Then, it wouldn't have been used against her.

Twelve

Mark was dispatched to be with the family, given he was the only one from Major Crimes who had met with them.

Emily would be similarly dispatched elsewhere soon enough. Straight to the hospital morgue, to await identification by the family.

'That's all we know for now,' Mark said, finishing his stilted update. He'd arrived thirty minutes earlier, knowing word had already reached them of the discovery that morning. Uniforms had beaten him there.

'They're going to let me know when we'll be taking the next step, but for now, I'm afraid we'll have to wait for more news.'

He'd be done with the case by the end of the day, he thought.

He hoped they wouldn't be able to see much when they ID'd her. That this wouldn't be made even worse.

There was no sign of the younger brother but Julie and Stephanie were sitting together on one sofa. Stephanie with a hand on her mother's, the other softly caressing her back. The uncle was currently pacing up and down the small back yard.

'They don't know if it's her though,' Stephanie said. Her voice was still as solid and confident as it had been the previous day.

She was being strong for her mum, Mark thought.

'I mean, it could be anyone,' Stephanie continued, fixing Mark with a blue-eyed stare. Daring him to disagree with her, it seemed.

'Yes, that's true,' Mark said, treading carefully as he spoke. From what he'd seen of the body, he knew the odds were slim. That it was only a formality now. Yet, he couldn't come out and say that for sure, so he had to dance around the subject, as if there was another answer for them. As if they could still hope for a different outcome.

Mark felt that a narrative was being created already, now they had a body. He was being pushed in one direction, one he couldn't really argue against. The possible lines of enquiry he might approach the family with, the questions he could ask.

Suicide.

Self-harm, which caused the blood they found. When she couldn't see that through, or lost her nerve, she found an easier way. It was possible she could see the student flats from where she was standing, he thought. On the riverside, a new addition to the waterfront, a mile or so from the old dockyards and a little further still to the Albert Dock and Liver Building.

Yards away from where her blood was left to pool and be washed away.

'Do you think I'll have to see her?' Julie said, speaking for the first time since Mark had arrived. 'Like, identify her or something?'

'We'll deal with that as it comes, Julie,' Mark replied, trying to catch her eye and give her his patented caring look. Knowing the answer was yes, but knowing there was no good way to tell someone that within hours, they would see a dead body. Her eyes were fixed on a spot over his shoulder, towards the window. As if she was waiting to see Emily walk up the path to the front door.

He watched Julie's hands tremble, the same rhythmic motions they'd been making since he'd arrived. The electricity running through her body, struggling to be contained. The grief and horror that wanted to be released.

'We don't know if it's her yet, Mum,' Stephanie said again, continuing to hold on to her mother's hand, as if she could absorb whatever she was wanting to let out. 'Let's not get ahead of ourselves. Until we know for certain, Emily might come back at any moment.'

Mark had been around people who had lost loved ones in this type of situation before. Quite a few times, in fact. Yet each time seemed like the first.

No. That wasn't quite true, he thought.

Each time just became a little harder to get past. To put away and draw a close on. It sometimes felt like he left a little of himself behind with each family he dealt with. As if they were each taking a portion of his soul and keeping hold of it.

Mark shook his head, catching a frown from Stephanie as he did so. The radio was playing softly in the background, before a grave news voice kicked in.

'*A body has been found on Liverpool's waterfront area this morning, in the search for missing teenager Emily Burns . . .*'

Mark reached across and shut off the radio before

standing up, hoping to distract the two women. 'Shall I put the kettle on?'

'Seems like the good British thing to do,' Stephanie replied, as Julie continued to stare out of the window. 'You know where it is.'

It wasn't a question. He nodded and stood up, making his way towards the kitchen. He lifted the kettle and filled it, spying the big man out in the back garden through the window. He had his back turned to him, phone clasped to one ear, as the other hand gesticulated wildly. Mark stepped away, his eyes still on the man's back, clicking the kettle back into its base and flicking it on.

He wondered what the uncle was doing out there. Who he was talking to. What he was saying.

He took a few mugs down from the cupboard, rinsed them and put a teabag in each, lost for a few seconds in the mundanity of it. It wasn't exactly in the training, making cups of tea for grieving family members.

'Is my sister dead?'

Mark had been pulling the cutlery drawer open when the voice jumped into the silence behind him. He banged the thing shut, knives and forks startling themselves with a clang. He turned, breathing harder than he wanted to show.

'Charlie,' he said, trying to calm himself. 'I didn't hear you come in.'

'Is she dead?'

Mark cocked his head, quickly working out how best to approach the youngest member of the Burns family who had been mute up to now. 'I'm afraid we don't know. We're waiting to hear what's happening at the moment. Nothing has been confirmed yet. We should have more information about the next steps soon.'

'Why won't you answer the question properly? She's either alive or not. She's not Schrödinger's cat.'

Mark considered the young lad more closely, the way his arms folded across his chest, chin jutting forward with barely disguised disdain for him. The typical teenage pose when confronted with authority. There was something else there though. Something barely constrained, under the surface. He wasn't sure what it was. 'Someone has died,' he said, choosing his words ever more carefully. 'We don't know if it's Emily or not right now. As I said, we have to wait for more information.'

'I knew she would be,' Charlie replied. He was playing the role of unaffected teen well. But when Mark had spoken, he'd noticed a slight clouding of his eyes. As if he'd been expecting to hear something else. Had knowledge of something else.

'People like her don't just disappear,' Charlie said, the stock pose back, more confident now. 'Something happens to them. Or because of them. I'm just surprised she wasn't found sooner.'

'Well, we don't know it's her for certain yet . . .'

'Yeah, because there's loads of fat nineteen-year-old girls from Liverpool missing right now.'

Probably way more than you realise, Mark thought, but kept his mouth shut. He knew Charlie was trying to provoke a reaction from him. It seemed that was the trade when it came to teenagers. Always trying to get attention from you. Yet, it didn't feel as real coming from this young lad. The lack of sympathy for Emily was jarring, but Mark thought it might all be part of the same act. 'We're doing all we can to get you and your family the answers quickly. These things take time though. I'm sorry.'

'Doesn't bother me. Won't make much difference to my life if she's here or not.'

Mark couldn't work out why he would be saying this. A plea for attention? Wanting to be noticed? Or was there something else he wasn't saying? 'We haven't really had a chance to talk.'

'That's because you've been too busy chatting up the sexy half of the twins,' Charlie said, a wry smile appearing as he studied Mark's face for a reaction. 'It's okay, I'm used to that by now. We all are. We know Stephanie is the star of the show in our family. Everyone can't wait to speak to her. Didn't expect you lot to be any different.'

Mark leaned back against the kitchen counter, struggling to keep his eyebrows from raising in surprise. He may not have had much to say the previous day, but it seemed Charlie had a lot of thoughts rolling around in his head. 'You didn't get on with Emily then?'

'Can't really speak ill of the dead, can I?'

'We don't know if it's her yet . . .'

'Yeah, yeah, we all have to wait around to find out,' Charlie cut in, his voice affecting a mocking tone now. 'I know how this works. She'll have to be identified and then there'll be a funeral and all of that. I just want it all to be over with already.'

Mark narrowed his eyes at the boy, but he couldn't work out if this was unfocused anger. Grief. Or something more.

'I guess she's finally getting the attention she always wanted, anyway,' Charlie continued, tapping fingers against the wall behind him. His eyes flicked from Mark's towards the window and the uncle, still pacing outside. 'A better kind of attention, anyway.'

Mark took note of the implication. 'How did Emily get on with everyone? Your mum, your uncle?'

Charlie gave an exaggerated roll of his eyes. 'Everyone basically left her to it. She'd have tantrums sometimes, but she'd been quieter lately. I was glad of that. She didn't have any friends. Maybe if she spent more time with people in real life, than online, it would be different. It's not like anyone cares what I think anyway. As long as I'm going to school and keeping out of sight, everyone's happy. No one gives one if *I'm* happy or not. It was all about the twins.'

'Is your Uncle Rich around a lot?'

A shrug of the shoulders. 'I don't really notice anymore. I try and keep out of their way. I just want to get out of here as soon as possible.'

'Still, it must have been a shock when Emily went missing.'

Charlie didn't answer for a few seconds, looking away from Mark again. When he spoke, his voice had softened somewhat. 'Not really. She is ... she was ... different. Always living in Stephanie's shadow. Like we all were. Only it was probably harder for her. You ask me, if she didn't top herself ... if something actually happened *to* her, I wouldn't go looking very far for answers.'

Mark watched as Charlie's eyes flicked towards the back garden again. He turned to look and by the time he'd turned back around, Charlie had disappeared from the kitchen.

Mark turned back to the counter, glancing up at the window, averting his eyes when he saw the uncle outside.

Watching him.

Thirteen

The journey to the morgue had been quiet, the back of the car thick with tension. Mark was sitting in the passenger seat, Julie and Stephanie in the back. The driver had picked them up without a word, knowing this wasn't the time to talk, thankfully. Before then, it had been a rough few hours back at the house, endless questions he couldn't answer, thrown at him with increasing venom.

Charlie had skulked off back upstairs, which had been a relief. He knew he needed to speak to him more, but that morning wasn't the time. He had been hesitant to leave him alone with the uncle, but a uniform was now at the house and would be on a more permanent basis, if his growing suspicion about Emily's death was eventually confirmed.

He didn't think it was suicide. Others would call it a gut feeling, but he just felt there was something more to this. The conversation with Charlie had helped bolster that idea. There was some part of the story he wasn't quite seeing clearly.

Yet.

Now, this. A family IDing a body. Another of those parts of his jobs he hated the most.

At last count, there were at least seven or eight things he hated the most.

DI Bennett had told him over the phone that nothing had been found on the body. Not a broken phone, a purse; nothing personal at all. Mark could tell how odd his boss had found this, the items a nineteen-year-old girl – woman – was likely to have on her being missing. It meant that the search had been widened along the waterfront – he'd be helping out with that, as soon as he was finished with the family, he guessed.

It made sense why they hadn't been able to track her phone to that location now. It was probably as dead as she was, travelling up the River Mersey, to somewhere it would never be found.

The car pulled to a stop in the hospital car park, Mark exiting and moving quickly to open the back door for the two women. They shuffled out, following close behind him as he led the way. He had done this a few times before, but he felt the same dread and anxiety as the first time he had done it. Knowing they would be looking to him afterwards for words of comfort and justice. For things he might not be able to give them.

Within a few minutes, they were waiting in a brightly lit corridor in the bowels of the hospital. Through double doors at the end lay a number of cold rooms, filled with the bodies of all those who had died in the past few days. He tried not to think of how many that would be, how many lay waiting behind thin doors. Instead, he talked Julie and Stephanie through what was going to happen next. Carefully, trying to keep them from not breaking down any further.

'You'll see her, you'll be asked to confirm if it's her or not. Don't worry if you can't. If you need to stop at any time, just tell me, or the coroner's assistant who'll be with us. If you need to take your time, that's fine. If you don't, that's fine too. We'll do this exactly how you need to.'

'Will I be able to touch her?' Julie said, her voice breaking, as Stephanie took hold of her hand. 'I just want to hold her – would that be okay?'

Mark paused, knowing the answer he had to give, but not looking forward to the response to it. 'I'm afraid not. It's a case of not wanting to disturb any evidence. Hopefully that part will be cleared quickly. You'll have the chance at some point.'

He knew the likelihood was that Julie would never touch her daughter again. That she wouldn't be buried for a while and that it would be too late when the body was released to the family. Not that he thought it would stop her. She would need that final touch. That final contact. It would haunt her forever that she wouldn't get it.

'We don't know if it's her yet, Mum,' Stephanie cut in, standing up from the chair and slouching against the wall opposite, repeating her now-familiar refrain. She'd been saying that a lot over the past couple of hours, as if doing so could make it true. 'Let's not get ahead of ourselves. It could be someone else for all we know. It's not like people haven't made mistakes before.'

Mark could feel Stephanie's eyes on him, but he chose to look at Julie instead. She was staring at the floor, but he could still see the dark marks underneath her bloodshot eyes. Her hands were cradled together, almost clasped in prayer. 'If you have any questions, just ask, okay, Julie? We want to make this as painless as possible.'

That earned a scoff from Stephanie, which Mark ignored. He knew he was there as support first and foremost, but also as a punching bag of sorts. He would have to take the anger and hurt the family would soon be feeling. The endless questions they would have. The answers he couldn't provide, leaving him looking toothless and pointless.

That's how it always was.

He wished he'd taken the previous day off work. Called in sick or something. Stayed in bed with Natasha and missed all of this entirely.

'What's taking so long?' Stephanie asked, pushing herself away from the wall and walking towards the double doors separating them from the inner corridors of the morgue. Mark watched as she peered through the frosted glass. He didn't make any move, knowing they were locked and she wouldn't be able to get through.

'They'll be with us any minute,' Mark replied, shifting forward in his seat. 'They'll be making sure everything is prepared for us to go in and out, that's all.'

'I've never seen a dead body before,' Stephanie said, moving back towards them now. She swiped a hand through her blonde hair, pulling it back from her face. She let it linger on the back of her neck as she did so. 'I don't know what to expect.'

Her voice was quieter now and Mark could see the strain creeping into her otherwise flawless features. She didn't have the same dark rings under her eyes as her mum, but for the first time, he could sense that the weight of holding things together was becoming a burden.

'I have,' Julie said, her voice barely above a whisper. 'Your nan. They never let me see your granddad, but I was with your nan at the end. And afterwards. I had to put her make-up on for the funeral because they didn't do it right. Made her look like a clown. I couldn't have her looking like that. She wouldn't have liked what they did.'

'I didn't know that,' Stephanie replied, coming back to sit next to her mum. Mark stood up, moving away to give them some space. Not that he could go very far.

'She was always particular about how she looked,' Julie continued, still unmoved from her position. 'It didn't seem right that she went out looking less than perfect. It was only right. There's so much to think about now. Everyone we'll have to tell, the plans we'll have to make, where we'll have the wake, the church part ... everything.'

'Shush, Mum,' Stephanie said, talking over her mother as she continued to mumble about the things she had to do. 'We can sort all that out if we have to. We can't get ahead of ourselves yet.'

Mark watched the two of them together, Stephanie comforting her mum as she continued to shut down. From the outside, if you couldn't see the age difference, you'd be forgiven for thinking Stephanie was the older of the pair: the mother figure, comforting her daughter. Telling her everything was going to be all right, even when the evidence suggested otherwise. He imagined that in years to come, this would be a moment Stephanie would look back on as the time she really became an adult. She was about to turn twenty, but he didn't really believe she would have experienced anything like what she was about to go through.

There was movement behind the doors and then they were pulled open, cool air rushing towards them. A woman in a long white coat, hair scraped back and glasses perched on her face, appeared and looked towards him first, then at the other two women.

'You can follow me through now,' she said, giving Mark a quick glance. 'We're ready for you.'

Julie got to her feet first, slowly and with a deep intake of breath. Stephanie followed her up, reaching out to grasp her mother's hand. Mark fell into step behind the pair, then took hold of the door as the woman directing them moved ahead of the group.

They passed a few rooms on either side of the dimly lit corridor, the temperature seeming to drop with each step.

'Here we are,' the woman said, coming to a stop next to a viewing window. Mark leaned against the wall a few feet away from Julie and Stephanie, waiting to jump in if necessary. For now, he was content to stand back and try to not get in the way.

'When you're ready, he'll pull the cover back and you'll be able to see her,' the assistant continued, her voice level and precise. 'I'll ask you to confirm if it is Emily or not.'

'We can't even be in the same room as her?' Stephanie asked, almost aggressive in her tone. Mark could see it having no effect on the assistant though. He knew she would have been through worse. Much worse.

'I'm afraid not,' the assistant said, turning back to the window. 'Just let me know when you're ready.'

Stephanie looked towards her mother, who was refusing to look up. Her eyes were fixed to the floor, her head shaking from side to side. Mark wondered if she was ready for what was to come. If you could ever be ready for something like this.

'Mum?'

'Okay,' Julie said after a few seconds, slowly lifting her head up, her voice cracking, tears springing to her eyes. 'Please.'

Stephanie used both hands to hold on to her mum, as the assistant gave the nod to the man behind the window. He carefully removed the blanket covering the bump on the stretcher. Julie leaned forward half a step, peering towards the young woman lying there. Mark walked forward, in line with the women now, and waited.

There was a sharp intake of breath from Stephanie as the cadaver came into view. A noise escaped from Julie, a choked sob. Mark waited for the inevitable breakdown, the rush of emotion.

'It's not her,' Stephanie said, soft and faltering. 'That's not Emily.'

'Stephanie, don't,' Julie began, but she was frowning towards the woman on the table as well.

'Mum, that's not her, I can tell.'

'This is a common reaction,' the assistant said, moving closer to the two women. 'Just make sure. Look at her and see if anything looks familiar about her.'

'She's about the same age, the same hair colour, but that's about it,' Stephanie said, becoming more sure of herself. 'That's not my sister. Mum, tell them. Tell them it's not Emily.'

Julie's hand was over her mouth.

'Can we see her shoulder,' Stephanie said suddenly, turning first to Mark, then the assistant and touching her own back. 'She had a birthmark, like me, only bigger. We should be able to see that.'

Mark looked towards the assistant, who turned towards the window and motioned towards the guy next to the body. He turned the body over and moved the gown down over the woman's back.

Stephanie made a noise at the back of her throat and staggered back. Julie collapsed to her knees, a mixture of sobs and incredulous laughter escaping from her.

'It's not her,' she gasped. 'Thank god, it's not her.'

Mark's eyes narrowed as the man behind the window dropped the body back on the gurney.

If it wasn't Emily, where was she?

And whose body was this?

Fourteen

The atmosphere in the car was more charged than on the way to the hospital. Mark listened as Julie and Stephanie chatted animatedly in the backseat. The events of the past couple of hours seemed to have reinvigorated them somehow. As if before there was no hope, but now anything was possible.

Like Emily had been brought back to life.

Mark had heard Julie call the big fella, Uncle Rich, first, almost breathless with excitement as she'd informed him. A short, punctured conversation with her other child followed. The content didn't seem to go much further than *Your sister's alive!* before the phone had been handed back to Rich.

He was itching to get back so he could speak with DI Bennett and find out what the hell was going on. Why no one had checked the body for a birthmark. If they even knew she'd had one. He'd managed less than a minute on the phone to her earlier, giving her the update on the body's identification. An expletive-ridden ten seconds had followed, before she'd ended the call abruptly.

It wasn't going to be as easy as they'd hoped.

'Do you know who it could be then?' Stephanie said, leaning forward, her head between the seats in front.

'We're going to find that out now,' Mark replied, propping an elbow on the passenger window lip and turning slightly to face Stephanie. 'I'm just sorry you both had to go through that. I can promise you that it's never happened to me before.'

'It's not your fault. We're just relieved it wasn't Emily.'

'Still ... that's not an experience I enjoy inflicting on people.'

Stephanie caught his eye and held it. 'We're just happy to have you supporting us through this. Isn't that right, Mum?'

Julie hummed a reply, her gaze fixed to the mobile phone screen in her hand. He glanced her way, wondering how long this change in her would last.

Mark didn't think it would be long before they would be returning to the hospital. He couldn't work out why he felt that way.

Maybe it was the fact that the dead girl in the morgue had been found within shouting distance of where Emily's blood had been found.

'Did she look familiar at all to you?' Mark said, turning in his seat as far as his seatbelt would allow him. 'Did you recognise her? Maybe you've seen her somewhere else, or with someone?'

Stephanie shook her head. 'I couldn't really tell what she looked like – she didn't look good. There wasn't much to see.'

Even despite the coroner's best efforts, the young woman at the morgue was in a terrible state. A fall from a height had a way of changing the look of someone.

At least it hadn't been face first, Mark thought. It would have been a much longer wait to find out it wasn't Emily. He wondered what the family of the actual victim was going through now. Whether they even knew their daughter, their sister, their granddaughter, was missing and now dead.

Mark felt there would have to be some kind of link between the two women, but he didn't think it would prove easy to find. Especially considering they didn't currently know who the dead girl was.

Thoughts shot through his mind, even as Stephanie continued to lean in between him and the driver. He could feel the pull of the investigation – wanting to get back on the streets, back in the office, working out what the answers to all of this were. Even as another part of him wished to be back at home, in relative safety.

'It doesn't explain the blood,' Stephanie said quietly, almost mumbling it under her breath. 'Unless it's not Emily's, but this other girl's? I guess this isn't over yet. Probably got way ahead of ourselves.'

'There's a long way to go, yes,' Mark replied. Stephanie looked away, but didn't lean back into her seat. 'Best thing to do is stay positive. I'm sure things will change now. More answers will be coming.'

Stephanie seemed to accept this, flopping back in her seat. She began gnawing away on one of her painted fingernails, Mark watching her for a second or two before settling back into his seat.

He wasn't sure what was going to happen next, but he knew it wouldn't be anything good.

It'll be media, he thought. A circus, from now on. One missing, one dead. The way Mark thought now, there were only two options. Either this was a massive coincidence, or the missing Emily and unknown dead woman were connected.

That threw up two more options. Either Emily was still in danger or there was another scenario. That Emily's blood was there following an altercation with whoever ended up at the bottom of that building.

That Emily was on the run.

Not enough evidence for that yet, Mark thought, but it was another wrinkle to an already pretty screwed-up picture that was forming.

Either way, he needed to find Emily. And that meant media. It meant people looking for her. It meant her face being shared by everyone in the area. It would have been one of the next steps anyway, even before the body had been found. With her family reporting her missing, it made sense to get them out in front of the cameras, just as the media glare was trained on the story. It would lodge in the minds of people watching.

You can't hide for long when the world is looking for you.

Fifteen

Mark walked through the kitchen and into the back garden, where he could talk a little more privately. The family were now ensconced in the living room, a renewed sense of hope tangible among them all.

From the sound of DI Bennett's voice, things had clearly changed now the body had turned out to be some other poor girl.

'Any news on ID?'

He imagined there would be a few people being shouted at back at the station for being too quick to believe the body was Emily Burns. He had no doubt he would've been on the end of one of those bollockings if he'd been there as well.

'Joanna Carter,' DI Bennett said, once Mark was outside. 'Has that name come up at all?'

'Not from my investigations so far,' Mark replied, shaking his head. 'I've not got very far with the social media aspect though, so can't say if they're connected online or something. It's all moved on a bit since yesterday afternoon. Is that the dead girl?'

'Woman,' DI Bennett corrected, tutting to herself over

the phone. 'Twenty years old. Student, from down south originally, so I imagine it's unlikely she'd know Emily.'

'Not that unlikely, if there's been contact online.'

'Nonetheless, she lived in the building where we found her. Private student accommodation. Not cheap either. She was studying medicine, at the City university. A world away from a place like your missing girl's house. She hadn't been seen for a few days, but didn't exactly have many friends in the building. Kept herself to herself, according to a whole bunch of students we've been speaking to today. None of them knew Emily when her name was mentioned. Seems like Joanna was a bit of a loner. Would have made things a bit easier if she had a boyfriend or girlfriend, at least. Once we realised it wasn't Emily, we went back over those who lived in the building. Should have been our first action really, but I guess we all just thought it would be too much of a coincidence, that we would find a body a few yards from where Emily's blood was found and it not be her. A mistake that won't be happening again.'

'So, you think there's some kind of connection?'

'What do you think?' DI Bennett said, a patronising tone creeping into her voice, which made Mark grit his teeth a little. 'Dead woman, found not that far from Emily's last known location. Blood found at that location – nothing else. Emily goes missing in the same area. Doesn't exactly take Sherlock to work this one out. Come on, Mark. I know you like the family, but there's something not right with this whole picture. With this *Emily*.'

'What about the blood? Or the fact Emily has been missing for three days and we've only just found Joanna Carter's body?'

'Maybe there was some kind of altercation between the

two,' DI Bennett replied, not seeming sure of anything she was saying now. 'It's not that far from where we found this woman. Maybe she kept her on the roof for a day or two, not knowing what to do, before coming up with this ... plan. Make it look like suicide. Only, she didn't think of what would happen next. Lots of options. We just need to find the link. We're going over Joanna's personal effects now. Her family will be up here any time now to identify her properly. Let's hope we've got it right this time.'

'This feels like a rush to cover a mistake,' Mark said, then instantly regretted it. 'I mean, we've got no evidence to suggest Emily could be a suspect. Right?'

'What are your theories?' DI Bennett said, sidestepping the question. 'If the two are related, that seems to be the most logical outcome.'

Mark blew out a breath and swept a hand through his hair. 'As I said, I haven't been working on this long enough to have much to go on. If she's involved with Joanna's death, then either she was the only one involved, or there's more to it. For now, she's simply a person of interest. Maybe they were in some kind of relationship or something? Or they liked the same bloke and it bubbled over. I don't know right now. All we do know is that we need to track down Emily and fill in the missing blanks to this story.'

'You know what we need to do, right?'

'We need to put the family out in front of the media ...' Mark said, wishing he hadn't been right in what was coming. Not really understanding why he felt that way. 'Tricky situation, if what you're thinking is even close to what has actually happened.'

'Very true, but we need to flush her out,' DI Bennett

replied. 'I'll explain how it should be presented to the family. I don't want it getting out that there's possibly a link between the two of them. Just in case there isn't and we look even worse than we do right now. For the moment, we'll treat the two cases with a quiet bond. You continue your investigation into Emily's disappearance and I'll have DS Cavanagh involved with the Joanna Carter death. See if we can figure out if there's a connection at all between the two. Everything goes through me and then the DCI and DSI. Whether it's murder or suicide, hopefully we can find out quickly.'

'You think it was a fall, a push, or ...' Mark didn't need to finish. He never liked the S word. It felt wrong, somehow. 'I mean, was any evidence found on the roof of the building that could give any indication?'

'No obvious signs of a struggle or someone being held against their will, if that's what you mean. Doesn't mean that didn't happen though. Could have been cleaned up in an attempt to hide the truth. Forensics are going over the rooftop as we speak. The building is over fifteen floors high. She lived on the fourth floor. Seems an odd place to find yourself, that far up.'

'CCTV in the building proving useful at all? Does it cover much of the inside?'

DI Bennett hummed an agreement. 'Lobby and entrance. And lifts. We're going over the footage now. Her phone had a few missed calls, but that was it. They were all from her family. We've spoken to one of the other students who said she tried knocking at her room last night, but when she didn't get an answer, she just assumed she had earphones in.'

'No easy answers from me, boss,' Mark said, moving his

hand to the back of his head and massaging some life into his neck. 'All I can tell you is that even if Emily is involved, I doubt you'll get far with the family. All they can say at the moment is that she was "troubled", whatever that means. There is one more thing though ...'

'What's that?' DI Bennett replied.

'I spoke to the youngest kid earlier. Just before we had to leave to go to the Royal to identify the body. He said something about the uncle, which is an avenue we really should consider alongside all of this. He made a comment that if something had happened to Emily, then we should possibly look towards him. And there was something about Emily getting attention, implying that maybe the uncle had been giving her unwanted attention. Which would make him a much better suspect than Emily herself, if you know what I mean?'

'This is becoming more convoluted by the minute. At the moment, we have nothing to tie that in with the actual dead woman we've found. So, if something was happening with the uncle, that might be secondary?'

'Possibly,' Mark replied, turning the thought over in his mind to see how it fit. Realised quickly that nothing did. 'Something to consider down the line, maybe? Always best to be ahead of the game, I suppose.'

'You've been on this twenty-four hours now,' DI Bennett said finally, after a few moments of silence. 'Setting the other death to one side, what have been your initial thoughts – the disappearance, intentional or not? What do you think about this family?'

Mark paused, trying to shake his thoughts into some semblance of order. 'There's something there, under the surface. Something we're not being told. I've got no idea what it is, or if it's even anything to do with either Emily's disappearance or the dead woman. Could just be like every other family we know.'

'What's that?'

'Secrets and lies. Every family has those. I can only keep digging. People don't go missing out of the blue – well, not often, anyway. Not without some kind of reason. She's out there and we need to find her. Every minute that passes, well, I don't have to tell you what the likely outcome will be.'

'No, you don't,' DI Bennett said with a sigh. There was a pause, then she continued. 'This is why I hate missing person cases. Far too many questions and never enough answers. How are the family holding up?'

'As best as they can, under the circumstances. I really wish I hadn't had to take them to the Royal though. Doesn't exactly make us look good.'

'No, you're right. But there was nothing in the initial report that mentioned distinguishing features. If there was, we wouldn't have done that. Don't worry. I've made sure that uniform will be told of proper practices.'

Mark ended the call and opened the door back inside. He needed to prepare the family for the next stage. How would they react to having to appear in front of a bunch of cameras? How would they cope with the scrutiny they were about to expose themselves to?

Sixteen

Mark hovered in the doorway of the living room. He could see the youngest in the family, scowling at the television in the corner. He turned over the boy's words from earlier that day, trying to find a way of fitting in Joanna Carter if the uncle was involved.

His phone buzzed in his pocket.

Natasha.

He checked it in the kitchen, putting his half-drunk cup of tea on the side. Smiled at the sight of her name and the message attached.

Thinking of you.

Mark fired off a quick response in kind, then pocketed his phone. A thought flashed through his head as he did so, the worry that things were moving too quickly between them. He quickly banished it, hoping that he was wrong. That sometimes, things are just right.

He shook his head and tried to forget what was happening a world away from where he was. Where his life was. Went back to work.

Charlie seemed to relax a little once his uncle left, something Mark noted. It had been almost imperceptible, but he had noticed the lad's shoulders lose a little tension. But Mark still wasn't sure if he was reading into things that weren't there. He'd tried to engage Charlie in conversation again, but had seen all his attempts swatted back at him.

'I'm going upstairs,' Charlie mumbled, pushing past Mark as he continued to stand half-in and half-out of the living room. Mark waited for Julie to protest, but she barely acknowledged him leaving. Stephanie was staring at the phone in her hand, her thumb resting on the screen and then scrolling down.

'Have you been sharing the story around?' Mark said, walking into the room. He placed his file of notes down on the windowsill for a few seconds, trying to make the next transition as easy as possible. He needed to go upstairs and look over Emily's bedroom. 'Don't let yourself get bogged down in all that social media stuff.'

'What else am I supposed to do?' Stephanie replied, glancing up at him then returning her gaze back to the screen. 'Her photo has been shared a few thousand times now. I'm just making sure nothing gets missed.'

'I understand, but there are people checking into that sort of thing.'

'Yeah, well, it doesn't hurt to have another set of eyes on it as well, does it?'

Mark didn't have an answer for her, so instead turned to Julie, who hadn't reacted. She was watching the television in the corner of the room, a twenty-four-hour news channel playing quietly. It wouldn't be long before Joanna Carter was named as the body found earlier, which would drive it home to this family that Emily was still out there. Still unfound.

'All the time in the world to talk about some no-mark

celeb, but nothing about my girl,' Julie said, the words spat out of her mouth with more vehemence than Mark had been expecting. 'You'd think they'd be at least a little interested.'

'People go missing every day,' Stephanie replied, before Mark had a chance to say anything. 'They'd never talk about anything else if they just talked about all the young people who had disappeared.'

Julie shaped as if to turn on her daughter and say something, but she closed her mouth instead. Mark guessed what she was about to say.

It mattered more when it was your own. You wanted everyone to feel the same way as you. To care as much. And it was never going to be that way and you knew it to be true. You never know the moment your life changes forever. Not until later, when you can look back and pinpoint it. He thought that would be what Julie would be doing now, going over every single moment she could possibly remember, trying to discover the moment when things had changed. When her daughter could have been saved from whatever was happening to her.

Mark knew it was never that simple.

He also knew the odds in play now. No suggestion of issues, no history of running away, no reason to leave ... a young woman going missing in those circumstances usually doesn't end well. Or they're hiding something big enough that their life is never the same even if they do return.

But the blood. Mark kept returning to the blood that had been found.

Red equals danger.

*

'I just keep thinking of that poor girl's parents,' Julie said, a flicker of sadness flashing across her face. 'They won't get a second chance like we have.'

'Do you mind if I take another look in Emily's room?' Mark said, on his feet before he'd finished the question. 'I know uniformed police have already gone through it, but I want to make sure we haven't overlooked anything at all. Even the smallest thing might help.'

Julie nodded, waving him away with one hand as she turned the volume up on the television. Stephanie caught his eye as he slipped past, but he didn't stop.

Mark heard soft music escaping from underneath a door as he reached the top of the stairs. Charlie – secluding himself away and listening to something vaguely familiar to him. A voice he'd heard on the radio or somewhere recently. He paused outside the door, trying to place the artist's name, but eventually gave up. Downstairs, he heard mumbled voices, but couldn't make out what was being said.

He walked across and pushed down on the handle to another room on the landing. He didn't need to go inside, recognising the room as belonging to an older woman. The dressing table on view, the carefully placed ornaments, perfumes. He decided it was Julie's room and turned back around. Down a short passage, he knew from an earlier trip, lay the bathroom, so he pushed open the door leading to the only other room leading off.

Stepping inside, Mark felt a wave of emotion hit him. The reality of what was left behind, now stark and uncompromising. He shuffled forwards, leaving the door open behind him as he walked further into the room.

It was always this way for him. The smallest details

suddenly hitting him the hardest. It was never the feelings of those waiting for a loved one to reappear. It was the items the person missing had held dear to them. The things and objects that they had kept closest to them, in the one room where they probably felt safest.

Not always, of course. He'd dealt with enough cases over the years to know that for some, it was the bedroom which became a prison. The abuse they would suffer, the pain and hurt that would occur.

He hoped that wasn't the case for Emily. Mark thought of the burly Uncle Rich – the manner of him. The way he filled any space he occupied. He heard the words of his superior echoing around his mind. *It's usually someone close to them.*

Charlie's words rolled around there too.

The room was larger than he'd expected, but then he imagined until recently, both twins would have been sleeping there. That would have vastly reduced the space, but he knew Stephanie had moved out and away to university a year or so earlier. The room had a dark vibe to it, but elements of typical teenage girl life also. A few posters dotted the walls, some canvas art prints which depicted some film stars he recognised. A book cover he didn't – a pale hand holding a green apple, the black background giving the image a sinister overtone. The words *Life* and *Death* emblazoned above it.

The bed was between single and double sized. A bookcase, filled with what he imagined was the past decade of Emily's reading habits. He scanned the titles, recognising some of the more well-known names. He'd never really been a reader, so it impressed him somewhat that Emily seemed to be. The small flat-screen television perched atop a chest of drawers next to it looked dusty and unused. Compared to everything else in the room, it looked as if it were the only thing that wasn't kept to a certain ... standard.

There was a desk-slash-dressing table underneath the window, a few nick-nacks left behind on the surface. A mirror on a pedestal towards the back of the desk had been swivelled around so its back faced into the room.

He looked around more, noticing the absence of anything beauty-related. No hair straighteners or dryer. No make-up or nail varnish bottles. Mark pursed his lips and shook his head slightly. What on the surface looked normal began to strike him as odd.

He moved to the bedside cabinet and opened the drawers slowly. Inside, a few things had been left behind by the uniforms who had initially investigated her disappearance. Mark knew some items would be waiting for his further inspection now, the uniforms handing over evidence to the Major Crimes Unit. For now, it would be his job to piece it all together.

From the report, he knew notebooks had been taken. They had been checked for a possible note left behind, but he imagined it would have been mentioned if one had been found. Another thing he would have to go over – the task of poring over its contents, trying to ascertain whether the words of a teenage girl meant anything in relation to her disappearance.

Mark sat down on the bed, pausing for a second and sighing loudly. He stood up, pulling back the covers, then the sheet underneath. Against the mottled white of the mattress lay a navy blue-coloured diary, a small sticker on its cover. One word scrawled across the white of it.

THOUGHTS

He picked it up, turning it over in his hand, noting its thickness. He tucked the sheet back in with one hand, then lay the duvet over it, and sat down on the edge of the bed.

The first page was blank, but the next one was filled with tiny, slanted handwriting, taking up all the available space. He continued to flick through the pages, seeing most of the same writing, interspersed with thick, black blocks of words. Words which took up entire pages by themselves.

The notebook was almost to its end, with only a few blank pages left to fill. Mark turned back to the beginning, reading a few lines and immediately feeling a sense of guilt for doing so.

I'm seventeen years old and no one has even looked at me. They barely know I exist. If I wasn't a twin, I reckon everyone in school would have had trouble picking me out of a lineup. S has never had that problem, of course. Everyone knows who she is. They've never bothered with me though. I could be invisible for all I know. It would explain a few things, I suppose. Even the geekier boys leave me alone. I'm not even good enough for them. I thought it would get better once out of high school, but if anything it's got worse. I have no friends, I have no boys interested in me. I'm alone. I don't have anything to look forward to. I don't have anything to remember. I wake up every single day and wonder what the point of all this is? I wonder if it's worth it. Whether I should even try anymore.

Mark read on, scanning the pages, also filled with similar feelings of woe and loneliness. The handwriting began as precise and neat, before slipping into angry block capitals, the ink almost bleeding from the page.

Further in, there was a list.

Initials. He wasn't sure what they meant.

JS
MK
AP

He wanted to reach out to the person writing these words and tell them it would be okay. Then, a thought came to him thick and hard. A realisation.

It was probably already too late for that.

'Enjoying the read?'

Mark's head shot up towards the voice from the doorway, closing the notebook in his hands with a snap. 'I . . . I found it under the bed. Thought it might be important.' He didn't know why he was trying to justify himself, but couldn't help it.

Stephanie leaned against the doorframe, seemingly studying him for something. 'Well, I guess it might be.'

'You've read it?'

Now it was Stephanie's turn to look towards the floor. 'Yes, a while ago. I wouldn't expect to find many answers in there. Emily . . . she was troubled.'

'How troubled are we talking here? Because I thought before that it was just, you know, the normal amount for a teenager?'

Stephanie sighed deeply, then looked up at him. 'If I tell you something, do you promise it won't change your opinion of her? That you won't let them stop looking for her, even if it means Emily isn't who you thought she was?'

Mark swallowed, trying to work out the best answer to her questions. 'No one will stop looking for her, Stephanie. But, this is the kind of thing we need to know. What kind of trouble was she in?'

'No, you've got it wrong,' Stephanie replied, a small chuckle escaping from her lips. She walked into the room, her voice dropping lower as she spoke. 'She wasn't the one who was in trouble. She *was* the trouble. I think . . . I think she might have done something stupid.'

Seventeen

'So you can see why I say she was trouble,' Stephanie continued, sitting down next to Mark on the bed. The perfume he'd smelled in the car earlier had faded somewhat now, but a little still lingered.

'How?'

'You were reading her book,' Stephanie replied, a hand gesturing towards the notebook in his hands. She was looking down at the floor, not at him. Her blonde hair covered the side of her face, cascading down like a waterfall of colour. 'You can see her state of mind.'

'I didn't get very far.'

'We used to share this room before I moved away. Just the two of us in here, every day. Barely enough room for both of us. Looking at it now, I don't know how we managed it. Everyone expected us to be like two peas in a pod because we're twins, but we were very different people. We had to share a room when we both wanted our own space. I remember the first night in student halls. My own room. It was like the noise finally came to an end. I'm not talking like Emily was noisy, it just . . . You live so close to someone, you can't help but hear every single sound they make. Even when they're quiet as a mouse.'

'I shared a room with my younger brother for a few years,' Mark said, still looking at Stephanie in profile as she continued to stare at the floor. 'I know exactly what you mean. You're never alone. I couldn't wait to move out. We were constantly getting into fights and stuff. Did that happen with the two of you? Was this book an outlet?'

'We never fought,' Stephanie replied, shooting him a glance. 'Nothing like that. We just tolerated each other, I suppose. We knew there was no other way, so that's just how things were. No other option but to grin and bear it. I guess if we'd actually had things in common, then it would have been different, but we didn't. Nothing at all really. Other than DNA.'

'Tell me how she was trouble, as you said.'

Stephanie nodded, gripping the edge of the mattress. 'You can tell from the first page that she wasn't happy. That she thought she deserved more than she had. I found the book accidentally. I couldn't help myself. I ... I read it, because by then I didn't know who she was anymore. I remember feeling sorry for her. Also, really pissed off because she says some nasty things in it about me. I understood, though. I knew it was hard for her at school. What she never understood was that it was hard for me as well.'

Mark kept his face straight, but wondered how true that actually was. It might have been just over a decade since he was in school, but he remembered girls like Stephanie. The popular ones. They never had to work at it, it just seemed like one day the hierarchy was decided and that was that.

He imagined being a twin where one had a certain social

status and the other was forgotten. It would have been hard to live with for Emily.

'We went to different colleges in the end,' Stephanie continued, sliding a manicured fingernail through her hair, sweeping it back behind her ear. 'I stayed in the school's sixth form, while she needed to go somewhere else. She needed the change. I don't think it got any easier for her. I *know* it didn't.'

'So she struggled to fit in at school and college. That doesn't sound too different to thousands of other kids out there. Why was she in trouble?'

'No, I told you, she *caused* the trouble,' Stephanie replied, her tone sharp suddenly. 'You keep getting it wrong. She wasn't some little innocent. I guess she decided enough was enough one day and decided to start fighting back. You ask me, it was about six years too late.'

'She fought back against who?'

'Other kids in the college, people from her old school, anyone she was angry with, basically.'

Mark could hear something being left unsaid. Thought for a second or two, then decided to ask, 'You?'

Stephanie didn't answer immediately, smoothing her jeans down over her thigh. 'She must have bottled it all up for so long. I wish she'd said something to me sooner. Instead of letting me read it in there.'

Mark noted the non-response to his actual question. 'You didn't know what she was going through in school?'

'I had an inkling, of course. She wouldn't really talk to me about it though. Even when we were on our own. We were close in some ways – like, we always looked out for each other academically and whatever. She'd help me with English, I'd help her with maths, that sort of thing. When it came to our social lives, we just never talked about it. We were in different classes, different circles. We just didn't socialise in that way. I know it sounds bad, but we just weren't into the same things.'

Mark held up a hand, sensing Stephanie slipping away from what he needed to learn from this conversation. 'It doesn't sound bad at all. I understand what you mean. Everyone thinks twins should be exactly the same, but I guess it's not always true. Me and my brother – we couldn't be more different. We don't watch the same stuff on telly or listen to the same bands. We have a few things in common, but not much, and only more recently, as we've got older. When we were younger and sharing a room, we didn't like the same things at all. In my teenage years especially. Doesn't mean we're not still close now. Things can change. There's still time, but I need to know everything.'

'I think she hated me,' Stephanie said in a low voice. 'I know that now. She always did, I guess. She wanted what I had, but didn't know how to get it. I wish she'd said something. Maybe I could have changed things. Instead of letting her fight a battle she had no chance of winning.'

'How did she fight back?'

'She was vindictive eventually,' Stephanie replied, relaxing a little on the bed, as her voice lowered even further. Mark had to lean forward to hear her. 'I think she just wanted to get back at people she believed had done her wrong. She would spread rumours online. Catfish people, that sort of thing.'

'Catfish?' Mark said, the term vaguely ringing a bell.

'It's where you pretend to be someone you're not online. Talk to people, become friends, then get in a relationship with that person, but all the time you're pretending you're someone else. Fat people usually do it so they can have nice-looking boyfriends and girlfriends.'

'How do you get away with that, though?' Mark said, ignoring the *fat* comment. Stephanie's filter seemed to be non-existent. 'Wouldn't it be all over the second they met each other?'

'Some people can keep the pretence going on for years. Problems with webcams, no video calling on their phones, whatever.'

'And Emily did this?'

Stephanie nodded, catching his eye for a second before looking away once more. 'Loads of times. She would string people along for months, before breaking their hearts. She seemed to get off on it. When I found out about it, I went off my head at her. She didn't seem to care though. It was like she'd finally found a way of being noticed that didn't take any effort. Nothing I said to her seemed to make any difference.'

'How did you find out about it?'

'She was going after people we knew. People from high school, lads and girls. She must have had dozens of accounts on the go. Someone worked it out and realised it was her.'

Mark shook his head, trying to work out why this hadn't come out sooner. 'This could mean something. If she hurt the wrong person, it could mean someone decided to get their own back on her.'

'I never thought about it like that,' Stephanie said, suddenly seeming smaller. 'I suppose you're right. I just thought it was all ridiculous, but she did hurt people. It was all online though, so I didn't really think much of it. It's not really real on there.'

'Did anyone threaten to do anything?'

There was a moment of hesitation, as Stephanie seemed to turn over the question in her mind before answering. 'Not that I know of, no. I've got no idea, though, really. You've got her computer, maybe you'll be able to find out.

'I didn't really make much of an effort,' Stephanie continued, standing up from the bed and crossing the room to the window. Mark turned to look at her, seeing only the back of her as she looked out over the back garden. He opted to stay quiet as she continued to talk. 'I suppose I could have tried harder. I *should* have tried harder. I've just had my own stuff to deal with over the years, you know? I couldn't carry her. Now I wish I had.'

'You can't look back and start questioning yourself now,' Mark replied softly. 'You'll drive yourself mad if you do that. You have to concentrate on what's best now. And that's telling us everything you know about what kind of things she was doing before she went missing, no matter how small you think they might be. We need to know everything.'

Stephanie nodded without turning around, but Mark could see her reflection in the window. The vacant look she had on her face as she stared out.

'She spent so much of her life online,' Stephanie said, breaking the silence. 'If there are answers to be found, I bet they're there. I just . . . I've had this thought in the back of my mind since the beginning. That this could all be just some kind of game she's playing with us all.'

'You think she'd do that?'

He was struggling to hide his growing sense of unease at what he was hearing. The revelations about Emily's life. It was exciting, but daunting. More questions to investigate.

'I don't know what to think,' Stephanie said, breaking

into Mark's disordered thinking. 'I just want her to come through the front door like nothing's happened. It doesn't matter why she's gone; I just want her to come back. I want to try again. Be a better sister this time.'

Mark stayed quiet, letting Stephanie process the emotions she was battling to keep under the surface.

Waiting for the moment he could get out of that place and start finding answers to the multitude of questions he now had.

Eighteen

The clouds had parted at some point during his return to the station, yet Mark couldn't enjoy the cool autumn evening. He was instead back at his favourite place at work – his desk. Although this was tainted somewhat by the fact that he seemed to be working on the case alone. The others were distracted by the small matter of Joanna Carter's body being found.

There was limited information to work with: her online accounts, the little contact she had outside her home, dropping out of college a few weeks earlier. She hadn't told anyone, which suggested to him that she was trying to keep something quiet at least. Didn't want to disappoint her family, he guessed. He knew her mum worked, and maybe didn't notice her daughter wasn't in college, but it still seemed a big thing for Emily to have been able to keep quiet. Which made him wonder what she was doing after leaving college, the people she was talking to.

Then he'd started reading through Emily's social media accounts.

He had access to Emily's main Facebook page, a Twitter account and Instagram. The Instagram page was blank, so she obviously hadn't been one for taking photographs. The Twitter account had followers barely in three figures, most of which looked like spam accounts. The Facebook page was similarly empty.

It was her email account that got his attention.

Mark wasn't exactly in touch with all the tricks of the online trade, but he knew enough to struggle through. He accessed the account with the information the family had provided for the security questions, but it turned out they'd already done that when they'd realised she was missing. What he noticed instantly was the number of times her main email address was used as a recovery address for another email address. A result of the family trying to gain access to her various social media accounts after she'd gone missing, he guessed. He began making a list of each individual email address, so he could collect them all in one place, before working on getting access to each of them.

The inbox also had messages from Emily's Facebook messaging account.

Dozens of individual messages. Some group chats.

All of them from people she'd catfished.

It was difficult to read for the most part – an unending litany of badly spelled, hate-filled messages, which didn't seem to ever generate a response.

U NEED TO STP DIS!

Y????? I NVR DID ANYTHIN TO U!!!!

JUMP OF A BUILDIN OR SOMETIN. I H8 U

KILL URSELF!! UR SCUM

LEAVE MEALONE!!

UR PROB A UGLY FAT B1TCH.
KILL URSELF! DO US A FVOUR

Each message became worse as he scrolled through them. A whole range of different people, who all wanted to get back at her in some way, for something.

Mark knew what she'd done, of course, he knew about her way of getting back at these people she'd gone to school with. Now, he could see their reaction.

What puzzled him was the lack of replies from Emily herself. He continued going through them all, but couldn't find a single time she had responded to any message she received. It was almost like having invited this sort of reaction, Emily had then ignored it entirely.

From the dates of the messages, she had continued on also. More people tricked, more people sending obscenities to her when they found out.

More victims.

They stretched back over months, the first occurring a year earlier. Mark wondered how this hadn't spilled over into her real life, but then realised it probably had.

He would need to talk to the family again.

Mark was ignoring the main question – of what the messages probably meant. What they would do to someone over a sustained period of time.

'I think she did something to herself,' he said, under his breath. Everything about the way the case was going now pointed to this. The isolation, the way Emily had turned her anger outwards, then received attention in return. Yet, what started as just attention – albeit only the bad kind – would have begun to hurt. It would have been a slow build, a snowball rolling down a mountain, gathering and gathering, until it finally became an avalanche of hate.

He suddenly felt sorry for the girl, imagining what it must have felt like to be on the receiving end of those messages. The way they must have made her feel.

Yet, he also knew he couldn't totally blame the people sending them.

He imagined most of them had probably forgotten about the whole thing by now, though. An internet drama that was over before it had even really begun, but felt like the end of the world at the time. People move on quickly, on to the next drama in their lives.

Most were probably embarrassed and wanted to forget.

For Emily, it would have been different, Mark thought. This would have been her life.

The last message had been sent around a week earlier. Then, nothing. As if it had been wiped clean, or she had suddenly stopped.

He flicked the screen to Emily's Twitter page, but her direct messages – private and unseen from anyone without access to her account – were much the same. Here, the angry messages were few and far between and the oldest a few weeks past.

Then Mark started looking for a link to Joanna Carter. Placing the names together, running through all the messages looking for Joanna's name; everything he could think of, he tried.

Nothing.

Gaining access to all the other accounts Emily had set up on social media would take a long time, and he probably wouldn't get help. He looked at the list of possible login details – all the various email addresses Emily had used over the past year –and wondered where to start.

Well, he knew *how* to start.

Gaining entry into someone's Facebook account is quite simple when you know how. It didn't matter how many security measures were put up, there was usually a way around them. For this, he just needed to note one of the email addresses that had been used to set up the various Facebook accounts and gain access to that first. He went on the first email provider's website and typed in an email address on his list. Then, he went to *Forgot Password* and had a new password set up and sent to the recovery address for that email.

Within seconds, a new email pinged into Emily's main email inbox, setting up a new password for that email address.

It was easy from there.

Within ten minutes, Mark was able to log into a Facebook account for an Isabel Thomas, an account which seemed to have been active for a year or so, then abandoned. It only contained a few photos and from a quick glance, they all seemed to be of the same young woman. A tanned brunette, with athletic legs and a penchant for doing the splits in photographs. Mark didn't expect the girl in the photos to have any knowledge that Emily had done this.

The inbox contained only a few different message threads. A conversation over a number of weeks with someone called Jack Marland. He tried to scroll to the beginning of it, but it went on for hundreds of messages. It would take longer than he had to go through each of them. Already, he could see some of them were sexual in nature. He scrolled past them for now and went to the end.

cant believe u did dis 2 me

ur messed up

u need help!

no1 does dis 2 me

**IF I EVA SEE U UR DEAD
AND I NO WHO DIS IS**

Emily had never replied, it seemed. The messages simply ended, along with the posts. Mark knew she'd moved on to someone else after that.

He needed a list of all the victims. All of the people Emily had targeted and angered. If Jack's last message to her was anything to go by, he imagined there'd be more threats to read. More warnings.

As Mark continued to read on, he discovered it wasn't just romantic catfishing Emily was doing online. She was using information about people to mess with their lives, playing people off against each other, trying to destroy relationships.

It was Machiavellian in nature. All of it.

And now Emily was missing.

He knew the case could disappear within seconds if Emily's body was found with a likely cause of death being suicide. It would change everything he was looking at.

Mark made his way over to DI Bennett's office and filled her in on what he'd discovered. She hummed and hawed over the social media information, but seemed to perk up when Emily's writing in her personal notepad was mentioned again.

'Go over the notebook in more detail,' DI Bennett said, motioning towards the book in a new evidence bag on her desk. 'And also find out who missed it in the first place. Who doesn't look under the mattress, I ask you? Sometimes I wonder about this lot.'

'Easy mistake to make, I suppose,' Mark replied, half-heartedly. It's not like they were all friends out in the bull-pen, but he imagined there was a nervous sergeant or – more likely – a lowly uniform who had made that mistake. 'At least we have it now. More likely than not, it's probably not going to give us much anyway. From a quick scan of it, it's just private complaints. Nothing to suggest outside involvement or anything like that.'

'Still, it could prove useful. An insight into her mindset, that type of thing. I don't think we're going to get much further tonight. You can knock it on the head for now.'

Mark stood up, turning his back and walking towards the door. He had one hand on the handle before the DI spoke again.

'One more thing, Mark,' DI Bennett said, sliding her chair back slightly from her desk. 'I know you have thoughts about whether the Burns and Carter cases are linked, but the evidence we have points towards a suicide, so I need you to see if we might be right. Without anything better than a hunch about them being linked, at the moment I should add, it's a pretty difficult sell.'

'I understand,' Mark replied, feeling a little better for hearing DI Bennett say that, but also wondering how long it would be until that tone changed. Whether he would be shoved to the side when it did. If he found the link, would he be congratulated, or cast aside? He wasn't sure.

Mark left the station not long after, driving his car out

into the dark of night, winding his way out of the city centre and into its suburbs. Or what there is of them, in a city like Liverpool. The city centre was its hub, but the various council and housing estates bordering it had to be traversed before you found the so-called nicer areas. He'd grown up over the water, in a place called Wallasey. A town which had seen better days, his parents had always told him.

Thinking of them reminded him that he'd not spoken to his parents in a few days. He knew they'd be worried, as they always seemed to be.

They weren't far off turning sixty now, still wondering how they'd allowed their son to move across to what they'd always viewed as the less affluent side of the River Mersey. Liverpool was the large city on their doorstep, one they had treated not with contempt, but with an air of something approaching fear. As if it held secrets they could never unlock. Now, their son was not only working in a dangerous job, but one which had taken their little boy to the bad side.

He'd always been attracted to the city.

His mum was always carrying on about why no one should ever leave the house. The dangers that lurked when you escaped the safety of the home. He'd long since given up telling her that the biggest dangers lay in your own house. The vast majority of the cases he dealt with occurred behind closed doors.

Once he'd landed the job in the Major Crimes Unit in the city centre's station, his mum's worries had kicked into overdrive. He knew she'd be happier if he was working in a quiet area. Somewhere in the leafier parts of the Wirral, where she could imagine he'd be dealing with lower-level crimes, if any at all.

It had never been a consideration for him.

He pulled up outside his house and killed the engine. Stepped out the car and glanced at the place he called home. He'd been saving for two years now for a deposit, but didn't think he'd be buying any time soon. The rent was just high enough on his house to leave a slim amount to stash away each month. He liked the area though – quiet and less rough than places a short drive away. He walked around his car, pushing open the metal gate and making his way up the short path. Wondering how long he'd give it before giving in and calling Natasha.

Or if she was already around, waiting for him to arrive home again.

He heard a noise from behind him and smiled. A shift of feet on the pavement. He turned to look, but there was nothing in his sightline, just an empty street, a dull light emanating from the streetlight a few feet away. An almost amber yellow. A noise again and Mark's heart rate increased. Beating against his chest, he could almost hear the pound of it.

'Natasha?'

There was no answer. He didn't think it was her anyway.

Yet, someone was out there.

He didn't know where that thought came from, but it was suddenly stark in his mind. Eyes watching him, unseen. Lurking in what was now a multitude of shadows outside his front door. He heard the scrape of shoes against concrete again and forced himself to walk back up the path, his breaths coming in short bursts.

Mark leaned against the gate, looking left and right, watching for any movement. Still, the feeling of being watched lingered, as he peered into the gloom of the evening.

Nothing moved, nothing shifted. The only noise he could hear was traffic in the far distance, blown towards him on a wind which seemed to increase in strength the longer he stood there.

He waited for another noise, but when none greeted him, he made his way back to the front door, pausing as he held his keys near the lock, waiting.

No sound came.

He shook his head and let himself inside. Almost rushing to close it behind him, as he imagined something out there.

Watching him.

Waiting for him.

Nineteen

NEW GAME

PLAYER ONE

She was standing in the darkness, watching a stranger walk into his house.

Her hands shaking with nerves, as she waited and waited for him to go inside. To not see her.

Holly didn't know who the man was.

She could feel the tears stinging her eyes, as her throat swelled up with fear. As she took her phone from her pocket, she almost dropped it. She righted it, and took dimly lit photographs. Swearing internally to herself, she switched to video and began filming instead.

Hoping, praying, this would get better. That it would be okay.

It had started with a phone call.

She had been sitting alone when her phone started ringing. Nothing unusual about the being alone part. That was the norm since she'd lost her only friend. A mix of misunderstandings had led to her being on her own. Again.

Most of the time she could handle it.

The phone had vibrated three times before she'd answered it. Heard the words that started it all.

'Hello, Holly. Do you know who this is?'

The voice had sounded unnatural, robotic almost. Like a computer was talking to her. 'Should I?'

'Not yet,' the voice said, flat and emotionless. 'I hope you will soon, though.

'I don't want to scare you, Holly,' the voice had said, as Holly sat open-mouthed, unable to speak. 'I just want you to listen. We know what you've been doing. And we're going to tell everyone who you really are. Unless you do exactly as we say.'

She had been playing The Game since that moment six hours ago.

Holly tried to remember a time when she'd been comfortable in her own skin. When she didn't feel lost. Out of place. Anywhere she'd been in her life – all seventeen, almost eighteen, years of it – she'd always felt like she didn't belong, no matter where it was. At school, at parties – when she'd still been invited to them – at gigs, anywhere. It didn't matter, it had always felt the same.

Now, she *was* a part of something.

A game.

This was the first part of it. Watching the stranger on her camera come into view finally, then disappear almost as quickly. Into his house.

She breathed silently, wondering what the next step would be. How far she would have to go.

Level One.

How far was she *willing* to go?

And she knew, right then, that she was ready to do whatever it would take to finish The Game. Was ready to do anything she was asked to do to stop people finding out about what she'd done.

Pretending to have cancer wasn't something people would understand. Not something her mum would understand, more than anyone else. Not after losing her own mother and sister in the same year to the disease.

That had given her the idea. Finding the support group online, the people reading Holly's invented story, giving her the time of day for once.

The story growing bigger and bigger. The lies becoming harder to hide.

Yet, they were there for her. More than anyone else.

Someone had found out what she'd done. And she couldn't let her mum know about it.

She had to play their game.

The alternative was too difficult to imagine.

Her phone buzzed in her hand. She lifted it to her ear and listened to the words. The instructions.

Then, walked out of the shadows and towards the house.

PLAYER TWO

Rob was standing outside the station, his body shivering as the cold air swirled around him, making him nervous.

This was the first level.

That's what he had been told.

He didn't know how many there would be. Just that he had to keep going, or they would tell everyone what he'd done. His family would find out. His wife.

Every time he thought about it, guilt and shame hit him again.

No one would know though. As long as he just played The Game and did what they said, no one would find out.

First level.

It didn't make sense, what was being asked of him. When he'd tried to question it, all they had repeated was that it was a game. That he had to do what he was told and not ask why. Rob thought it was simple enough.

They wanted to humiliate him enough that he would still be punished, without revealing his greater crime.

He didn't know how they'd found out. Rob had been careful, he thought. Been online using anonymous names.

It wasn't like he was really a right-wing sexist bigot. It was just a laugh. Bit of trolling. They were asking for it, most of the time. Moaning snowflakes. That's what they were.

Okay, some of the death threats and lies were a bit far, but it wasn't serious.

He'd lose his job if he was exposed.

He didn't think he would ever reach the end of the levels. And that scared him almost as much as being found out.

The train pulled into the station and came to a stop. Doors swishing open and a few people disembarking onto the platform. Going about their normal evening. Maybe going home after working late. Maybe they'd had dinner in the city centre after work, possibly a date.

He stood at the exit, blocking the way. Some of them had already spotted him standing there, his arms outstretched, blocking the doorway that led to the small concourse. Maybe that was why this station had been chosen for him – they knew he would have been able to block their only way out.

When he spoke, he didn't sound like himself.

'No one is getting out,' he said, his voice, uncertain at first, rose with every word. 'You all live here now. With me. On this train station. No one is getting past.'

A couple of them laughed quietly, not really under-standing the joke. One guy had headphones in and didn't even flinch.

As they reached him, he didn't move.

Five against one.

He held on for as long as he could, but once the guy took his headphones out to see what was going on, it didn't last long.

He fought back.

Ended up on the ground with a bloodied nose for his troubles.

Level One complete.

Twenty

Mark busied himself in the kitchen to shake off the sensation of being watched. He yawned as he clicked on the microwave, the plate holding the frozen meal spinning around until his eyes began to feel heavy. He breathed in deeply and stood up taller. Widened his eyes and hoped he'd stay awake long enough to eat.

Too many late nights and early mornings, he thought. Long days after long evenings with Natasha were probably also to blame.

His eyes closed briefly as he leaned against the kitchen counter, almost dozing within seconds.

A noise shook him awake. At first he thought it was the microwave finishing, but when he opened his eyes, it was still going.

The noise came again. A bang. Against the front door. He shook his head, trying to decide if he was happy that Natasha had come over, or if he would have preferred a solid eight hours of sleep.

He moved down the hallway, opening the door as he reached it, a small smile on his face.

No one was outside.

He stepped out on his front step, moving quicker down his path as he heard footsteps running up the street.

He saw a blur of movement in the distance, turning the corner. Out of sight. Confusion washed over him as he looked back at his house. Nothing out of place. Nothing left there.

He remembered as a kid they would play a game of 'knock a door run'. Banging on some poor person's door and then running away quickly.

It was too late at night for that, he thought. He considered running after whoever it was, but his hesitation had already left him far behind.

Instead, he moved back towards his house and went inside. His heart rate returned to normal a few minutes after he closed the door behind him and heard the microwave ping.

He ate his meal in silence, reading over the notes he'd collected, trying to ignore the nagging feeling in the back of his mind.

That someone was watching him. Had been at his house, banged on the door and ran away. For a reason.

He fell asleep on the sofa, thinking about one thing.

His next step.

NOW

Twenty-One

The Second Interview

Tuesday 30th October
Interview Room One
Lancaster Police Station – sixty miles from Liverpool City Centre

It was later in the day now. A tired and tepid air had settled over them as they sat down for the next stage. Another interview. More questions, when all he wanted to do was sleep.

He was a mixture of emotions. Boredom had set in earlier, while he was sitting in the cell alone. Then, there was another part of him that wanted to shout and scream at the top of his lungs. To tear the place apart in frustration.

'This interview is being recorded both visually and audibly. Investigating officers are Detective Inspector Patrick Hicks and Detective Sergeant Victoria Lee. Suspect still refuses to give us his name.'

The same spiel as earlier. He continued to stare at the table, trying to quieten the other side of him. The voices straining to be noticed in his head. Feeling his grip on reality start to slip.

'We would like to talk about the woman you were found with,' Hicks said, his voice steady and strong.

He thought that inside, Hicks would be anything but steady and strong. He could almost smell the revulsion the detective was feeling for him. 'And I said she wasn't important. Not yet.'

'We want to talk about her,' Hicks said, more forcefully now. 'Why were you there with her?'

'Why are we anywhere? I had something to do. She was there, too.'

'What's her name?'

He shrugged his shoulders and then enjoyed the silence that followed. The seconds slipping by, closer and closer to the end.

'How did you end up there? What contact did you have with the victim previously?'

He almost laughed at that. *Victim*. As if that's all she was. 'That was the plan. She would be there and I would be, too. That's how the story goes. I was just playing my part in it.'

'Just another victim to you,' Hicks said, barely containing his anger towards him now. He could feel it coming off him like heat from an open flame.

'I wouldn't say that.'

Beside him, the solicitor coughed, but at least he'd stopped trying to interrupt him. Probably just wanted to get out of there. Back to his wife and kids, away from all of this madness.

'Okay, if you like, we can go one by one. Would that be better?'

He didn't respond, looking at the bare walls around him instead. The seconds continued to tick by.

'Stacey Green, twenty-two years of age,' Hicks said finally, reading from his notes. 'Worked in the local cinema. Youngest of three children. Single, lived with her doting parents. Your second victim.'

He didn't say anything, waiting for a question to appear. He knew this was just a technique, humanising the dead, trying to provoke an emotional response.

He couldn't give them that.

'How did you get in contact with her? How did you two cross paths?'

'How does anyone meet these days? All that matters is that I killed them. All of them. One by one. So, why don't we stop messing around with all these stupid little details and charge me? I mean, we both know that's what's going to happen, so let's get it over and done with. Stop wasting my time with these questions.'

'We need to go over the details first . . .'

'That's what I want to do,' he said, interrupting the detective. His voice reverberated around them, but the two detectives didn't even flinch. 'You're just not asking the right questions. You should be looking into all those deaths and seeing the connection between them all. Instead, you keep messing around with diversions. Let me talk and I'll tell you what you need to know.'

There was a pause. A glance between the two detectives. The solicitor sitting next to him seemed to shift away from him slightly, as if distance would help him. 'Why don't you ask about all the other victims? How I convinced them to believe a story and then die.'

He could see the anger return to DI Hicks's eyes. He needed that.

He needed his judgement to be clouded.

He was desperate.

'We've gone over some of the names you've given us,' DS Lee said, a pen in her hand, scoring down a list on one of the files in front of her. 'They were found dead in a few different locations, but concentrated in the north-west region mostly. Different ages, split between genders. You've been concentrating on women more recently, I see. Your first named victim was male. The male is the only one classed as an unsolved murder. The rest are all apparent suicides. Over the past eleven months, all of them were found dead. That was all that linked them together until you told us you killed them. Why now?'

'Because you found me.'

'How did we find you?'

He paused, wishing he'd accepted a drink of water now. His mouth had been going dry, but the last question had finished the job. 'You'd have to ask someone else. I don't know. Luck?'

'Perhaps it is just luck,' DS Lee said, looking back at her notes and not giving anything away. 'Shall we talk about your fourth victim – Melissa Carmichael – what can you tell me about her?'

'What do you want to know?'

'Everything,' DS Lee replied, her face inscrutable. 'Start from when you chose her as a victim. How did you meet her?'

He didn't like the way she had taken charge of the interview, leaving DI Hicks to sit in silence. He had found it easier to deal with the barely constrained anger of the man. The blankness of DS Lee's features troubled him.

'She told lies. So I told her to go to a certain place. Perform certain tasks. She didn't question me. She did as she was told and she became my fourth victim because of it.'

'What did you ask her to do?'

He didn't answer, staring back at her instead. Not sure what she was trying to achieve. She didn't strike him as someone who could be intimidated.

He didn't want to answer.

That was the truth.

He didn't want to reveal the full extent of The Game. Not now.

It was almost fun, in a delirious sort of way, watching them try to work out what was sitting in front of them.

Perhaps he really was losing his mind. Perhaps he'd already lost it. They would believe that, quite easily. Someone rocks up and confesses to killing eight people, over an extended period of time – it doesn't look sane.

Maybe it would be easier if they believed he was mad and that would be that. Lock him up in a secure hospital and never worry about him again.

Maybe that would be for the best.

'You do something bad and you have to try and atone for your lies. Butyou never realise you're playing with a loaded dice. And no one has won yet. Charge me with eight counts of murder and it'll be over. Until then, it goes on.'

He knew on some level that wouldn't be the outcome. That soon, the house of cards he'd tried to construct would come tumbling down. He didn't know how to stop it. Didn't know what he should do.

He wasn't sure of anything. Only that the story hadn't finished yet.

BEFORE

Twenty-Two

Mark suppressed a yawn as he left his car and made his way up the path the next morning. He rang the bell. The house seemed like any other in the area. Small, a decade or so old, with that new-build brick colour. To him, they've always looked like a strong wind could blow them over. He knew this was what would soon be the norm – that every house in the country would look like these at some point. Smaller, less weathered. Communities changing before his eyes. As more investment came into the city, this was how the future would look.

He shook his head and checked his notes again.

Chris Jackson. One of the names that had stood out when he'd gone through all the messages to Emily again that morning. The most vitriolic, the most threatening. Mark was standing on the doorstep, about to ring the bell again, when the door opened. A lad of about twenty stood before him, arms bulging from a tight white V-neck, showing the tufts of dark chest hair poking out. Tattoos fighting for freedom from the sleeves. Skin the colour of a burnt orange. Hair swept over his head in a manner that probably took hours to perfect.

'Yeah?'

'Chris Jackson?'

The lad slouched, one hand still holding on to the door. 'Yeah, who are you?'

Mark produced his identification. 'Detective Constable Mark Flynn. I was wondering if you'd be able to answer a few questions, related to a current investigation.'

Whatever or whoever Chris had been expecting, it quite obviously wasn't a detective wanting to ask questions. He stammered a couple of times, then nodded a little too enthusiastically and showed him inside. Mark walked through into what he assumed was the living room and turned to see him still standing by the front door. 'You can come back inside with me, it's okay.'

'I probably shouldn't have let you in,' Chris said, seeming smaller now, even as the muscles on his biceps struggled to be contained. 'My mum and dad are both out.'

'That's okay. I think you'll want this conversation to be between us for now.'

Chris was still hovering in the doorway, seemingly lost in the strange direction his morning had suddenly taken. The room smelled of lavender and Lynx Africa, the television in the corner paused in the middle of a game of FIFA. Mark sat down on the smaller of two sofas, taking up most of the space, even with his small stature. Eventually Chris was sitting down on the opposite seat, putting his controller on the table.

'What's this about then?'

Mark took a few seconds, then began taking printouts out of the black folder he'd been carrying. 'It's about these communications you sent a few months ago.'

Chris took the sheets of paper from him as Mark leaned

across to hand them over. He began reading them, a look of confusion sweeping across his face as he did so. Mark spoke as he continued to scour them. 'I'm investigating the disappearance of Emily Burns. I gather you know who that is.'

'I don't understand . . .'

'It's quite simple really,' Mark said, placing the folder back in his lap and staring at Chris as he talked. 'Emily has gone missing in suspicious circumstances and we're looking into all aspects of her life. It seems you've had some interaction with her in the past. I'd like to talk about that with you.'

'I don't even know her,' Chris said, but his voice was quieter now. The semblance of confidence he'd been holding on to evaporated with each passing second.

'Really? That's strange, as it looks to me like you were speaking to her for a long time. The first messages you exchanged with her were over a year ago now.'

'No, I mean, I . . . I didn't really know her at all.'

'You've said that. Yet, it looks like you were in some kind of online relationship for quite a while. It didn't end well though, did it?'

Chris hesitated, clearly working out if he should continue the lie. Finally, he spoke. 'No.'

'I think the last message you sent was "If I ever see you on the street I'll push you into the road in front of a car." That sound about right?'

Chris didn't answer, his Adam's apple bobbing up and down as he dry-swallowed a few times.

'How about an easier question,' Mark said, when it became clear Chris was struggling. 'How did you know Emily Burns?'

The silence was shorter this time. 'I didn't really know her. I knew the girl she pretended to be.'

'And who was that?

'Jenny Ward.'

'You didn't know her before then?'

'No . . . well, no, not really. She told me . . . afterwards, that she knew me from school, but I had no idea who she was. I thought I was talking to someone from Canada. She'd ring me and everything. She somehow found out I was planning on moving over there to do a sports degree. She made it seem like I'd have someone waiting for me.'

'And this went on for over a year without you knowing who it was?'

Chris made as if to answer quickly, then stopped himself. Mark imagined he wasn't used to being made to look a fool. His entire demeanour when he'd first opened the door had screamed entitlement. He would be the lad at school who was good at everything. Had his pick of a number of girls, loads of friends. Always listened to, never maligned.

Exactly the type of person Emily would have wanted to teach a lesson, it seemed.

'I didn't really think it was real,' Chris said, holding on to the sheets of paper still, but no longer looking at them now. 'She was just there, with a nice comment, or a message that would make me smile.'

'There was more to it than that,' Mark said, knowing some of the comments that had been shared. Intimate discussions . . . well, intimate was probably too delicate a term to use. 'You sent her pictures of yourself. That must have been embarrassing when you realised the girl you were supposedly talking to was someone else entirely. Someone you knew, who knew your friends.'

'Yeah, it was,' Chris replied, his grip on the printouts tightening now. 'I didn't like the fact that I'd been played with. I was supposed to be going over to Canada in the summer, but I didn't in the end.'

'That was Emily's fault?'

'Yeah . . . well, no, not really. But it didn't help. When I found out she wasn't who she said she was . . . I went crazy for a bit.'

'You were scared of being thought of as someone who could be played like that. You were worried that she would share some of the things you'd shared with her. Does that sound about right, Chris?'

'I wasn't happy about it,' Chris said, trying to keep his voice level and calm, but it was painfully obvious he was still angry. Hurt. Embarrassed. All wrapped up in one combustible ball. 'You can't just mess with someone like that. It's not right. She made me think she was some fit girl in Toronto – a cheerleader and everything – and it turned out to be some fat bird from round the corner. That's not right.'

'How did you find out you weren't talking to who you thought you were?'

'I got a message from someone else she had been messing with,' Chris said, finally laying the paper to the side. 'It was out of the blue. I knew something wasn't right when she wouldn't FaceTime me, she would only speak on the phone. And a few times the accent would slip, like. Then I got a message from someone who told me her real name. I didn't remember her at all, but a couple of lads from school did. She's a proper nutcase, man.'

'And how did you take the news?'

Chris smiled without showing his teeth, shrugged and

then sighed. 'I think you can tell not that well. I was angry. You would be too if you'd been strung along like I was.'

'What do you think of those messages you sent now?'

'I don't know. She kinda deserved it, don't you think? She made me look like a complete idiot. I couldn't just let that go, you know. It wasn't right, what she did. I know other people probably got it worse.'

'And the person who told you who she really was?'

Chris shook his head. 'No idea who it was. Anonymous. I didn't believe them at first, but you know, I put it together and couldn't believe how stupid I'd been.'

'You know others who this happened to?'

'Has to be others, right? It wasn't just me. There were probably loads of people she had on.'

'There was more, though, wasn't there?' Mark said, trusting his instincts. Something had been bugging him since he'd started going through all the communication Emily had with all these people . . . these *victims*. There was something he wasn't seeing. Something that happened outside of the social media circle he'd been allowed a glimpse into, something that would trigger the rage that was directed back at her. 'She did more,' he probed.

Chris breathed deeply, looking towards the floor as if it contained the answer. 'She had pictures. Stuff I didn't want people to see, you know? She threatened me. Said she would share them with everyone I knew. Family, friends, the lot. Unless I kept talking to her. But I couldn't. I didn't think she'd go through with it.'

'She didn't share yours, did she?'

Chris didn't answer, but Mark could feel the answer hanging in the air between them.

'I promised not to tell anyone what she'd been doing. That was the deal we made. I was one of the lucky ones.'

'How did she do it?'

'Through email. Said she was going to send them to everyone she could, post them everywhere, if I ever said anything about what she'd done. I took it serious, like. I was too scared about what would happen, so I didn't say a word. She's a nutcase.'

'Still, the messages you sent to her ... they weren't friendly.'

'I didn't have nothing to do with her going missing, if that's what you mean. I'm over it, man, haven't even thought about it in months.'

That's the only lie he felt Chris had spoken in the time he'd been sitting in his parent's living room. The fact he'd been taken for a ride probably slipped into his thoughts at night. His pride had been hurt.

'You said you wanted to kill her ...'

'I didn't mean it, not really,' Chris said, his voice getting louder now. He half rose out of his seat then thought better of it. 'Have you never said something like that before? *I'll bloody kill you*. It doesn't mean you're actually going to kill that person. I swear on my life I didn't even know she'd gone missing until the tweets were getting shared around and that. I saw them and that's all I know.'

'What did you think when you saw that she'd gone missing?'

Chris didn't answer, his hand curling into a fist and resting against his mouth. He shook his head and sniffed. 'I thought, good, hopefully she's topped herself. Done herself in. Before she screwed over the wrong person and they did it for her. I don't think that's what happened though. I reckon she's just done it for atten-tion, because that's all she ever did anything for, in the end. No one paid her any attention in school and this is her way of finally getting some. She shared pictures of us. You know what I'm talking about? Pictures, and stuff we'd said, that should have stayed private. It's embar-rassing, you know? She made us all look like idiots. Only, that wasn't enough for her so now she's gone one better. She's "disappeared". She'll be back by the end of the week, I bet.'

'If something's happened to her though . . .'

'Then there's about fifty people at least who would prob-ably want to throw a party. She's evil. She knew what she was doing to me. She knows what she did to other people. I'm not going to lose any sleep over it. She played me and didn't care how I felt. Why should I care about her?'

Mark's brain decided to throw in an unwanted thought. Like those times when you're stood on a train platform and wonder what would happen if you pushed the obnoxious bloke standing near the edge in front of an oncoming train. Or strangled the person who just pushed in front of you in a queue.

He really wanted Emily's body to suddenly turn up, so he could get out of this nightmare of teenagers and their problems.

That wasn't an option. He felt another part of him shift, a weight of responsibility.

This was his job.

He was going to find out what happened to Emily. He was going to find answers.

And as he felt that, a rush of adrenaline ran through his body and he almost smiled.

'I need the names of everyone you know that she did this to.'

He was sitting in the car, making sure his notes were thorough enough, when his mobile buzzed on the dashboard where he'd left it. Mark reached across, looked at the screen and smiled. He should have ignored it, but decided he needed to hear a friendly voice.

'Hi,' Mark said, laying his notes down beside him with one hand. 'Sorry ...'

'For what? It's me that should be saying sorry. I just crashed out last night. Had a long day of it.' Natasha's voice was light, but he could hear eagerness behind it. He felt soothed by it. 'I hope you didn't get too lonely.'

'It's okay,' Mark replied. 'I probably wouldn't have been much use anyway. Really busy couple of days.'

'I saw. Was it the missing woman?'

Mark hesitated, wanting to be open with her, but remembering they didn't really know each other that well. 'No. Well ... I don't know yet. The body found wasn't her, but we're not sure if it's linked yet.'

'Ah, right. What was I saying to you the other night, hey? All these young women – it's an epidemic. I got caught up in the same kind of thing yesterday.'

Mark listened, happy to hear her voice. It felt right, though he couldn't help but wonder how this could have happened in such a short space of time.

He realised he missed her.

'Listen, I'll see you later. What time do you think you'll finish?'

Mark looked at the clock, then shrugged his shoulders, as if she could see him. 'Not sure. I'll message you, if that's okay?'

'No problem,' Natasha replied, giving him a cheery goodbye. Mark stared at his phone a little longer after the call ended, smiling to himself. He thought about finishing early and seeing her now. Shook his head at that and knew it was a ridiculous idea.

He wished, not for the first time, that he had someone he could talk to about things like this. Relationship stuff. Someone who could keep him from rushing into things. Was that what he was doing? He wasn't sure.

He had friends, but apart from playing five-a-side with them every few weeks, he didn't really keep in contact all that much. They were acquaintances more than friends, really. He had a few mates from his days at college, but that was about it.

Sometimes he missed being part of a group, but he knew it made more sense this way. To keep his private life small. Just in case.

Mark leaned forward and turned on the ignition, trying to focus on what was important at that moment.

Everything else could wait.

Twenty-Three

When Mark returned to the station, he could feel the atmosphere had changed since he'd left a few hours earlier. The place was busier now, people moving to and fro with purpose. He wondered for a few seconds what he'd missed, but knew he probably wouldn't get a straight answer if he asked his so-called colleagues. He left his jacket on his desk and went in search of DI Bennett, ready to update her on the little he'd learned since leaving.

It didn't amount to much, in the end. He'd spoken to two other former school attendees of Emily's – each with similar stories to Chris's. He doubted any of them had anything to do with Emily's disappearance. They were all wide-eyed and astonished by his presence.

Scared too.

For them, the comments they had made against Emily had been silly and forgotten about within a few days. Now they could see what the implications were. All of them eager to say they didn't mean it *really*. That it was all heat of the moment anger. None of them were sorry to see her go and all of them thought she was probably attention-seeking, like Chris had said.

There were more names on the list. More people Emily had hoodwinked with lies.

DI Bennett's office was empty when he crossed over to see her. He was about to go back to his desk and start typing up his notes when she appeared.

'Mark, just the man I was looking for,' she said, her cheeks red with blush and sounding a little breathless. 'You need to come and see this.'

Mark was about to ask her what was going on, but she had already turned and walked away quickly. He raised his eyebrows and followed her.

In the meeting room, which was close to the main office, the blinds had been closed and a screen erected on one wall. As Mark walked in, a few heads turned, but no one acknowledged him. The images on the screen stopped as Mark noticed that DS Cavanagh was controlling the playback.

'Wind it back and show Mark what we've got,' DI Bennett said, her eyes lit with a mixture of excitement and nervousness.

'Must be good,' Mark replied, taking up a position closer to the screen. 'What is it?'

'We've got CCTV from the student accommodation block where Joanna Carter lived,' DS Cavanagh said, fingering the remote in his hand. 'It's the most bizarre thing you'll ever see.'

The screen changed to black, then started up again. The camera angle was in the top corner of a lift. The door opened, no one appeared, then it closed again. A few seconds passed by; the door opened again.

'This is her,' DS Cavanagh said, his voice soft and quiet in the still of the room.

On screen, a young woman appeared, dressed in a red top with a black cardigan over it. Some kind of jogging pants on. What Joanna Carter's body had been found wearing. Similar to what Emily Burns had been wearing when they saw her on CCTV last. Even now, knowing it wasn't her, Mark could see the similarities between the pair.

Joanna Carter entered the lift, walked to the far corner, then turned towards the panel. She leaned over, a finger extended, and proceeded to press buttons in a seemingly precise manner.

More than one button.

She stood back up, waited. Then she crossed to the still-open lift doors, looking out left and right. She moved back inside, standing in the corner again for a few seconds.

'The doors aren't closing,' Mark said under his breath, but everyone was still looking at the screen as Joanna moved forwards again, creeping to the opening, then she jumped through, twisting her head left and right, as if she were trying to surprise someone waiting there for her. She stepped back into the middle of the lift, her hands loosely clasped in front of her. She took a sidestep to the right, turned so her back was against the lift wall, and stepped towards the lift controls again, like she was trying to hide away from the opening.

The doors closed, Joanna unmoved from her position. The lift seemed to ascend, but it was difficult to tell. The doors opened again, but what little could be seen outside looked exactly as the previous floor did. The same corridor, the same blurred furnishings.

Joanna moved slowly, peering around the corner of the opening, then stepping out of the lift. The doors remained open as she disappeared from screen for a few seconds, then walked across the frame. She backed into the lift again, moving in a stilted fashion, seeming to count her steps as she did so.

She moved back to the same position again, her back to the lift near the controls. The doors remained open.

'Watch now,' DS Cavanagh said, turning to Mark, shaking his head. 'This is where it gets weird.'

Mark nodded and continued to watch, thinking it was pretty weird already. On screen, Joanna stood for a little while longer, the doors remaining open. She moved forward tentatively, her feet stopping in the lift opening, her head attempting to peer around its corners and into the corridors. She then jumped out, two feet planted together. She was there, looking around yet again, then sidestepped to her left a few times, then back again. Then walked forwards two steps, then all the way backwards into the lift again.

Once inside, she began dragging her left foot in a circle. Then she did the same with her right. She peered out of the doors again, standing there for around ten seconds, her head jutting out of the doorway repeatedly. Then she stepped again, standing to the side, so only one of her arms and a slight portion of her lower body were visible. Mark watched as she lifted her arm up, moved it around for ten seconds, then let it drop to her body again.

She walked back into the lift, pressing buttons on the controls again, stepping to the side as the doors closed. She stood there, rocking on her heels, as her lips moved soundlessly.

'You're right,' Mark said, his eyes stuck to the screen now, watching every moment as the images unfolded. 'It is weird.'

DS Cavanagh sniffed, but didn't say anything. The doors of the lift opened again, the same pattern as before emerging. Joanna peering out into the corridor. Joanna stepping to the side and backwards, in a seemingly random pattern. Joanna walking out into the corridor and moving in an odd fashion. Then she went back into the lift and began pressing buttons again.

This repeated for the next three or so minutes, the lift opening on different floors of the building and Joanna seeming to perform the same ritual each time.

Until what Mark assumed was the top floor.

Joanna seemed to pause this time, taking deep, slow breaths, shaking her hands out as she did so. She suddenly looked nervous, whereas before she looked assured, even while doing increasingly bizarre things.

Mark watched the counter on the top of the screen tick by, five seconds, then ten, as Joanna continued to stand in the middle of the lift.

The doors continued to stay open.

Then, without warning, she almost bolted out, disappearing from view quickly in a flash of colour. The CCTV images continued, the doors to the lift eventually closing.

'Wait,' DI Bennett said, a small smile curling her lips.

Mark could see Joanna walking off into the distance. A few seconds went by, then someone else appeared.

A figure dressed in dark clothes. A hood covering his head, his footsteps purposeful and stalking.

'Someone followed her,' Mark said, squinting at the screen, as if he could magically make the figure turn around so he could see whoever it was.

'That's the last time we see Joanna,' DS Cavanagh said, pausing the video and turning back towards him.

'She's followed onto the roof, then a few minutes later, this happens.'

The person who had followed Joanna appeared again. Mark held his breath, waiting to see the face of the person, then frowned when he could only see black.

'He walks backwards,' DS Cavanagh said, his voice flat and emotionless. 'We've gone through the entire CCTV and he is always shielded from view.'

'He knew where the cameras were,' Mark replied, for his own benefit, rather than anyone else's. 'And it is a he, I'm guessing.'

'It certainly looks that way from his build and the way he moves,' DI Bennett said, turning away from the screen and facing Mark again. 'Which means . . .'

'Emily's disappearance is probably unconnected,' Mark finished for her. Although he could see that DI Bennett wasn't exactly buying that thought. 'As in, she wasn't with Joanna on the roof of that building. Still, it's some coincidence.'

'It is,' DI Bennett said, perching herself on the long table that took up most of the room. 'Joanna hadn't been seen for two days before this happens. Before she's found at the bottom of the building, dead, yards away from Emily's last known whereabouts.'

'We need to find Emily,' Mark said, understanding why he'd been brought in to see the video. 'Even if we think they're unconnected, we can't say for certain.'

Bennett glanced across at DS Cavanagh, the look not really answering anything for Mark.

'They're possibly unconnected, but we don't know. If there's a chance they are connected, then obviously we can't rule that out,' DS Cavanagh said finally, unable to keep the look of confusion from his face. 'Because, right now, we haven't got a clue. The best we can come up with is that Joanna was having some sort of mental breakdown and that someone took advantage of that fact. We need to find Emily to make sure either she wasn't involved, or . . .'

'She hasn't been a victim like Joanna too.'

'Exactly,' Cavanagh continued, standing up and leaning on the back of the chair with two hands. 'We've been going through Joanna's phone, her laptop, everything we could possibly find. We don't have a single link to Emily whatsoever. There's nothing on social media, nothing in her emails, nothing at all. Even those names that came up with Emily – all the fake personas she created – not a single one seems to have had any interaction with Joanna at all. So why is Emily last seen a hundred yards away two nights earlier? It doesn't make sense.'

'Not without Emily,' Mark said, mirroring Cavanagh and leaning on a chair himself.

'Precisely,' DI Bennett said, standing up and crossing towards the door. 'At the moment, however, I think we have to go with the obvious here. Emily's disappearance may not be connected. Still, we need to find her to make sure.'

'I'm working on it,' Mark said, then felt the need to continue. 'If someone doesn't want to be found, it makes everything more difficult.'

Which wasn't his first understatement of the week and he felt it wouldn't be the last.

Twenty-Four

PLAYER ONE

This was the part she hated most.

The waiting.

She couldn't stand the waiting.

Downstairs, she could hear her mum singing along to music in the kitchen. Some old song she'd never heard before, or was likely to again.

'*Alexa,*' Holly heard her mum shout, too loud for the new device she'd picked up for herself on sale a week earlier. She'd laughed when her mum had told her about the purchase, thinking she'd never be able to use the thing properly. Turned out it was more user-friendly than Holly had realised. Which meant all she heard when her mum was home was that stupid name shouted loud enough for the neighbours to hear.

'*Alexa – play "Heaven Is a Place on Earth" by Belinda Carlisle.*'

Holly sighed and grabbed her headphones, set her iTunes playlist to shuffle and placed her phone back on the bed beside her. The pink laptop she'd had for three years was perched on her legs, running slower now than when she'd first got it.

She still hated the colour of it. When she'd unwrapped it, she had smiled and said thank you, thinking the entire time *this isn't what I wanted*. Still, at least her parents had got her something that was useable. Other years, they'd given her cheap hair straighteners she'd never get out of the box, or vouchers for places she never shopped at.

With the laptop, she now had a reason to spend more of her time in her room, instead of having to do her home-work on the ancient desktop they had in the dining room. The thing that took half an hour to send a document to the printer, even though it was sitting right next to it.

It had made schoolwork a little easier, but it had also helped in other ways.

It was getting dark outside, the glow from her laptop screen straining her eyes. She looked over at the light switch and decided it was too far away. Continued to lie on her bed and wait.

Her eighteenth birthday was seven weeks away and she didn't have any friends she could invite to a party. No one to go out clubbing with, or to a local bar. To go for a night into town to celebrate her coming of age.

No one to make her feel better.

All she had was the knowledge of the things she had done and the only way to make sure no one found out about them.

Level One – Spying on some random bloke she'd never seen before. Trying to break into his house and failing. She'd thought then that it would be over, but it hadn't been enough apparently.

Level Two – Vandalism. Breaking panes of glass in bus

stops, late at night, in different areas of the city. A few other things too, but she didn't want to remember.

The Game.

She could feel her pulse begin to beat faster than the music blaring in her ears. The nervous feeling of being found out. The lies she'd told.

Just keep playing and it'll all be okay. Just got to keep going.

Her bag lay on the floor where she'd slung it ten minutes earlier, the college books spilling from the top. The folder which contained notes she never imagined she'd read again. The exam preparation she wouldn't need. The course had been something her parents thought would be a good idea. Away from the high school she'd grown to loathe. A fresh start, outside of that place, those girls and boys who had made her life a misery.

That's what it was supposed to be.

Instead, it was the same old story. Sitting alone, no one bothering to make any effort to engage in conversation with her. No one caring that she was on her own, no one trying to become her friend. She was invisible to them all.

It didn't take long for her to go back to her old ways. Sitting at the back, feigning interest every now and again, but really just seeing out the minutes until she could leave. Escaping from that prison cell and into the online world to have at least a little interaction in her life. People she didn't know in the real world, who wouldn't judge her, who accepted her for who she was.

That's what she'd done instead of bothering with all the fakeness she witnessed every single day in that college.

Instead, she'd created a fake life all of her own.

She wondered if there was ever going to be a final

level to this game. Whether she would have to play forever and ever.

Imagined the look on her mum's face if she found out what she'd been doing.

It wasn't all bad. Her life was easy in so many ways. Her mum loved her, she wasn't ill, she wasn't poor.

Her dad had already left for work and they both earned a good wage, provided all the things she could ever want.

She'd had enough to make her life easy, if you ignored the loneliness.

Beside her, the mobile phone lit up and began to buzz. It made her jump, her heart pounding, knowing who it would be. She swiped to answer and lifted it to her ear.

'You're almost there, Holly,' the voice said, the flat, robotic tone filling the silence. 'Only a couple more levels . . .'

'Please, let this be over,' Holly replied, feeling a huge lump grow in her throat. She wanted this done. To move on. To go back to loneliness. 'I've done enough for you.'

'Too late, Holly. You know the rules by now. Everyone is going to know what a dirty little liar you are, if you don't do exactly as we say.'

For the first time, Holly realised the reality of it all. That it would never be over. Not really.

'I'll do anything, please,' she heard herself say, and realised it was true. She wanted to take it all back. She didn't want the attention anymore. She didn't want to live like this anymore.

The voice had scared her the first time. The emotionlessness of it. She had no idea if it was a man or woman on the other end; no idea if they knew *everything*. There was no doubt now, though.

'But please,' Holly said, her voice soft and pleading, 'I can't do anymore. I've done enough. Let me go.'

'It's too late for begging,' the voice replied, and there was almost a humour to the tone now. As if it was excited. 'There's only one way out. And that's to play. To the end. Unless you want me to tell everyone what you've been doing.'

She breathed in and closed her eyes for a second. Leaned her head back and nodded to herself. 'I'll do anything. Just please, don't tell anyone what I've done.'

'I knew you would make the right choice,' the voice said, its monotone purring through the phone. Holly felt she could almost hear emotion in its void.

'What do I have to do now?' Holly said finally, thinking she wouldn't go near the internet ever again. Wouldn't look for validation there, for comfort. She wanted nothing but boredom from now on.

Something else.

A life.

PLAYER TWO

Rob couldn't play anymore.

Ending up in hospital hadn't been part of the plan. Now, he dreamed. Soundlessly, endlessly.

His wife and parents sat at his bedside, waiting for him to wake up.

They had been called late at night.

After the incident at the train station, he had walked for a long time. Considered his options and then walked out into traffic at Switch Island.

A rather large lorry had hit him and left him like this.

Where he slept peacefully, without any clue that's what he was doing.

They would sit with him, praying, hoping, pleading, for an outcome that was never going to happen.

At some point, a doctor with kind eyes and grey, thinning hair would take them into a room. Sit them down and ask them to make a decision.

And, they would make it.

Rob couldn't play. He wouldn't play.

He failed at Level One.

Twenty-Five

Mark was a little disappointed by the turnout, but it was becoming the norm now. Unless the story had already taken off, or had some juicy elements to it, very few actual news journalists would show up at this point. Now that everything revolved around twenty-four-hour rolling coverage, they could afford to crib the footage from local stations, without the need to send anyone up to cities outside of London.

He wondered if the attention would have been different if they'd told them it was connected to the death of Joanna. Or, more annoyingly, if the victim had been a pretty blonde girl from a middle-class family.

The press had been more interested in Joanna's death anyway. This was a silly distraction from what they saw as the main story.

That said, he could still see there were a few cameras around the room. A smattering of print journalists sitting patiently waiting, before going on to the next story they'd be working on. For them, he imagined it was business as usual.

He could already hear some of them taking bets on which of the family would actually be the culprit.

Mark listened to them speculate, wondering how long it would be until Uncle Rich found himself in the middle of the odds. He couldn't blame them – they weren't wrong. It was one of those clichés that was actually true. In most cases he'd been involved with – however tangentially – it normally turned out to be someone close to the family. Usually a parent. Usually a male.

Something told him that this wasn't the case here.

It was over twenty-four hours since Joanna's body had been found. In that time, he'd taken Emily Burns's family on a wasted identification and spent long hours reading endless conversations between Emily and various other teenagers. All of them nonsensical, ridiculous discussions, which always ended with threats and anger towards her. Once they'd discovered her true identity.

DI Bennett was leading the press conference, which had surprised him at first. He was preparing to do it himself, when she'd announced it. Now, his job there seemed to be almost like a liaison officer. To be on hand for the family. For afterwards. He'd left them in the corridor with DI Bennett, so he'd be better positioned to observe, but even now, he was anxious for them. Knowing what was to come, once they were in the spotlight.

Trying not to let his annoyance at being shoved aside show.

Mark moved closer to the door they would soon be coming through, standing with his hands loosely linked in front of him, watching those in the room. Wondering how they would report this, how they would react to the story. Whether they would even think it was one worth telling.

He wondered if they'd been tipped off to anything

yet. Whether any of them realised they were being used somewhat.

Flashes of light blurred his vision momentarily, as the doors opened and DI Bennett walked in first. Julie was close behind, followed by Stephanie. The only two family members needed, it had been decided.

'What about the uncle?' Mark had asked earlier, still unsure of his role in this. 'Might be good to get his face out there. See if anyone in his past has something to say?'

'Too soon. We need to make sure he doesn't get spooked.'

Mark had accepted DI Bennett's words, wondering if he was a man who was easily worried.

He watched as DI Bennett waited for Julie and Stephanie to sit down behind the table, Emily's last known photograph on a screen to the side of them. Waited to see if either of them looked towards it at any point. They were both looking out into the room, wide-eyed, almost wincing at the sight. Mark knew they'd be nervous, but he didn't think they'd even get a sentence out. Both pale and, likely, dry-mouthed. Reality setting in now, the adrenaline of that morning disappearing.

'Thank you all for coming,' DI Bennett said, quietening down the camera clicks and low murmur of voices. 'On Sunday 21st October, Emily Burns – a nineteen-year-old woman – left her home without saying where she was going to anyone. Four days later, the family has had no word from her. She has no known means of travel or plans to meet anyone.'

Mark listened to the normal spiel DI Bennett said, detailing the circumstances of Emily's disappearance. He watched the faces of Julie and Stephanie first, before turning back to the room. Most of the people there listened seemingly attentively, but he could see a few blank faces there. Some who had become more seasoned to this type of show. Just another missing person. Another name they would struggle to remember in a month's time.

Never making a dent in their consciousness.

'Emily is a bright, intelligent young woman,' DI Bennett continued, playing her part well. Mark knew some of the reporters in the audience would already be questioning why someone of her rank was conducting this press conference. Wondering why a detective inspector was seemingly leading this investigation.

'We are increasingly worried about her safety. She has no history of running away. No history of going missing. This is a situation which is greatly worrying. Her last movements have been shared, but I'll go over them again. She was last seen on CCTV, at two-twenty a.m., making her way into a disused warehouse yard on the Liverpool waterfront, off Sefton Street. Brunswick Business Park is close by, as is the old Century building. While this is not a heavily trafficked area during the early hours of the morning, we believe there may have been some witnesses who may have noticed Emily's movements at this time. We'd urge anyone with information to come forward and provide that to us. No matter how small or insignificant you may think it is.'

Mark watched Stephanie, as DI Bennett continued to talk. Her lips were pursed together, her blonde hair hanging past her shoulders. Sitting beside her, Julie seemed to withdraw further into herself.

'Emily, it's Mum,' Julie said, when it was her turn to speak, her voice cracking, stilted, as she struggled to get those words out. 'We're all worried about you. We just want you to come home. You're not in any trouble.'

Maybe, maybe not, Mark thought.

'We all want you back home and safe with us. That's all we need. Just get in touch and let us know you're okay, if you can't come home yet. Everyone misses you. Charlie, Uncle Rich. We just need to know you're okay.'

Mark watched a few exchanged glances between the reporters at the mention of the uncle. Eyebrows raised as they began to wonder how this story would play out.

'We just want to know you're safe, Emily,' Stephanie said, the moment to speak passing to her. 'And if you're in trouble, then you have people who will support you no matter what. Please, just get in touch. And if anyone out there has seen Emily, or spoken to her, get in contact and let us know.'

Mark was impressed by the pair, their heartfelt pleas coming across as genuine and just needy enough to be effective. He wasn't sure how much play they would get on local news channels, but he thought it would be all over social media within an hour at least.

Another tweet that could be shared over and over, as if they really had any effect.

The press conference was wrapped up a few minutes later, more words shared by DI Bennett, information doled out once again. Mark held the door open for Julie and Stephanie as they walked out, away from the media, cameras still snapping pictures as they left.

Stephanie turned to him once the door was closed, wide-eyed and shaking.

'Did that go okay?'

'You both did excellently,' Mark replied, a tight smile shared with them both. 'Hopefully it'll jog some people's memories, get some of them thinking back on that night.'

'Someone must have seen her,' Julie said, quieter now, as if all her energy had been expended in there. 'That's all I keep thinking. Someone knows something.'

DI Bennett joined them, giving the same words of encouragement Mark had already given them. He liked to think his had a little more conviction than hers did, but by that point, he doubted Julie and Stephanie were even listening.

It was moments like these that they would play over and over in their minds later, when sleep became a distant stranger. Wondering if they could have said more, whether they had said the right things.

Whether they had done enough.

'The girl they found yesterday near where Emily was last seen,' Stephanie said, turning to DI Bennett now. 'Who was she? Did she know Emily? Do you know that yet?'

'We know who she is,' DI Bennett replied, treading carefully, Mark felt. 'We now have someone travelling to identify her for sure.'

'Is it someone we know, or Emily knew?'

'Why do you ask?' DI Bennett said, eyes narrowing a little as she spoke.

'It just seems weird that someone around the same age, same look, almost, would be found so close to where Emily was seen last.'

'That's something we're looking into,' DI Bennett said, shooting Mark a quick look. One he couldn't quite read. 'We'll let you know if anything comes up in the investigation that is a possible link. DC Flynn here will still be leading the search for Emily.'

They seemed to buy that explanation easily. As the seconds went by, the minutes, the hours, Mark was believing less and less that there was no link between them. The proximity, the ages, the gender ... too much of a coincidence. Mark took them home a little while later, driving in silence as the two women stared out at the disappearing city centre on the journey back to the estate. He didn't stay with them long.

There were only so many times he could tell them everything was being done to find Emily and make it sound believable.

Mark pulled his car to a stop outside his house after 9 p.m. Worn out, the muscles in his body aching and begging for rest. A flash of guilt washed over him as he remembered the looks on the Burns family earlier. Like rabbits in a hundred pairs of headlights.

With that image, the feeling of being watched returned once again.

He couldn't quite work it out, yet the hairs on the back of his neck stood on end as he stepped out of his car, closing the door as quietly as possible behind him. On the empty street, darkness staring back at him from every corner, he couldn't help but feel that someone was out there. Hidden in the shadows.

Mark decided to take a walk.

He made his way down the street, slowly, methodically, eyes scanning the area. Listening for any noise, like the one from the previous night. Each step made him a little more anxious, as if he was going towards the danger, rather than away from it.

Which was his job, he supposed.

He walked the length of the street and back again, hearing and seeing nothing. The feeling remained, but he shook it off and eventually made his way up the path to his house. Let himself inside, gave it a few seconds, then called Natasha.

She arrived twenty minutes later.

He sat down next to her on the sofa, muting the television in the corner. 'Have you eaten?'

'Yeah, was starving when I got home from work,' Natasha replied, running her hands through her hair and sitting back further into the sofa. 'Couldn't wait for you to finish. Wasn't sure if you'd be calling. Still busy?'

'Yeah,' Mark said, grimacing at the thought of having to go back there again the next day. 'You didn't have to come round if you were tired or something.'

'I know, but I'd rather be here than at home on my own,' Natasha said. 'Don't worry, I'm not expecting us to move in together after so short a time. But don't you think this has been ... easy? None of the weird awkwardness that's usually there at the start of relationships?'

'No, I guess not. Just let me know if things are moving too fast though. I don't want you thinking I expect you to come round at the drop of a hat if you don't want to.'

'You're sweet for someone who obviously doesn't have any problem getting people to "come round".'

'That's not true ...'

'You keep saying that,' Natasha said, turning to him and lifting her feet onto the sofa. 'What do you mean?'

'Let's just say when I was younger, I looked a lot different.'

'How so?'

Mark sighed. 'I was a heavy teenager. Acne, sweaty, the lot. You wouldn't have looked twice at me.'

'How do you know that?'

'Because no one did,' Mark said quickly, then closed his mouth as the familiar feeling he'd lived with as a teenager bubbled its way to the surface. 'I didn't know how to talk to anyone really. I thought if I spoke up, I'd just be laughed at. Then puberty hit, and it just made things worse, I suppose. I was bullied for a while, but even they moved on. I was too boring to make fun of, so they just left me alone. I barely spoke to anyone from the age of fourteen to eighteen. Just got used to it. I don't know why I'm telling you this.'

'It's fine,' Natasha said, and Mark believed her.

They sat quietly for a minute or so, before Mark felt her eyes on him again. He turned to her and opened his mouth to say something, but stopped.

'It's okay, I can feel it too,' Natasha said, speaking for him. 'This is the good bit though. Talking to each other and learning. I don't usually get this close to someone after a month or so. I guess this is moving quicker than I realised.'

'I'm sorry,' Mark replied, but didn't feel like Natasha was really sorry about what was happening.

The start of something.

Natasha laughed at his apology and shook her head. 'It's fine. I'm ...'

'Comfortable?' Mark finished for her, smiling as she nodded in agreement. 'Good.'

'Doesn't mean if I find out you're secretly a Marmite lover or enjoy *Love Island*, I won't be running for the door though.'

Mark laughed now and felt good for it. 'No on both counts. But I do like those reality TV shows about emergency services, if that's a problem?'

'I'll let it slide.'

'What about you?' Mark said, as Natasha shifted on the sofa, moving closer to him. 'Any tales of woe from your teenage years?'

He couldn't see her face now, as she turned and leaned on his legs. 'Nothing that'd interest you.'

Mark shaped to say something, push her on what was quite plainly untrue, but instead closed his mouth and stayed silent.

It could wait.

Around midnight, with Natasha asleep in bed, Mark stretched out on the single sofa in the tiny living room, overpowered by the ridiculously huge television he'd spent far too much money on a year earlier. The Sky+ box was almost full, so he started watching a programme from it, turning the volume down so as not to wake Natasha. A half-hour panel show, he thought, would bring on sleep more quickly.

An hour later, he was still awake. He took his phone off the coffee table where he'd left it earlier that night and started scrolling through the local newspaper's Facebook feed. He quickly found the story he was looking for.

The press conference for the Burns family. Julie and Stephanie centre stage. DI Bennett sitting next to them. He watched the video again.

Mark switched back to the Facebook link, when the video autoplayed on his phone once again. He scanned the few comments left, the usual stream of *thoughts and prayers* and sycophantic declarations. A few troll-like comments appeared, as was the norm now.

Shouldnt b out that late on her own round there. Askin for it, ya ask me.

'No one is ever asking you,' Mark said under his breath, continuing to scroll through the comments.

Near the end, there was one which seemed to jump out from the page. Made him frown at his phone and read it again.

She played the game and lost. Shame it wasn't the other twin. Would have been more fun.

He wondered what had prompted such a strange response, but carried on reading through. Combed through the comments to see if there was anything similar he'd missed.

Seems like a Game to me. Another girl going missing – probably turn up in a day or two.

Who cares? More important things going on than a stupid girl playing around.

He'd seen comments like these before. Social media – the refuge of annoying opinions. He took a screenshot of the comments on his phone, without knowing why, and then switched to the main story on the page.

The death of Joanna Carter.

It seemed that this story had the same kind of people commenting, but with a few more fools tossed into the pile. The ones who couldn't wait to post that someone was *selfish* for possibly ending their own life. The same idiotic words that were always used. *Coward, attention-seeking, stupid*. It was always the same.

They would soon change their tune, once the fact it wasn't suicide became known.

Mark switched back to the story on Emily Burns when it became too much. There were a few more comments trickling in that he was interested in. Names he recognised from trawling through her fake social media accounts. Those who had been targeted by her, victimised and shamed. They would feel vindicated now; still too embarrassed to tell anyone what she had done.

Hope she regrets wat she did.

No1 will miss her.

More to this than anyone knows. She wasn't a goody two shoes.

The anger Emily had left behind, like a stain on their lives. Mark couldn't read anymore, but forced himself to make a note of the names.

She played The Game and lost . . .

When Mark finally fell asleep three hours later – Natasha asleep beside him, silent – he was still thinking about that comment.

Twenty-Six

Mark was bleary-eyed and tired when he arrived at the station the next morning. His eventual sleep was fitful, disturbed by the guilt of not working every hour, every minute of the day, to try and track Emily down.

To work out what connected her to Joanna Carter.

The usual early morning meeting was about to start when he arrived in the room, taking a seat near the back. Filled with faces he recognised, but couldn't name.

'Joanna Carter,' DI Bennett said, bringing the room to a quiet. 'Positively identified by family and we're treating it as a suspicious death now.'

'Not suicide?'

'Highly unlikely, I would say, given the CCTV,' DI Bennett said, turning to Mark's least-favourite fellow DC. The smarmy Dale Williams. 'We're going through the last of the CCTV now, but it looks like whoever was with Joanna that night knew to keep themselves hidden.'

On the screen behind her, there was a blown-up image of the figure that Mark had seen the day before, following Joanna onto the roof. He still couldn't see any facial features, but he leaned forward anyway, trying to see anything recognisable at all.

'So, we're trying to track down whoever this person is,' DI Bennett continued, gesturing behind her to the screen. 'This is our most important piece of evidence at the moment. Tech officers are going through the victim's computer and phone as we speak. At the moment, we don't have even a possible ID for this person yet, but that doesn't mean we can't find him. I want this to be the main focus of today. Take this picture around the building, to all the occupants. The photograph will also be released to the media in a couple of hours. Someone, somewhere, knows who this man is.'

Mark listened as DI Bennett went on, talking about a case he increasingly felt was way out of his control now. He waited until the meeting had ended before speaking to her. She was expecting him, it seemed, as he made his way past the other people in the room to the front, where she was leaning against the table, arms folded across her chest.

'So . . .'

'It would have been much easier if there was a link, Mark,' DI Bennett said, shrugging as she finished. 'We still haven't found any link between the two and you would think in this day and age that wouldn't be difficult to find. They're not Facebook friends, don't follow each other on Twitter, no emails or WhatsApp messages. We can't find a single thing. Plus, it doesn't look like Emily in the CCTV. I'm positive about that.'

'So am I,' Mark replied, as DS Cavanagh joined them. The room had emptied out now, leaving them alone. 'I don't like coincidences though.'

'None of us do.'

'So, what if Emily is a victim as well? What if she saw something that night and has been dealt with in the same way?'

'Until we have something concrete, we don't have the manpower to cover that angle at this time. We need something to connect them, Mark. You know the score.'

Mark shook his head, trying to contain his frustration. 'We're just waiting for her body to show up, is that what you're suggesting?'

DS Cavanagh stepped forwards, fixing Mark with a stare. 'That's not what is being said, Mark. At the moment, Emily is still missing. Your job is to find her, or give us something more to work on, right?'

Mark swallowed and averted his eyes. 'I understand.'

'Good,' DI Bennett replied, cocking her head to one side and giving him a look of concern that disappeared as quickly as it had appeared. 'Have you tracked down the father yet?'

'I think so,' Mark said. 'I'm going to speak to him now.'

DI Bennett nodded, then turned to DS Cavanagh to discuss Joanna Carter again.

Mark left them to it and went out.

Alone.

Driving through the city was something Mark enjoyed. Back when he'd started working that side of the water, he was always driving. Exploring the way it was constantly changing before his eyes, the buildings and people shifting with each passing month. It was still all fresh to him, seeing it through new eyes every day.

It meant he still viewed the city as almost another world. One with hidden secrets he wanted to uncover.

After pretending to himself he knew where he was going, he eventually conceded defeat and plugged the street name into his sat nav. The city was a sprawling landscape of towns and estates. He couldn't know it all. No one did. Still, he wanted to try.

Mark pulled the car to a stop outside a tired-looking block of flats, half an hour outside the city centre. It could have been a different place entirely, a different city. This one seemed to still be clinging on to its past with whitened fingertips: the faded green facade of the building, peeling paint each way you turned. Even the graffiti looked like it was of a different time. As he left the car, he heard shouts and cackling laughter swept on the wind towards him, but the street was empty, apart from a crisp packet swirling in the breeze.

The door that led into the block was ajar, held open by a bit of cardboard so it didn't close properly. He pushed it open and made his way up the concrete stairs to the second floor, trying to breathe through his mouth as he did so. The cloying smell of decay and ammonia was seeping out of every surface.

This was the forgotten land. The side of the city people elsewhere tried to pretend didn't exist. The money spent on the waterfront and beyond not stretching this far.

Yet. He hoped that would change.

He rapped his knuckles on the door, stood back and waited a few seconds. He didn't think it was likely that Barry Usher was going to be at work. Not with his knowledge of the type of people who lived in this area and what he knew about the bloke. He tried knocking again, harder this time. The wooden door rattled a little on its hinges. Another minute went by and he reached out to knock again, when the door behind him swung open with a creak that echoed around the small walkway.

'He's not in,' a voice said, gruff and raspy, thick with years of smoking and drinking, Mark thought. He turned to see the woman it belonged to. 'He'll be in the pub by now.'

Mark smiled at the older woman, taking in her large stature and bent posture. She was propping herself up on a walking frame, staring him down. 'I'm from Merseyside Police . . .'

'That's nice for you, but he's still not in.'

'Where does he drink these days?'

'You'll find him at the Peg,' the woman said, already turning around to go back into the flat. 'Do me a favour and tell him to pick me up a pint of milk on his way back. He's a good lad. Don't go nicking him or anything.'

Mark shaped to answer, but the door was already closing.

He pulled out his phone for directions once he was back at the car, the sat nav finding the right pub within a minute. It was no better than the block of flats he'd just left – a pub that was probably last booming twenty years ago.

Mark wondered how he would find the man, given he had no idea what he looked like. He pushed open the door to the pub, walking inside with his shoulders back and chest out, waiting for trouble as soon as he entered.

He needn't have worried.

Inside, a fat barman sat precariously on a barstool staring at a quiet television in the corner. The only other sign of life was an older bloke, sitting a little further down the bar, a newspaper open in front of him. A pint of something dark next to his hand.

Mark made his way over towards the bar, feeling

more overdressed than he ever had, in his suit and tie and black polished shoes. He didn't belong there. The barman gave him a cursory glance up and down, then turned back to the television. Marked out within seconds, he thought.

'Barry?'

'Who wants to know?' the man sitting at the bar said without turning around.

'Detective Constable Mark Flynn. You got a minute?'

Barry Usher looked at him for the first time, then turned back to his paper. 'I don't know nothing about anything.'

'I'm here about Emily. Your daughter.'

'Is that right?' Barry replied, lifting his pint and draining a third of it in one slug. 'What's that got to do with me?'

'You don't know?' Mark said, wishing he was suddenly anywhere else. 'We've been trying to track you down for a couple of days now. She's missing. It's been on the news, online and that.'

'I don't bother reading all that shite. It's usually all lies. Anyway, she's twenty-odd years old now, I'm sure she can look after herself.'

'She's nineteen,' Mark corrected, trying to keep his voice calm and steady. 'And we're worried she may have come to some harm.'

'And what do you need me for? It's not like I know where she is. I've not seen her in over ten years. Thanks to that bint of a mother she's got. Should I be worried?'

'That's not for me to say.'

Barry considered this and sniffed. 'I'm sure she'll be fine. It's not like they need my help anyway. Wouldn't piss on me if I was on fire, thanks to their mother. She'll turn up soon enough, no doubt. And won't thank me for caring.'

'I'm guessing my next question is going to be easily answered then.'

'No, I haven't seen her. Wouldn't even know what she looked like now. Any of the kids. They don't want to know me, so what can I do? It's not like they're missing out on anything. They'd only want to know why I wasn't around when they were growing up. All that touchy-feely Jeremy Kyle bollocks. It's not like I could give them an answer they'd like. I'd only be landing their mum in it.'

'She kept you from seeing them?'

'She didn't want me having anything to do with the kids,' Barry said, stroking the side of his pint glass with an idle hand. From the look of him – and the smell – Mark guessed it wasn't his first pint of the afternoon. 'I was a bad influence because I wouldn't put up with the shite she would. They needed discipline, not a friend. That's what she wanted to be. I wanted to be a dad. Show them the right way about things. Real-life stuff, you know? Especially the boy. He was soft as shite, even as a baby.'

'So, you haven't heard from any of them in years?'

Barry paused, then lifted his pint to his mouth. Motioned towards the barman for a refill. He didn't move. 'Not a word in at least four or five years. Their head will be full of crap by now. Their mum never had a good word to say about me and I can only imagine what she's said since then. All lies, of course.'

'Really?'

There was a moment when Mark thought he'd pushed it too hard, even though he'd only asked a simple question. That's all it could take in a place like this – one bad word, one wrong look.

'I never did anything bad to her,' Barry said, a look of

anger sweeping across his face, gone in a second. 'Nothing like as bad as she told your lot anyway. We had some arguments, me and her. Some doozies. She could give as good as she got, that Julie. What happened to me was never talked about – it was always what happened to her. She always came running back, though.'

'Until the last time,' Mark said, watching as Barry's face darkened yet again, before the fresh pint was plonked in front of him on the bar. A curled fist went round it and Barry supped greedily.

'Yeah, until the last time,' Barry replied, wiping a grimy sleeve across his bearded face. Mark wondered where he'd been for the past decade, as his son and daughters grew older, became adults. Whether he'd been waiting in this pub, for someone like him to come along and tell him how his kids were doing.

'I tried for a bit,' Barry continued, patting his pockets and eventually finding what he was looking for – a pouch of tobacco, which he opened and began rolling a cigarette. 'Used to have them round to this little flat I had back when I moved out. Tiny place it was and *she* wouldn't let me put some sleeping bags down so they could sleep over. Not my fault, that. They would have loved it, I reckon. Would've been like they were camping. That bint wasn't having any of it. She hated me by that point, even though she still loved me as well. I could tell, when I would drop them off – there was always a part of her that wanted me to just walk through that door like nothing had happened and take over the house again. She needed it, but I wasn't going to give it to her. Not anymore. Bet she's still waiting for me to come back. She could never cope without me.'

She seems to have done fine without you, Mark thought.

'Do you keep in touch with any of that side of the family? Ever had any run-ins with them perhaps?'

Barry barked out a short laugh, then, a little sliver of tongue slipped out of his mouth as it ran along the cigarette paper, sealing it shut. 'You've met her brother then, I'm guessing. Richie Burns. Is he still a big, jumped-up lump? You know, he never said a word to me, in all those years me and his sister were having *problems*. All talk, that one. Don't let him make you think different. He'd sooner beat up some poor drunk bloke a foot shorter than him, than actually take on someone who could fight back. His reputation is not well earned, I'll tell you.'

'So, you've not seen Emily, or any of your kids in over a decade. Or their mum. Or any of their family.'

Another short pause. 'That's right.'

'Emily is missing . . .'

'You said that when you first came in and I told you then – I can't help you.'

Barry stood up with the easy grace of someone used to alighting from a bar stool, even with a bellyful of booze inside him. He stopped in front of Mark, scratching at his face and looking up towards him. He was smaller than Mark had been expecting, with the air of a man who had spent his life trying to make up for the fact. 'Look, it's sad that the kid has done one, but I've got nothing to do with it. She probably just got sick and tired of that woman and her mind games. She'll turn up sooner or later. And she still won't want to have anything to do with me, so why should I care now? It's not like it's going to end in some lovely reunion or some such bollocks. No, best leave me out of it. We've all moved on. Those kids probably don't even know my last name anymore.'

Mark stood aside as Barry shuffled off towards the exit, wondering if he should try one more time. Whether he should make the man see sense and actually care about his own flesh and blood.

Yet, he knew he wasn't there to be Jeremy Kyle, as Barry had said.

'Your neighbour from across the way wants you to bring her back a pint of milk.'

Barry lifted a hand in response, but didn't turn around.

He clearly didn't care, but Mark couldn't worry about that. He only needed to find out one thing. What happened to Emily Burns.

And the answer to that wasn't there, in that pub, with its fat barman and a man who looked twenty years older than he was.

The barman gave him a look as he walked away, but went back to staring at the television. Mark waited, knowing what was coming.

'He's not letting on about something, am I right?' Mark said, when he'd waited long enough to know he would have to talk first. 'Want to help me find a missing girl?'

The barman sniffed, but turned to face Mark. 'It's probably nothing . . .'

'Could be something though.'

'Listen, Barry is messed up. An alcoholic, just like his old fella. And his old fella before him. Doesn't mean he doesn't love his kids.'

'They always do,' Mark said, leaning on the bar and eyeing the beer on draught. Wishing he could have a quick pint before going back out onto the street. 'He's not exactly willing to do anything to help though.'

'He doesn't know anything.'

'What's not being said here?'

The barman shifted on his stool. 'We've heard some weird things about the girl for the past few weeks. Someone who knows the family told Barry about it last week.'

'What kind of things?' Mark said, trying to keep his voice level. He straightened up at the bar. 'It could be important.'

'Some guy came in last week and said he'd heard one of Barry's girls had been seen in town stopping random people and asking weird questions. Like she was on drugs or something.'

'Weird how?'

'I don't know, about their sex lives, stuff like that.'

'What do you mean? Sex lives?'

'Like, pretending to interview people, but getting very personal.'

Mark shook his head and made a mental note to ask Emily's family about this. If some randomer in a pub knew about it, no doubt they would. He wanted to know why they hadn't told him. 'What did Barry say about it?'

'Just laughed and said something about the mum. He's always banging on about her. All women, I guess. You get that kind of thing a lot in here. Should have seen it during the Women's World Cup on the big screen. Thought there was going to be a riot.'

Mark shook his head at the ridiculousness of that, but continued on regardless. Tried to get more out of the bloke, but didn't get very far.

Tried to work out what he'd learned and whether this was just another wasted trip.

The words from that Facebook comment came back to him then. A game.

That's how he felt. As if he was in a big game, that he was being played with. Batted around from side to side, with no real clue of how to stop it.

He straightened up and made a decision.

There was no way he was going to let that happen.

Twenty-Seven

Mark tried to talk to Barry again later at home, but the absentee father was having none of it. Mark gave up eventually, but only when the older man went silent for five minutes, ignoring his questions entirely.

Barry's head was firmly in the sand now.

He travelled back across the city, making his way to the Burns's house. It was a twenty-minute drive, giving Mark a chance to get his thoughts in order. The discovery of Joanna Carter had proven to be an unwelcome distraction from what was happening to the Burns family. He could feel the doubt from DI Bennett and DS Cavanagh that the two were connected, but he was increasingly sure that his instinct was right.

There was a reason Emily was there that night. That time. There was a reason Joanna Carter was found dead and why someone on CCTV followed her up to that rooftop.

With every passing moment, it became more and more unlikely they would find Emily alive.

Stephanie opened the door for him, giving him a good morning, then making her way back to the kitchen. He popped his head around the living-room door, firing off a greeting to Julie as he did so. She was curled up on one sofa, a blanket over her body, but she was wide awake. As awake as she could be, anyway. She had slid back into silence since the press conference, the energy after the identification evaporating.

He wanted to ask about Emily's odd behaviour, but didn't think he'd receive an answer while Julie was in that state.

Mark moved through to the kitchen, sitting down at the table as Stephanie switched on the kettle. She busied herself with rinsing mugs – just the two cups. He guessed she knew her mum wasn't in the mood.

He had a quick look past her, out into the back yard for the uncle. He breathed a sigh of relief when he saw it was empty.

'No Rich this morning?' Mark said, as Stephanie handed him coffee and sat down opposite him. 'Thought he'd be waiting for me.'

'He was out late apparently,' Stephanie replied, looking fresh and alert, despite the pressure, the weight of what the family was going through. 'Scouring the streets for Emily, he told Mum. Probably had some jobs on and didn't want to be lumbered with all of this anymore.'

'Jobs?'

Stephanie didn't answer, giving him a look he knew meant he should drop the subject. Something illegal, no doubt. It made little difference to Mark what he was doing, he was just glad he wasn't around. His aggression was barely contained the more the days went on.

'Uncle Rich,' Mark began, trying to sound calm and relaxed. 'I think we both know what his *jobs* entail, right?'

He waited for a few seconds for Stephanie to answer, but she looked away from him nervously.

'Does he deal with students?'

Stephanie shook her head. 'I don't know.'

'You might have heard something though? Maybe from friends, or the like?'

'Maybe, I don't really pay attention,' Stephanie said, raising a finger to her mouth and chewing on a nail without biting into it. 'I don't want to know.'

Mark nodded, knowing there was probably some truth to that. He thought about probing further, but it was only a semi-formed thought at that moment and he needed more time to go over it.

A drugs angle. He'd have to ask Pathology if they'd had a report of anything in Joanna Carter's body at her time of death. Could be something to it. He stored it at the back of his mind for now and continued talking to Stephanie, changing the subject.

'Have you thought about going back to classes on Monday?'

'Not really,' Stephanie replied, cradling the mug in front of her. 'I don't think it's a very good idea. I'd only be thinking about Emily and what's going on back here. It's not like I'd be able to concentrate on anything they were saying.'

'The distraction might be a good thing, you know? A way of forgetting what's been happening, even if it's just for a few hours.'

'Why would I want to forget?'

Mark cleared his throat, annoyed with himself for the poor choice of words. 'Sorry, that came out wrong. I mean . . . a way of putting it to the back of your mind for a little while. It's not healthy to live with this much anxiety. You need a break from it.'

'I'm fine.'

The words sounded final, yet Mark could see she was thinking it over. This was something he tried to do often while investigating cases: encourage them to do tasks, any little thing to take their minds off what was happening. He'd witnessed too many families driving themselves into unending angst when they thought of nothing else but the situation they were in.

He also needed them to see a way out.

'I'm doing everything I can to find out what happened to Emily. I need you to level with me though – if there's something, anything, you can think of that might be important or not, I need to know it.'

Stephanie was silent for a few seconds, looking away from Mark, before she turned back to him. She shook her head. 'There's nothing else.'

Mark didn't believe her. Instinct again, he thought.

'It's not going to have a happy ending, is it?'

Mark didn't reply, taking a moment to choose his words carefully. 'I was involved in a case back when I was in uniform. I was about twenty-one, twenty-two, so must be about eight years ago now. I had just finished probation, so had only been a copper for two years. Anyone will tell you, you're still the new kid even then. Still am, to some degree. There was a call about a teenager gone missing – young girl, about seventeen. I recognised the address straight away when they gave it to us over the radio. Been over there a fair few times for a load of different reasons. The usual council estate stuff: fights, domestics, thefts, you know the score. This family was pretty notorious, but only in the few streets around where they lived. Anyway, we were always getting called out there for some reason or other. The girl, she was in the middle of five kids. Had a younger sister, but three older brothers who were nightmares. She'd disappeared before, getting up to all sorts, no doubt. It was always only for a day, tops. She'd waltz back in, usually just around the same time we'd show up. I hadn't dealt with that side of them before, but I knew about it. I didn't think this time would be any different.'

'It was though, right?' Stephanie said, as Mark paused.

'She'd left the house the day before, about five p.m., they said. Just said she was going out, nothing more. Took the details and told them we'd keep an eye out for her, that sort of thing, thinking she'd be back soon enough.'

Mark had a clear image in his head of that house. So different to the one he'd spent almost a week in now. The smell of damp and despair seeping out of every wall. The yellowed wallpaper, the nicotine stains on the dad's fingers, as they prised open another can of cheap lager. The lines on the mum's face, crevices deeper than were normal on the face of someone in their forties. The shouting and arguing from other, unseen places within the house.

'She wasn't, was she?'

'No,' Mark replied, shaking his head. 'I heard a few days later that it had been passed to CID. I kept up to date with the case, though. Think it was the look on her mum's face that did it for me. Like she couldn't work out why this had happened to her. Anyway, they found her bag a day or so later. Whatever money she'd had in it had gone, along with her phone, but other stuff was in there. You start fearing the worst then. They said as much – the detectives working it, I mean – when I asked, that they were probably looking for a body. The bag was found in a park somewhere, can't remember now. They found a piece of clothing, torn off, hanging from a bush. The mum thought it looked like something her daughter had been wearing.'

'As bad as blood, I imagine,' Stephanie said quietly, staring at Mark as he continued to talk.

'Numerous calls came in. Someone had seen her being dragged off the street, another person saw her hitchhiking out the city. Talking to men who had angry looks on their faces, or wandering the streets late at night, looking the worse for wear. It seemed like everyone and no one had seen her. The family went on telly, like you did, and I remember watching it thinking, this story is only going to end one way.'

'And it didn't?'

'No,' Mark replied, attempting a half-smile across the table at Stephanie. 'She knocked on the door a week later, like nothing had happened. She'd gone to a house party on a whim. Didn't really know anyone there, except some lad she'd been chatting to online. Lost her bag while she was drunk, but was having too good a time to care. Drink and drugs involved, and the attention of a good-looking older lad. Spent a week getting off her head and whatever else you can imagine in this lad's bedsit. No contact with the outside world at all. The lad didn't have a TV, no internet. Basically, they stayed in that room for a week – eating pot noodles, smoking weed, and getting drunk and ... well, you can imagine. She – they – had no idea anyone was even looking for her. She was as shocked as anyone when she came back to police being involved and all that.'

'That doesn't sound like something Emily would ... *could* do.'

'Maybe,' Mark said, holding his hands up in mid-air. 'Maybe not. But that doesn't mean there isn't something else keeping her away. Something stupid, something that'll make no sense. It doesn't have to be the exact same story to have the same outcome. I'm not saying it's what's happened, but I'm saying you never know. That's why you can never give up hope. People are just full of surprises. You can never tell what they're going to do next. You can never predict their behaviour, their choices, their decisions. Life would be easier if you could, but there you go.'

'Thanks for trying,' Stephanie said after a few seconds of silence, staring into Mark's eyes. They lingered for a moment, then she turned away. 'I just can't see it. Something bad has happened to her. I can feel it.'

'You can't know that . . .'

'I know something, Mark,' Stephanie said, her voice louder now, interrupting his. 'I don't know what it is, but I can feel it here, in the pit of my stomach. Eating away at me. Like it's a part of me dying off or something. Something bad has happened to her. I know it.'

'That's just your fear, Stephanie,' Mark tried, keeping his voice level and soothing. Or trying to at least. He was never sure if it came out as soothing or patronising. 'You've been through a lot this week. You need a break.'

'I don't need a break,' Stephanie replied, her raised voice reverberating around them, bouncing off the walls and shifting the atmosphere in the house. She slumped back in the chair and covered her face with her hands. 'I'm sorry. It's just . . . I need my sister back.'

She began to crumple in front of him, his chair scraping back before he realised it was happening, moving across towards her as she dissolved into tears.

'It's okay,' he said, an arm around her shoulders as he squatted down next to her. 'I know you want her back. We're trying all we can to bring her home.'

'I know,' Stephanie said through gulps of air. Her body shook with emotion, as the week's events finally caught up with her. 'I just can't live like this anymore, with the not knowing. That's what's killing me. The fact I have no idea where Emily is, or what's happened.'

'I know, I know.'

'But ...'

'What is it?' Mark said, his arm still around her, as she grasped on to him with one arm and wiped the other across her face. 'I'm here to listen to anything you have to say.'

'Part of me ... part of me hopes she never comes back. That she's found a place for herself. Away from all of this. A better life. One where she fits in properly and isn't angry or upset. Not lashing out at people. Somewhere she belongs.'

'I understand,' Mark said, hoping she believed him. 'I need some more answers though, before I can find her, okay? There's things that aren't being said that need to be.' Stephanie shook her head, frowning towards him. 'We've told you everything ...'

Mark held a hand up. 'I'm not accusing anyone of leaving things out, or not telling the truth. It's just ... I've heard some things about Emily. About her behaviour over the past few weeks.'

'I don't know,' Stephanie began, then stopped herself, wrapping her arms around herself. 'It was just stupid games, that was all.'

'What kind of game are you talking about?'

Twenty-Eight

Mark waited for Stephanie to compose herself once again, allowing the atmosphere to settle before tackling the next step. It was almost like a play running in his head – the lines and actions he had to act out so he could look for the correct responses, the real ones.

Mark sat back down at the small table, finished his coffee in a long swig and set the cup down. Looked across at Stephanie, who was still cradling her own drink.

'I know we've been over this before, but I need to have everything in the right order here. There's still so much I don't know and I need the whole story right. Have you been back much in the past few months? Home, I mean?'

'Not really,' Stephanie replied, staring at her mug. 'I've been busy and that. I rang Mum as much as I could, but you know how it is.'

'How were things with Emily during that time?'

Stephanie shook her head. 'We weren't really talking. Not for a couple of months. I'm sure it would have sorted itself out, but you know ... Sometimes when you think you have the time to let things happen naturally, it turns out you don't.'

'Did you hear anything about Emily while you were away? Her behaviour?'

Stephanie shifted, her chair scraping back as she stood and walked over to the sink. 'Not really.'

Mark watched her empty her cup and then stay with her back to him. 'I've been told she was doing some odd things lately.'

'What do you mean?' Stephanie replied, turning to face him, arms folded across her chest. 'I don't understand.'

'That perhaps she was witnessed doing weird stuff in town, things like that?'

'Who told you that?'

Mark shook his head. 'It's not important right now. I just wondered if you'd heard of her doing anything like that.'

'Look, we both know she was a little messed up. Doesn't mean she was losing her mind, or whatever you think it was.'

'I wasn't suggesting that,' Mark said, standing up, as Stephanie's voice began to rise. He heard movement behind him, but didn't turn. 'I'm just asking because I need to know everything.'

'I don't know anything about that.'

'So, you hadn't heard of her talking to people in strange ways, or anything of that sort?'

Stephanie shook her head, but Mark could feel something unsaid in the air between them. He hesitated, wondering how to approach this now. 'If Emily was doing something out of the ordinary, it might be helpful to know now. While we're still looking for her.'

'There's nothing . . .'

'Anything, no matter how small, it might be important.'

'Who told you?'

Mark turned to see Julie Burns standing in the kitchen doorway, staring at him with bloodshot eyes that probably hadn't been closed in a day or more. He kept himself calm and continued. 'Told me what, Julie?'

'There's nothing to say. She's missing and needs to be found. This has nothing to do with anything.'

'It's just that we've had some reports about possible strange events Emily might have been involved in recently.'

Julie shook her head. 'Whatever it is, it's got nothing to do with what's happened now. She . . . she was just messing around, that's all.'

'How?'

'There's nothing. Who told you this?'

Mark opened his mouth to answer, then closed it to consider his words more carefully. 'What was Emily doing?'

'It was all just pranks, she told me,' Julie said, waving her hands as if none of it mattered. 'Nothing important. It was just silly stuff, that's all. You know what teenagers are like.'

'What kind of pranks, Julie?'

There was a huff, hands went to her hips. 'I don't really know.'

'I was told about something that happened while she was in town. Approaching people there and asking personal questions.'

'I don't know . . .'

'Mum, how many times were there?'

Mark kept his eyes on Julie, even as Stephanie moved away from the countertop and towards her mother.

'She said it was just some pranks that she was doing with people in college,' Julie said finally, leaning one shoulder against the doorway. 'It's got nothing to do with her going missing.'

'Unless this is a prank too,' Stephanie said, before Mark had a chance to.

'Julie,' Mark began, then stopped himself, finding the right words. 'Emily hasn't been in college this term. At all. She hasn't attended since last June.'

'It can't have been that long . . .'

'I spoke to them myself,' Mark continued, hoping to be believed, if for nothing else than to move the conversation back to what was important. 'There's no doubt. She wasn't there. So, if she was playing pranks, who would it be with? And what were they?'

Julie shrugged her shoulders in response, but didn't argue with him further. He turned to Stephanie, who was now standing nearer to him. 'What about you? Do you know who she could be doing this with? You've told me she had no friends, but your mum is saying something different. You can't both be right.'

Stephanie seemed to think for a moment or two, then shook her head. Mark looked from one woman to the other, trying to figure out what wasn't being said.

'She said it was just a game,' Julie said finally, her voice quiet and flat. 'That it was nothing to worry about. That she was just messing around. I didn't think it was anything to do with what happened.'

Mark sighed, wondering if he would be so blind in the same position. 'What else was she doing?'

'Just silly things. I didn't really take much notice. She wasn't getting into trouble, so I just left her to it.'

'I went to see her dad,' Mark said, moving away from the pair and sitting down at the table. 'That's how I found out about this.'

'You can't believe a word that man says,' Julie spat out,

before checking herself with a look at her daughter. Even now, she wanted to be the bigger person, it seemed to Mark. 'He's a known liar. Whatever he's told you, none of it's true.'

'He didn't tell me a lot and I can't see him rushing back to be involved. He wasn't the one to tell me anyway. Another source close to him told me that Emily's . . . antics were the cause of some discussion. So much, that they made it back to her father.'

'It was nothing.'

Mark sighed, knowing he wasn't getting very far, but also that he had to keep pushing. 'Did you ever hear her talk about the other people involved, any names?'

Julie shook her head. 'She didn't talk about it. I had to hear these things from other people. When I asked her about it, she just glossed over it, like it didn't matter. So I didn't think it did.'

'Julie, why didn't you tell me this?'

She rolled her eyes, looking tired just from that simple action. When she spoke, her voice was quiet enough that Mark had to strain to hear it. 'I thought you might just think she was mad and not bother trying to find her. She wasn't mad.'

Mark understood. Slightly. He was worried this was his fault though. That if he'd questioned harder at the beginning, it wouldn't have taken this long to discover. 'This could be important. If anything, it says something about her state of mind in the past few months. Were there any other changes in her behaviour you haven't told me about? Anything else she was involved with, people she was talking to?'

'No, she was fine,' Julie replied, but even now Mark

could see she was questioning herself. 'I . . . I don't think any of this has anything to do with her going missing.'

'Okay,' Mark said, holding his hands up and standing. 'It's okay. I'll look into this a bit further and see if I can find the people who she was doing this with.'

'You think it might be a prank?' Stephanie asked, moving towards her mother and placing a hand on her shoulder. Julie shrank back and slipped away silently. Back into the living room, no doubt. Stephanie turned to Mark again. 'Is that what you're thinking now? That she might have done this as another weird thing?'

'I don't know,' Mark replied, truthfully. He wasn't sure of anything at that moment. None of it made any sense. 'There's obviously been something happening with her. She wasn't going to college, but no one realised. She doesn't have any friends, but suddenly she's playing pranks with people that none of you know. She spent the past year and a half catfishing people online and people knew it was her. Now, she's missing.'

'What about the people she was going after then? Maybe they've got something to do with it?'

Mark shook his head. 'I've already spoken to them. There's nothing to suggest they were involved in Emily's disappearance. We're keeping an eye on that, but at the moment, none of the people we know of is under suspicion. Can you think of anything else that we may need to know?'

There was a moment of hesitation that Mark didn't miss. When she was silent for a little longer, he spoke again. 'It's important I know everything. I need to know it all, even if you don't think I or anyone else needs to.'

'She was talking to someone before I left for uni,'

Stephanie said with a sigh. 'It was over before I'd even unpacked though, so it's probably nothing.'

'A boyfriend?'

'No,' Stephanie replied, shaking her head and smiling thinly. 'Nothing like that. It was an online thing. An anti-bullying group. Like a helpline, but done on the internet. Locally, from what I can gather. I looked it up at the time and it seemed like you spoke to someone on a message board type of thing, then you could see them face-to-face if you wanted to. I saw Emily looking at it one day, but she closed her laptop when she realised I'd seen it. I googled the name of it and found out what it was.'

'Did you talk to her about it?'

'I tried to, but she wasn't having any of it. She never talked to me about anything.'

Mark nodded and pulled out his notepad. 'What was the name of this company?'

'The Huddle,' Stephanie said, then pulled her phone out from her pocket and checked again. 'Yeah, there it is. I don't know what it's all about, but I know she was using it. I tried talking to her about it more, but by that point we weren't really getting along.'

'Why was that?'

Stephanie sighed, putting her phone away. 'I've told you. Nothing important. Just silly stuff. I wanted to help her, but she just wasn't seeing sense. I couldn't get her away from her screen long enough to have a proper conversation with her and probably didn't try hard enough. I should have made more of an effort, I suppose.'

'You did the best you could, I'm sure of it.' Mark smiled thinly, which turned into a grimace as she looked away.

Maybe she could feel the insincerity of his statement as much as he could.

He wasn't sure of anything. Other than he needed to speak to the people supposedly helping Emily.

Twenty-Nine

PLAYER ONE

Another phone call.

The next level.

Giving her the instructions. Telling her what they wanted.

She had tried to question it, tried to back out and find another way. It had been pointless. There was no reasoning with the voice.

She knew now that they had been watching everything. Checking her old posts, the way she had spoken online, what she'd talked about. Waiting for her to make one last mistake. Take it too far.

Holly lay in bed, waiting for the alarm on her phone to sound one more time before finally moving. She could hear her parents pottering about in the kitchen, directly beneath her bedroom. The sound of the kettle boiling, of plates and mugs being moved about. Every morning was the same. Her mum doing breakfast – cereal in a bowl, some toast on the table, a giant mug of tea – all waiting for her when she went down. They would have been up for an hour already – awake and ready to leave for work.

Dad would probably be out the door before Holly made it down. Mum would wait to make sure her daughter had been fed and watered.

Every day the same thing.

Over and over.

Holly hadn't been able to take it anymore. That's why she'd taken to lying about her life online. It could have been any group of people. Why did she have to pick that one?

They had made her feel less alone.

She'd tried talking to her mum about the way she felt. About the difficulties she was going through. But she had only tried a few times. Seeing the pain etched across her mum's face was too much. She didn't want her mum blaming herself, as if she was the reason Holly's life sucked so bad.

Her mother had done nothing wrong.

Next to her head, Holly's phone trilled with an alarm once more. She reached across and slid a finger across its screen, silencing it. Heard her dad shout a muffled farewell and then the front door shut. She lifted the bed covers and got up, getting dressed in silence. She went to the bathroom, gave her face and hands a cursory wash. Ran a hairbrush through her hair.

She could hear her mum singing along to music in the kitchen again. Another old song. She recognised it this time at least.

'Morning,' her mum said, a big smile plastered across her face. Holly returned it, but didn't feel it inside. More fakery.

'Ran out of Coco Pops yesterday,' her mum continued, tipping her the wink as she did so. 'I'll pick some up today. Sugar Puffs okay?'

Holly nodded and stifled a yawn, as her mum placed a bowl in front of her.

If her mum knew she'd pretended to be dying of cancer to a whole bunch of people, there would be none of this normality. It would forever be tainted.

'What time are you in college today?'

'Not sure,' Holly replied, staring at the bowl in front of her. 'Need to check my timetable. Might try and get some work done at home if there's not much on.'

'Well, make sure you have something to eat. There's stuff in the cupboards. There's lasagne in the freezer for tea. You sure you're going to be okay later? We'll be home by midnight, I think.'

'I'm old enough to look after myself now, Mum.'

'I know, I'm just making sure,' her mum replied, looking around the kitchen counters for something, then grabbing her keys finally. 'I'm not sure if I'll be able to call later on – I've got a bunch of meetings before we go over to the place, but I'll try and ring around lunchtime.'

Holly nodded at her mother, as she picked up a slice of toast smothered in butter and shoved it in her mouth. Her mum was doing the same as she shouted at the speaker to stop, putting her coat on.

'Speak to you later, love you,' her mum said, planting a crumbed mouth on Holly's forehead before leaving. She heard the door close at the front of the house and breathed out.

There was silence then, Holly eating her cereal, her phone on the table in front of her. Inside, her mind continued to tick over. She could almost hear the thoughts as stark words, being shouted into her ear.

You're going to lose. They're just messing with you. There is no way to win.

She tried to ignore them. To shut out the fears and doubts that were now beginning to creep in.

To not think about the decision she had made and what it would mean if it didn't work.

She needed it to work because she couldn't live like this anymore.

The fear of being found out. She had seen what happened to people on social media, once the drums began to beat and people were castigated. Thousands, millions of voices shouting, all directed at her. The anger that would come her way. Her mum's way.

She couldn't let that happen.

Holly finished eating, swallowed what was now lukewarm tea and stared at the mobile phone. For a few minutes, she enjoyed the glowing and airy kitchen. The way the sunlight danced through the windows and settled around her. She had become used to shutting herself away when at home, almost running from the light, the radiance of an autumn day. Barricading herself in her room, shutting the curtains, sitting in near-darkness.

She had forgotten what beauty could be derived from simple everyday occurrences.

Holly closed her eyes for a second or two, breathing in and out slowly, enjoying the quiet and the warmth. The silence. Her thoughts quietened and stilled, allowing her to simply feel calm.

Holly stood up from the kitchen table, clearing away the dishes, and padded back up the stairs.

Entered her bedroom and closed the door behind her. Let the darkness back into her life.

As soon as she'd sat down on the bed, her phone had

rung. As if the voice would know her mum had left and she was alone.

'Hello?'

'Last chance,' the voice said, the same flat tone coming through the phone. There was a new background noise on the call though. Wind, or something. 'Level Four. Are you playing?'

'I haven't got a choice,' Holly said, her breath catching in her throat as she spoke. She stood up, crossing the room and opening the curtains slightly. 'I want this to be over. Will it be over?' She looked out onto the street, hoping to catch a glimpse of someone nearby.

Someone on a phone.

She knew they were out there. Watching her. They had seen her mum leave.

Holly listened as she was given her instructions. Waiting for the call to end, before standing up and leaving her bedroom. She went downstairs, back into the kitchen. Half an hour earlier, she had been swapping pleasantries with her mum.

Now, she crossed to the knife block next to the microwave, paused to consider each one in turn, then selected the largest. She held it up in the light, searching the blade for a reason to stop playing, and found nothing.

Holly slipped a jacket on, slid the knife up her sleeve and then left the house.

Thirty

The website for whatever the 'Huddle' was didn't really give Mark all that much to go on. A landing page with a few lines of text, stock photographs of sad-looking people being comforted. A 'Contact us' box, and a few testimonials on another tab.

He wondered if there was more information to be found if he accessed it from an actual computer, rather than his mobile, but figured it'd be much the same. From the look of the site, the dates on some of the supposed testimonials, it hadn't been updated in a few years.

A few phone calls later, a name procured and checked, he was pulling up outside a detached home in a leafy cul-de-sac on the outskirts of the city. The echo of his car door closing was the only sound as he made his way up a meticulously well-maintained path, next to a well-kept patch of grass. The stone bordering and hanging baskets further projected an image of normality.

He rang the doorbell and stepped back, one hand on his ID in case it was asked for, which it increasingly was now. People were getting more security conscious by the day, Mark thought, as he spotted a camera affixed to the house above him.

The door opened, a tanned man in his fifties looking him up and down, one hand on the door. 'Yes?'

'Hi, I'm Detective Constable Mark Flynn,' Mark said, trying a disarming smile that didn't quite land. 'Are you Kevin Blackhurst?'

A frown and then a slight pause. 'Yes.'

'I was wondering if you could spare a few minutes to talk about an ongoing investigation.'

The man hesitated, before giving Mark a broad smile, as if he'd suddenly had a personality transplant. His shirt was open at the neck, dark trousers over polished shoes. He dressed as immaculately as his front visage. 'Of course. Come in, please. Excuse the mess. You've caught me in the middle of a busy time.'

Mark was shown through to a pristine-looking living room, which left him searching for what could be considered a 'mess'. There wasn't a thing out of place. A smell of lavender air freshener was all that seemed to give it life.

'Please, sit,' Kevin said, gesturing to a beige-backed armchair. 'What can I help you with?'

Mark sat on the chair slowly, as Kevin Blackhurst took a seat opposite him on a matching sofa. 'Are you aware of the missing person case regarding Emily Burns?'

Kevin paused again, his smile slipping a little. 'I can't say I am, I'm afraid.'

Mark nodded, trying to place the accent. Not Liverpudlian, that was certain, but it wasn't northern either. Anything south of Nottingham and he started to struggle to place them, he supposed. 'She's a nineteen-year-old who hasn't been seen for almost five days now. The name doesn't ring a bell?'

'Can't say it does.'

Mark consulted his notes again, leaving a gap for him to elaborate, but Kevin didn't take the bait. 'You are the owner of something called "The Huddle", right?'

'Well, owner is probably pushing things a little,' Kevin replied, smoothing down an unseen crease on his trousers. 'I was somewhat involved in the creation of the website, but I left the day-to-day running of it to others. It's been disbanded now.'

'The website is still live . . .'

'I don't think they're taking on any new cases, though.'

Mark nodded again, wondering why he felt as if Kevin was choosing his words a little too carefully. 'What was it set up for, if you don't mind me asking?'

'Of course not. It was intended to be a sort of hub for people experiencing bullying. In schools, colleges, even workplaces; anywhere where bullying was occurring. The Huddle was set up to help those in need.'

'How did it work?'

'It was an online support forum. You could get in touch and talk to others who had been in the same situation you had. It was supposed to help and give advice, that type of thing. That then branched out into a couple of sessions held in real life. That wasn't as successful though.'

'No?'

Kevin sighed and ran a hand through his hair. 'From what I heard, there were some issues with those who had been tasked with running the sessions and those who attended.'

'And what was your involvement in all of this? Were you just the money behind it, or something like that?'

'Something like that.'

Mark tilted his head, trying to maintain eye contact with Kevin, but he looked away and out of the large bay window.

'I had a son,' Kevin said after a few moments had passed. There was a weary look on his face now, as if the memory had changed him somehow. 'Andrew. He was a good lad. Always did well at school, played rugby and cricket. Was near the top of each class he was in, until he was around fourteen. Then things changed with him. He wasn't the same boy. It suddenly didn't matter to him about his future, or anything of that sort. We tried everything to get him out of it, but nothing worked. He just shut down.'

'He was being bullied,' Mark said quietly, beginning to understand what Kevin was telling him now.

Kevin nodded silently. 'We didn't know until it was too late. A group of boys he'd once been friends with turned against him. I imagine at first he didn't understand what was happening; he was a little naïve, I suppose. That's the thing; it doesn't matter what you have at home. The money, the luxuries . . . Then, it just becomes about differences. Perhaps today he would have been given some kind of diagnosis, but we just put it down to a little eccentricity. Thing is, at that age, anything outside of the norm is a target. That's what he became.'

'What happened to Andrew?'

Kevin hesitated and when he finally spoke, it was as if every word was painful to say out loud. 'He died two days before his sixteenth birthday. His mother found him in his bedroom. It was too late. He left a note.'

Mark wondered how long ago this had happened. It probably didn't matter; the wound would always be open.

'So, you created The Huddle as a reaction to what happened to your son.'

'Yes. Not just that one. I've been involved in a number of different organisations that have tried to combat and help within that arena. I've been incredibly lucky over the years and have the means to do so. What else am I meant to do with my money? Andrew was our only child and by the time he was gone, it was too late to have any more. He died fourteen years ago this year, but no matter what we do, it only seems to get worse. When social media became the new way of victimising people, I got involved with The Huddle, hoping we could at least have a force for good available online. There are countless others trying to do the same thing, but it only seems to be getting worse.'

'If someone was to get in touch with The Huddle now, what would happen?'

Kevin shrugged his shoulders. 'Once I became aware that the face-to-face sessions weren't really helping anyone, I withdrew my financial support and supported other places.'

'That seems a big decision to make. There wasn't more to it than that?'

Mark held his gaze until the man finally looked away.

'What really happened?' Mark said, when it became clear Kevin wasn't going to continue. 'I'm not buying that you would make a decision like that lightly.'

'It became … It became clear that it wasn't helping anyone. They turned it into something else. A revenge mission, of sorts. The sessions became more heated, I was told. Less structured. The people running them lost control, I guess. I got reports back that some of them had been found stalking people, getting into trouble. A lot of different things. So I got out of it before it went even further south. My name might be on there, but I don't have anything to do with it now. As I said, as far as I know, it's not live. There's no money to pay anyone to work for them since I walked away from it, so I wouldn't think it's still running. All those requests would just disappear.'

'And none of these people have an outlet anymore,' Mark said. He could see it still pained the man that it had been a failure. He wasn't sure why it had been, however. 'It must have been pretty bad for you to have walked away.'

'I trusted the wrong people,' Kevin replied, shaking his head and pinching his nose at the bridge. 'What I've learned in being involved with this sort of thing, with people from all kinds of different backgrounds and experiences, is that there are some who have been bullied who will take any opportunity of power to then *become* what they had once despised. Give them control and it's like a drug. They just want more and more.'

'According to Emily Burns's family, it's possible she may have been in touch with someone on The Huddle. Before she went missing. Who could that have been?'

'I have no idea.'

'I'll need the names of those who ran these sessions. And who had access to the website. Just to eliminate them from our enquiries.'

'You think this girl disappearing might have had something to do with the website?'

Mark blew out a breath. 'I hope not, as it seems to have been set up with good intentions. I'm just looking into every possible avenue at this time.'

'Was she being bullied?'

'From the information we have, it looks as if this was

something she may have experienced in the past. Possibly still. As I said, it's about looking into everything we can.'

Kevin nodded, his hands linking together in his lap. The man looked to have aged at least a decade since Mark had arrived. 'Andrew's death is something that never disappears. No matter what you do, it's always there, even if it's faded. That's what I've learned in the years since his death. All the people it affects, how they carry that forever.'

'What happened in those sessions, Kevin? What was so bad that you pulled out from something that you had so much passion for?'

'Some of them didn't want help,' Kevin replied, closing his eyes and leaning back into the sofa. 'That wasn't ever going to be enough for those who had tasted power and didn't want it to end. They wanted something more.'

'What was that?'

'They wanted revenge. They wanted to make those who had treated them so badly pay for what they had done. In the end, it didn't matter who their own personal bully was, they wanted all those who they believed had transgressed to pay. Even those within the group who were there for help – if they didn't meet expectations, they were attacked. Not physically, but in other ways. The atmosphere was described to me as toxic. That was enough for me. That's not what it was meant to be.'

'Does the name Joanna Carter mean anything to you?'

Kevin thought for a second and there was a momentary blip of hope in Mark. Then he shook his head and seemed certain. 'Sorry, doesn't sound familiar.'

'I'll need the names of anyone you can remember . . .'

'Okay, I'll give them to you. I don't think they'll have anything to do with your case, but it can't hurt, I suppose.'

Mark wrote down the names Kevin gave him, then an email address and a phone number that he found in his mobile. It was clear that Kevin was only the face of The Huddle. That he'd handed over responsibility to others, then shut it down when it became something toxic.

Absolving himself and moving on.

'I hope you find her,' Kevin said, as he was showing Mark out of the house. Outside, it had grown overcast, turning the world grey and dull. 'I really do.'

Mark nodded, then turned and made his way back to his car.

Thirty-One

PLAYER ONE

It was time.

This is how it ends.

Game over.

Game *completed*.

She hoped, anyway.

It wouldn't be over really. She knew that. Not with what they were making her do. It would just put her into another bad situation.

They wouldn't believe her. That would be obvious. They would think her mad and that would be it.

She hoped.

Holly looked around her, then out across the water. The river was choppy, the water foaming as it settled against the wall below the promenade and dispersed backwards. The wind was stronger here, lifting her hair from her shoulders and rippling through her jacket. Dull conversation from other people standing nearby, words she couldn't quite decipher.

A world away from the bedroom that had almost

become a prison to her. Locked away, so she couldn't be hurt out in the real world. And it had only succeeded in bringing the hurt even closer.

What had been an escape had instead cornered and trapped her.

She gazed out across the Mersey, the view staring back at her blandly.

No note. You can't tell anyone where you've gone. We'll know.

Holly traced a pattern on the concrete she was standing upon with her right foot, stealing a glance at those closest by. The knife up her sleeve was weighing heavy against her arm. She imagined the blade slicing into her flesh, drawing a line of blood from underneath the skin. The release and relief it would give her.

She turned and looked at the people on the waterfront. The tourists, the day-trippers, the unemployed, the workers on their lunch break. The sounds drifted towards her but didn't permeate the shell. Lost in a void she had created for herself. A barrier, so they couldn't get in.

Just the one thing and it's over.

Holly felt as if everyone could hear the sound of her heart beating, crashing against her chest. The sound of her breaths shortening, the sound of her hands shaking, tapping against the top of her legs. She was a shuddering ball, a cacophony of noise and anger and fear.

Do it.

Do it.

Please.

She took the knife out and waited for the shouts to begin. The shock, the exhalations and alarm. Instead, there was silence. As if she was invisible. Holly looked around, almost daring someone to make eye contact with her, to notice what she was doing.

But there was nothing.

Simply holding a knife in public wasn't enough, it seemed. She would have to go through with it.

Complete the level.

End the Game.

Holly began screaming.

'JOANNA CARTER.'

Over and over.

Then, as instructed, she ran across the busy A road that ran down the waterfront. She felt she could hear footsteps following her, but she didn't risk a look over her shoulder. Instead, she kept running and screaming over and over. Holding the knife up, against her neck, swishing it in the air around her. The faces around her became a blur. Tears dampened her cheeks, her throat stung.

'I killed Joanna Carter. I killed her. Joanna Carter. I'm going to do it again and again!'

She didn't think. She could see the confusion playing across the faces of those who were now surrounding her as she continued to scream over and over.

A young woman holding a knife in the air, shouting until her voice was hoarse and sore. Repeating the same thing over and over.

It didn't take long for the police to arrive.

Thirty-Two

Mark sat in a café, going over his notes as a waitress placed another cup of coffee in front of him.

What he'd learned only served to confuse things further. How had Emily been implicated in this group? What had been the result? And was Joanna Carter a part of this, too?

He didn't have long to go over things before Natasha joined him, so he quickly tried to make some sense of all he had learned.

Before he had a chance to make some order of his thoughts, his phone started buzzing on the table.

'Hello?'

The normally calm tone of DI Bennett sounded different. An almost excited feel to her words. 'Thought you'd like to be updated.'

'Of course.'

'We've made an arrest in the Joanna Carter murder. Teenage. Female. Looks like she's had some kind of breakdown.'

Mark sat back in his chair, his free hand reaching the back of his head. 'That's ... that's good news. Is it Emily Burns?'

'Sorry, no.'

'Who is she then? How did you find her?'

'She wasn't really found. She was waving a knife around screaming Joanna's name as loud as she could. Uniforms first on scene said she made some kind of confession. Same age as Joanna, but didn't say a lot when she was booked in. Looked relieved, apparently. No solicitor yet, just keeps asking for her mum. Interviewing her soon, so hopefully she just cops to the lot of it and we can close it.'

'Fingers crossed for you,' Mark replied, looking for the sugar and opening the packets with one hand. 'I think Emily Burns needs to be brought up in questioning. We need to know of any connection.'

'We will, but you should know we've discovered quite a bit more about Joanna in the past few hours. Seems like she had some interesting habits, according to fellow students. I think this will be either jealousy or a revenge killing.'

'What kind of habits?'

'We're preparing a report as we speak. I'll make sure you get a read. How are you getting on?'

Mark sighed, stirring his coffee and placing the spoon quietly down on the surface. 'Not very far. Looking into a few different things, but not really any closer to an answer. I've learned that Emily has been doing some odd things lately. And that there was something called The Huddle – some sort of support group that went downhill. It's all kinds of messed up.'

'I like that term. Well, if that's your final assessment . . .'

'No, not in the slightest. I think there's a connection to Joanna Carter. Emily had her own issues too, which, if what you're saying about Joanna is true, means someone could have been out for revenge against her as well. I could do with more help, though.'

'Not much chance at the moment, but hopefully this arrest checks out and I can help you out with that. Just keep on top of things for now.'

Still on his own then, Mark thought. 'Good luck with the interview.' He ended the call as Natasha entered the café, smiling at him as she spotted where he was sitting. She took the seat opposite, catching the waitress's eye as she did so. 'Thanks for coming over my way. I don't get much of a lunch break.'

'It's no problem,' Mark replied, taking a sip of his coffee. 'Could do with the distraction to be honest.'

Natasha ordered and then turned back to Mark. 'Everything okay?'

'Yeah, just work stuff.'

'Would it help to share the pain? I can be a good listener, you know. And you know, a problem shared . . .'

'Honestly, it's nothing you want to know.'

'Don't be so sure,' Natasha said, shaking her head and holding her hands out in front of her. 'Anything to take my mind off my own work issues.'

'I shouldn't . . .'

'I won't tell a soul.' Natasha placed a hand over her heart, as if that was all that was needed.

It turned out to be enough.

Mark breathed in, then began talking. He was careful to keep his voice low, so the two other people in the café couldn't hear him, and also didn't name anyone involved. Apart from that, he found himself telling Natasha everything that had occurred in the past few days. The missing teenager. The dead woman. The murky hidden life online that Emily had. The family left behind waiting for answers. The non-connection between the missing and the dead.

It wasn't until he mentioned the anti-bullying website that he got the sense that Natasha wanted to interrupt. As the waitress took that moment to deliver plates to the table, he stopped and waited for her to speak.

She stayed silent.

'Have you heard of them?' Mark said, looking down at the decidedly limp chicken salad on his plate and wondering if it was too late to change it to the bacon on toast that was sitting in front of Natasha. Doorstop bread, as well, he thought. He could smell the grease dripping onto the plate beneath it and almost drooled. 'The Huddle?'

'I have,' Natasha replied, but didn't elaborate. Instead, she stared towards the main road outside.

'Well, don't leave me hanging. What do you know about them?'

Natasha finished another bite of her toast, then wiped her mouth free of crumbs. 'I don't know much. We've had a few clients who have used their . . . services, shall we say? I tried to get more information about them for a long time, but ran into a brick wall. Seemed like they'd disappeared, but I wouldn't be surprised to hear they've just found another avenue to make nuisances of themselves.'

'Nuisances?'

Natasha made as if to speak, then hesitated. Thought for a second, then opened her mouth again. 'I think you have a good idea what I'm talking about.'

Mark smiled. Tried not to slip. 'What do you know about them? It might be helpful.'

'They were set up by some rich bloke who lost his son,'

Natasha said, after she'd let a few seconds of silence grow between them. 'Killed himself because he was being bullied. From what I can gather, he was just the money in the operation. Had no idea what was going on behind closed doors.'

'And how did you become aware of it, as a social worker, I mean?'

'We had a few kids who'd been on the website and spoken to the people behind it. Counselled, was the term they used. A couple of the kids thought it helped them. Said it gave them some skills to cope, that sort of thing.'

'Not all of them, though,' Mark said, shifting uneasily in his chair, the salad in front of him picked at, but mostly untouched. 'How much reach did this website have?'

'I could never really work that out – how many local kids used the site before it went dark. I know of five who came through our service, but it was probably more than that. Then, if you go nationwide – worldwide even – you're into god knows how many people. From what I could gather though, there were only a few face-to-face meetings. And they were all local.'

'What happened to make you so interested in it?'

'There's not much I can tell you on that. All I know is that a couple of those kids went to separate meetings and both of them were very scared to say anything about it at all. I tried – we all tried – to get more out of them, but they just refused to say a word. Something very shady about that, I thought. So I started looking into it a bit more. Didn't get very far. I spoke to the rich bloke . . .'

'Kevin Blackhurst.'

'That's his name,' Natasha replied, but Mark suddenly had a feeling she knew his name quite well. She wanted to see how much *he* knew.

'I spoke to him about it,' Natasha continued, as if he hadn't interrupted. 'Tried to gauge what had happened, if there was something we should be worried about. It seemed like it was brushed under the carpet a bit, given it was just shut down with no warning.'

Mark thought for a second. 'What happened to these kids that it created such a worry in the first place? I don't quite understand what actually went on during these meetings.'

'I don't know myself for sure,' Natasha said, hesitating over each word. 'I think there was talk of violence. About making yourself a victim and how to combat that. That wasn't the main problem with it though. It was a toxic atmosphere for the girls there. As if it were solely their issue. The men in charge didn't believe they could be bullied or have any negative effects from it.'

'That sounds ridiculous – why go in the first place?'

'If we're going to try and work out why certain things are ridiculous towards certain genders, we could be here a long time.'

Mark held his hands up in mock surrender. 'Okay, but what happened to stop you looking into them? You haven't exactly struck me as the type to give up easily.'

'I was met with silence,' Natasha replied, shaking her head with frustration. 'And the caseload. I was asked to leave it alone, given it had shut down and the kids involved weren't interested in doing anything with it anymore. Doesn't mean I was happy about it, but sometimes you have to move on.'

'I guess it wasn't really your job,' Mark said, feeling for the first time since they'd met that he wasn't getting the full truth from her. That there was something being left unsaid. He mused for a moment or two on whether to push it further, but decided against it. 'Well, it looks as though my missing person had some contact with them or someone pretending to be them at least. And that's in the past couple of months. Which only makes this whole case that bit more complicated, if it has you worried as a social worker.'

Natasha shrugged but didn't say anything more, finishing her lunch in silence. Mark picked at the salad a little more, before pushing it to one side. 'Listen, sorry for bringing up my work problems. Probably not what you were hoping for when I asked to meet up.'

'It's okay,' Natasha replied and sounded genuine about it. 'Although, this is the second or third time we've eaten together and I'm still not sitting in a fancy restaurant.'

'I'll book somewhere,' Mark said instantly, swearing at himself internally. 'It's on my list. We've gone at this a bit backwards, I suppose.'

'Don't worry. My fault as much as yours. It would be nice to go out properly though. I feel like this is going somewhere.'

'I agree,' Mark said, and meant it. It wasn't how he thought it was going to happen, but he was happy, he realised.

Then he thought of Emily Burns and her family waiting for answers. He felt immediately guilty about his own happiness.

He didn't have to wait long for that guilt to grow.

Thirty-three

The call came with no warning. A breathless detective inspector, telling him to get down to a place he didn't recognise.

Her name, her body.

This time it was real. This time there was no doubt.

His fears were proven correct.

Emily was dead.

Mark had hoped that another mistake had been made, but it became clear quite quickly that there was no doubt among the team about who they had found.

They'd checked for a birthmark this time.

The temperature was low, becoming chilling each time the wind whipped up around him and crashed into his face. Mark was standing in an old builder's yard, the detritus and decay of it indicating it hadn't been used for a long time. Just another abandoned piece of land that would spend years lying empty until someone eventually came and built tiny thin-walled flats on it. He looked around, unable to see anything past the high walls that bordered almost the entire yard. At the far end, metal railings backed onto the disused train line behind. A forgotten place. Like the place where they'd first found her blood.

Which wasn't that far away. If he'd craned his neck, he could make out an edge of the entrance to the place. He looked up and there was the top of the building where Joanna Carter's body had been found.

Too close.

'She was discovered behind one of those burnt-out cars,' DI Bennett said, pointing into the distance, where officers in protective clothing ducked down out of sight. 'When the uniforms who were dealing with the young girl with the knife moved the crowd back, there were a few reports about a suspicious smell. She's in a bad state, so I'm guessing it's likely she's been here since the night she went missing.'

'What is this yard? Is it still in use?'

'It's been abandoned for years. We're trying to track the owner, but odds are it's part of someone's extensive portfolio of land; just another old place waiting to be renovated into houses or something similar. They probably won't have a clue what goes on here on a regular basis. But guess who does some of his business here? Our favourite nutcase, who just so happens to be related to the dead woman over there . . .'

'Uncle Rich . . .' Mark said under his breath.

'Of course,' DI Bennett replied, a slight smirk appearing on her face. 'Nothing legal, oh no. This was information we managed to get from our friends in drug squad. They've been monitoring his movements for a number of months now. He visits this place at least once a month. They're on the verge of getting the go-ahead to have full surveillance put on him. Apparently he's a big player in the drug world.

Or at least in the know of those who are. Doesn't really matter. There are already enough meetings taking place about why this information wasn't shared with us earlier. Anyway, he's linked to the yard and we reckon we'll find more evidence in his house.'

'Getting a warrant?'

'On its way now.'

'This is going to destroy that family,' Mark said, scratching at his increasingly stubbled face. 'He was like a surrogate dad to them, by the looks of things.'

'You said it yourself. The younger one, he didn't think he was going to be blameless here. We're going to need to talk to him again.'

'What about Joanna Carter . . .'

'Yes, yes, I know,' DI Bennett snapped back. Mark was surprised by her irritated tone. 'The girl I mentioned earlier, the one with the knife saying she killed her?'

'She said that?'

'The arrest didn't go well. Turns out she had no idea how Joanna died. The young woman was referred to Psych. We don't think she was involved at all. Just a very mixed-up girl.'

'Boss . . .'

'I know, I know,' DI Bennett said, exasperation flowing from every word. 'Cavanagh finished questioning her about thirty minutes ago. She has an alibi. For basically every single day since before and after Joanna's death. Which we know includes the time Emily went missing too. She wasn't even in England. Her mum provided proof that they were on holiday last week. No way she could have been involved. We think she was just mixed up.'

'And made her way to where Emily was eventually found?'

'It's across the road. Hardly that much of a coincidence. One of the uniforms could smell something and checked it out.'

'What was her name?'

'Holly Edwards. Nothing to link her to Joanna whatsoever. We think it was just a breakdown of sorts.'

'Joanna and Emily being found dead so close together – that's no coincidence.'

'It doesn't quite fit yet, but I have a theory on that one.'

'Really?' Mark replied, wondering why it had taken so long to get to this point.

'Rich killed them both. I know it sounds like a coincidence, but maybe Joanna saw what he did to Emily. That's how Emily ended up here. He needed to chase her down or something, after being disturbed. He went back to deal with Joanna, realising he had to kill her or she would say something.'

'It's a stretch . . .'

'I know, but it wouldn't be the first time we've seen something like this.'

Mark tried to remember a time he'd heard a similar thing happening, but was struggling. 'I just think we're missing part of the story here. It doesn't make much sense to not kill Joanna that same night. If it was Rich, he would kill her at the same time, surely? He knew Emily's blood was in that place, why not plant that near the body or on the roof if he was trying to frame her or something?'

'I don't know why yet. I'm hoping to find out though. Maybe he just thought it was enough to keep us running in circles.'

Mark shaped to talk again, but DI Bennett cut him off. 'For now, we have to concentrate on what we have so far,' she said, pulling her jacket closer to her body as the wind hit them again. 'And that's Emily's body found somewhere her uncle – who has prior history of violence against women and a possible statement coming from Emily's brother – uses frequently. Obviously, he would know of its existence when there are loads who wouldn't. You could walk past this place and not know it existed. No cameras pointing towards it, not overlooked. It's perfect.'

'What's the motive?'

DI Bennett cocked an eyebrow at him. 'Drugs or sexual abuse. That's the odds.'

'I suppose so,' Mark replied, wondering what this would mean for the family. Emily's mum, having to deal with the fact her own brother was under suspicion for her daughter's murder. *If* it was murder. 'Has she been beaten? Any signs of violence?'

'We think the blood came from an injury to her arm. She's got a deep gash along the outside of the left one. From the bruises around her neck, it looks likely that death will have been caused by strangulation, but she wasn't in the best shape. Those bruises could be anything. Won't know the truth until the post-mortem.'

Mark looked towards where the forensic techs were shuttling back and forth. They were standing on the periphery of the yard, keen to keep any contamination down to a minimum. He felt a pull towards them, wanting to see for himself that she was really there. To know that there was nothing he could have done differently to find her sooner the past few days. That he'd be able to look the family in the eye and do so without guilt.

He didn't think that was possible.

Truth was, he felt very out of his depth now.

He wanted to find whoever did this to her. To Emily.

That gut feeling again. That it wasn't Rich. There were too many unanswered questions. Too many other parts to the story that didn't make sense.

He wanted to run away from it all, but his body wouldn't let him. Maybe, that was what being a detective was really about. Wanting to run, but continuing on in spite of that.

'I think it's best you inform the family,' DI Bennett said, turning back to him and pocketing her phone. 'You have a relationship with them already and they'll be more willing to trust that this time it's for real. They'll be expecting it to come from you, given you've been the one leading the investigation.'

'What happens next?'

'They identify her, we confirm cause of death, we arrest the uncle. Hopefully he confesses and we're back to domestic violence cases and scrambler bike deaths by the end of the week.'

Mark didn't reply, sighing almost inaudibly and crossing his arms against his chest. One of the officers walked towards them, holding a camera. He didn't want to see, but knew he wouldn't be able to resist.

He stood at DI Bennett's shoulder as the officer flicked through the photographs that had been taken, leaving each image on the screen for a few seconds. At first, you could be mistaken for not knowing what you were looking at. Then she came into view properly.

There was anger bubbling up inside him as he watched the slideshow of horror. She was lying on her side, wearing the clothes they'd seen on the CCTV images. Her body had bloated somewhat, the decomposition period settling in. Mark glanced up at the tech officer, seeing only blankness in his eyes. No sign of what he'd seen and experienced having any effect at all.

Mark envied him.

The photographs became more graphic, closer-up images of her face, her neck. There was angry red and purple bruising to her neck, blackened in places. He could see her face, round and discoloured. Lines of red bursting from the surface as the capillaries fought to break out.

It was her.

Mark wanted to take the camera and throw it as far away as he could.

Instead, he continued to stand almost at attention, watching as the photos of Emily Burns's dead body flicked past the screen.

'We good?' the officer said, looking towards DI Bennett. She gave him a nod and he was gone before her head had returned to centre.

'Look, I know you wanted a better outcome here,' DI Bennett said, moving closer to him and tilting her head sideways as she looked up at him. 'This one got a little bigger than I was expecting, so it's my fault you've been dealing with it on your own. I also know it's not your first suspicious death, or even murder. We don't always save them, Mark. Sometimes we're too late, sometimes we don't have enough. We learn and we move on. We try to make sure we help the next people.'

There was a practised tone to the speech, which caused Mark to bite down a little on his lower lip. He wanted to say something in response but held back, not wanting to show any kind of emotion.

'I told you it wasn't a pretty picture. Poor woman. We have to make sure this is airtight. I don't want this guy getting away with it. Will you speak to the son?'

Mark nodded, but was still refraining from actually speaking. He didn't trust himself. He knew he would have to eventually, but still needed a few more seconds.

'After they've been to identify her, of course,' DI Bennett continued, as another tech officer approached them. 'They need to absorb the news first. We're going to need to move fast on the uncle's arrest though. I don't want him having any more time.'

'Emily's phone,' Mark said, breaking his silence. He could still feel the anger within himself, but felt he had swallowed it down enough now. 'The last ping was near to the yard where her blood was found. That's, what, a good hundred yards away from here? Emily magically moves from there to here. How does that happen and where's her phone?'

'That's information I'm hoping her uncle will be able to provide. CCTV only covers so much around that area, so it's not out of the question that he brought her here. Tried to hide her body somewhere he knows for as long as possible. Then, all this heat, maybe he was waiting for it to die down a bit before moving her.'

'Maybe,' Mark replied, but nothing about it felt right. He couldn't buy into the coincidence of Joanna Carter's death a day later, the bodies being found so close together. Or the feeling that Rich wasn't the answer.

Mark tuned into the conversation that was now happening beside him; DI Bennett scowling at a short tech officer, who looked like he could be blown away if the wind picked up any further.

'Show me,' DI Bennett said, Mark surprised at the harshness of her tone. Something had been said and now he was annoyed with himself for allowing his thoughts to run away with themselves.

The tech officer revealed what he was holding – an evidence bag with a piece of paper in it. Mark leaned forward, trying to read what was printed on it.

'It was in her pocket? Are you sure?'

'Yes,' the tech officer replied, his hand lingering in mid-air in front of DI Bennett. 'They told me to come and show it to you. There's nothing else on her. Just this scrap of paper in her right trouser pocket.'

Mark read the paper again, feeling a surge of something rush through him. Excitement wasn't the correct word.

But this proved he was right. He had known there was more.

DI Bennett was already turning towards him, her face suddenly drawn.

'What is this?'

Mark wished he could answer the question.

Thirty-Four

It had only been a couple of days since Mark had asked the family to identify the wrong body, but it felt much longer. As if time had ceased to follow its normal rhythm.

Now he was standing in the same spot in the bowels of the Royal Hospital, the air somehow cooler and more still, watching Emily's body being unveiled. The same spot where Joanna Carter had been revealed and the relief which had come next for Julie and Stephanie.

It wouldn't be that way this time.

He had tried to prepare the women for that, but he could tell in the car journey over that they still thought that was a possible outcome. Julie almost chanting it over and over again.

They've made a mistake again. They've made a mistake again.

'Ready?' Mark said, as if this could be avoided if it needed to be. He watched as Julie stared at the window and said nothing. Stephanie stared at him, willing him to say something else. As if he could change what was about to happen.

Stephanie shook her head and muttered under her breath. 'It's not her, it's not her.'

Julie showed no sign of having heard her daughter talk. Mark turned to the window and nodded towards the coroner's assistant inside the room. He bowed his head and lifted back the sheet covering the body.

Mark forced himself to look in the same direction as the two women. Emily's body was covered for the most part, only her face on display. They were only a few feet away, separated by glass, but the effect wasn't diminished in any way.

Her face was discoloured, distended. Her features were all there, but just different enough to hammer home the fact she wasn't there anymore. That they were looking only at a shell of a person.

He turned to the two women beside him; they were staring intently at the body, searching the small visible area for dissimilarities.

The quiet was suffocating. The tick of a clock somewhere down the corridor broke it, sounding insufferably loud suddenly.

It's her,' Stephanie said, her voice flat and lifeless. Back to stoic mode, holding on to her mother as Julie staggered back in the corridor. A noise rumbled within her, before a howl escaped her lips, echoing off the walls as it increased in volume. Mark felt his body tense at the sound of it, watching as Stephanie gripped her mother harder trying to quieten her. With little effect.

It had been ten hours since he'd been sitting at their kitchen table, watching Stephanie break down. Now, he was watching her try to comfort her mother. This time, she knew. They both did.

Emily was gone.

Julie's cries filled the corridor as she sank to her knees,

her body finally giving up. Stephanie held on to her, slowly moving down with her, holding her in her arms. Stroking her back, crying with her, silently.

Mark watched them for a few seconds, feeling the lump at the back of his throat grow. Watching as reality took hold and their lives changed in an instant.

'What do we do now?'

Mark didn't have an answer for Stephanie, as she looked up towards him. He stammered, knowing he needed to stay professional and give them something. He couldn't. There was nothing he could say in that moment that would provide solace.

Stephanie had already turned back to her mum, helping her to her feet, as Julie's cries still filled the corridor. He shepherded them away, finding a relative's room quickly and sitting them down.

'What happened to her?' Stephanie said, her own eyes filled with tears. 'Was she ... Who did this to her?'

'They're going to do a post-mortem and find out,' Mark replied, talking low as Julie moaned and rocked in her chair. 'Once we know, you'll be told. We'll tell Charlie and your Uncle Rich as well. You can stay here for as long as you need, but there'll be more questions. I need to prepare you for that. Now we've found her, we have to make sure we find the person who did this.'

Stephanie nodded, then hugged her mum and stood up. She placed a hand on Mark's arm and guided him out into the corridor. She left the door open behind her, but spoke in a hushed tone.

'We need answers. We need to know what happened. You can't leave us without them. Promise? Only, my mum ... she's not going to come back from this without knowing. This is going to destroy her and I can't lose both of them.'

'I'll ... We'll do everything we can,' Mark replied, staring into Stephanie's blue, filmy eyes. 'We have every resource on this. Forensics, the works. If there's something to find, it'll be found. Hopefully answers will be easy to come by. If not, I guarantee we won't leave any stone unturned to find them.'

'I knew it was coming,' Stephanie said, trying to keep her words from sticking in the back of her throat. She coughed and blinked back tears. 'I could feel it. It doesn't make it any easier. I thought it might, you know, if I prepared myself for this to be the end. I just feel empty.'

'You're going to need time to let this sink in,' Mark said, moving his hand to her shoulder. 'You need to be with your mum for now. Help each other. A family liaison officer is on her way here now. They'll be with you for the foreseeable future. They'll be able to help you as well.'

Mark removed his hand and guided her back to her mum, leaving them ensconced in the relative's room, still holding on to each other. He closed the door behind him and felt only anger at what was about to happen to them. The multitude of police detectives who would now become part of their daily lives, especially once Rich was arrested. It was bad enough for them when it was only him – now, there would be a whole team they would have to deal with. Asking questions they probably couldn't answer. Keeping things from them. They would almost become ancillary to the entire story, as the truth became the only thing of interest.

He didn't want to think about how their lives would be if DI Bennett's theory was correct. That someone in their own family was responsible.

He knew Bennett would be here, waiting for a moment to step in and speak to him face to face. Probably overseeing the entire process. Watching their reactions, looking for something that didn't fit.

He found her leaning against the wall with her arms folded. Mark came to a stop and then slumped next to her. 'If they've got anything to do with her death, they're bloody amazing actors.'

'I've seen better,' DI Bennett replied, unmoved from her spot. 'But it doesn't matter anyway. They're not involved. It's the uncle.'

'You're sure now?' Mark replied, standing up slightly, trying not to let tiredness wash over him. 'What do we know really?'

'It's his yard, Mark. And really, come on, how often is it a stranger? Really, when we start looking at every murder we investigate, you've got to play the odds. It's always someone known to the victim.'

'Not always,' Mark said, but he didn't trust his words enough to have any conviction behind them. 'I just don't want us wasting time on him if there's someone else out there.'

'Someone she met online, or the like?'

'That's what I've been looking into the past couple of days. Emily had a whole network of people on the hook on the internet. One of them might have been disgruntled enough to do this.'

'How many of them have you spoken to now?'

'A few more since Chris Jackson,' Mark replied, wishing he had something more. Knowing that he didn't have enough. 'They were all angry about what she did, but I can't say for certain any of them were angry enough to do something like this to her. It doesn't make sense though. If she was doing something like that online, that all of them are level-headed enough to just move on from it. She did some pretty nasty things. Messed with people's lives. Embarrassed them. Maybe there's more to this than what we're thinking.'

'You're overthinking this, Mark.'

'What about what was found on Emily's body?'

It wasn't much to go on, but it was enough to set Mark's heart racing. Even now, as he remembered it.

I LOST THE GAME.

'It could be anything,' DI Bennett said, shaking her head as she did so. She didn't believe it herself, it seemed. 'Just another thing to put us off track. Rich is cunning. He knew the more the water was muddied, the less chance we'd have of nailing him.'

'I just don't think we should totally dismiss this other angle and expect it all to be on the uncle. That's all. If I should shut my mouth, just tell me now.'

Mark could see she was growing tired of his interjections now. He stood up away from the wall, waiting for her to tell him to stop.

She didn't.

'Well, you keep looking into that if you think it'll come to anything,' DI Bennett said, as if she were a teacher dismissing one of her unruly children from her office. 'In the meantime, I want you to talk to the boy and see if he will give you any more on the uncle. I need you to do that, given the prior relationship. You're in the best position to get as much out of him as possible. Do it at his home, but make sure it's all above board.'

'He's not going to be happy about that . . .'

'I don't care,' DI Bennett said, smoothing down her jacket and stepping away. 'Meet us at the house. FLO will be here in a few minutes, so the mum and sister will be looked after. Once you're done with the kid, get a uniform to take him to the station to meet these two there. They're going to be questioned as well.'

Mark ran a hand through his hair, letting it travel back and massage his own neck. 'Right, no problem boss.'

'I know it's a difficult one, Mark, but we have to go with what we know so far. Once that's over, we can move the investigation further afield. For now, our resources are best spent on the more likely answers, but I can give you some time to make sure what you've found out has nothing to do with it.'

Mark nodded, but didn't feel confident in the choices being made. There was something about the whole thing that didn't feel right. The way Rich had acted over Emily's disappearance, the fact he'd been there for days, supporting his sister. The fact he had no history of anything untoward with the family.

The fact of the note.

Another mention of some kind of game.

'One more thing, Mark,' DI Bennett said, as she turned to leave. 'If you feel this is all a bit much for you, please say something. I don't want you burning yourself out. It's a difficult case, this, but you need to show you can deal with this sort of thing, okay? I think you've been a good addition to the team, but you've been with us long enough now. I don't want you getting bogged down in something that doesn't fit, so don't take too long on this.'

Mark didn't respond, letting her walk away without

another word. He could feel the anger like a ball of fire in his stomach. He wasn't a child. He didn't need to be spoken to like one.

He breathed in and forced himself to relax.

Thirty-Five

The house felt different with Julie and Stephanie gone. As if a part of it was missing. All that was left behind was an eerie, still silence. Mark had arrived with two uniforms, directing them to the back of the house to where he expected the uncle to be.

Charlie had opened the front door for them, rolled his eyes and not said a word. Mark had tried to stop him, but he was already back up the stairs, his bedroom door closing behind him. He waited for the uniforms to make their way through the house, then walked up the stairs to the only bedroom he hadn't seen yet.

He was standing on the landing, knocking on the door for at least a minute before Charlie opened it. The teen stood at the threshold, his hair hanging dankly, almost covering his eyes.

'Can I talk to you?'

Charlie slouched against the doorframe, crossed his arms and said, 'What?'

'You might want to sit down,' Mark said, keeping his patience in check.

'It's about her, isn't it?'

'Can you just let me in so we can talk it over.'

There were a few seconds of silence, before he eventually relented and walked back into his room. Mark followed him, closing the door over a little. Charlie had already slumped into a gaming chair facing the television propped up on a chest of drawers in a corner. The curtains were drawn close, barely any light breaking into the room. Mark considered opening them, then settled for turning on the light instead. The teenager blinked, but showed no other sign of a response.

The room was small, but seemed to have been filled with more things than the rest of the house. Each available surface was being used, including the countless shelves that were on every wall. They held various figurines, which probably meant much to Charlie, but left Mark confused. Gnarled and misshapen figures, which seemed to be mixtures of monsters and mythological beings. Winged beasts, malformed humanistic types. The walls were similarly covered in posters that depicted various metal bands and horror films. On the television, a video game had been paused. Red and black splashed across the screen. A character holding some type of gun that probably didn't exist in the real world.

When Mark had been younger, they would have termed Charlie as a 'Goth' or 'Mosher'. Something told him the names were probably the same now. The weird kids who seemed to have their own language, to be mocked and mistreated by those higher up in the social chain.

Mark decided to stand and try not to slouch over himself. 'Your mum and sister have confirmed that it's Emily that we found.'

'Yeah, I guessed that,' Charlie replied, folding his hands

into his lap and staring away from him. 'Not sure what else there is to be said. I told you she was dead.'

'Yes, I know. Someone will come by to pick you up soon, so you can be with them.'

Charlie rolled his eyes far too dramatically for it not to be for effect. 'All they're going to do is cry. Do I have to be around for that?'

'They're going to be very sad, Charlie,' Mark said, wondering why he had to talk to this lad like he was a five-year-old. Why he didn't seem bothered at all that his sister was dead and his family was in tatters. Was it all part of the same act? 'I'm sure you will be as well. It's best you're with your family at the moment. You're going to need them.'

Charlie shrugged, but didn't push back any further.

'We're treating her death as suspicious right now,' Mark continued, when it became obvious he wasn't going to get an immediate response. 'You know what that means?'

'It means you think someone might have killed her. Yeah, I'm not an idiot.'

'Okay, well, because of that, we're going to have some questions for all of you.'

A shift in the chair, Charlie now looking towards him with something approaching a smirk on his face. 'Am I going to need a lawyer?'

'Do you think you need one?'

'Probably not. Can't see me being arrested for killing her. Look, we weren't, like, close or anything. It's not like I'm not sad that she's gone, but it's like if I heard the next-door neighbour had died. I don't know what to tell you. Emily not being around isn't really going to have much effect on my life. They'll still ignore me, act like I'm an annoyance, rather than a member of the family, and that'll be that. The only thing that'll be different is that Mum will be talking about it every five seconds.'

Mark took a few moments to work out how to move forward. The lack of empathy, of sympathy, any kind of emotion, rocked him. He wanted to reach out and shake some reality into him. Switch off the computer and try to explain that this was real. Not like one of his video games.

Instead, he breathed in and tried to go on.

'Look, she was your sister. You don't have to put up a front with me. I'm not one of your mates. I'm here to help you.'

'I'm sure you are, but honestly, I'm okay with it. I knew something like this could happen as soon as she didn't come home in the first twenty-four hours. I guessed after that, well, she was either gonna be dead or never found. It's not nice, but that's life, isn't it? We've all got to go some time. I guess this was just hers. I feel bad for my mum. This is going to destroy her. She'll blame herself, even though it's not her fault at all. Not her fault Emily's weak. That's just the way it is. Princess Stephanie will probably find a way to use it to her advantage. She knows how to use her best features. You know what I'm talking about.'

Mark ignored the sick smile Charlie gave him. 'The other day, you said something about your uncle. About him and Emily . . .'

'I knew that wasn't going to be the end of it,' Charlie said, the words emphasised by a teenage sigh. 'Look, I don't know what was going on. You'd have to speak to him. It's not like you can speak to her anymore.'

'What makes you think something was wrong between them?'

'You don't know what it's like around here. No one

cares if I come or go and that was doubly so for Emily. She had her own shit going on and we all had to walk on eggshells around her, just because she was fat and ugly. She had some desperate lads who were interested in her, but she didn't even care. It was just constant moaning about never being liked. All it comes down to is that she wasn't Princess Stephanie, so that was enough to spend all day, every day, in a shitty mood. Last couple of years though, Uncle Rich has taken more of an interest in her.'

'An interest?'

'I don't know,' Charlie said, scratching his head, dandruff flakes floating in the air and onto his shoulders. 'Just making comments and that. He was coming round all the time because Mum thinks I needed some "male influence". Like that drug-dealing idiot could teach me anything about being a man.'

'You don't get on with him then?'

'Could you? He would come in here, sit there and just run down everything I like. It was stupid. He's stupid. Just a Neanderthal wanker, who thinks everything can be solved with a fight or a fuck. I don't need him. Never did. I've got my own thing going on.'

Mark followed Charlie's glance towards a lifeless computer screen on a small desk. Dreaded to think about what lurked on that hard drive. 'So when he failed to make an impact on you, are you saying he tried to help Emily?'

A snort of derision. 'Help is probably too strong a word. Like I said, he had two ways of solving a problem – he wasn't going to fight her . . .'

Mark waited for him to say something more, but he didn't finish the thought. 'You have to be very clear with me here, Charlie. This is important. Do you know anything about possible abuse or otherwise between Rich and Emily?'

Charlie averted his eyes, picking a stray thread on his black jeans. 'I can't give you anything. It's just the way they were with each other, the last few months. The past year, to be honest. He would go in her room and stay in there for ages. I tried listening, but couldn't hear anything. When he came out, she'd be quiet for hours. To be fair, it was the only time we didn't hear her whining about something or other.'

'Do you think he . . . did something to her?'

'I doubt it,' Charlie said, leaning back in the gaming chair now, hands interlocked over his skinny midriff. 'He could probably get his pick out there. Big stedhead-looking dealer? There's a load of sluts out there who love that kind of thing. See them all the time. Especially round here. Skanky bitches, you know what I mean? No idea what they did for all that time in her room, though.'

Mark stared at him for a few seconds, fighting the urge to slap him. 'I don't think that's the best language to use, Charlie. Especially given what's happened to your sister.'

Charlie rolled his eyes at him. 'Honestly, are you one of those white knight idiots? Social justice warrior and all that? You need to wake up. Women are taking over the world and we're just sitting back and letting them. They've changed the rules and we're losing. We need to start winning, take back control. Get back to being alphas again. I've lived my whole life surrounded by women. I know them inside out. I can't wait to get out of here and away from them. Find a proper woman. Am I sad Emily is dead? A bit. I suppose she was my sister. Thing is, I bet she wouldn't have batted an eyelid if it was me. She barely even spoke to me in the last couple of years. Didn't even know I existed. I can't wait to get away from them all.'

'You're a teenager, Charlie,' Mark said, choosing his words carefully. *He's just lost his sister.* 'Plenty of time to experience life a little more.'

'Yeah, that's what I plan on doing,' Charlie replied, sniffing and standing up in one motion. 'Is that it then? Are we done?'

Mark was too shocked to do anything other than watch as the boy walked to the doorway and turned, waiting for him to follow. He hadn't been expecting Charlie to talk all that much, but it seemed he'd been waiting for someone to engage him in conversation. Although the situation wasn't any clearer to Mark.

He walked out of the room, unable to decide on the worst thing he'd heard. The diatribe Charlie had given him, or the suspicions he had about his own uncle and sister.

It took him a second to realise it was definitely the latter.

Mark walked down the stairs ahead of Charlie, remembering the uniforms who were in the house. Wondering how they'd dealt with Rich. Whether two of them would have been enough to handle the big man.

He paused at the bottom of the stairs, looking back down the hallway towards the back garden. He could see a flash of fluorescent, so made a decision to take Charlie down to his mum and sister at the station himself.

Let them deal with the huge lummox. He was someone else's problem for the time being.

Thirty-Six

Mark wasn't sure what more could be found, but it had been decided a thorough search of the house was the next port of call. Julie had given permission, which Mark guessed was probably done through a fugue state. He'd left Charlie with his mum and sister, hoping he'd go back to being the quiet teenager he usually was, rather than the one he'd discovered in the comfort of his bedroom.

Something he'd said was gnawing away at him. A memory which refused to make itself known. One of those things that would annoy him while he was trying to sleep. Whenever that would be.

A makeshift investigation team had been put together to search the house, which now suddenly seemed the best chance they had to find any more evidence towards Rich's possible involvement. Mark had been tagged on, DS Cavanagh the obvious lead. A couple of other DCs and a uniform or three. It was quite the party. He'd considered leaving them to it, going back to the office and continuing his search for other answers. But he wanted to know what could be hiding in the house. Each previous search had been done with the family over their shoulders. This would be different. No questions, no awkwardness. Just a blank canvas, ready to be filled with anything Emily may have left behind.

The house wasn't a crime scene – yet – which meant he didn't have to don the obligatory white forensic suit he hated so much. Still, if they found anything, that would change in an instant. Mark held back, allowing the others to move ahead of him, waiting to see the rooms they would decide to search first.

'Okay, here's what the plan is,' Cavanagh said, speaking to the team in the living room. 'Ash and Jill, you take the downstairs rooms. Go through everything you can, remove all furniture away from walls, check the back of cupboards, you know the score. Me and Hale will take the upstairs rooms.'

'And what'll Mark be doing?' Ash said, a DC Mark had never really got a handle on. Ash was a hard-eyed, hard-headed bloke. 'Sticking him on post duty?'

Mark looked at DS Cavanagh, ignoring the sniggering that floated his way from one of the others in the room.

'He's been in and out of here for days,' DS Cavanagh said, not rising to the bait, it seemed. 'He knows the layout. I want him checking places he couldn't easily do with the family here.'

Mark gave the DS a short nod, watching as they scuttled off, wondering how long it would take before they realised the likelihood of them finding anything of any use was zilch. Not without tearing up the carpets and hoping for secret plans. Maybe evidence that Emily had been killed there and then moved twenty minutes down the road. That would be for the CSIs to sort out, of course, but it would be much better if they could find something at least.

He followed DS Cavanagh out of the living room and up the stairs. He glanced in the other two bedrooms before finding what he was looking for in the bathroom.

'Who still has carpet in their bathrooms these days,' Mark said to himself, barely audible in the small room. A faded white-coloured bath took up most of the space. There were various bath products perched on a small shelf which ran across the width of the bathtub. A couple of bottles of cheap shampoo and conditioner took up the space at the end. The windowsill held a beaker and a toothbrush holder. Toilet roll sat on top of the cistern, a broken roll holder lying on the floor. He could smell wet, that damp aroma he hated so much.

Above him was what he had been looking for.

A square insert into the ceiling, just low enough for him to reach with his fingertips, if he stood on tiptoes. The attic door was scuffed on one side, a latch which looked rusty on the other. Mark looked around, considered standing on the bathtub and reaching across for entry, but thought better of it.

He left the bathroom, peeking into rooms for something to stand on for easier access, headed downstairs and returned with a chair from the kitchen. He stood on top of it, testing to see if he was going to be tall enough now. Just about. Mark unlatched the hook on the attic door and lifted up the panel. Snapped on a pair of white gloves and retrieved the torch he'd left on the side of the bathroom sink. Stuck it in his trouser pocket, and lifted himself back up onto the chair.

He should have looked for a stepladder.

Mark gripped each side of the opening, lifting himself up with difficulty, his arms barely supporting his weight.

It took a few seconds longer than his body wished, before he finally got some upward momentum and was inside the roof space.

He removed the torch from his pocket and switched it on, illuminating the darkness only slightly. Mark waited a few seconds for his eyes to grow accustomed to the dark. He could see outlines of shapes, but the space wasn't exactly vast. He imagined walking into something and wondered how soon he could get out of there.

He had wanted to do this earlier, but felt it wouldn't have been right. To ask to go up into an attic – it would have been odd. But every house search he'd been involved in, he'd always ended up there eventually. Not once had he ever found anything, but it had become something he had to do now. He'd wanted to search it the first day he'd arrived, but had managed to ignore the gnawing voice in his head.

Mark wasn't exactly afraid of the dark, but he didn't welcome it. The torch in his hand was helping a little, but he could picture himself crashing down into a bedroom. Standing between the wooden beams under his feet would do it. Only soft insulation and the thickness of a ceiling keeping him from falling.

He probably should have let them know what he was doing, but he imagined they'd hear him soon enough. He was the second-largest member of the team who'd been assembled, after DS Cavanagh, which meant it was arguably a mistake that he'd chosen this job for himself. He was almost bent over double, the roof above him much lower than he'd anticipated. He was up there now though, so he may as well keep going, he thought.

Mark pointed the torch downwards so he could see

the beams properly in the darkness, carefully placing one foot down on the wood to make sure it supported his weight. He got himself into a rhythm. Pointing the torch at his feet, moving a couple of steps, then moving the light around him.

The air was cooler up there. Bitter, biting into his face, as he moved further forward. A draught blew from an unseen source. The smell of damp and abandonment. Mark didn't think they used the space for anything. In other houses, he'd found all kinds of discarded things. Old boxes, Christmas trees ... Once he'd found a bag full of broken marionette dolls and nearly screamed when he saw their eyes glinting in the darkness.

The attic space opened up a little more, so he could see how empty it was up there. Yellowed insulation was between each of the wooden beams he was standing on, some of it carefully laid in place, some rising over the beams. He stopped for a second, moving the torchlight around, to see if he could spot anything of interest.

Mark moved again, steadying himself as he almost lost his balance. He looked to his left where he'd placed his hand, lifted the light and shone it at the brick which stood there. It was in good condition for the most part, not crumbling around him as he'd imagined.

As he moved the light away, his attention was grabbed by something. A gap in the floor below him. Mark crouched down towards it, shifting his feet slowly along the wooden beam as he did so. It took him a minute to make his way there, crossing slowly and painfully, as his legs began to protest at the movement.

It was as if a part of the insulation had been removed purposely, a perfect gap in the floor. He shone the torch around the space, seeing it was next to where the chimney stack was, jutting out of the wall to the right. The air seemed colder the further he got into the attic. He shivered and almost lost his balance again, steadying himself once more. He breathed a few times, then pointed the torch at the gap.

There was something snagged in the wood there.

An envelope. He picked it up carefully, shining his torch across the front of it.

Written across it, in block capital letters, were the words THE GAME.

Mark shifted his position and swept his torch across the envelope. As he did so, something caused him to look down and see what had been at his feet the entire time. He could suddenly hear the voices that had been muffled until then, clearly echoing up at him.

A hole, which he'd uncovered accidentally. The piece of wood that had covered it, now lying a few inches away.

He was above Emily's bedroom.

Thirty-Seven

Mark was sitting down on the chair in the bathroom, wishing he'd left it for someone else to check. That he had ignored the part of his mind that had screamed to look and instead searched under beds like a normal detective.

His hands were shaking slightly, the white forensic gloves still adorning his hands, as he read the words printed on paper inside the envelope. He swallowed back saliva and fear.

And excitement. Tried to keep it all inside him.

He stopped reading, looking up at the attic opening and wondering how or why Emily would have gone up there to leave behind something like this. How long it had been up there for, how long she had planned to leave this, waiting for someone to discover it.

Mark blinked down at the page again and read it through.

This is for anyone who happens to find it.
  They're making me play.
  I don't want to do it.
  They're calling it a game, but I don't think it's

anything like that. I have to do what they say and not question it at all. If I don't, they'll tell everyone what I've done.

It doesn't matter what I think anymore. I've lost all control.

I don't think this will ever be found. I hid it well enough. Could be that it'll stay here forever – never being read by another person. That might be apt. It's not like anyone listened to me before. Why should it change now? Anyway, I wanted to leave something behind, just in case. I have no idea if this will ever be needed, but it's my security blanket now.

Things have been weird between us for ages. It's like she never accepted my apology. Like it meant nothing to her.

I didn't mean for her to take it that seriously. I was doing it to everyone and she deserved the same treatment. All of them treated me like shit and she was no different. Not once did she help me. Not once did she make sure I was okay. She was happy doing her own thing, living her amazing life, while I was drowning. She knew how sad I was and just ignored it. She's my sister and she didn't help me at all.

She could have put me first for once. She could have helped me. We could have been friends.

She wasn't interested in that. It's all about her. That's how she's always been.

I shouldn't have done it, though.

I shouldn't have done any of it.

I'm not sorry. Not really. They did worse to me. And she was the same as them.

But I know what I did to her was the worst.

This isn't a suicide letter. I would never do that. I just can't let them win.

That's why I have to play the game.

Level One was easy enough.

Then it became harder.

Then they wanted blood.

I'm not writing down what I did. Not the thing that is making me play.

I have to prove I've learned my lesson. Then, no one will know what I've done.

I think she was the one who brought this on me. I can't be sure, but I heard her say it. The words.

The Game.

She could be the one making me play.

I know after this, I'll never do anything like it again. This is a fresh start.

A way out without it being the end of everything.

That's what I've always wanted. Another chance at being someone else. A new start.

I can't trust her. She was never my sister. Not really. We share the same blood, we come from the same place. But she's never really cared about me.

I used to think she hated me, but it was always worse than that.

She just didn't care about me in the slightest. Never ever. She didn't think about me, didn't even know I was in pain. She felt nothing for me at all. I was just someone who shared a house with her. She never spoke to me about real stuff. About feelings, about our lives. She simply didn't care one bit about me.

That's worse than hate. At least with hate, there's

an emotion. People have hated me and I hated them right back.

She's supposed to be more than that. More than them.

The Voice tries to tell me that I just have to play through The Game, and that's it. I play the game and it's all over. We all move on. But the doubt is still there, despite the voice.

Am I The Game?

If she has done this to me, then I will never forgive her. I will spend the rest of my life making sure she never forgets what she did.

She will pay.

She can't be trusted. It's all about her.

Uncle Rich thinks I could be "someone". Reckons I have something about me. Maybe I have.

Maybe that would be enough.

Maybe that would be the end.

I know I did wrong. I know that's why I have to play The Game. I've nearly completed it now. I think I'm close to the final level.

If something goes wrong, I'll know it was her.

And this will be waiting for me. This proof. That I always knew she would get payback.

I read to escape. It taught me to take chances. Every story has a beginning, a middle and an end. I thought my end would be soon. I thought that I could never survive what has happened to me the last few years.

If she takes hope away from me, I'll show her what pain is.

This is the beginning of my real story.

The end of The Game. The last time I have to

*play by their rules. They'll get rid of all the evidence
of what I did, no one will ever find out. People will
forget everything I've done in the past few weeks and
I can go back to normal.*

I can get back to my life.

Whatever that is.

Emily Burns.

Emily's last words, Mark guessed. Before that night when
it had all ended.

Stephanie. Her sister.

She was talking about not trusting her own sister.
Mark stared down at the words, hoping they would
change somehow.

He had watched Stephanie when she'd seen Emily's body
earlier that day. That wasn't someone who didn't care. He
had watched her face as the truth crashed into it and her
world changed in an instant.

Emily had been wrong. Stephanie had cared deeply. He
didn't know why Emily didn't know that.

Mark didn't know what to do.

No one was meant to see this letter. It was the random
words of someone who was seriously troubled. She had
got herself into a situation she couldn't control and come
to harm. There was a mental slip happening before Emily
disappeared, that was clear now.

It wasn't Stephanie's fault. It couldn't be.

Mark slid the paper back into the envelope, letting it
dangle in his hands, working out what to do next.

Mark could feel his hands shaking as he held the envelope tighter. He knew what he was going to do, without
knowing why.

He needed to make them see that there was more to this than just a couple of unconnected bodies, found on the streets of the city within days of each other.

He heard footsteps in the corridor behind him, coming towards the bathroom. Mark stood up quickly, looked down at the envelope, at the door.

Then, as a voice called his name, he thought about stuffing the envelope in his pocket and doing this alone.

Instead, he shouted back through the door.

'Coming out now.'

He needed to make them see.

To know that he wasn't what they thought of him. That he was good enough for this job.

That he knew what he was doing.

He needed to find out what The Game was.

That was the key to all of this.

Thirty-Eight

DS Cavanagh was waiting for him outside the bathroom, his head tilted to one side as Mark emerged, realising quickly that something had been found.

'Come on, out with it,' DS Cavanagh said, leaning against the wall opposite. 'You look like the cat that got the cream – or the milk – whatever it is.'

'I've found something,' Mark replied, unable to keep the excitement from his voice now. 'There is more to all of this than just randomness. There's something called The Game—'

'What did you find?' DS Cavanagh interrupted, holding out his hand.

Mark handed over the letter and watched as the DS scanned the contents, his gloved hands crinkling the paper. 'It's all connected,' he said, as Cavanagh continued to read. 'I think all the odd things Emily has been doing are part of it.'

'What odd things?'

'I don't know everything, but Emily was witnessed behaving strangely in public before she went missing.'

DS Cavanagh stopped reading and looked up.

'Approaching members of the public, saying odd things, like that?'

Mark nodded, opened his mouth to talk but was stopped by DS Cavanagh continuing.

'Joanna Carter did something similar.'

'There you go,' Mark said, then began pacing in the small hallway outside the bathroom, head down, trying to work it out. 'There's someone making them do this.'

'I don't know—'

'You can't call Emily's death anything other than a murder,' Mark said, taking his turn to interrupt now. 'And we saw the CCTV of someone following Joanna onto that roof. Did it look like Emily's uncle? There must be a link between the two. We need to speak to Emily's sister, Stephanie. Find out why she couldn't be trusted, or what was going on.'

'Possibly,' DS Cavanagh replied, but didn't sound convinced. 'We'll continue the search, see if there's anything more to find, then take this back to the boss. See what she has to say about it. I still don't like the uncle. I think he has to be involved in some way.'

Mark wanted to pick DS Cavanagh up and shake him. He thought of a few comebacks, but kept them to himself and decided to bide his time, more sure than ever that Uncle Rich wasn't the person responsible for any of the events that had occurred in the previous few days.

Which left him wondering again who was.

Mark waited for the rest of the search team to find the grand total of nothing. He made a show of helping them out, ripping apart Emily's bedroom, going through every single square inch of the place.

The sky was black outside as they continued on, hoping

that an answer was going to be forthcoming. All the while, grumbling that it wasn't *that* house they should be searching. All the time, becoming more ingrained in the idea that it was Emily's uncle who should have his house ransacked. That the answers would be there instead.

Mark didn't know what to think anymore. All that kept playing in his mind was the need to speak to Stephanie and find out her side of the story. To see what she knew.

There was something going on and he didn't think anyone on that team was prepared to see it.

DS Cavanagh's face was lined with annoyance and acceptance. He exchanged looks with Mark, a quiet nod of recognition that at least one of them had found something of note. Mark kept quiet, trying to figure out what he was going to do next.

How to find out more.

Back at the station, things had moved on in their absence. Emily's uncle had been brought in and was currently being questioned. Answering 'no comment' to everything, Mark imagined. Another group of detectives were searching his house and car, looking for anything to tie him to the scene. The officers who had searched Emily's house all looked a little relieved about that. The team were gathered quickly, ready for an impromptu update on what was happening. Mark lurked near the back of the group as his phone buzzed away in his pocket. He ignored it.

The investigation team had grown in size since a few days earlier. Faces he'd never noticed before were suddenly a part of what had been a one-man band two days earlier.

Just him and a missing girl.

'Right, so the latest we've got back from the team searching Richard Burns's house and car is that several items of interest have been found. Forensics are going over the car, as you'd expect. Unfortunately, nothing was found in the victim's home that was evidence of anything happening there. We're not ruling out that Joanna Carter's death is linked at this stage.'

DI Bennett continued on, listing what they still didn't know, as she perched on a desk addressing the room. Phones rang and were cut off mid-ring. Feet shuffled about, someone coughed.

'With regards to Joanna Carter. The man we saw on CCTV didn't look big enough to be Rich Burns,' DS Cavanagh said, arms folded across his chest, muscles in his neck straining against the surface. 'I think Mark was right though. I don't like the coincidence at all. If the two are connected – and we have to be seriously asking ourselves why they wouldn't be – there's the possibility of another person's involvement. Plus, we now have another angle to consider.'

A few heads turned his way, but Mark ignored them. He stared straight ahead, at the wall to the left of DI Bennett.

'It's not enough at the moment,' DI Bennett said, a touch of irritation in her voice at the interruption from Cavanagh. 'All our concentration needs to be on nailing him for Emily's death first. He's giving away nothing in interview at the moment, other than veiled threats and barely contained anger. At least it's not a "no comment" interview at the moment. I'm hoping they can break him down quickly.'

Rich was talking then, Mark thought with surprise. He glanced at the clock on the wall and wondered how much longer this would go on for. The urge to slip away quietly was becoming difficult to ignore.

Stephanie was in the building somewhere. Probably in the family room on the third floor, he guessed. He thought they'd be still be in shock, trying to deal with what had taken place that day.

'Mark spoke to the son,' DI Bennett said, bringing him back into the room. 'He didn't exactly give up his uncle, but made some interesting statements we can use. The family are together and will be returning home soon. A family liaison officer will be accompanying them, who will keep an eye on them. I don't need to tell any of you of the importance of keeping this all quiet at the moment. That means not telling family members, friends, anyone, about what's going on right now. And definitely no media at all. They're camped outside at the moment, looking for someone to let something slip. We can't give them anything. It'll only screw us up at this point. Let them speculate and come up with non-stories. We'll keep doing our own work.'

As DI Bennett spoke, the television on the wall in the corner of the room flickered silently. One of the twenty-four-hour news channels was on screen, the yellow breaking news banner running across the bottom.

Mark turned away from it, not wanting to see what was being reported.

'Some of you are staying on to continue working the case, but it's been a long day for the rest. I want those who have been here since eight this morning to clock off and get some sleep. We've got two pieces of evidence that I need final reports on by the morning: Emily's diary of "thoughts" and her social media accounts. Mark has been working on them the last couple of days and done as much as he could, but they're extensive and long. I want a couple each on both. Work through them quickly but diligently. Find me something that we can use against the uncle.'

They wouldn't find anything, Mark thought, but didn't say. He needed to scour those pages himself and try to find any references to a game. He wanted to know why she wasn't putting more stock in what he had discovered, but was prepared to wait.

Someone was killing these women – two so far – and he didn't think for one second that it was a low-life drug dealer with an anger issue.

His phone buzzed again in his pocket, as DI Bennett continued talking for a few more minutes. When she eventually dismissed them, she grabbed hold of his arm as he walked past her.

'A quick word first,' she said, letting go and walking into her office. Mark looked across at DS Cavanagh, who seemed to stay in place for a second, before deciding to follow them.

'Yeah, boss,' Mark said, surprised at how calm and level his voice sounded. 'The letter we found, I'm guessing?'

'Yes, the letter,' DI Bennett replied, standing behind her desk, one hand resting on top of her chair. 'I've had a quick look through it, but I'm not sure what we can take from it right now.'

'A few things,' Mark said, shooting a hopeful look towards DS Cavanagh for back-up. 'First, we have the odd events before both Emily and Joanna were found dead. The things they've been doing in public, etcetera. Then you have this mention of some kind of game and the fear behind it. Also we have the online element of it all. Emily was targeting people online. And I've heard Joanna might have been doing similar things. Ostracised, all of that.'

'I agree that things aren't adding up,' DI Bennett replied, placing her hands on her hips. 'But I need to play the odds here. Occam's Razor, you know? I think there's something to suggest there's some kind of game, but that could just be something new that teenagers are doing, and we're getting side-tracked by it. At the moment, evidence is leading us away from something like what you're suggesting, and towards abuse and a closer connection.'

'The uncle ...'

'Yes, the uncle. It's been a crazy couple of days. If I had any idea what was going to happen, I would never have sent you to that house on your own.'

'No one could have seen it coming. I just ... Are you sure that this isn't all connected?'

'Mark ...'

Mark tried to quieten down the part of him that wanted to make her see sense, but he didn't know how to do that. 'It's not right. None of this. I found absolutely nothing to suggest Emily's uncle was abusing her. Only a sulky teenage boy, who has an axe to grind by the looks of things. It seems a huge stretch to think that Rich killed her and Joanna Carter. Do you really think that's him on that CCTV?'

'You don't think he could find someone to do his dirty work for him?'

Mark hesitated, then shook his head. 'It just doesn't make sense.'

'It does, Mark,' DI Bennett said, correcting him, her face now blank and unreadable. 'I understand your concerns and don't think that I don't share them. That's why we're looking at the most logical option right now, in her uncle being the one who killed her.'

'It doesn't seem that logical to me . . .'

'Careful, Mark,' DI Bennett said, before he had chance to say any more. 'You've done well this week, so don't make a mistake.'

'There's absolutely nothing in anything she's written down or online about her uncle,' Mark said, unable to stop himself. He wanted to take the letter Emily had written before her death and thrust it in her face. Thankfully, his body didn't let him. 'It's all about the people from her life, yet only mentions him in a positive way. Look, she went after people online, got her revenge and didn't seem to have a problem doing that, so if her uncle was abusing her, why wouldn't she mention it in a hidden note? Charlie could be lying. Or, if Rich had been spending more time with Emily, maybe it's because he was trying to help her? Doesn't it make sense that if he'd done something to her, she'd go after him? Or at least leave something behind saying so? That's before we get into the whole blood in one place, body in another, with some random other girl at the bottom of a building, who was known to be doing certain acts in public that Emily was doing as well.'

'I agree, it's starting to come together in a certain way, but that doesn't mean I can ignore what's right in front of us. This could just be a distraction, an attempt to make us do what you're trying to do right now. Waste time instead of concentrating on the one man who has the capacity to do this.'

Mark could see himself losing an argument he didn't even want to have. Still, he couldn't let it go. There was more to this than just coincidence and an abusive family member. He could feel it. He just couldn't voice it. Not without making himself look out of his depth.

'Just keep an open mind, that's all I'm saying,' Mark said eventually, pleased to hear his tone had calmed somewhat. 'I don't think this feels right at all. If we were to miss something because we spent all our time on the wrong man, that'd be wrong too.'

DI Bennett fixed him with a stare, but he could see by the way her shoulders dropped a little that she'd heard him.

'What do you think, Cav?' DI Bennett said, turning to the DS standing in the doorway now. 'Is Mark right?'

'I think he knows this case better than all of us right now. If Mark thinks there's more to it than just the uncle, I reckon it's on us to listen to him.'

Mark could feel his eyebrows raise in surprise, but didn't say anything, and certainly didn't look at DS Cavanagh.

DI Bennett sighed and moved her chair out to sit down. 'Fine, why don't you two take over the questioning of the uncle. See if that changes your mind.' She looked at her watch and made a decision. 'Take him into a room now before you call it a day. There's another sixteen hours on the clock, so we have the time.'

'Thanks, boss,' Mark said, opening the door and leaving the office before she had a chance to change her mind. He waited outside for DS Cavanagh, who joined him a few seconds later. The two men looked at each other, Cavanagh breaking it with a small nod, then they set off for the custody suites on the bottom floor.

He'd managed to get much more than he'd thought was possible. Now, he just had to work out what he wanted to ask Rich.

Mark tried not to smile as he made his way down the corridor. He could feel himself becoming part of the team finally.

There was something nagging at him still. Something he wasn't seeing yet. Something he was missing.

He tried to shake the feeling, but it wouldn't let go.

NOW

Thirty-Nine

The Third Interview

Tuesday 30th October
Interview Room One
Lancaster Police Station – sixty miles from Liverpool City Centre

They had about an hour and a half left on the clock before they'd have to decide whether to charge him or not. He thought it was an absolute certainty that they'd have enough to get at least one charge, but he wondered about the rest he had said. They had left him in the cell for about six hours before they'd brought him back.

He didn't like the way they'd been looking at him. As if they had a secret they couldn't wait to share.

Surely they would have been looking into his confessions, rather than anything else?

He was just nervous, he decided. He needed this last hurdle to be crossed and then he would be remanded and everything would be okay.

He thought of the dead girl they had found him with.

The looks on the faces of the uniformed officers as they handcuffed him and bundled him into the back of the van. The waves of hate that had streamed across the table from the detectives in the two previous visits to this interview room.

They all looked and felt the same. There was no chance they had looked into who he was. His past, his life.

Of course, they'd want to identify him. Have a name, so they could do this properly. He was still weighing up the pros and cons of giving them that.

They hadn't tried talking to him on the walk to the room. Or now they were inside. He was glad of that. Didn't want them to try and engage him in idle chit-chat, as they had done previously.

This had to go one way only.

'This interview is being recorded both visually and audibly. Investigating officers are Detective Inspector Patrick Hicks and Detective Sergeant Victoria Lee. Still not ready to tell us your name?'

He shook his head, then said 'no' for the benefit of the tape. He looked up at the camera in the corner of the room, wondering if anyone would ever see this video. If it would go that far. At the beginning of the day, he had no doubts it would. That he would be charged with multiple murders, plead guilty, and go quietly inside a prison for the rest of his life.

But that couldn't happen without him giving them something tangible, rather than just stories.

'That's fine, we'll come back to that,' Hicks said, shuffling the paper in front of him. 'We've identified the young woman whose body you were found with, you'll be pleased to know. Holly Edwards.'

He kept a straight face. He'd known it would be coming eventually, but had hoped it would take a little longer to get to that point. He didn't like the way Hicks was looking at him. Holding back a smirk, almost. Hiding something from him.

'She was reported missing in Liverpool. How did she end up so far away from home?'

He was becoming nervous now, thinking of all the strands he'd left hanging. The threads he hadn't been able to keep a handle on, before he'd been arrested.

The question still hung in the air between them, as he tried to think of the correct way to answer. He shrugged his shoulders instead of talking.

'Not important right now, I suppose,' Hicks said, as he shared a quick look with the detective sitting next to him. 'We can get back to that. I think the bigger question is how you came to be a serial killer, as you tell us. The fact you've been running around this country, killing all these people without being caught out. We'd have no idea, if you didn't sit down there and tell us, either ... which doesn't make much sense. Especially when of the eight names you've given us, only one, before this last week in Liverpool, has been determined to be a suspicious death.'

'Maybe you weren't looking hard enough?' he replied, but he could feel it all slipping away from him. He placed his hands under the table, so they couldn't see them shake and tremble. Gripped a hold of his leg to stop it jumping up and down in response. 'It's not my fault if you've missed it all this time. That's for you to sort out.'

'So, we started looking into this missing girl and who she was,' Hicks continued, ignoring the accusation. There was a definite hard smirk on his face now. 'It seemed bizarre to have someone just completely confess to a bunch of murders no one was even looking into. We knew we had to step back and look at the facts only. Holly Edwards. You're found next to her body, but you don't have any blood on you, no signs of injury whatsoever. And we think she put up a fight, would that be right?'

He didn't respond, seeing where this was all going.

They knew.

'We spoke to our colleagues in Merseyside,' Hicks said, elbows on the table between them, arms lowering and folded in front of him. Staring into his eyes. 'Turns out, she'd been linked to a string of disappearances over the past week or so. Two other young women, both found dead.'

'Both victims of mine—'

'I didn't ask a question,' Hicks cut in, before he could say anything more. 'You should know better than that. As I was saying, the Major Crimes Unit down there were informed of her having gone missing, only this morning. The events of the past week made them take it very seriously indeed. Another young girl going missing in their city.'

He put his head in his hands, wanting to curl up and disappear. Become invisible.

'A third disappearance and now another body,' Hicks said, and now his tone was softer somewhat. 'They're understandably upset that the body was found. Yet, with someone in custody, hopeful that this could all be sorted out. Especially when that person in custody is confessing to not just those three deaths, but a string of others.'

He could feel it coming now. The final nail. He was just waiting for it to happen. Unable to say anything to stop it.

He wondered if it was enough. If all of this was going to be sufficient to stop The Game.

'Tell me, why did you do this? Why are you here? If you knew where Holly was, why didn't you just tell someone, call it in?'

He couldn't lift his head up. Couldn't look them in the eyes and explain it all. He couldn't. He wasn't allowed.

He thought of her, of what would happen now.

There was no way of keeping her safe now.

'We just want to help,' Hicks said, his voice full of concern and pity. He hated that. 'What happened?'

He wanted to tell them everything. Try and explain how he had ended up there. Tell them what he had discovered. About The Game.

Instead, he continued to sit there, his head buried in his arms, and waited for the inevitable to happen. It had never been possible, this. To just be charged and end it all. That had been certain from the start. He thought he'd been stopping it all, but they were going to believe he was making it all up.

Or worse.

DI Hicks cleared his throat, waiting for him to answer. When it became clear that he wasn't prepared to, he sighed loudly then finally spoke.

'We know who you really are.'

BEFORE

Forty

PLAYER ONE

Her mum finally let her escape an hour or so after they arrived home. Left her in her bedroom alone, while she cried on the phone to Holly's dad about how she didn't know what was wrong with their daughter.

When she'd arrived at the police station, Holly had quickly realised that she didn't have a clue what to do next. In that sense, she supposed there was no real plan. She was being pulled into something that she'd never really had any control over. That was clear now.

Yet, she was in it until the end. There was no turning back.

What had happened at the police station would follow her for years to come. They had bailed her, which meant there would be more to come. Her mother had arrived from work, face lined with tension, trying to work out what her daughter had done. This happened to other people – not them.

Hours later the house was quiet, after every attempt to talk had been batted back by Holly. She had listened to her mum cry herself to sleep as her dad tried to soothe her. She wanted to stay curled up on her bed, ignore what she'd brought into their lives.

She thought this was worse than them finding out what she'd done. Yes, her aunty and her nan had died of cancer recently. Yes, she'd been pretending to have it, just to get sympathy.

What this had done to her mum . . .

Her phone buzzed.

She knew the voice was waiting to give her more instructions.

Holly answered and listened. Whispered her acceptance and felt the tears slowly crawl down her cheeks.

Level Five.

They wanted blood.

When the call was over, she crossed the room silently, picked up a red felt-tip pen from the small desk near the television, and pulled a piece of paper from the ream underneath. She drew a heart in the darkness, I love you both underneath.

That would be fine, she thought. It would be okay.

It was just in case.

The house was silent. Cold. She passed her parent's room, moving as slowly and quietly as she possibly could, not wanting to be discovered. Her phone told her it was 02:03, even if she didn't believe it. Crept towards the stairs as if any noise could permeate the darkness and wake her parents. Alert them that something was wrong and that their only daughter was sneaking out. She reached the top of the stairs and avoided the squeaky floorboard on the fifth step down. In the hall, the clock was silhouetted, the ghostly outline of time shown.

Two-ten.

She had never been out of the house at that time. Never needed to be. No late nights out, in town with a group of friends. No late-night parties. Nothing. She had always been tucked up in bed by this time every night.

That was about to change.

Holly slipped on her coat, picked her keys up from the hook where they lived near the front door, and turned them in the lock slowly. She heard the click and pulled down the handle. A rush of cold air came in as she stepped outside, pulling the door closed behind her. She moved the handle up and locked the door.

She didn't know if she could do what she'd been told to. The fear of her secrets being discovered was enough to get her this far, but whether it would be sufficient to take the next step, she didn't know.

Forty minutes later, on the banks of the River Mersey, she broke out onto the waterfront. She was at the outer edges of the city now, before it turned into Southport, into Lancashire. The north of the city where she'd grown up, living her boring, uneventful life.

Holly looked at the phone in her hand, knowing one phone call would bring them running to her. Driving their little car in pyjamas and slippers, that worried look plastered across her mum's face. Exasperation on her dad's. They would pull up and wrap her in their arms and tell her everything was going to be okay.

And then, well, hundreds, thousands of people everywhere, knowing she was a liar. That she had told people she was dying and it hadn't been true.

As she looked down at the phone, it began to vibrate, making her jump in shock. She almost dropped it in surprise, but then composed herself quickly. 'It'll all be over soon,' she found herself whispering, and she almost believed the words.

She answered and lifted it to her ear.

'Second thoughts?' the voice said, and it was an oddly comforting sound.

'No,' Holly replied, but she could feel her own tone betray her. 'I just . . .'

'You finish playing The Game and no one will ever know what you've done.'

'Why make me do something like this?' Holly said quickly, almost a little too loudly. 'I don't understand. How much longer do I have to do this?'

'You like playing games with people. With their emotions, their lives. Now it's your turn. You're going to finish this.'

'Why here? Why this late?'

'I thought you'd know the place . . .'

Holly frowned, looking around, trying to remember where she was. Another time she had been there. A glimpse of memory came to her, but disappeared just as quick. 'I don't. I'm sorry.'

The static on the line went silent. Holly thought the voice had hung up on her and she felt a momentary lapse of reason. Imagined being left there alone, no way out. The darkness around her became suffocating. It all became too much in an instant. The thought of being exposed. The thought of being ridiculed and shamed.

'No, you can go on,' the voice said finally, relief flooding Holly's veins at the sound of it.

'Okay, I'm sorry,' Holly replied, hearing the earnest whisper escape her mouth. 'I know I've done something wrong. Please, don't tell anyone . . .'

'Stop your whining. Carry out the instructions. Good luck.'

The voice talked her through The Game again, not that she understood much of what was said. She listened to every word intently, scared of missing something.

Why are you doing this? It's obviously crazy.

She ignored her own voice, screaming inside her. Listened carefully to the words, hoping it was enough to just do whatever it said and be done with it all.

No more worry.

She could fix things with her parents. Tell them she'd gone slightly crazy for a day. That it didn't mean anything, all that trouble with the police. Tell them anything so they wouldn't look at her with that worried look in their eyes.

The call ended abruptly. She kept hold of her phone, thinking it would buzz again within seconds. Every step memorised, she walked further up the promenade, feeling the chill in the air. Out on the beach, she knew the Gormley statues would be looking out on the same vista as she had. They were a secondary thought to her now, as she soon found the secluded place that had been described to her.

'One, two, three,' she whispered, the air silent and still around her. She walked three paces forward, then two to her right-hand side. 'One, two, three, four.'

She continued for another two minutes, walking back and forth and side to side. A pattern that she'd had to commit to memory.

Holly turned in a circle, recited words, and then went back to the beginning. Began the process all over again.

Repeated it twice.

On the fifth time – the final time – she felt as if she could feel the air around her change. Her heart began to beat quicker, as fear built within her. She wasn't sure what was happening, but there was a definite shift in the atmosphere.

She could hear sounds around her, but they were lost in her repetitive words. She didn't want to look up, staring at her feet and chanting the words she hoped would be enough to not be exposed.

Inside, she screamed at herself for being so stupid.

The world became bright suddenly, her face illuminated in light. She screwed her eyes shut, but didn't stop chanting numbers that meant nothing to her. Moving in small steps, side to side.

Until the young man stepped out of the shadows and came to meet her, his body shaking with fear, tears cascading down his screwed-up face.

Until the sound stopped and the world turned black.

Forty-One

Mark and DS Cavanagh were sitting across the table from Rich Burns, the small space seemingly doubling the size of the man. His arms were bulging against his chest as he folded them and leaned back in the chair. There was a calmness to him that spoke of being in the same room, the same scenario, countless times.

He was used to this.

His eyes betrayed him, though. The hurt etched into them. The redness underneath, a sign he had been crying recently.

Away from this place, the grief had grabbed hold of the man. Now, he was only going to show the detectives what he wanted to show them. And it wasn't going to be nice.

No solicitor, which Mark guessed wasn't usual for him. He'd done enough interviews in the past to know the type of career criminal Rich was and their usual modus operandi. An endless stream of 'no comments' until the interviewer became tired.

This was different and Mark knew why. Rich wanted to talk and knew nothing he could say would mean he was guilty. Because he wasn't.

Mark made himself useful setting up the recording machine, as Cavanagh reeled off the usual talk about his rights and options. Rich once more confirmed he was happy to continue without representation and then leaned forward to take a sip of the coffee he'd asked for before they'd entered.

He was like a coiled spring, which set Mark on edge. Rich wanted to be out of there, looking for whoever had killed his niece. That much was obvious just from looking at him. He expected that Cavanagh had made the same observation. His head was more red than usual, the bulging neck muscles and veins popping to attention. The hands curling in and out of fists.

They would have to tread carefully. Although Mark expected Cavanagh could give the big man a run for his money in a straight fight.

Rich's clothes had been taken from him, sent for the same testing that would be done on the rest of his belongings. The jumper he'd been given to wear was too small for him, the material straining against his build. The tattoos on his neck seemed to be struggling against his skin to break free.

Mark looked down, so he didn't have to feel intimidated any longer.

'Please state your name for the recording,' Cavanagh said, once Mark had given him the nod.

'Richard Burns.'

'You're uncle to Emily Burns,' Cavanagh said, quickly and without pause. 'Is that right?'

'You know it is.'

'Now, you've already been asked about your movements of the past few days. Before and after Emily's death.'

'Yes. And you can't say I haven't told you everything. Anything to get this out of the way so you can concentrate on finding out who actually did this.'

'Rich, that's what we all want here, but you have to agree that there are unanswered questions you have to answer. Does that seem fair?'

Rich sighed and lowered his head. He laid his hands on the table, palms down, and looked at Mark. 'I know my past. You know it. I've done things I'm not proud of, still do some things I won't mention. When it comes to family though, that's different. I'm different. I wasn't as lucky as some others. By the time I was doing the stuff you wouldn't like to hear about, it was already too late. Mark, you've been around me, the family, all week now. You should know I wouldn't be capable of doing anything like this.'

Mark shifted uncomfortably in his seat, aware of the recording of familiarity that would now be on file. 'Rich, just answer honestly and we can move on. Right?'

Rich nodded at him in response, sitting up and then leaning back again. Mark looked at Cavanagh and received a nod in return.

'Your relationship with Emily, how was it?'

'It was close,' Rich replied, his voice low and cold. He shook his head; sadly, it seemed. 'More so recently. She was getting down on herself a lot. I heard some stuff and just thought she might be heading down a dark path. I've seen it before and didn't want that for her. For our Julie. And now look – I've failed them all.'

'And you didn't think to tell us what was happening?'

'And have you think she was just depressed? You think we would have got a detective in our house every day if you just thought she was gonna top herself?'

Mark shaped to answer, but anything he said would have been a lie. Instead he moved back to what he wanted to know. 'What was going on with her? Was it the online stuff?'

'What else?' Rich said with a dismissive bark. 'That's all kids these days are obsessed with, isn't it? Spending all day staring at phones, never talking to each other like normal people. It's all about likes and comments. They put their whole lives on the internet and expect nothing bad to ever happen, then act all surprised when it does.'

'How did this start?' Mark said, discarding the short notes he'd made for himself and trusting his own instincts. 'She came to you for advice?'

'Something like that,' Rich replied, shaking his head again, as if the idea had been ridiculous. 'Like I know anything of that world. What I do know, though, is people and maybe that's why she came to me. Something had kicked off around her and she wasn't sure how to deal with it. I spent some time with her, trying to talk some sense into her.'

'What kind of sense?'

'That it didn't matter. That in a few days everyone would have forgotten about it and moved on to the next thing. And I thought it had. She didn't talk about it for weeks. I think we know I was wrong.'

'She was in some kind of trouble then? Before she went missing?'

'No, that was ages ago. It was all sorted out, she told me. You know how it is with these kids. She never made out it was anything bad. She didn't know how to get out of it, that was all. A few nasty messages, but she told me it was nothing that bad. She just didn't know how to deal with it.'

'We have information that Emily was doing something on the internet – do you know what that was?'

'The pretending to be other people thing?' Rich said, now looking at Mark and ignoring the mute DS Cavanagh. 'That what you're talking about?'

'I think the term is catfishing,' Mark replied, earning a dismissive wave from Rich.

'Whatever it's called, still the same bollocks as the rest of it. They said she was pretending to be other people online and going after that lot who bullied her in school. Making them do things and say things that would embarrass them, stuff like that. Kiddy stuff, you know. I didn't understand it when Emily told me about it and I still don't. Seems like no one online is who they say they really are. That's just another part of it. All the fights take place on Facebook or whatever and then when they see each other in person they don't know what to do. The world's changing.'

'Emily was targeting people who had bullied her online.'

'That's the thing, no she wasn't. Not anymore. She was caught out a year or two ago and stopped. She said someone was doing it again and was pretending to be her, pretending to be someone else . . .'

'What?' DS Cavanagh said. 'I don't get that.'

'Someone pretended that she was still doing it to those people. It wasn't her. She was keeping her head down and just trying to get on with her life. Then this happens and it just destroyed her. She was a wreck. Julie couldn't get her out of her room for a week, before I went in and started talking to her. But this was ages ago. At least a couple of months.'

'Let me get this straight,' Mark said, wondering how this would fit in, if at all, with what he'd discovered in the letter. 'She wasn't the one behind the catfishing, or target-ing of people online? Someone pretended that it was her doing it, so she would get the blame for it?'

'That's right.'

'Why? Why would someone do that?'

'I don't know,' Rich said, his head lolling back and looking up towards the ceiling. 'Maybe she was an easy target. She ... she wasn't the most switched-on girl. Not streetwise at all. Easily led, easily manipulated. She just wanted to be liked, but it never seemed to happen. It didn't help that it came easy to her twin. She was forever in her shadow. So she tried to make friends, but ended up being bullied. She tried to be different, but that didn't help at all. Nothing she seemed to do worked, so she stopped trying.'

'And when someone came along and did this to her, it just made things worse.'

Rich sighed and looked at Mark. His eyes were red now, shiny with tears that hadn't been shed in a long time. 'She never had a chance to just ... be. There was always something holding her back, or someone. She was going to college and changing her path, but then this happens and it all falls apart. I stepped in because I knew what was going to happen next. You see it all the time these days. All these kids being bullied who end up topping themselves because of it. I didn't want her to be another one.'

'When was the last time you spoke to her?'

'A couple of days before she went missing,' Rich replied, wiping his face with the sleeve of his jumper. 'She seemed better. I didn't get much out of her, but she was excited about something it seemed. I thought she was finally seeing some kind of light out of the darkness she'd been feeling. I know what I am. I know what you think about me and what I do, but don't for a second think that I don't love my family – I'd do anything for them. I had nothing to do with what happened to Emily.'

Mark believed him. Despite what they knew about the man and what he'd done – the violence he'd been a part of, the criminal activity – there was no way he was this amazing an actor on top of that. 'She was excited – about what?'

'I don't know,' Rich said, holding his hands out in front of him. 'I wish I could tell you.'

'Did she mention any kind of game?' Mark replied, trying to keep his voice from showing any excitement. 'Something she had to play?'

Rich stared back at him, then leaned back as if thinking about it carefully. 'Don't think so. She was talking about some kind of self-help thing, where she was moving through levels. Think she was on Level Three or something.'

Mark looked at DS Cavanagh, who stared back with wide eyes. He sat back, taking it all in. The whole story. The Game he'd now heard about a few times, Emily saying she just had to play and everything would be solved.

'Who do you think could have done this to her?' DS Cavanagh said, as Mark tried to make the pieces fit together.

'I don't know,' Rich replied, his voice changing. Hard and devoid of light. 'But I hope I find out before you lot do, so I can get proper justice. That's all I'm going to say.'

Forty-Two

Him

It was becoming too much for him to handle. The waiting. It was endless, the seconds ticking by with nothing happening.

He couldn't deal with it.

He checked the phone sitting beside him for the fifteenth time in the past minute, placing it back down on the bed when he saw nothing new. The laptop was perched on his crotch and stomach, heat pouring from it.

He had chosen her. There was no turning back from that.

He just needed them all to see the proof, so he could get that feeling again.

That acceptance. They would all know he'd been brave enough to allow this to happen.

Maybe, now, his life would get better. Maybe *he* would be better.

First, she'd had to be dealt with. That was all.

His choice. His decision.

He wanted to be sure he would never be found out. Wanted to make sure he had his story straight, if they ever knocked on his door.

He was safe.

Your hands are clean.

Soon, his screen was filled with photographs.

There she was, standing near the waterfront, looking out. He could only see the back of her head, but that was enough to recognise her.

Then, he could see her face as she turned around and the photographs became almost like a flick book of small drawings. In each picture, she moved slightly closer to the camera. Unaware of its existence. The streetlights around her provided some illumination, but otherwise, she was a blurry form in the dull light.

His heart began to quicken as he saw her arms extended out in the correct manner. The way she'd been told.

The sequence of photographs shortened, became duller and more difficult to make out. Finally, near the end of the thumbnails that had filled his screen, there was what everyone on the forum had been waiting for, all this time. Since the last one.

His choice.

He clicked play on the video, then made it full screen.

The image was barely clear enough to make out more than a motion of movement, but he could hear her voice. A hand went to his mouth, as he choked back something he hadn't been aware he was feeling. A sob, a cry of delight at what he had been responsible for creating. A memory.

He watched it again and again, as if each time it was the first time he was seeing it.

On screen, he could hear her breathless chants. The numbers she was reeling off. The movements she was making. In the background, he could hear nothing but the waves and the wind.

The blood.

Then, the screen went black and the video ended.

That was all there was.

She was gone.

Suddenly, his mind was filled with regret and darkness. Thoughts of the family, how they wouldn't understand. How they would never know the truth.

He would have to watch them grieve, never knowing where she was or what had happened to her.

It was over.

Now, he could move on. Begin a new chapter.

He wasn't sure what that would be. What he should do. What he should be.

A thought came to his mind, pushing its way to the surface above the noise.

If it's over for her, is it over for you as well?

He didn't know the answer.

Forty-three

Mark checked the time and suppressed a yawn. It was late, even as the adrenaline inside him increased. He was getting close, he felt, to something approaching an answer.

'You don't think it's too late?'

Mark shook his head to DS Cavanagh's question. 'It'll be fine. I just want to make sure you're okay with me talking to her alone.'

'It should be fine. She trusts you and it's not an interview under caution. If she's willing to talk to you now, then I say go for it. I'll find out where she is and then probably take the boss's advice and get some rest. See if I can work out what the hell we're dealing with here.'

'Thanks,' Mark replied, pulling out the letter he'd found in the attic of Emily's house out and reading it over again. He tried to work out how best to tackle what he needed to ask Stephanie.

'By the way,' DS Cavanagh said, turning back to him as he walked away. 'For what it's worth, you've still got my backing. I think it's all connected. I don't like coincidences. Well done for not letting it drop. Other newbies would have just got their head down and done as they were told. The boss won't forget that; especially if it leads to us figuring this all out.'

With that, DS Cavanagh left Mark alone in the corridor as he tried not to punch the air at the compliment.

There was still too much to do.

Half an hour later, Stephanie was led into the family room by DS Cavanagh and left alone with Mark. Her eyes were red and puffy from hours of tears. Her skin was pale. She looked so different than when he'd last seen her. Burdened with pain.

'What's going on?' Stephanie said, her hair hanging limply over her cheeks. 'How come you didn't just come to the house tomorrow or something?'

Mark realised he wasn't sure how to begin. Stammered out a response. 'I thought it better we talk straight away. It's not too late, is it? I mean, if you're tired or ...'

Stephanie shifted in her seat, trying to sit up straighter. 'No, it's fine. What is this about, Mark?'

'We found something. In the house, earlier.'

'Yeah, thanks for that,' Stephanie said, before he had a chance to say anything more. 'As if things weren't bad enough, now my mum's house has been turned upside down. Honestly, you couldn't have given us a little more time? We've only just found out she's dead. We could have done without that. Or at least had some warning.'

'I'm sorry,' Mark replied, stuck for anything else to say. 'It's what happens in these types of cases ...'

'And now you're interviewing our Uncle Rich, as if he had something to do with it? It's just not right.'

Mark could see she was on the brink of breaking down again, but resisted the urge to reach out and comfort her.

'She was found somewhere he's known to have a connection to, Stephanie. That can't be ignored.'

'He would never hurt her,' Stephanie said, a grit to her tone of voice. As if she was holding back from raising her voice in the small space. 'I know that's what you people always think, but this time, it's different. He didn't do this.'

'That's why I need to talk to you. What I'm going to tell you here, I want you to think about carefully. If there's anything sensitive, I promise it'll be dealt with properly. I just need the truth, that's all. I need your trust here. Okay? Can you trust me?'

Stephanie nodded, her eyes now wide, staring at Mark. Her face gave away nothing and Mark felt that he was either dealing with an incredible liar or someone who genuinely had no clue what Emily had been thinking.

'We found something,' Mark said. The letter was in an evidence bag inside the folder sitting on his lap. He opened the file as he talked. 'When we were searching the house. It was hidden in the attic.'

He glanced across at Stephanie, who had turned in her seat and was now staring at the floor. The striplight on the ceiling above them was dim and cast an almost amber light on her. She had a jacket on, but he could see she was cold from the way she held herself.

'I found it by chance,' he continued, reaching down to grasp the evidence bag and move it to the front of the folder. 'There's a gap in the ceiling in your old bedroom, it seems. Wouldn't take much to stand on a chair, shift the tile and stuff something in the attic. If I hadn't flashed my torch across that particular bit of floor, I would have missed it. I don't think anyone was supposed to find it. It's almost like I was meant to.'

He pulled out the letter and held it in his hands. Turned it over and held it in mid-air between them. 'Have you seen this before?'

Stephanie looked at what he was holding, squinting across at him to try and read what was written on it. Mark held it out further towards her and waited. She shook her head, but he couldn't tell if that was in response to his question or not.

'That's Emily's writing, isn't it?' Mark said, trying to prompt her into talking. 'I recognised it from the journal she kept hidden in her bedroom.'

'Yes,' Stephanie replied, her voice quiet and thick with emotion. 'It is. But I don't understand . . .'

'Neither did I,' Mark said. 'Do you want to read what she wrote, or do you want me to read it?'

She didn't answer, simply extending a hand and taking the bag from his hands. He sat back in the seat, staring at the various leaflets and posters attached to the wall. Stephanie read silently opposite him, as he listened for any reaction from her. He remembered most of what was written there and the space was small enough for him to notice a sound without her even realising.

Stephanie read through it in a few minutes, then turned back and read it again. When she was finished, she let the bag rest on her lap and clasped her hands together as if she were offering a silent prayer for an answer to what was happening.

'She's wrong,' Stephanie said finally. 'She got it so wrong.'

'Which part?'

'All of it,' Stephanie replied, and now all tears had disappeared. 'She was stupid. A stupid little girl. I told her . . .

I told her not to mess with things she didn't understand, but did she listen? Of course not.'

'What are you saying?' Mark said, feeling more confused than ever. 'I'm not following you.'

'"I didn't care?" How dare she say that? She knew I did. I spent years trying to help her, but she never listened. Never. She'd just sit there, nodding her head like an idiot and not taking anything in, apparently. And now, she blames me? How could she?'

'Stephanie, you need to calm down—'

'Calm down?' Stephanie shouted, her voice echoing around the room. Mark glanced towards the door, wondering if DS Cavanagh was out there, listening, or if he'd really gone home as he'd said.

'How can I be calm?' Stephanie continued. 'That little bitch could have been like me any time she wanted, but she wasn't willing to be. She could have been friends with my friends. She could have been *my* friend, but she was never willing to do anything about it. She was too lazy. And now ... and now she leaves this behind, just to try and twist the knife a little bit more. I should have known.'

Mark sat open-mouthed, trying to work out what she'd told him. The reaction wasn't at all what he'd expected. He breathed in deeply, let his mind clear. 'She was obviously angry when she wrote this. Why would she be like that towards you? I know you said things hadn't been great between you two, but I didn't get the sense that it was this bad.'

'Neither did I. Guess I got that wrong, just like everything else about us. I spent so long trying to get her to fit in, but she would never listen to me. It was like she was punishing herself, for no damn reason. I had my own shit to deal with as well, so I had to give up eventually. No one was all that nasty to her, they just didn't bother. It didn't mean they didn't care though. They just gave up trying as well.'

'What she says in the note, about doing something to you, what was that about?'

Stephanie sighed, the bag in her hand almost crumpled in her grip. Mark reached across and took it from her before she destroyed it entirely.

'It was nothing. I'd forgotten about it. She obviously thought it affected me more than it actually did. I didn't care.'

'What did she do?'

'She put private pictures of me on a message board. She went through my phone somehow and got them. They were just silly little selfies I sent to someone I was seeing at the time. Nothing fully nude, thankfully, but enough to embarrass me, that was all. Nothing with my face, either, which was something at least. She was angry. I didn't tell anyone because it didn't matter. They were taken down and no one even knew about it. There's enough out there already that no one even cared enough to start sharing them round or anything. No one knew it was me. She told me herself and that was that. We had a row, but it was all sorted.'

'Still, it must have been difficult,' Mark said, trying to take it all in. 'Given everything else she was doing, to other people I mean, you can't have taken it too well. Being lumped in with all of the others.'

'She was angry at herself. We all just got caught in the crossfire. I got off lightly and I don't think that was accidental. She knew I hadn't really done anything wrong to her, despite what she writes in that letter. Honestly, if she had just chilled out a bit, then everything would have been different for her. She couldn't do that though. It doesn't mean what she wrote here is true though. I had nothing to do with what happened to her.'

'You said she had messed with things she didn't understand . . .'

Stephanie made a noise as if to speak, then stopped herself. She seemed to grow smaller in her seat, as Mark looked at her. She opened her mouth, then closed it again.

'What?'

'I shouldn't have said anything, it doesn't mean anything.'

'You need to tell me,' Mark said, firmer now, seeing that, if anything, he'd only made the whole case even more incomprehensible. He began to feel out of his depth, but ploughed on regardless. He couldn't just let it all go. 'I've taken a chance on trusting that you had nothing to do with what happened. That's why we're in here and not an interview room under caution. Now, you need to trust me.'

'It's nothing. It's silly.'

He remembered the words written in the letter, what Emily had mentioned, and knew there was only one question to ask her now.

'Stephanie,' Mark said, reaching out a hand and resting it close to where she was sitting. 'What's The Game?'

She didn't answer immediately, swallowing hard and rubbing a hand across her face. 'It could be why she's dead.'

Forty-Four

Mark waited for Stephanie to explain what she meant, but she had gone suddenly quiet. Her eyes glistened as he waited, unable to take his eyes away from her. He wanted to push her, to force her to explain, but he didn't think that would work.

'It's not supposed to be a real thing,' Stephanie said, almost at a whisper, without conviction. 'It's just a stupid thing that got passed around school one year.'

'What is it?'

'There's this story. Started online. Someone finds out some kind of secret you have and makes you play some kind of game. It erases the bad thing you've done and makes it all forgotten. You just had to do certain tasks first. Like levels in a video game. We scared each other with it, that sort of thing. It wasn't like anyone actually did anything with the secrets.'

'Emily talks about it differently though, as if it's really happening to her. As if she was being made to play it,' Mark replied, leaving the words he almost said safely unspoken.

Or she did.

'I never thought it was a real thing people did. No one

did, not really. We all knew it was just something that had been made up. Some stupid, online bullshit that didn't really mean anything.'

'Why would she think it was real though?'

Stephanie shrugged in response, but Mark could see there was something she wasn't saying either. He decided to try a different tack.

'Where did it start?'

'I don't know. It was one of those things, you know, that just gets passed around school and that. A group of us talked about it in school and that was it. There's a whole bunch of people who talk about it online though. Emily must have heard about it. That's all.'

'Why would she be interested in it? Do you think she would have believed in it?'

'I . . . I don't know. Maybe, if she'd done something even worse than we know about, someone could have made her play The Game or something. But it's not a real thing. It's just a story. No one actually makes anyone do anything like this.'

Mark leaned back in his chair, closed his eyes and stroked his forehead with his fingers. Wondered how the hell he'd ended up in a mess such as this. 'Is it possible someone used this thing to get back at her? Made her think if she played this game, she could make up for something?'

'We spoke about it. Once.'

'What did she say?'

'I can't really remember. It was a while ago.'

This time, Mark didn't hide his disappointment in her answer. He gave her a look to tell her so. 'Come on, you know that's not true as much as I do. You spoke to Emily about this game . . .'

'The Game.'

'Right, "The Game",' Mark said, using his fingers to emphasise the point that he didn't really understand what this was all about. 'Is it possible, with all the things that she's done over the past year or so, that it could have been used against her?'

'I don't know . . .'

'Obviously she said something, or did something, that resonated. Otherwise you wouldn't remember it. You need to start telling me everything. This is too serious now. No one thinks you have anything to do with Emily's death at the moment, but that can change if you keep things from me. People will think you're lying by omission and think you have something to hide. You've got to give me something to work with here.'

'I never asked you to do anything.'

Mark sighed and leaned forward in his seat. 'I know you didn't, but you need answers. Your mum and the rest of the family need them as well. Right now, this is what we have. I need you to start talking to me.'

It was Stephanie's turn to sigh. 'It was a few months back, when I came home from university for the summer. I was going to be living back at the house, but I decided to stay with some mates instead. One of them had digs and a spare bed, which made more sense than moving back home for a couple of months. Easier all round. Emily wasn't happy, but I didn't understand why. Whether it was the thought of being on her own, even though we both hated sharing a bedroom. Or that I had friends and she didn't. I don't know. I went round there and wanted to pick up some of the clothes I'd left at home. She came in the bedroom while I was going through them. She asked me about it. The Game, I mean. Asked if I knew anyone who had actually done it. Played. I said no, because it wasn't real.'

'Did she tell you why she was asking?'

Stephanie nodded her head, her hands clasped together in her lap. 'Yeah, she said she'd been looking into The Game. Said she'd found some things online that had made her interested in it. Looking back now, I think she wanted to talk to me more about it because of what I'd done in sixth form.'

'Sixth form?'

'Oh, I did some kind of project about it,' Stephanie replied, her hands unclasping quickly. 'About modern-day myths and how they become part of wider societal thinking. Proper college level, pseudo-intellectual bullshit. Stories interwoven into the fabric of how we think, how we act ... all that rubbish. I'd used The Game as an example and talked about some real-life examples of mysterious disappearances, to do with other kinds of online games of this sort. That kind of thing. There's very little out there about it, to be honest. Some forums online that talk about it, but it's always different. All with different rules.'

Mark began to see things becoming clearer, but still wasn't sure if he could make this even slightly believable to DI Bennett. 'And Emily asked you about it?'

'She had obviously read my essays on it and had her own questions. Problem was, she didn't want to talk to me. It was still tense between us. Not from my side, but I think she still felt guilty about what she'd done. She wanted to know if I'd ever found a case where it was proven that someone had actually played it. Of course, I couldn't give her that. It's not like it's a real thing. And even if it was, it's not like we'd ever know for sure. It was a day or so later that it all came out anyway, so it was forgotten about.'

'What came out?'

'All the stuff she was doing to people online,' Stephanie said, another dismissive wave of the hand. He guessed she had been more bothered when what Emily had been doing was first revealed, but had a little perspective now. 'That came out and it was just endless after that. I was doing damage control for her from that point until I went back to university. People wanted blood, but I managed to keep the worst of it controlled. She denied doing it, but the evidence was all there. That was bad enough when it got out, but if she'd done something even worse, it could be the reason someone could have forced her to play The Game. And she didn't think she had any choice.'

'The pictures, of you – when did that happen?'

'Around the same time. She denied doing that as well, but I knew when she was lying. Mum never found out, thankfully, and hopefully she never will. Emily was . . .'

'Troubled?' Mark said for her, when it became clear Stephanie was struggling to find the right word. He used the one she'd given him a few days earlier, when they'd been sitting in her bedroom. When they had still hoped to find her alive. 'So, I think I'm starting to put this together.'

'Really? Because to me, it all seems so much more difficult to work out. If this was someone online, it could be anyone.'

'There is that,' Mark replied, leaning back and scratching the growing stubble on his cheek. Made a decision. 'There was another girl found dead this week. A student living in the new block, down past the Baltic Quarter on the waterfront.'

'The one we saw . . .'

'Yes. She was called Joanna Carter, not sure if you were ever told her name?'

'We were, to see if we recognised it or if it might have been someone Emily was talking to. You asked us.'

Mark nodded slowly, remembering. His memory of the week's events was already becoming jumbled up, he realised. 'Right, of course. Anyway, they think she was killed after seeing what happened to Emily. She was a witness and paid for it. Yards away from where Emily was seen last. Only there was something more. She was a loner, like Emily. Struggled to make friends and seemed to live her life online. And there were some reports that she was doing some strange things in the weeks leading up to her death. I've not found anything to suggest she was doing what Emily was doing to people . . .'

'Catfishing.'

'Right, catfishing. Joanna just seemed to live her life in anonymity on the internet, rather than making friends in the real world. We haven't dug deep enough yet, so maybe she was doing something similar online. Even so, it's sort of similar to what Emily was doing; not living in the real world, finding herself on the internet, etcetera etcetera. On the night of her death – two days after Emily goes missing – the only thing we know for certain is that she was caught on CCTV in the student building. She was in the lift, doing some weird stuff, then outside of it, then she is followed by someone up to the roof. The next morning, her body is found.'

Mark stopped talking, as Stephanie's eyes widened with alarm. He could see flecks of red in the white around her pupils. 'What is it?' he said, pausing from his speech.

'Was she like, pushing buttons and going in and out?'

'Something like that,' Mark replied, about to continue but Stephanie wasn't going to let him.

'That's a version of it. Of a game, I mean. It's called the Elevator Game. That's all online, you can look it up.'

'This just gets better and better,' Mark said, covering his face with both hands. 'So, there's different versions of this game and they're being used to, what, make people pay for things they've done wrong?'

Stephanie opened her mouth to speak, but nothing came out. Instead, she shook her head and shrugged her shoulders. 'I don't know. It all sounds stupid when you say it out loud.'

Mark didn't want to hear any more of this, but couldn't stop it now. He realised what a mistake he had made. Being drawn into this.

He breathed through it and tried to ignore the feeling. Tried to remember why he was there. Why he *wanted* to be there to hear this.

'Emily wouldn't have believed this,' Stephanie said, her voice shaking now, as she struggled to hold back the events of that day. 'She was smarter than that. It's all so stupid. It doesn't even make sense.'

'Could someone have noticed she was talking about it?'

Stephanie shrugged, but didn't say no. Mark tried to walk it back, work out what he actually understood, what would make sense.

'If Joanna Carter had been discovered doing something bad to people, was told the same story, was in the same situation, then it makes sense that the two things could be linked. That someone was making both Joanna and Emily play this game and they were killed at the end of it.'

'Are you saying they both killed themselves or that someone killed them?' Stephanie replied, carefully. 'Because there's a big difference. And Emily definitely didn't kill herself. Maybe that's part of what happened – she fought back. Could that be it? Because she didn't really do anything wrong?'

'I don't know yet,' Mark said, but he felt he was close. Closer than he had been all week. Not to actually finding the person who had done this, but closer to a reason why it had happened.

'I need to find out more about this. It's going to take some time to get people to believe this is a possibility . . . I mean, that both girls were involved in some sort of game and were pushed into doing it.'

'Thank you. For trusting me,' Stephanie replied, a smile briefly appearing on her face, before falling away.

Mark smiled thinly at her, the atmosphere thickening. He suddenly saw the weight she would carry for the foreseeable future. The twin left behind.

After a few seconds, he broke the silence. 'Go back to your mum. Get back home. She'll need you right now.'

He watched her leave as he remained sitting there, processing everything she'd said. Inside his pocket, his phone vibrated. He took it out, seeing Natasha's name on the screen. He paused, then let it go to voicemail. Another missed call from her, to join the others from earlier.

His private life would have to wait. He needed to think.

He needed to work out what to do next to find out who had done this.

Posted: TODAY
Status: Live

All players eliminated.
A new game has begun.
New players chosen.
Player One and Player Two.
They'll think they can bring this to an
end, but we've already won.
KEEP PLAYING THE GAME.
THIS IS OUR TIME.
TIME'S UP FOR THEM.
I'M WITH YOU ALL THE WAY.

Forty-Five

Mark woke to the sound of the vending machine being struck a few times, then a stream of expletives. He rubbed sleep from his eyes, wondering when the thing had been installed in his bedroom. A few moments later, he realised he was sitting upright in the small kitchen next to the incident room at the station.

'You not got a home to go to?'

Mark blinked in the direction of the voice, squinting at the harsh light that suddenly bothered him so much. 'I was working late,' he managed to croak out at the blurred figure of DS Cavanagh.

'Yeah, I can see that.'

As Mark gained more consciousness, he looked down to what DS Cavanagh was gesturing towards. The memories of the long night before came back to him. He began gathering up the mounds of paperwork he'd been working on overnight.

He didn't want anyone to see it all just yet.

'Just some stuff on the case. Came to me late on and I thought I'd get it sorted before the morning. Guess I underestimated how tired I actually was.'

Mark looked at the clock on the wall, seeing that he'd been asleep at least two hours in there. The pain in his neck attested that it hadn't been all that comfortable.

'Yeah, well, the boss isn't in yet,' Cavanagh said with a smirk, then turned back to the vending machine. 'So you've probably got away with it. She'd go mad if she knew you'd fallen asleep in here and not gone home for the night.'

'Course, right,' Mark replied, standing up and shuffling towards the doorway. Pins and needles hit his left leg, but he soldiered on. 'I need to put this together anyway, before she comes in.'

'How did it go with the twin?'

'Some useful stuff. Some not so useful stuff. I think I can say with some certainty that this was a targeted attack and it was from someone she did something to online. She was being made to do something . . .'

'I've got a feeling that something else has turned up on the uncle,' Cavanagh said, before Mark had the chance to continue. He looked back from the doorway, seeing Cavanagh leaning against the vending machine, his arms folded across his chest.

'What?'

'Not sure, but they've interviewed him again this morning already. Clock's running down. Forensics might have found something.'

'It wasn't him.'

'I think you're right,' DS Cavanagh said, then looked at what Mark was carrying. 'What is all that?'

'What?'

'All that stuff,' Cavanagh said, frowning at him. 'Doesn't look like normal paperwork to me. On the wrong paper, for a kick off. Is there evidence there?'

'It's information I printed out,' Mark managed to stutter out. He was suddenly aware of how this would look, how it would sound. He needed to get his story straight on it all, before talking to anyone. Even if Cavanagh was more accepting of his previous theories. 'I need to get it in some sort of order, if what you're saying about the uncle is right.'

'Must have been enough to make you sleep in this place. Can't even get a bloody Mars bar from the vending machine ...'

Mark managed to slip out of the room, as Cavanagh continued to grumble at the machinery. He shoved the papers in his desk drawer and then went into the bathroom. Splashed cold water on his face a few times, then over his hair as well. Ran fingers through it, then dried himself over.

It was ten by the time he was back at his desk, putting what he'd learned overnight in some sort of order. The information he'd managed to gather had been difficult to pull together – taken from a multitude of different websites and forums. He felt he had enough though.

Joanna Carter's email account had helped, along with the private messages in her social media. That might be an issue if he was wrong – it wasn't technically his case, but he'd managed to get access to it. He hoped it wouldn't count against him.

He waited for DI Bennett to arrive and settle into her office before taking a breath and making his way over there. He'd gone through half a pack of Polo mints and was currently chewing on gum. From DI Bennett's look as he entered the room, he didn't think he looked his best.

'I was working late,' Mark said, sitting down, the stack

of papers in his lap. 'Sorry about that. I know you wanted us to go home early—'

'It's fine,' DI Bennett replied, interrupting him with a wave of one hand. 'I've been dealing with delegating out another death this morning. Looks gang-related.'

'What is it?'

'Some young lad, beaten to death in Walton. I've handed it over to Matrix to deal with. They think it's a drug deal gone wrong. What have you got for me?'

'I think we're missing something with both Emily Burns and Joanna Carter. Something that links them together.'

'Really?'

'Yes, it's going to sound a little weird, but I need you to bear with me.'

Mark began to speak, telling her about The Game and the little history he had found on it. It was patchy, nowhere near extensive enough, he knew, but he was building a complete picture slowly. Hoping the amount of information would be hard to ignore.

'So, we have this thing online that is talked about a lot,' Mark said, continuing his monologue. He glanced up at DI Bennett, who was giving away nothing. 'We've seen this sort of thing before, but this seems to be more on the quiet. And it fits perfectly with what we saw Joanna doing on the CCTV. She was re-enacting the rules of one form of this game.'

'She was being made to play some sort of game – that's what you're telling me?' DI Bennett asked, and this time her expression had changed. 'And she was either killed at the end, or killed herself to really atone for her supposed crimes?'

'Yes . . . I mean, no, of course not really,' Mark replied,

hearing the eagerness in his tone. He couldn't let her dismiss this so easily. 'It doesn't really exist. That's not what I'm saying. It's ... it's a form of punishment. Joanna and Emily did something wrong and they had to play a game to atone for it. Say, you got found doing something you were ashamed of and someone came along and said play this game and it'll go away, you'd do it, right? If you struggle with life anyway, you might try it out, right? If you were desperate. Then, if it doesn't work, they're destroyed mentally.'

'So, you've spent all night proving Joanna Carter committed suicide?'

'No, that's not the point,' Mark said, unable to hide the irritation from his voice. Now he really was losing DI Bennett. 'The thing is, I think this is murder. And there are two victims in the past week alone. And more.'

'Go on.'

'Emily's sister spoke with her about this game a few months ago. Stephanie wrote about it in college for an assignment and Emily was asking lots of questions about it. I went through the reports from her laptop and she googled different versions of these games. Joanna Carter did the same thing.'

'I'm not following ...'

'It's a link,' Mark said, trying to keep his cool. To keep calm. 'And that's not all. It got me thinking, about the fact that Joanna's body was found before Emily's, but she died after. Something went wrong with both of these deaths – Joanna, we see someone following her on CCTV. And Emily was beaten before being killed. It was supposed to look like suicide. I started looking at missing people all over the country, who turned up dead.'

'That's a long list, I bet.'

'Of course. I found that pretty quickly. I've found a number of cases that are similar though.' He handed over a pile of printouts he'd been holding back for the right moment. This was it. 'That's six more deaths. Three in Newcastle. Three in Leeds. They were considered suicides, and someone noticed that each of them had displayed odd behaviour in the weeks leading up to them being found. And that's not all. There's probably more. This isn't all just a coincidence. They were all found within days of each other as well. They thought it was a suicide pact each time, but they could never find a link. Not until now. There has to be more out there as well.'

Mark waited as DI Bennett leafed through the pages, sitting back in his chair. It wasn't as heavy on detail as he would have liked, but he thought he'd done enough.

She would see what he could see now.

'I fail to see how any of this has any relation to our case.'

Mark thought he had heard her wrong. 'I don't . . .'

'Mark, you're clearly overworked and knackered. All you've given me here is a silly ghost story kids have told each other and some suicides hundreds of miles away. People kill themselves every day. They're not all connected.'

'Yes, but—'

'But nothing, Mark,' DI Bennett said, pushing the papers back his way and folding her arms across her chest. 'This is ridiculous. You're asking me to believe, what, exactly?'

'The Game . . . it's being used somehow. They've been chosen or volunteered to do it and then they're being murdered.'

'There's no evidence for that—'

'Yes, there is,' Mark said, and now he was shouting. He

didn't care anymore. 'Emily's blood being found away from her body was for a reason. It's because it was supposed to look like she killed herself in that yard. Only it didn't work out that way and she almost escaped. Then, whoever it was panicked and put her where she was found. Probably to frame her uncle when it became obvious she'd been strangled, rather than slit her wrists. It all fits. I bet you anything, if we look into those other deaths, we'd find the same thing. And there'll be more, I reckon. It's obvious.'

DI Bennett didn't say anything, staring him down. She cocked her head, studying his face.

'Look, I know this sounds crazy,' Mark said, lowering his voice and trying to salvage the moment. 'Nothing about this makes any sense, but we can't just ignore what's been happening here. This isn't what it looks like. And more people are in trouble. Holly Edwards, the girl who came in and confessed to Joanna's murder – that could be part of this game. We need to pick her up and find out.'

'We're charging Richard Burns with murder at around lunchtime, I think,' DI Bennett said, her voice betraying no reaction to what he'd just laid out for her. 'Forensics came back on his car this morning. They found Emily's hair in it and we also found blood. Will take a few days to confirm it, but it's enough for a charge for now.'

'Her hair? Of course it'll be in his car. She's his niece. The blood could be from any time—'

'That's enough, Mark,' DI Bennett said, talking over him. 'This is my fault. I should have noticed this was all a bit much for you. It's understandable, it really is, but you're seeing connections when there aren't any. The CCTV might not be as we see it – maybe Rich Burns was stooped over. It's only a short clip. It could be unconnected. Joanna could have seen something she shouldn't have and been killed to keep her quiet. Emily was definitely killed by her uncle. There's just not enough evidence to suggest otherwise. Holly Edwards is a troubled girl, who is now being assessed by the mental health team. That's all there is to this. Just look at the facts. That's all I'm asking you to do.'

'You can't ignore this.'

'I have to, Mark. For now.'

Mark closed his eyes and wished he could go back. To before this week, when all he had to contend with was being ignored or ridiculed. This was somehow worse.

God really hates a trier.

'Let me keep working on this angle. That's all I'm asking for, okay?'

DI Bennett stared at him, then stood up and walked closer to him. 'Take the day and consider things a little more clearly. I don't want to see you back here until tomorrow. You need to get some rest and let us get on with things. There's nothing here, Mark. Maybe a little space is what you need, so you can see what's really going on.'

'I don't want to do that,' Mark said, but could see it was too late. If this was a US cop show, it would be about the time he was being asked for his gun and badge, but it wasn't that. This was the UK and real life. He was being sent away so he couldn't interfere any longer. Quietly moved aside. 'You just want me out the way, isn't that right? So you can shut this case down, wrap it up in a neat little bow. Charge the uncle, because it's always a family member, right? That's what you said to me the other day. You can't see it being anything else, other than a man related to a dead girl.'

'It has nothing to do with that . . .'

'Really?' Mark shouted, and now he could see movement outside the office. 'I came to you because I thought you'd be willing to listen and understand that there's more to this than just a couple of dead teenagers. Instead, I get laughed at. Just like I have been since I joined the team. That's all you lot think of me. Not that I'm one of you, but someone to baby and treat like an interloper. That's right, isn't it? I should have known better.'

'It's time to leave, Mark,' DS Cavanagh said from behind him, standing in the doorway.

Mark looked at him, then back at DI Bennett. 'I thought you were better than ... than them out there. Guess I was wrong.'

He didn't say another word, grabbing his papers and walking out of DI Bennett's office. Mark grabbed his jacket from the back of his chair, sending it spinning a few feet as he did so. He heard the clatter of something falling to the floor as he left, the door slamming behind him.

DS Cavanagh caught up with him as he was waiting for the lift. He pressed the button a few more times, with increasing force, avoiding the man's gaze.

'What?' Mark said, when Cavanagh's presence at his side became too annoying.

'Get a couple of hours' sleep and then get back to it,' DS Cavanagh replied, leaning against the wall and folding his arms across his chest. 'There's something more going on. And if you're the only one who can see that, then so be it. If you need anything, give me a shout. I'm a phone call away. It's better if you're not here for now though.'

With that, DS Cavanagh walked away before Mark had a chance to say anything in response.

It wasn't until he was sitting in his car minutes later,

knuckles turning white on the steering wheel as he gripped it, that reality began to set in.

He'd probably just screwed himself up royally.

He wanted to bang the wheel in frustration. Wanted to scream and shout his feelings away, but it wouldn't help him. It wouldn't help anyone.

There was only way out.

He had to prove he was right.

Forty-Six

Mark drove from the station car park, then pulled into the new retail park further down Great Homer Street. His phone jittered in his hand, as the adrenaline running through him took hold. He forced himself to close his eyes and breathe in and out a few times, but it made no difference.

He looked at his phone and saw a number of missed calls from Natasha. A couple of messages asking him to call her. Mark navigated to the contacts on his phone, then pressed on the last number dialled. Heard the tone a few times, then voicemail kick in. Waited a few minutes, then tried again.

There was still no answer on Natasha's phone.

He closed his eyes again, phone in his hand, waiting for her to call him back.

Back to the case at hand, he thought. His personal life could wait.

There was no way that they would warn Emily's family off speaking to him. It hadn't been that bad, he thought. So he'd lost his temper a little bit – it wasn't like he'd smashed the incident room up or anything like that. He'd shouted and been thrown out. It could have been much worse.

He would put speaking to the family again on the list.

On the passenger seat, the information he'd gathered the previous night was stacked up. He opened his eyes, began leafing through some of the papers, hoping to find something more. Something else he could take back and show DI Bennett or any of the others. Something tangible. One part of him could see the reality of the situation. What he'd tried to pass on to DI Bennett and how stupid it had all sounded.

His phone lay dormant in his other hand, coming to life with a quick swipe. Something had been bugging him since the previous night – something he had read or heard. A distant memory he couldn't quite grasp.

He opened the anonymous Facebook account on his app and began looking around his feed. Saw the link to a news story from the *Liverpool Echo* article, which is when it finally clicked.

He'd seen a mention a few days earlier – before he'd known about the existence of The Game. He clicked on the page and began searching back to the previous news articles, looking for the correct one.

There were more than a few about the events of the previous week. He went through them all as quickly as he could, trying to find the one he'd seen. Reading through endless comments, searching for the one he could only just remember.

It had mentioned The Game. He was sure of it.

It took him ten minutes to finally find it. By that point, his phone was almost dead, so he had to attach the charger in his car to keep it going.

She played The Game and lost. Shame it wasn't the other twin. Would have been more fun.

The comment had been left a couple of days earlier, but now, it seemed like it was something he shouldn't have scrolled past. It was buried under a number of similar comments. Now, it took on a much different light, given what it said.

The Game ...

It was the capitalisation of the word, so odd in comparison to the rest of it. He had dismissed it without even thinking – yet, with what he knew now, it meant more.

It meant that whoever had left the comment could know something.

He clicked on the name of the person who'd left the comment, knowing what was probably going to be the result.

'Bastard.'

There were no details to be seen; all hidden from non-friends. He sent a friend request anyway, hoping it would be accepted without thinking. Then he looked at the name, expecting it to be as fake as the picture.

The picture ...

He clicked on the pictures that were on the profile, a vast array of different anonymous and cartoony characters coming on screen. Even on private profiles, the pictures were available. A history of profile photos switched over a number of years. He swiped through them, eventually finding one that he thought might be the real person.

He was young. Around fourteen or fifteen, he guessed. He looked at the date of the profile picture, realised it was around three years old.

The name could be real then, he thought.

Mark dialled another number. 'Cav, it's Mark,' he said, and heard an intake of breath over the phone.

'Didn't think you'd be calling me this quick,' DS

Cavanagh replied, trying to act cool and calm, he thought. People listening to his conversation possibly.

'Yeah, something has just come to me,' Mark replied, keeping his voice straight, trying to sound as normal as possible. 'I need an address . . .'

All he'd needed was a name and an area. That was enough to get an address for the lad. It sometimes worried him how easy it was to find people, but at that moment he was glad it was that way. DS Cavanagh had been almost entirely silent on the call, before texting him the address he'd needed.

That was two of them in the shit if he didn't get a result now.

He'd tried calling Natasha again on the drive there, but it was still ringing out and going to voicemail. He considered leaving a message, but thought better of it. It would only end up sounding garbled and desperate. He needed to wait until this was over.

The house was in a nice area to the north of the city, bordering the posh bit of Formby and beyond. It was situated in a small cul-de-sac of detached houses, all with their own driveways and manicured lawns. A world away from the council estates a mile or so down the road. He stood back on the doorstep and waited for an answer. Knocked again when a few more seconds went by.

A woman in her forties answered the door, a teatowel in her hands, soap bubbles running up her forearms. She was in full make-up and dress, as if she were about to go for a nice meal. It was almost lunchtime, Mark thought. How the other half live . . .

'Morning,' Mark said, wondering if she would give him even a little time before closing the door. His ID was in his hand just in case. 'I'm Detective Constable Mark Flynn, from the Merseyside Police. I'm looking for John Redwood. Is he home?'

From the look of surprise on her face, he guessed that was the last thing she'd been expecting him to say. She stood open-mouthed for a second, then seemed to find herself again. 'He's . . . he's in bed, I think.'

'Can I come in and have a chat with John? It's important.'

She still didn't move, so Mark lifted his warrant card, just to slam the point home a little further. He doubted she would remember his name very quickly, but he didn't let her linger too long on looking at it.

'Please, come in,' she said, stepping back and letting the teatowel hang at her side limply. She offered her hand and Mark took it, then wiped it discreetly on his trousers as he moved into the house; her hand was still damp, slick with some kind of cleaning product. Her voice was barely constrained Liverpool – the accent of the upper middle class in the city, just prim and proper enough to be accepted into different circles than the norm. 'Excuse the mess, but I wasn't expecting visitors.'

Mark turned to her and smiled. 'That's okay. You have a lovely home. He's upstairs. is he?'

He didn't wait for a response before stepping onto the stairs, hearing a little noise of agreement, before taking them two at a time. It was as much as he'd been expecting when he'd arrived – the rest of the house immaculate, doors opened, all of them apart from one.

He knocked, then let himself in.

'John,' he said, squinting into the darkness. The curtains were drawn, some kind of blackout thing attached to them. 'Get up.'

There was a lump in the bed, unmoving. Behind him, he could hear the mother climbing the stairs. She was making sounds, but none that sounded like actual words. Mark thought she'd finally woken up to the fact that he'd forced his way in and bounded up the stairs to talk to her son. Probably about to make some kind of complaint. He turned back to the door, waiting for her to appear, but a noise from the bed made him move back around.

'It's alright, Mum,' the lump said, sitting up and perching on the edge of the bed. 'I know what this is about. It's all okay.'

Mark turned to where John's mother was standing and smiled at her. She still seemed perturbed by the disturbance, but he knew what she was going to do. She would slip back downstairs and go into full British middle-class form and grumble to herself. Mark closed the door and felt for the light switch, turning it on. John was sitting fully clothed on the edge of his bed.

'You know, don't you?' John said, his shoulders slumping a little. 'I knew it wasn't going to be kept quiet.'

'Know what, John?' Mark replied, taking in the young lad sitting on the single bed. The room was almost exactly like Charlie Burns's had been – teenage angst seeping out of every surface of it. Only John Redwood was eighteen now, so really should have known better. John looked younger though – sixteen at most, Mark thought. His face was still pockmarked with acne, red and angry. His entire body seemed to be bearing a heavy load. Mark had heard the phrase *carrying the weight of the world on his shoulders,* but realised it could be true in this case. John seemed to be collapsing from the strain. Mark tried to breathe through his mouth to mask the smell emanating from him. Sweat and self-abuse. 'Do you want me to tell you who I am first?'

'I heard you talking to my mum downstairs,' John said, rubbing a sleeve of his jacket across his nose. His eyes were as red as the scars on his face. He'd been crying, Mark thought. Dark bags under his eyes, as if sleep was a distant memory.

'You know I'm a detective then,' Mark replied, watching him carefully. He was hoping to have had the upper hand in bursting inside, but he could see that John had almost been waiting for him. Like he knew he was coming, even before he'd knocked on the door. Lying in bed, fully clothed, waiting for the inevitable. 'You know what case I've been working on?'

John frowned, but then nodded his head. 'The dead girl. Emily Burns. And the other one. And you're here now because of her.'

Mark felt his heart quicken, but kept a straight face. 'Because of who, John?'

'Holly,' John said, then stood up. He looked at Mark, blinked a few times, as if he was making a decision. Then, he put his head down and started barrelling towards him.

Forty-Seven

It was hardly a fair fight.

What John had on Mark in weight, Mark had in experience and speed. Mark stood his ground, watching as the lad moved towards him. He grabbed a pudgy arm, twisted it behind John's back with ease, and used his momentum to push him back towards the bed. 'Easy does it, lad,' he said, whispering, hoping too much noise hadn't been made. Even if they'd wrecked the room, he didn't think John's mum was about to burst through the door. Still, he wanted to keep this as quiet as possible.

'Are you going to be good?' Mark said, keeping a grip on the lad's arm. He'd forced it behind his back, but wondered exactly how much damage he could do. He wasn't exactly pliable. He guessed John had used all his energy running the six-foot distance between them. Now he was out of breath and sweating even more. 'I'm not going to do anything but talk to you. If you want to make this more difficult, I'd rather know now.'

'Fine,' John replied, his shoulders sinking as his resistance fell. Mark let go of his arm and he promptly collapsed in a heap, his head dropping into his hands. 'I'm sorry, I just ... I just can't take this anymore. It's not fair.'

Mark shook his head, resisting the urge to sit down next to him and offer words of comfort. 'You need to start talking to me. Now, John.'

'I can't ...'

'I'm not interested in can't. This has gone too far. You need to tell me what's going on. With Holly.'

'You've found her, haven't you? I didn't think it would happen. Not really. She's gone, hasn't she? She's not coming back.'

Mark tried to think quickly, not willing to let on how little he actually knew. 'If you just tell me your side of things, we can sort this out. That sound fair?'

'It's not just her though, is it? It's everything. It all got out of hand. I thought I was doing the right thing. I thought it was going to be okay, but it's all gone wrong.'

'John, I need you to calm down and talk me through it all.' Mark still resisted sitting down, but placed a hand on a large dresser, which rocked a little as he did so. Even in the light from the lampshade above his head, it was still dark in the room. The bed was lying underneath the window, lengthways along the wall. It created a little space in the room, but it was still a small area. Not as claustrophobic as Charlie's box room, but close enough. He chose his next words carefully, hoping to make John think he knew more than he did. 'Start at the beginning. Tell me what you know about this Game.'

There was a sniff, but no tears. Not yet. 'I heard about it online and I realised there was something to it.'

'People online.'

'Yes,' John replied, even though it hadn't been a

question. 'There was this group of people, just like me. All around my age. I found somewhere I could finally be myself. It wasn't long until I saw a few mentions of The Game and what it could mean for people like us.'

'You used it to do what?'

John sighed, his face still mostly buried in his hands. He wouldn't look at Mark. 'It's a secret place we go to talk about it. Online. Only, I didn't think it would actually happen.'

Mark tried not to react. 'So, how did it come here?'

'Where?'

'To Liverpool,' Mark replied, trying to keep his anger in check. 'I know it's happened in other parts of the country.'

'It just happened one day. Someone talked about someone round here and there were a few people who needed to pay for things. That's what he told us.'

'Who told you?'

John acted as if he hadn't heard him and continued on. 'Each game needs two players. That's how it works. Then we all vote on who wins. From everything I know though, it's not like it's a bad thing, really. It's justice. Emily and Joanna were both the same – they needed to pay for what they'd done. And they lost. They were punished for what they had done. Only, I thought we were just messing about. I didn't expect anything to actually happen to her.'

'And what's the story with Holly?' Mark said, but he could already see it. It was crawling all over the room, embedded in the walls. This was just another sad, lonely, teenage boy, who hadn't got what he wanted.

'I was her only friend for years. She should have known what was right. These girls . . . they can't treat us like pets.

There at their beck and call, only to drop us as soon as we ask for more. She owed me. I treated her like a princess and she treated me like shit she'd found on her shoe. She just dropped me, out of the blue. Last year. Years of talking, then it just stopped. I was just, dead inside. All that time, only to have her dismiss me that way. I was upset, angry, everything. I knew her secret as well. What she did to people, but it didn't matter. She knew I'd never tell anyone. My parents took me to the Lake District to get my mind off it. Just a snap decision they made to take me up to the cottage we have up there. Didn't help though. Nothing did. Not until I found that place. The forum for The Game. I had all our conversations saved, so I could show everyone. They read them. All of them. And they could see how she'd manipulated me then thrown me away when she wouldn't accept that I was her best option. She should have been lying on her back, waiting for me, but instead she just used me for what she wanted, then I'm left with nothing. It's not right. Not only that, but what she was doing to people was evil. Something needed to be done. It was just a way of getting back at her. I didn't think anything bad would happen to them, not really.'

Mark listened, trying not to grab the lad by his throat there and then. 'And Emily and Joanna were both nominated by men with the same stories?'

'Pretty much,' John replied, sniffing again. There were still no tears though. 'It was Holly's fault, really. She asked for it. They all do. I tried to tell her that, but she wouldn't listen. If she had just given herself to me, this wouldn't have happened.'

'They're forced to do challenges. Show that they are atoning for their crimes.'

'Holly did some fucked up things online,' John said, wiping a sleeve across his face again. 'When she rejected me, she needed to pay for those things. She had to play The Game and she lost.'

'And they're supposed to be suicides,' Mark said, trying to follow all the lad was saying but failing to keep up with the bullshit. 'That's right, isn't it? So, you vote for the people who should play, then sit back and wait for the results? Is that right?'

'I didn't think anything would really happen to her. I thought it was just talk.'

'I saw Emily's body,' Mark said, his jaw tensing, knuckles turning white as they gripped the dresser. 'Joanna's too. They were both dead. You helped kill them. Those girls are dead because a bunch of little boys can't take rejection.'

'No . . .'

'Where's Holly?'

John's mouth hung open, his eyes glazing over with a film of tears finally. 'I don't know. She was supposed to have been found by now. We could have a say on how they were found. Emily wasn't supposed to be found like that. It was supposed to be like Joanna.'

'Tell me where you wanted Holly to be found.'

'It was supposed to be a nice place, not far from Crosby Beach. I thought that would help the family, you know? Help them get over it quickly. If she had chosen somewhere that seemed okay.'

'She hasn't even been reported missing yet,' Mark said, and enjoyed the reaction from John. He could see him take in the news; understand that he had revealed more than he'd needed. 'There might still be time to save her, do you understand?'

John shook his head. 'It's too late. She's gone. He showed us.'

'How?'

'On there,' John replied, gesturing towards the laptop perched on his bedside cabinet.

'Show me,' Mark said, then moved across to the laptop and picked it up. He dropped it on John's knees and finally sat down next to him. Being that close to the lad almost made him gag. He wanted more than anything to break something in his body, but resisted the urge. 'I want to see what you've been sent.'

John hesitated, then looked at Mark for a second and realised he had no choice. Mark watched as he opened the computer and begin inputting passwords to get onto the home screen.

'What's that?' Mark said, pointing to the screen. 'I've never seen that before.'

'It's a special browser,' John replied, his voice barely above a mumble. 'Helps me get into parts of the web that are hidden.'

Mark nodded, continuing to watch as John worked his way through a multitude of screens. He knew what he was looking at now. It had been part of his training, but not a major aspect of it. There were specialist officers who would deal with this sort of thing thankfully. The Dark Web, they called it. He'd only experienced it in relation to things like child abuse images being shared and the sale of drugs. It seemed like there was more to it than that, however.

'Here,' John said, after a minute or two. He sat back a little, allowing Mark to get a closer look at the screen. 'That's what was posted last night. As promised.'

Mark took the laptop from John's knees and shifted

away from him. On screen, a series of photographs were displayed. Each were blurred and in very little light, but he could see enough to realise what he was looking at.

A young girl. Woman. No more than eighteen, he thought. Her eyes were closed, no outward signs of injury. She was propped up against a tree, a rope beside her in further photographs. He kept looking through, hoping to see something that would suggest they weren't real, but nothing came.

'This is Holly?' Mark said, hearing the anger in his voice now. John recoiled at the sound of it. Mark turned towards him. 'Tell me.'

John nodded, teardrops escaping his eyes and falling down his cheeks. 'I know it doesn't look good, but you have to believe me, I didn't want this. I thought they would just scare her.'

Mark shook his head, trying to take in what he was seeing and hearing. The insanity of it. He laid the laptop on the bed and stood up, one hand going into his pocket and grasping his phone. He'd ring the station and explain it all. At least they would listen to him now.

'You know you're going to have to come with me, John,' Mark said, opening his phone from its lock screen and finding the direct number to the incident room. 'We're going to need to find Holly's body and you're going to tell us everything you know.'

'And the other one as well,' John replied, resigned to his fate it seemed. He shifted forward on the bed. 'I'm guessing that's how you found me.'

Mark frowned, his forehead creasing as he tried to work out exactly what John was talking about. 'Who else?'

'The other woman. The one he told us about,' John

said, as if Mark should have already known. 'You saw me, right? Outside her house? That's how you know it was me involved, with that woman you're always with? I thought that was why you were . . .'

It took Mark a second, then he understood. 'Natasha? What's happened to her?'

'He's taken her. She's the new player.'

Forty-Eight

She had been so close. To finding them. To stopping them.

She had been trying to call Mark – to tell him that she had names to give him. Young men, young women, all involved in an online ring.

It hadn't taken much to infiltrate their little place. Just one person who could see it wasn't just make-believe.

That they were really going through with their plans.

It ended with the feel of breath on her neck as she'd slept fitfully.

The sense of it, warm and balmy, had been almost a comfort. Rhythmically beating against her neck, as her eyes flickered open and shut. The room was still dark and she could hear the low murmur of her phone from the bedside table, playing music softly. Blurred notes, playing an unfamiliar melody.

She had been in the blissful moments between wakefulness and sleep, as the breathing warmed the skin of her neck. Soothing her into consciousness.

The music played on.

She hadn't wanted to move; the bed becoming like a cocoon. The weight of the blanket on top of her, almost wrapping her entire body in warmth. The presence of another person beside her.

The breath on her neck.

Her body had switched on in stages. Her head clearing the fog slowly, as she became aware of each part of herself. One arm had been trapped under her torso, her mind telling her to move from her side to her back.

Another part of her had wanted to stay in the bliss of sleep. Screw her eyes shut and ignore the outside world for longer.

Something stopped her from dropping back off, just as she would have done at any other time. A voice in her head, a warning. Something not right with what was happening.

A hand clamped over her mouth, just as she was about to scream.

Natasha didn't know where she was. What was happening? Did anyone know she had gone? She didn't know how long it had been since the previous night, when someone had taken her from her bed, hands grabbing and incapacitating her before she could react.

She could hear a noise, but couldn't place it. A low, humming sort of sound. She imagined it was what people who had tinnitus heard constantly. She was becoming more aware of the smaller things, now her other senses had been shut off. She couldn't see, couldn't touch. Couldn't move.

She could smell, but didn't want to think about what it was that was around her. The rotting smell of decay. Couldn't allow herself to consider what that might mean.

No one knew where she was.

There was only one reason for her being there.

Natasha tried to move again, screaming into the cloth in

her mouth. Her screams echoed back into her head, but they didn't escape her mouth. Her struggle to break the binds that tied her was similarly useless. She was unable to move much at all, a few inches with her hands, her legs. She was almost stuck fast, roped and bonded to whatever it was.

She didn't know how she had got there. It was a blur of darkness and noise. A hand over her mouth as she slept, then an arm across her throat until she had seen bright stars and then, nothingness.

There was no reason for her to be there.

If she had just ignored what she had found out, then she would never have put herself there.

She wanted to scream at that thought.

She needed to get free. She struggled again, a rumbling in the back of her throat, as she used all her strength to try and break whatever was holding her down.

It was no use. She wasn't going to escape.

Natasha thought of Mark. Imagined him bursting into the ... room? Warehouse? She didn't know what. It didn't matter. If he could find her, she knew he would help her get out of that place.

There was a noise somewhere in front of her, then a distinct changing of the atmosphere. It became colder somehow, as if the little heat that was in there had been sucked out.

Then, the voice again. Moving towards her. It set her back on edge, straining with everything she had, a noise escaping her throat. Instantly cut off before it could echo around her.

'Shhh,' the voice said, and it was somehow worse now. As if it had been merely playing with her until that point. 'Stay calm and nothing will happen to you.'

She couldn't place an accent or even something familiar

about it. He sounded young, but she wasn't sure if that was even right.

Natasha bucked and moved as she felt his breath again. His presence over her. Rocked back and forward, trying to do something. She needed to speak to him. Tell him he'd made a mistake.

'It'll all be okay soon,' the voice said, something inhuman and perverse about the way he spoke. 'He's coming for you and it'll all be over. The white knight, coming to save you. Riding in and saving the day. Only, we both know that won't be the end of it.'

Natasha gritted her teeth and tried even harder to move, but it was useless.

'There's going to be a new game,' the voice said, moving away now. His footsteps grew softer and quieter, as he crawled backwards. 'That's going to be your punishment for trying to stop us. You'll be nothing but a shell by the time I've shown you the way.'

More time passed.

She exhausted herself trying to escape. The smell and dampness of the air was suffocating. A fog she couldn't see, could almost feel.

There was no way out.

As the minutes ticked by on some unseen clock, the anger rose inside her. The silence became restrictive and mind-numbing.

Then, the presence came back. Hauled her to her feet and guided her on unsteady legs. When she fell over for the second time, she was lifted with ease. She struggled against it, but it was useless. Firm, painful hands pressed into her flesh, making her scream soundlessly with pain.

Seconds later, she could feel the atmosphere shift; cold air swirled around her as she realised she was outside. Not for long. Not long enough. The sounds turning again.

She wanted to cry, but gritted her teeth against her tears. She had to be strong. She had to find a way out of whatever situation she was in.

Her mind was blank, as the movement beneath her changed.

This was it.

The end.

Whatever that might be.

Forty-Nine

Mark was diving on John before he had the chance to react. His hands gripping his jacket below his shoulders and lifting the lad to his feet, with a great effort that Mark wasn't aware of. He came willingly, dragged into standing, a small whelp of surprise escaping from his mouth.

'What are you talking about?' Mark shouted, his voice bouncing off the walls around them. 'What have you done to her?'

'I thought you knew,' John replied, a whimper in reaction to Mark. 'I thought . . .'

'Where is she?' Mark moved the boy across the room with ease, running on autopilot now. He shoved him against the bedroom door, something falling to the floor as he did so. He was barely aware of noise from the stairs beyond, almost all his attention on John and his sweating face. 'Start talking now.' He slammed him into the door again, to make his point.

'I don't know, I really don't,' John replied, blubbering over his words now. 'Please, let me go, you're hurting me.'

'If you don't tell me, I'll really start hurting you, okay? What did you do?'

Outside the door, he heard a small voice. John's mum, coming up to check what was going on. Mark didn't care. He could only think of what was being said to him. Natasha.

'They saw you with her over the past few days,' John said, choking on every syllable. The faint aroma of urine drifted up from him. 'They . . . they thought you were on to us. What we were doing. He had to be told.'

'Who did?' Mark replied, stepping back slightly in disgust. 'Who is he? Tell me what you know. Tell me where he is.'

'I . . . I . . .'

On the door behind them, there was a knock. Quiet at first, then becoming more insistent. Mark grabbed John harder, moving him back across the room, and sitting him down on the bed. 'Get in contact with him now. Find out where he is. You'd best hope nothing has happened to her.'

Mark moved back towards the door, ran a hand through his hair, and then opened the door slightly ajar. He slipped out, without allowing John's mum to see inside. She was standing on the landing, stepping back as Mark came out. Her hands were on her hips now, more front than when he'd arrived.

'What's going on in there?' she said, indignant, voice shaky. 'I demand to know what you're doing to my son.'

'I'm afraid John is in a bit of trouble,' Mark replied, looking down at the woman and keeping his voice straight, free of the emotion that was coursing through his veins. 'I need you to understand this is serious, but if he cooperates, we might be able to get him out of this. Can you do me a favour?'

John's mum stammered out a reply, clearly reeling from what he'd said. 'What's he done?'

'He'll explain everything soon, but first, you need to do something for me. Okay? Don't worry. Hopefully this can all be sorted out quickly.'

She didn't answer at first, opening and closing her mouth, looking back down the stairs towards the front door. 'What do I have to do?'

'I want you to call this number,' Mark said, taking out a pen and his notebook. He wrote down the number and tore off the page. He handed it over to her. 'This is my direct superior's number. His name is Detective Sergeant Stuart Cavanagh. In five minutes, ring him, and say Detective Constable Mark Flynn told you to call about your son. Tell him he has information about Emily Burns, Joanna Carter and Holly Edwards.'

John's mum thrust her hand to her mouth. 'The dead girl . . .'

'Don't worry,' Mark said, swallowing his disgust and placing a hand on her shoulder. 'He's going to be okay. Don't let him leave if I have to go before they get here. Just explain everything to DS Cavanagh and he'll do the rest, okay?'

Mark could see she wasn't really taking in what he was saying. 'John's going to be fine,' he lied, knowing that there was nothing further from the truth. If he could get it out of him, he had no doubt that he'd break down completely after being properly arrested. This was coming to an end. 'He's just made a few silly mistakes that we need to sort out.'

'Did he . . .'

'No, he didn't kill them,' Mark said, when it became clear she couldn't finish the sentence. 'But he knows what happened. He's got involved in something he shouldn't have and now it's all gone too far to ignore.' The lies fell out of his mouth without him even thinking about them. 'It's going to be okay, but he needs to help the detectives who are working on the case ... alongside me. He needs to tell them everything, otherwise it won't end well for him. Now, go downstairs, and John will follow you down shortly.'

Mark waited to see if she would simply accept his instructions, knowing she would. Anywhere else in the city, he would expect an argument, but he knew this area. The people who were from these parts were too scared to open their mouths or disobey.

That's what he hoped. He couldn't talk to DS Cavanagh himself – he didn't want to give him the chance to talk him out of what he was going to do next.

She walked off down the stairs and Mark moved back into the bedroom, closing the door behind him. 'Well?'

'What?'

'Have you contacted him?'

John was choking on his sobs now, but the laptop was open beside him. 'I sent him a message, asking where he's taken Holly. I thought that would be the same place as your girlfriend.'

'Her name's Natasha and you'd best hope nothing has happened to her.'

'Right, right, okay, please ...'

Mark let go of John's jaw, wondering at what point he'd grabbed it. He was running on nothing but instinct now, making decisions before he'd had a chance to consider them. 'What happens, after you send him a message? Will he respond?'

'He should do. He always does. He talked me through

everything that would happen, then shared it on the forum. He told us exactly what happened with the others.'

'I don't understand how he gets them to do the things,' Mark said, motioning a whole lot of nothing with his hands. 'We saw one of them on CCTV – she was doing something in a lift ...'

'Joanna,' John cut in, then clamped a hand over his mouth. Mark was beginning to think John would be the worst person to turn to in a crisis. He crumpled under pressure far too easily.

'Yes, that's right,' Mark replied, swiping a hand across his own face, the sound of rough stubble bristling into his ear. 'If you just wanted them out of your life, if it was just about getting rid of them, then I don't understand the rest of it. Why make them do all the rest? Why not just go after them elsewhere?'

'Because it has to be that way,' John said, as if he were explaining something which didn't really need an explanation. As if it were normal. 'The rest ... it's just for fun. To see if they can be made to do anything they're asked to do. It's proper punishment.'

Mark rolled his eyes, trying to keep his composure. He winced as he bit into his lip too hard. 'I think it's more about making them look disturbed. You see that video of Joanna, doing her lift thing, and it looks like bizarre behaviour. It's designed to make people willing to accept she would commit suicide. It's a way of whoever this guy is covering his tracks.'

Which made it stranger that he was willing to snatch Natasha when they had no real idea of his existence anyway. An innocent man was on the verge of being charged with Emily's murder and Joanna's death was being treated as suicide.

Would he know that?

'It's the ritual,' John mumbled, but Mark could see his resolve on that idea was beginning to crumble as well. Given enough time, John could probably be convinced of anything.

Mark didn't think John believed what he was saying anymore. It had probably sounded right, back when it was just words on a screen, anonymity giving him a barrier between what was real and what wasn't. Now, a detective was standing in his bedroom, and he was confronted with the fact that what he'd set in motion had had consequences.

And all Mark could think about was Natasha and whether she would be just another victim.

What have you done?

John's head snapped towards the laptop as a low pinging sound came from the speakers.

'Is that him?' Mark said, moving closer, as John snatched up the computer.

'Yes, he's got back to me,' John said, motioning with his head towards the screen. 'I think he's told me where she is. He'll tell me the truth. He always has.'

'Right, yeah,' Mark replied, moving him to one side, so he could sit in front of the laptop and read the screen. There was a familiar-looking message box in the middle, but everything surrounding it was alien to him. The numbers in the address bar, the format of the site. It was all seemingly designed to stop people accidentally stumbling across it. He read the reply.

There was an address and one line of text and that was it. Nothing else to the message.

HE HAS TO COME ALONE OR SHE DIES.

Mark didn't think twice, pulling out his phone and typing into the search bar of his Maps app. It was a fair distance away, but he thought he could be there within a couple of hours.

'Stay here, John,' Mark said, standing up and closing the laptop over. Considered again, and then picked it up, placing it under his arm. 'They'll be on their way here now and you're best telling them exactly what you've told me. Try and escape – I'll track you down personally and that time I won't be so nice. Understand?'

John nodded his head, collapsing in on himself now. Disgusting, sobbing sounds fought their way from between the hands covering his face. 'I'm ... I'm sorry. I ... I don't want to go to prison. I ... I didn't do anything.'

'Tell them everything, John,' Mark repeated, making his way towards the bedroom door. 'That's your only hope. I'll tell you this, though – those girls are dead because of you and your friends. You're going to have to accept that. Those girls were murdered and it's your fault.'

Mark didn't wait to hear anymore, making his way out of the bedroom and down the stairs. John's mum was standing in the doorway to the living room, staring at him, shock plastered across her features.

'Call them,' Mark said, reaching for the front door. 'Now. You understand?'

'Yes,' she replied, nodding her head for extra effect. 'What's going on?'

'Ask your son. He needs to speak to the detectives and tell them everything.' Mark went to leave, then turned back. 'Tell them I'll be in touch soon, but I have to do something first.'

He left then, opening the front door and jogging to his

car. He threw the laptop into the backseat, then jumped in. He plugged his phone into the charger, then set up the navigation on the map, and started driving.

The message had been clear. Go alone, or she dies. It made the decision an easy one. He knew he should have ignored it – got in touch with Cavanagh and told him what was happening.

The only way to make sure nothing happened to her was to do it this way. It had to be just him.

He just hoped he was right and it wasn't already too late.

Fifty

Mark's phone buzzed in its cradle, but he ignored it. He was on his own again now, had to be. The voice on the sat nav guided him out of the city and further north. That was all he was interested in now. The destination. The rest of it could wait. He could worry about everything else later.

First, he had to get to Natasha.

Along the journey, his brain worked overtime. Doubt creeping in the entire time.

He continued to ignore it.

The day had passed in a blur. The sun had started disappearing an hour or so earlier, winter nights drawing in closer. He was barely more than sixty miles out of Liverpool, but travelling up the M6 had brought home the differences quickly. The countryside on both sides of the motorway – the Yorkshire Dales and Lake District only a little further up the road on either side. The city of Liverpool a distant memory.

'Your destination is two hundred yards away.'

He pulled his phone out of the cradle, switching off the

map after a glance to make sure he knew where he was going, then locked it and placed it in his pocket. Then thought again and pulled it out to check it.

A whole heap of missed calls, a series of text messages. They were all from the station, the texts from DS Cavanagh, all becoming increasingly fraught.

> Get in touch, now.

> You need to tell us what you're doing.

> We want to help you! Get back to us!

> What have you done?

> Where are you????

> You're not in trouble Mark. We need to hear your side of the story. You need to contact us.

He imagined by now that John had started talking. Probably making wild claims and accusations. Put together with Natasha disappearing overnight, they would become suspicious and wonder what he was doing. If someone had noticed Natasha had gone at all.

It was why John's laptop was currently sitting in his car. He didn't want to leave it there and give him a chance to erase every bit of evidence linking him to what had happened.

Mark considered ringing in and telling them everything, but there was another part of him louder and more insistent. Everything told him he needed to do this alone. That it was the only way to make sure she was safe.

If they came mob-handed, it would mean whoever was doing all of this would feel cornered. Trapped. Like an ensnared animal, they would panic and be liable to do anything.

He needed to do this alone.

Mark pocketed the phone and shook off his seat belt. Outside, the sky had turned black, clear and cold. He looked at the time, then got out of the car.

Up ahead, there were only bushes lining the narrow road. He stuck to the side, walking carefully and quickly. By now, he'd memorised the address. Only it wasn't really an address, he understood now. It was a road name, which thankfully the sat nav had recognised, but he imagined most people wouldn't even know this place existed. He was in an area that didn't see many visitors at all, he guessed. A narrow dirt track of a road, which led to the countryside beyond, away from civilisation.

A lock-up garage, number 2A.

The bushes came to an abrupt end, low-level garages appearing out of the ether almost. They were run-down, some of the doors rusted and overgrown with plants and other vegetation. Overhanging trees bordered the land, their branches drooping and touching the roofs of the small structures. They didn't look in use, abandoned and waiting to be levelled, so a new thing could take their place. Mark guessed this hadn't been a spur of the moment choice.

In the ten minutes since he'd got out of the car – longer since he'd driven down the back road – he hadn't heard a single engine. A single signifier of other life, that someone else knew this place existed. It was deserted, as if he had stepped into another world.

The thought made his heart beat a little faster.

He strained to hear any sort of noise – a cry or plea for release. He imagined Natasha wouldn't have come quietly, but there was nothing but the whisper of the wind, rippling through the branches and greenery that surrounded him.

The numbers on the garage doors were faded and peeling. They started at 14, going down sequentially. Soon, he was standing outside 2A, wishing he had a plan. He'd concentrated so hard on getting there that he hadn't thought about what he would actually do when he arrived.

In the middle of the door was a handle, flat and cold to the touch. The wind picked up, whipping across him and sending a shiver down his spine. He reached out and tried it, pushing in the centre lock and pulling it.

It was locked.

He looked around for something, anything, that might give him some inspiration for what to do next. All the garages were connected, so there was no side window for access. He walked around, hoping for a way in at the back. The terrain was worse here, overgrown brambles and countryside trying to reclaim the land. When he finally made it to the back, he only found a brick wall.

There was no way in other than via the door.

He walked back round, considering his next move. He grabbed the handle and started banging against the door.

'Is there anyone in there?'

His voice sounded odd in the silence. Filled with eagerness and fear. Now he was there, he realised how woefully out of his depth he was. He listened at the door, wondering if he'd already scared whoever was inside enough to do something stupid. He couldn't hear anything.

'Look, I just want to talk to you,' he tried, hoping this time he sounded a little more authoritative. In his pocket, his phone buzzed again, insistent against his leg. 'I just want to make sure she's okay.'

Still no answer.

Mark stepped back, trying to work out what his next move should be. He was lost, his brain insisting he do something, but not giving him a clue what that something should be. The buildings were old, under his feet the ground dirty and unkempt.

His phone buzzed again. He took it from his pocket, resigning himself to the fact he couldn't do this alone. That he'd have to call it in and try to explain what he was doing. The screen illuminated in the darkness, a withheld number calling him.

Mark swiped a finger across the screen, answering the call. Knowing who it was.

'*THANK YOU FOR COMING. PLEASE COME INSIDE. THE KEY IS UNDER THE MAT. WIPE YOUR FEET BEFORE ENTERING. SHE'S WAITING FOR YOU.*'

The call ended, the line going dead before Mark had a chance to say anything. The voice had been robotic – non-human – with no hint of tone about it at all. He took the phone from his ear, as the phone went to black. He checked the call log, but all that showed was PRIVATE NUMBER, which meant he couldn't call it back.

He checked over his shoulder, staring into the darkness of the fields in the distance. Looking for something that didn't fit with the rest of what he could see. He needn't have bothered. He could barely see further than the road.

Mark had that feeling of someone watching him again. He tried to ignore it, focusing instead on what the voice had said.

He moved quickly without further thought, dropping to his knees and swiping his hands at the foot of the door. There was no mat, of course, but he was hoping there was something that he could lay his hands on. He couldn't see what he was doing, considered walking back to the car and finding his torch, before remembering his phone had one of its own.

Mark switched it on and began sweeping the floor, looking for something that didn't belong. He found it quickly – a triangular structure, propped up against the brick to the side of the door. Unless you were looking for it, you wouldn't notice it, blending into the background, grass growing up and running up its side to mask it further. He grabbed it, moving it aside, underneath a key.

He picked it up, scrambling to his feet and holding his phone in one hand, slid it into the lock on the handle. It took a few seconds before he worked out how to open it up: pushing it in and then twisting the entire handle. Mark heard something click, then the door was rising up, the bottom half extending towards his legs. He stepped back, grasped the bottom of the door and pushed it up.

The smell hit him first.

It wasn't a foreign aroma. He'd experienced it before, several times. Part of his brain snapped into focus and reminded him what it was, while the other part tried to ignore his senses.

He could smell death.

Mark lowered his head, the phone in his hand now pointing the light towards the floor. He was too late. His legs turned to jelly, as a million butterflies took flight inside his abdomen.

He was too damn late.

A guttural noise rumbled in the back of his throat. The phone in his hand digging into his palms, as sound escaped him. A moan, a scream, a roar.

How was he too late?

Mark blinked into the present, his hands on his knees, a small spotlight shining into the floor behind him. His breaths came in short bursts, loud and filled with anger.

He straightened up, moving the phone in his hand to the wall nearest to him. He didn't want to see by the light of the torch on his phone; he would have to get too close for that, he thought. He didn't want to disturb the scene any more than he already had.

A dirty white light switch was on the brick. Mark moved his sleeve down his hand and carefully pressed it. A noise came from overhead, a few clinks and flashes of dim light, then a small strip of fluorescent illuminated the garage.

She was at the far wall.

She had been discarded, it seemed. Dragged along the floor, then placed against the wall. Her head lolled forwards, her hair covering her face. Her trousers had been torn apart, barely holding on to her hips, even as she was lying on them.

She wasn't long-haired.

She wasn't tall.

She wasn't Natasha.

The flash of relief was replaced quickly with shame. It still meant there was someone else dead in the garage and the likelihood was that it was Holly Edwards. He realised he didn't know anything about her. Who she was, where she came from. All he knew was what John Redwood had told him and he didn't want to take his word on anything.

He didn't know what to do next. Natasha was still missing and whoever had killed Holly Edwards knew he was there.

Had known he was coming.

He turned around quickly, expecting a shadow to be standing in the opening, but it was as he'd left it. The phone in his hand started buzzing again.

Mark lifted it to his ear, not having to look at the caller ID to know who was ringing him.

The robotic voice came over the speaker, into his ear.

'YOU'RE GOING TO PLAY A GAME.'

Fifty-One

'Where is she?'

Mark spat the words down the phone, but the voice remained robotic, emotionless.

'YOU'RE GOING TO PLAY THE GAME. PLAY OUR GAME OR NATASHA DIES. IT'S THAT SIMPLE. I HOPE YOU ENJOY IT.'

'Talk to me properly,' Mark said, walking towards the doorway and stepping back out into the road. 'Come out and face me.'

There was only static on the line, the call still open but no response coming back.

'Where are you?'

'WE ARE EVERYWHERE, MARK. YOU WANTED TO KNOW WHAT THE GAME WAS AND NOW YOU HAVE YOUR CHANCE. ONLY *YOUR* GAME WILL BE DIFFERENT.'

'How?' Mark said, looking all around him, hoping to see a glint of something in his surroundings. A movement, a figure. Anything that would give him a chance.

'YOU ARE GOING TO GIVE YOUR LIFE FOR HERS. IT IS VERY SIMPLE.'

Mark shook his head. 'I don't believe you. Show me her first.'

'THAT WILL NOT HAPPEN, MARK. YOU NEED TO HEAR THE RULES NOW. YOU DO NOT HAVE MUCH TIME. THEY WILL BE HERE VERY SOON. YOUR FIRST LEVEL IS APPROACHING. YOU NEED TO GET READY.'

'You can't make me kill myself,' Mark said, wondering if he could actually do that, whether he could sacrifice his own life for someone else's. He'd always thought he could; whether for a family member or someone he was protecting. Wasn't that what he was doing with Natasha anyway? Wasn't that why he was there, alone, trying to save the day?

'THAT IS NOT THE GAME. YOU ARE GOING TO END IT. HER LIFE FOR YOURS.'

Mark didn't understand, a wave of tiredness washing over him suddenly. He didn't want to be there anymore. He wanted to start over. Never hear the name Emily Burns again. Never hear about any damn game.

He wanted it to be over.

'WILL YOU ACCEPT?'

'What are the rules?' Mark said, hearing the resignation in his voice and being surprised by it. 'How do I play?'

'IT IS VERY SIMPLE. THE GAME NEEDS A WINNER. YOU WILL BE THAT WINNER.'

Mark wished for transparency. For normalcy. Anything that wasn't cryptic bullshit. 'You're going to have to give me more than that. Or just come out and face me like a man. Oh, sorry, I forgot what you're all like. Whiny little boys who can't take rejection. A woman doesn't like me, so I have to kill her.'

There was silence over the phone, then a scream. It lingered for a second or two, then was cut off and silence fell again.

'Was that . . .'

'I WILL KILL HER NOW, MARK. NO GAME. IS THAT WHAT YOU WANT?'

Mark gritted his teeth against the words that threatened to spill from his mouth. His jaw tensed, sharp pain in his knuckles, as he dragged a fist along the rough brick of the garages.

'ARE YOU READY TO PLAY?'

He thought about trying to find her instead. With no leads, no idea where she could be.

'Let me think,' Mark said quickly, trying to work out a way out of this. He could speak to Cavanagh, tell him the truth – what they were trying to make him do. He might believe him. They would see Natasha was missing and that could be enough, he thought.

'WE WILL KNOW,' the voice said, as if he was reading his mind. 'IF THEY COME LOOKING FOR US, WE WILL KNOW YOU LIED. THAT YOU ARE NOT PLAYING.'

Mark couldn't think straight. The only thought in his mind was of Natasha, alone and scared. That was enough. 'Fine,' Mark managed to say, the word being forced out through a barely open mouth.

'THEN I WILL TELL YOU THE RULES.'

'What does that mean?'

'FIRST LEVEL. YOU ARE GOING TO CONFESS.'

'That's ridiculous . . .'

'YOU WILL TAKE RESPONSIBILITY FOR THEM ALL. EVERY SINGLE ONE. YOU WILL ADMIT TO

KILLING THEM ALL YOURSELF. THAT IS THE
FIRST LEVEL.'

'You're crazy if you think this'll work,' Mark said, but
he was already turning it over in his mind. Seeing how it
would stick. Whether he could pull it off.

How far he was willing to go.

'IT WILL WORK IF YOU WANT NATASHA TO
LIVE. THAT IS THE GAME. IF YOU DO NOT WANT
TO PLAY, I WILL END IT ALL NOW AND SHE WILL
DIE. DO YOU UNDERSTAND?'

'I can't do this . . .'

'IS THAT YOUR DECISION?'

'No,' Mark said, loud enough that his voice echoed into
the darkness. The wind seemed to pick up at the sound of
it; whipping up around him once more to provide its own
noise in response to his. 'You want me to take the blame?
That's not going to work.'

'YOU ARE A DETECTIVE. YOU WILL FIGURE
THAT OUT, I AM SURE. THIS IS ALL YOU
NEED TO KNOW.'

Mark heard the robotic voice list the names, over and
over, repeated them back when asked. He knew three of
them fine.

Joanna Carter, Emily Burns, Holly Edwards.

It took a few more minutes before he could repeat the
other five back to the voice without pausing. They would
disappear quickly, he imagined, if he didn't keep turning
them over in his mind.

The methods of death took a little longer.

Thankfully, most of the deaths had been quite similar.
Joanna Carter's death had not been the first to be framed
as a suicide. Similarly, it seemed Emily Burns had been

destined to bleed to death in that yard. Mark wondered for a second what had transpired. How she had fought for her life.

He shook the thought from his head and tried to concentrate on the information being recited to him.

Mark wanted to run. Tell someone what was going on. The loss of control angered and scared him.

He was going to take responsibility for it all, probably so the real killer could make his escape. Even if they didn't believe him, his career would be over. And he would be shouting into the wind, while he was trying to tell them the truth. His life would be over.

He wasn't coming back from this.

Mark couldn't think of another way out.

'ONE MORE TIME.'

'Steven Hallet, hammer to back of his head.'

His first kill, but his first mistake. It obviously hadn't looked like suicide, so Mark imagined the death was still unexplained. 'M6, near the junction thirty-two services, grass verge.'

'GOOD. NEXT.'

Mark went through them all in turn, only pausing on one or two before finding the right answer. When he had them all down, he tried to talk again. 'You have to know this won't work. They'll work out who I am and it all ends, do you understand?'

'NOT MY PROBLEM.'

'There has to be something else I can do. Something else you want.'

'NO.'

Mark looked back and forth yet again. Still, there was nothing out there. He was alone, but he could feel eyes watching him. Out there, in the shadows, hidden from view. Watching to see what he would do. Watching to see if he would go through with his task.

'If they find out who I am – and they will – this will all fail.'

'I DON'T CARE—'

'You have to,' Mark said quickly, shouting into the darkness. Hoping he could be heard by whoever was watching him. Out there. 'I can't do this. It won't work.'

'THEN THE GAME IS OVER AND SHE IS DEAD.'

'No, listen, I spoke to John Redwood. The one who gave you Holly Edwards's name. He is going to the police and telling them everything . . .'

'JOHN KNOWS NOTHING. HE DIDN'T GO TO THE POLICE, HE IS CURRENTLY SITTING AT HOME. NO ONE KNOWS YOU ARE HERE OR WHAT YOU KNOW. THEY WILL HOLD YOU FOR TWENTY-FOUR HOURS AT LEAST. LONGER IF YOU CAN MAKE THEM BELIEVE YOU. TWENTY-FOUR HOURS IS THE MINIMUM TIME. IF YOU FAIL, SHE DIES.'

'His mum called them. They were coming.'

'ENOUGH. PLAY THE GAME OR SHE DIES. HAND YOURSELF OVER TO THEM. TELL THEM WHAT YOU DID. SHE CAN DIE NOW.'

'No, wait . . . I'll play. I just need time. I need the rules to change a little. They can hold me for twenty-four hours without charge. If I make it a full day, will that be enough? They won't charge me.'

'YOU DO NOT HAVE MUCH TIME NOW. THEY HAVE BEEN TOLD YOU ARE HERE. THEY WILL BE COMING SOON. GOODBYE AND GOOD LUCK.'

The call ended then, Mark still talking into nothingness. Wanting a little more time, more information. He placed the phone back in his pocket and began reciting the names. The methods of their deaths. He needed to keep them searching for that twenty-four hours.

Mark took off down the road, covering the two hundred yards to his car quickly. He didn't pause, jumping inside and turning on the engine. He drove past the open garage, not looking at the dead girl inside, a pang of guilt hitting him as he did so. Kept driving, until he was further past it. Eventually, a minute or so further down the road, he came to a clearing in the field. More outhouses.

It would have to do.

If they found his car near the scene, it would be over before it had begun. They would run the number plate, discover his real name, and he would be carted off to a mental institution before the next day's sunrise, he guessed.

He left the keys under one of the wheel arches and jogged back to the garage. The air was still and silent. The wind had died down around him, in the time it had taken him to hear all the names of the people who had been killed.

He just needed to make it to a full day. He could do that. 'Steven Hallet . . .'

Mark heard sirens in the distance, coming closer to him. He walked back into the garage, pacing up and down. Trying to remember every single name, chanting them over and over to himself. 'Steven Hallet . . . Stacey Green . . . Melissa Carmichael . . .'

Over and over, until he had the names and how they had died lodged in his head. He couldn't mess this up, not now. It would take only a momentary lapse and it would be all over. He needed to save Natasha.

That was all he could think of, in that moment. That his actions would keep her alive.

He ignored the rational part of his brain, even if it was currently making more sense than the rest of it. He had to concentrate on the names. The methods of death. His story.

The Game.

The sirens sounded closer, drifting on the wind towards him. He had seconds left before they arrived and he would have to start telling his story.

They would arrest him. Place him in handcuffs and put him in a cell. Within a matter of hours, they would start interviewing him.

He wondered how long it would take for them to identify him. He wouldn't be able to give his own name, not at the beginning. He would be anonymous for as long as he possibly could. Long enough for them to believe his story.

The sirens were close now.

'Steven Hallet ... motorway ... Stacey Green ...'

He could hear engines outside on the road. Mark lifted his head and opened his eyes. Red and blue lights streaked across the darkness out on the road. He heard doors slamming closed.

Mark dropped to his knees. Holly Edwards lay motionless behind him. He placed his hands behind his head.

'I'm in here,' he said, his voice bouncing off the walls. 'I did it.'

NOW

Fifty-Two

The Third Interview

Tuesday 30th October
Interview Room One
Lancaster Police Station – sixty miles from Liverpool
City Centre

'We know who you really are.'

The words hung in the air between them. He kept his face as straight as possible, trying to work out how much time he had left.

'Does it matter who I am? I did this. You have me. Charge me.'

'Under what name, exactly?' DI Hicks said, and now there was a look of pity on his face. 'We could charge you as a John Doe, I suppose, but we both know that wouldn't last long. CPS would have a fit.'

'You have enough,' Mark said, feeling the sweat running down the back of his neck. He imagined what he looked like to them now. Too eager, too willing.

Too scared.

'We had enough just finding you there, probably,' DI Hicks replied, leaning back in his chair, his hands folded over his stomach. 'Even if you'd given us some story about just turning up and finding her there, I doubt it would have been enough. Not for a civilian. But, then, we're not dealing with that here, are we?'

Mark lowered his head, knowing it was done. He wondered how they had found out, what he had left behind as a clue. There was nothing in his pockets when he'd been arrested; he'd left everything in the car.

The car?

Next to him, the solicitor shifted in his seat and cleared his throat. Clearly he hadn't been informed of what was happening. And DI Hicks was taking his time in dropping the hammer.

Let him, Mark thought. He was getting ever closer to the twenty-four-hour mark. He considered the words he'd heard over the phone – the robotic voice and its stilted cadence. The almost palpable violence and anger in something that couldn't express emotion.

Mark was tired. His thoughts mudded up and crashing into each other. A robotic voice couldn't do those things, he thought.

He realised no one had spoken for almost half a minute; both detectives stared at him from across the table. They were waiting for him to say something.

They were going to have to do better than that.

'Why were you there?'

'Because that's where I had to be,' Mark replied, staring back at DI Hicks. Daring him to maintain eye contact with him. He wondered if he thought he was crazy or if he believed Mark had actually done something to Holly

Edwards. He supposed he'd find out soon enough. 'That's the Game.'

'See, now we know who you are, we got the chance to do a little digging.'

'I'm sorry, can I just interject?' the solicitor said, interrupting for the first time in what felt like forever. 'Could you tell me what's going on here?'

All three detectives turned to the weedy little man. He lowered his head in response and stayed quiet.

'As I was saying,' DI Hicks continued, giving the solicitor one last look of annoyance, 'we've done a bit of digging. Turns out you weren't even in the country for two of the people you claim to have murdered. Also, Steven Hallet died the same night you were on duty in Liverpool. So, unless you have a special transporter you'd like to tell us about, why don't you start telling us the truth?'

Mark swallowed, his mouth dry. There was a horrible taste in his mouth. 'What time is it now?'

DI Hicks glanced at his fellow detective, who looked down at her wrist. 'Six-fifteen p.m.,' she said, then went back to writing on her notepad.

'I need another hour.'

'I'm afraid not,' DI Hicks said, shaking his head. He reached across and turned off the recorder, the numbered lights pausing in place. 'Look, we've seen this before. Both of us. We understand ...'

'No, you don't,' Mark said, his shoulders slumping down as he waited for the inevitable.

'We've spoken to your friends in Liverpool,' DI Hicks continued, as if Mark hadn't interrupted. 'They've told us how much strain you've been under. It's understandable. We just don't understand how you found her body. What you know about it. We don't think you killed her. So, how did you find her?'

Mark sighed deeply, feeling it all fall away from him. He could only hope that it had been enough. He could stay silent for another hour, but he didn't think there would be much use. They had already decided what they were going to do.

They thought they would be helping him. A fellow detective.

'Information from John Redwood led me there,' Mark said quietly, thinking about how to word it. 'I'm guessing he didn't talk.'

'Can't say I've ever heard the name mentioned.'

John's mother hadn't called, as he'd instructed. As he'd expected her to. He shook his head at believing she would. Based on an assumption about where she lived. He should have known that her bond to her son would be greater. He wondered how long it would have taken to just do that small thing, call DS Cavanagh. Even if that meant Natasha would be dead already.

If she wasn't all along and he had just been played with.

The dice had been loaded. The cards marked. He never had a shot.

'What happens next?'

'You tell us who John Redwood is, for starters.'

Mark explained how he had found the boy. His story. He could see the doubt in their faces, the pity. They seemed to accept enough of it to not push him too far.

'But, why have you pretended to kill eight people, Mark?' DI Hicks asked, concern dripping from every syllable. 'What's made you do that?'

There wasn't an easy answer. Not without leaving him

with zero chance of finding Natasha alive. He would tell them all once he found her. Alive or dead. For now, he had to shift his plan a little. That was all. Even with so little sleep in the previous few days, his mind was still working sharply. Connecting things together, making clear decisions.

'I guess, finding Holly Edwards like that, something just ... snapped,' Mark replied, rubbing his temples and closing his eyes for a second or two. 'I thought she'd be alive. That was how I'd redeem myself. Prove I was right about those people being mixed up in something no one was willing to accept.'

'The Game.'

Mark nodded slowly, already planning his first move, when they eventually released him. There were things he could do. Still time. It's unlikely that *he* would be out there, watching to see if he was released. Whoever he was, he would be sitting back and waiting. Watching the news or something similar.

Keeping Natasha captive.

If she was still alive, of course.

She had to be, Mark thought. Hope is a dangerous thing, but he needed to hold on to it.

'And how do you feel now?' DS Lee said, her soft Lancastrian tones reaching over the table and giving him comfort.

'Tired,' Mark replied, telling the truth. He could feel the weight of exhaustion bearing down on him. Determination battling against it. 'Sorry, too, if I'm honest. I've wasted your time. I guess I just need to sleep. Forget about all of this for a while.'

'There's nothing we could charge you with ... other than

making false statements and wasting police resources,' DI Hicks said, closing over the folder he'd brought in with him for the last time. 'I think we both know how well they'd hold up. I want to tell you something though: if you were on my team, I'd bounce you out so fast, you wouldn't know your arse from your feet. If – and I don't think you need me to tell you, it's a pretty damn big if – they let you back in MCU, you need to get some help, mate. Cracking when you've found a body is the last thing you should be doing. Going off on your own is fine and dandy if you want to be a fake cop on a TV show, but this is the real world. You never do that.'

'Thank you,' Mark replied, leaving off the rest of the sentence. *For the lecture, Einstein.* This was how it worked for them. If he'd been a normal person off the street, he would have been charged with every single thing they could throw at him. For him, the rules were different. Some part of him had known that, he thought. That's why he'd been willing to at least try it.

He knew he wouldn't be left in jail to rot on remand.

'Your car is in our car park,' DI Hicks said, standing up and folding his arms across his chest. 'We found your keys in the wheel arch. You should be more careful where you leave them. They'll be given back to you, but I've asked someone to come and pick you up and take you back to Liverpool. They're going to check you over down there.'

Mark continued to sit, brushing his hands through his hair. 'Right, good.'

'You can wait downstairs if you want, or up here with us.'

'I think I'd rather wait out of sight, if that's okay. Feel a bit embarrassed, now my head's started coming back into focus.'

Mark waited, the shared glance between the two detectives, the quiet nod. He followed them out of the room, leaving the solicitor in there, probably still trying to work out what had happened in the past twelve or so hours. He couldn't be bothered trying to explain anything to him.

Once he was downstairs, he knew it was just a matter of time.

The keys were in his pocket. Digging into his thigh. DS Lee stayed with him, any attempts at small talk with her being quickly dismissed.

He knew he had an hour to do something. In the end, it was twenty minutes before the opening came.

DS Lee got a phone call, excused herself and walked away a little. Mark didn't hesitate – approached the guy on the front desk and smiled. 'You don't smoke, do you?'

'Afraid to say I do,' the guy said, overhead light shining off his bald head. He could carry small children in the bags under his eyes. 'Been trying to quit, but I'm guessing you know how it is.'

'Can I nick one off you?'

Less than a minute later, he was outside. Finding the car park, then his car.

As easy as that.

Fifty-Three

It didn't take long before he realised he didn't have a plan. Not one that was further than getting away from the police station in his own car. Rather than waiting for some no-mark to turn up from Liverpool. Judging him silently all the way back.

He didn't want to know what could have been in store for him. Instant assessments, mental health checks.

Mark didn't need any of that.

Didn't *want* any of that. He needed to do something first. So they would realise he'd been right. So they would welcome him back.

So his life wouldn't be over.

He drove quickly, hoping they wouldn't follow him soon. Maybe give up entirely and let other officers deal with him. He wondered what their thinking had been anyway. To just allow him out of custody, given what had been discovered. Then he thought of DI Bennett, and the way she had treated him. Kid gloves. She had put in a call, Mark thought. Talked them out of doing what they should have. Sent DS Cavanagh to pick him up, probably. They would try to find him, he decided. Would be out there now, on the unfamiliar roads he was travelling, trying to track him down. That couldn't happen. He needed some time. Some space.

He needed to think. To find Natasha.

Mark drove without direction, his phone sitting safely in the false box underneath his seat. That meant he didn't know where he was going, but that was okay right then. Any direction would do. He'd accomplished a lot in those minutes before they'd arrived at that garage.

He drove for fifteen minutes, taking turns at random, waiting to see the perfect place he could stop and take a breath. Formulate his next move. His mind was working overtime, trying to come up with a plan. Something, anything, that could work.

In the distance, he saw a small clearing at the side of a country road. He turned into it, parking up and turning the engine off. Outside, it was pitch black. The surroundings plunged into darkness, once his headlights and dashboard ceased illuminating the way.

Mark put his hand underneath the seat and removed his phone. Switched it on and keyed his passcode into it. It seemed to take an age to come on, then boot up. He couldn't stay in one spot for very long if they were out looking for him, but he should have enough time, he thought. They could track his phone easily enough, but he doubted that would be their first port of call. That would come later.

There were no notifications. No missed calls or voicemails. No robotic voice to tell him what the next steps would be. Just the same stream of messages he'd had earlier, from DS Cavanagh.

Nothing.

When he'd pulled out the phone, his hand had brushed against something. At that point, he'd only been thinking about retrieving the phone, but now his mind reminded him of it.

The laptop. John's laptop.

He didn't think twice, reaching underneath and taking it out. He prayed it would still have a little battery left, enough for him to see the forum John had on screen earlier. There had to be a clue there, something that could lead him to wherever he might be. A little kernel of information he could use.

Mark opened the laptop, the screen coming to life. The background image was some kind of picture, the date and time in the foreground, the battery life meter in the bottom right-hand corner. It wasn't in percentage, but he could see it was almost out.

He had to work fast.

He pressed the space bar, hoping that the screen saver would disappear if he did so.

It did.

Replaced by a password box.

'No . . .'

He tried everything he knew to get past it, but failed at every turn. It was no use. There was no option to bypass it, no cancel button to log in as a guest, no clues to the password. Mark began inputting random words. Strings of numbers. Anything he could think of, in order to get in.

Every single one failed.

Eventually, it stopped allowing him to put them in, locking him out indefinitely. Mark sat back in the driver's seat, defeated. The screen changed back to its screen saver, the battery icon flashing red.

He didn't know what to do next, other than to tell the truth. To have the full weight of Major Crimes helping, and hopefully save Natasha. His career was probably still over, but he had to do something.

It wouldn't help, of course; she would be killed so he, whoever he was, wouldn't be caught. If she wasn't already dead, he thought. He'd been played with, just like everyone else involved. It was all a game and there were no winners.

The laptop shifted on his knees, as he dropped his head back onto the seat rest. Screwed his eyes shut and tried to think of a way in which all of this could be sorted out. A way in which he could save his career, save Natasha, stop the madness.

Nothing came.

Mark was out of ideas, he realised. He had nothing left. Every single decision he'd made had been wrong. A day spent in custody, pretending to be a serial killer for what looked like no reason. He'd listened to some robotic voice over his phone, decided to follow it, and tried the ridiculous. And for what? To save someone who was probably already dead.

Mark rubbed against his forehead with the palms of his hands, wondering how long it would take for someone to find him. To take him back to Liverpool in disgrace. He'd only narrowly escaped being charged for something back at the police station. Now he imagined an investigation against him would find plenty of reasons to make sure he was gone from the police for good.

He had destroyed his life.

Just like he'd been told to do.

Maybe he had won then, Mark thought. Probably not in time to save Natasha's life, but he could claim a victory of sorts. Even if it meant the loss of everything.

There was nothing left to do, but go back to Liverpool. Face the music, which had been playing him offstage for the past week without him even realising – it was the only logical next step, the only chance at finding Natasha. He dropped his head down and placed a hand on the lid of the laptop to close it, hoping it would at least give the IT techs some information. They could scour it and find exactly what John Redwood had done. He wouldn't be getting away with it for much longer, even if he had managed to convince his mum not to call DS Cavanagh as he'd asked her to.

Then he thought of the missed calls and messages he'd been receiving the previous day. He thought about the increasing amount he'd been getting, which meant they knew he had been out there somewhere, doing something he shouldn't have.

Which meant John Redwood's mother *had* called them. And John had not told the truth. He should have stayed with him, explained to the team what he'd done. He could have gone after that, or at least taken DS Cavanagh with him. Anything other than the giant mistake he'd made instead.

Natasha had already been taken at that point though, Mark thought. Perhaps The Game had started before he'd even realised.

The phone started buzzing in his lap. Mark glanced down at it, seeing PRIVATE NUMBER flash up and answered quickly. 'I tried . . .'

'Mark, where are you?'

Mark swore quietly and thought about hanging up on DI Bennett straight away. Instead, he responded. 'What's going on?'

'I was hoping you'd tell us.'

'I don't know,' Mark replied, swiping a hand across his face and feeling the tiredness enveloping his skin. 'I thought I was doing the right thing.'

'You need to tell me where you are,' DI Bennett said, a catch in her voice. Mark began to frown. There was something she wasn't saying. 'We know about Natasha.'

'Is she okay?'

'We don't know where she is. Her mum has reported her missing and mentioned you. So, I think you can help us with finding her, right?'

'I don't know,' Mark repeated, still hearing something unfamiliar in DI Bennett's voice. 'I've been trying to find her.'

'Mark, why don't you tell me where you are, so we can sort all of this out. I don't want to do this over the phone. We're worried about you.'

'I'm sure,' Mark replied, leaning back into the headrest and closing his eyes. 'There's something else though, right? Why you're so keen to get me back?'

'I think it's best if we talk about that in person, Mark.'

'You keep saying my name, boss. Why is that?'

There was a long sigh through the phone, then the sound of something tapping against a desk. 'What happened last year. What's happening now. Stephanie's brother has made a statement ...'

'What are you talking about?'

'Why, Mark? What did you do?'

Mark couldn't make sense of what was being said.

What he was being asked. Yet there was a sureness to DI Bennett's tone. As if he was the one who was mistaken, who had forgotten something he'd actually done. 'I haven't done anything.'

'Then come in and tell us the truth. What's happened to Natasha, Mark? Is she safe?'

'I don't think so, but I had nothing to do with that. I'm trying to find her.'

'You've made mistakes, but we can fix them together. I just need you to come back and sit down with us properly. Talk us through what's happened.'

Mark made to answer then closed his mouth, realising what she was implying now. They thought he'd completely lost it. Admitted to murders he hadn't committed because there was something else he'd done wrong. 'It's not like what you think,' he said, after a few more seconds of silence. 'I was just doing what I thought was best.'

'This is not helping you, Mark,' DI Bennett said, and now her voice was soft and motherly. 'The only way to do that is to let me help you.'

It was Mark's turn to sigh. He opened his eyes, his lids heavy with tiredness. Looked down at the laptop and its flashing red light. He paused as he lowered the lid on the dying laptop, something in the background image catching his eye. He realised there was more than one picture captured on it. It was actually a collage of different images.

Mark recognised some of them.

He traced a finger across the screen, seeing them all in turn.

'Steven Hallet . . . Melissa Carmichael . . . Stacey Green,' Mark whispered, as his finger shuffled across the screen, capturing each image in turn. 'The building Joanna Carter lived in ... the scrapyard where Emily was found.'

'What's that?'

Mark ignored DI Bennett's voice, looking through the pictures on the laptop screen. They were all there in front of him.

And in the top right-hand corner ... the outside of the garage where Holly Edwards had been waiting for Mark to arrive.

All of the places where the bodies had been found.

There was a moment when he couldn't quite understand what he was seeing. What was in front of him. Then, it all coalesced and came into focus.

The dates all those people had been killed. How close together they all were. Eight dead in less than a year – seemingly unrelated, only one death really unexplained. All the rest, dismissed as someone taking their own life.

The first, the aberration. The violence used. Impossible to hide.

It was because the first was unplanned. A random act of violence from someone who didn't have a way of controlling himself.

Not yet.

The timing.

He heard DI Bennett's voice in the background, but he wasn't focusing on that any longer. Her increasing pleas to be answered only distracted him. 'I've got to go,' he mumbled, ending the call and switching off his phone in one movement, as his mind continued to turn.

When Holly Edwards had rejected John Redwood for the last time. When she had stopped answering his messages, his pleas.

He didn't need to check to make sure. He was almost positive it would have been mere days before Steven Hallet had been killed.

'My parents took me to the Lake District to get my mind off it. Just a snap decision they made to take me up to the cottage we have up there. It was night by the time we arrived.'

They would have stopped at the services. John, filled with anger and rage. Chances upon Steven Hallet and beats him to death.

Enjoys it. Feels satisfaction from what he's done.

'You bastard . . .'

Mark looked at the images on screen, knowing what each represented, all except for one.

One he recognised.

It was his last shot. He might be too late, he knew that, but he had to try.

The laptop finally died, so he took it from his knees and placed in the passenger footwell. Turned his phone back on for a few seconds and checked the map. Memorised the route back to the motorway, then turned it off again. Turned the engine on and blinked as light entered the world around him once more.

It was time to end this.

Fifty-Four

It had been a long time since he'd last been at the place. Mark had at one time been a regular visitor – when he'd first moved over to Liverpool, on his days away from the police training. Walking and taking in the beauty that could be found there.

Sefton Park. Only it was more like a different world. Over two hundred acres in size, Mark had discovered new things every time he'd visited. He hadn't been for a while, but still remembered parts of it vividly. Others were a little less memorable, but he knew where he was going. He knew the way.

The place that had been in an image on John's laptop screen. A statue and fountain. Modelled on Eros, the Greek god of love, or attraction. He had walked past it years earlier. He might have ignored it completely if he hadn't been struck by how much it had reminded him of a similar statue in London. Turned out, when Mark had investigated a little further, the two statues were in fact related. The Liverpool version had been created by the same people behind the capital's version.

He knew John had chosen this place. Probably thought it meant something, it being Eros.

The fountain was located near the middle of the park – a good fifteen-minute walk from the car park on Mossley Hill Drive. It was pitch black when he parked up, the clock on the dashboard blinking almost midnight. Fear hit him, as he thought about the time it had taken him to get back.

Mark got out of the car and started walking, unsure what he would actually find at the fountain. The thought of John just waiting there for him seemed a stretch, but he had been wrong about him before. Taken in by his crying act, the way he'd dismissed him as just a little boy in over his head.

Mark had been wrong. So wrong.

It took him a while to find it, coming to it from a different way than he was used to. In the dark, everything looked slightly different also. The paths merged into one, nothing to differentiate one from the other. The trees around him, stripped of their leaves as autumn took hold. Underfoot, the constant swish of walking through them was the only sound he could hear.

Then, he heard something else.

It was soft at first, as if it were only his imagination, then it became more prominent.

The thought made him nervous, his heart beating against his chest as he grew closer to the sounds. Every step felt like a mistake. A betrayal to himself. He could run away and be safe, but that wasn't happening.

Always running towards the danger, not away from it.

He kept moving forwards. It was too late to turn back now.

Mark rounded a final corner, seeing dim light in the distance. A single beam of light. The chanting became clearer now, driven to him with force on a gust of wind.

'One ... two ... three.'

The numbers being recited. A male's voice encouraging, disparaging. A female, stilted and slow. Treading over the words as if they were hot coals.

Mark broke out into a run. Within half a minute he was standing at the edge of the stone path that surrounded the fountain.

Took in what he was seeing.

Natasha, a rope around her neck, around her body. Her hands tied in front of her. All interlocked. She was walking slowly around the base of the fountain, the other end of the rope being held by him.

John Redwood.

'Thought you could stop us,' he said, talking to Natasha. 'You never had a chance. Now it's the last level.'

Mark moved closer, his feet scraping on the gravel path. John slowly turned to greet him, his sorry look of yesterday replaced with emptiness. A smile slowly crawled across his face.

Mark had done exactly what he'd expected him to do.

'Glad you can finally join us,' John said; even his voice was different. More confident, more sure. 'I wasn't sure if you'd work out where we'd be. Was going to call, but thought it'd be more fun to see if you could get here to watch the grand finale.'

'Let her go,' Mark said, stepping closer to them. He could see John's hand on the end of the rope, knowing one forceful tug and he would start strangling Natasha. Possibly even break her neck. He moved slower. 'This is all over, John. You don't need to do this.'

'I think I do,' John replied, moving his hand so it was firmly on the rope now. 'This is the last one. This is my gift to you. She's been playing too.'

'Holly Edwards was all you were working towards.

Natasha hasn't done anything wrong. She wasn't on the forum. She wasn't a choice. No one wants her gone. No one wants her punished.'

'I disagree,' John said, the single beam of light coming across and shining into Mark's eyes. It was coming from something in his free hand – a phone or camera. He couldn't be sure.

'I've been watching you for days,' John continued, following Natasha as she walked a little further around the fountain. 'You're just like us. Alone, betrayed. Even looking the way you do, they've still broken you.'

Mark tried to get a good look at Natasha, but she was masked by John's body. He could hear her voice, however, soft and scared. She was whispering under her breath. 'There is nothing I need you to do right now, other than to let her go and talk to me. It's over, John.'

'You know who this statue is?' John said, pulling the rope tighter and bringing Natasha to a halt.

'Eros. God of love,' Mark replied, trying to move a little closer. He wanted to see Natasha. Try to let her know he was there and she was going to be safe. 'It's a grand gesture. I'm guessing you picked it for its history.'

'You're wrong. On both counts. It's actually Anteros. Said to be the brother of Eros. They did the same in London – depicted the wrong god of sorts. Do you know what Anteros was?'

'Can't say I do,' Mark said, risking another step forward. He was blinded for a split second, as John moved whatever was in his hand, light blasting into his eyes. 'Not all that good with Greek gods.'

'He was the punisher of scorned love. He avenged unrequited love. Now, that's more apt, don't you think?'

Natasha was standing still, head bowed, defeated. Mark side-stepped and brought himself further in line with her, working out what his next move should be. 'Apt if you think the way you do, I suppose.'

'Why don't you tell me how I think? That'll be interesting.'

'Well, apart from the obvious wanting to be caught part, you think unreturned love is something that should be punished. This isn't to do with the lies they were telling to people online. This is all personal. The whole Game thing was just a cover. You used it to kill Holly. You found other people like you online and they built this into this game, where you were supposedly killing people to punish them, only that's not what happened. Joanna, Emily, all of them – they didn't deserve to die, but you still did it. You're not even sure if they've done anything wrong, really. Holly didn't want you and you couldn't handle that. It doesn't leave much room for freedom, does it? No room for people to make their own decisions. All of this was just a mask to put off what you wanted to do last year. You wanted to kill Holly Edwards because she turned you down, but you didn't have the capacity to do so.'

'I killed Holly Edwards because she deserved it. All of them did.'

Mark stopped, as John tightened his grip on the rope. 'No one deserves to die for not loving someone. That's just life.'

'Like that's all they did. These people needed taking care of. *That's just life?* That's a simple way of looking at it. It doesn't mean a thing though, really. You want to know the dirty little secret, Mark?'

'What's that?'

John grinned and now Mark saw him for something else than he'd seen in the bedroom the previous day. He wasn't a scared little boy. He wasn't weak. He was stronger now. He had power, probably for the first time in his life.

'I enjoy it,' John said, a sparkle in his eyes. 'This is the greatest feeling in the world. The fact that I can do this. Set myself free of these people. It's incredible. And it's not just me. There's hundreds of us out there; so many people you will never know. You can't stop us all. We've all found the truth and now there's no turning back. The days of hurting people with no recourse are over. It's our time now. The forgotten ones. Men and a few women too, the whole world over. All finding a truth you can't ignore.'

'This isn't the way, John,' Mark said, but he knew there was no way of getting through to the boy. And that's all he was. A boy. One who had suffered some kind of *mental break* but a boy all the same.

Which meant, it shouldn't be all that difficult to stop him doing whatever he was planning to do.

'I've been talking to her, you know,' John said, winding the rope closer to him and pulling Natasha closer. He angled the light so it illuminated her face. 'She used you. She wanted to find us and that's why she was with you. She thought she could find us through someone in the police and maybe that's true. She knows what you've been doing and what you were prepared to do for her and she doesn't care. I bet you think you'll save her and all of this will be over. Then you can ride off into the sunset with a beautiful young thing on your arm. You don't care she's so much younger than you and that your entire relationship so far is based on her giving you sex and that's it – you want her, so you'll have her. She'll come running to you because you've saved her life. Is that right?'

'Let her go, John . . .'

'Tell the truth,' John replied, his shout echoing around the empty park. 'You think she'll fall for you, just as you've fallen for her. It's wrong. You're wrong. She doesn't like you. You repulse her. No matter what you've done for her, she thinks you're just a weird bloke, who even though he's good-looking, is smarmy with it. She's thought that from the beginning. She was playing with you. Just so she could get what she wanted.'

'That . . . that doesn't mean anything,' Mark said, but he could feel something building inside him. A feeling of betrayal, of jealousy.

'Of course it does. I can see it written all over your face. The only reason you have ruined your career, your life, in the past twenty-four hours, is for her. And she doesn't even care.'

'That's not why I did it.'

'And this isn't even the first time,' John said, his voice dripping with a mixture of pleading and derision. 'This is what these types of people do. They bleed us dry. I mean, look at you. You have everything, but you're still the same person you always were.'

'We can talk about this . . .'

'Tell him, Natasha. Tell him you don't want him and never would.'

Mark opened his mouth to talk, but Natasha raised her head to look at him. Her eyes were glassy and she was shivering against an unseen wind. Her body was shaking, even as she tried to look at him.

'He's . . . he was just a way for me to find you and stop

you,' Natasha said, her voice stilted and breathless. She sounded unfocused, seemingly out of it, but was somehow still standing. 'I was only with him to get what I wanted.'

Mark listened as Natasha began to sniff and chuckle, trying to ignore the knot in his stomach that began tightening. In her place was another woman. And another. A long line of teenage girls and, then, women in their twenties. All who had laughed at him. All who had dismissed him easily.

And he didn't care.

Because he was better than that.

He watched the rope around her neck pull her back, saw her face contort in dull pain.

He couldn't ignore the anger, but he could beat it.

He was aware of more breathing, of more eyes. There were faces appearing in the darkness, but he ignored them.

They weren't alone there.

Fifty-Five

The feeling of anger dissipated, but Mark still felt bitter and desperate. He was a young boy again, being talked about behind his back. A lonely teenager, shunned by the pack.

Then, that feeling was gone. Years of hurt, blinked out with experience.

He was better than this.

He wasn't going to let John see that.

He had one chance.

'It doesn't matter who you are now,' John said. 'You'll always have the same thoughts as you did then.'

'You don't know a thing about me.'

John chuckled softly, then sniffed. Beside him, more people appeared. More boys. They were as young as John and one significantly older. Mark ignored them. The light from the phone in John's hand drifted across Mark's face for an instant.

'I know more than you realise. We all do,' John said, the phone in his hand revealing the five men who now stood in line with him. 'I watched you, looked into your past. You shouldn't be surprised the amount of information we were able to gather about you. I've seen who you were when you were my age. You were just like me. Like all of us. You've changed a bit now, but it doesn't matter, does it? You're still the same person you always were. You sleep with women and then discard them just as quickly. Why do you think you do that?'

Mark shifted closer to him, his insides churning as the words hit home. 'I grew up. That's all. I became a man and things changed.'

'Oh yeah, a new man,' John replied, his voice breaking a little as he spoke. 'They've convinced you that's what you had to be. You discard them because you still want to punish those girls from back then. All those who turned their back on you. Going to the gym, getting your hair cut, paying over the odds for clothes . . . these are all the things they *want* us to think make a difference. It's not true. What makes a difference is getting rid of them. That's how we punish them.'

'Killing them,' Mark said, taking another step closer. He scanned the faces of the silent men standing with John. He was vastly outnumbered, but it didn't stop him. 'That's what you're doing. Because you can't get women out of your league to sleep with you, you kill them. All of them. Is that what you're really telling me?'

'*Punishing* them. This isn't about killing them. This is about taking back control. Without the punishment, it wouldn't mean anything. They pay for what they did to us.'

Mark didn't believe a word he was saying, but he knew John believed it. Every word. 'And that's what they deserve?'

'Of course,' John said, surprise in his voice now, as if he couldn't believe he had to explain it. 'Look what they've done to us. For years and years and years. How have we let them get away with it for this long? And it's only getting worse. They hold all the power and they *know* it. It's not right. This is about taking it back. I know you're like us. I know you won't stop me.'

This was never about blackmail. This was simply about power.

Mark opened his mouth to answer, but Natasha was laughing again. He stopped himself, watching as she turned to him again and sneered.

'You were just going to use me as well,' Natasha said, her words tumbling into each other and barely making sense. 'Why not get what I wanted first? You should just go, Mark. You've embarrassed yourself enough.'

'See,' John said, giggling like a child now. 'She's just like the rest of them. She could see you for what you really were. Not good enough for her, not good enough for any of them. You're still like me.'

'I'm nothing like you.'

'You keep saying that,' John interrupted, irritation entering his tone. 'It's meaningless though. You know the truth. We all know the truth. You don't have to keep lying. This woman is nobody to you, so why still protect her? She treated you like shit on her shoe and you still can't accept it. The things you did for her, for all of them, because you felt like you had to. You don't anymore.'

'That's not how I feel,' Mark replied, adding a touch of defeat to his tone that he hoped John could detect. From the smirk on his face, he thought it was working. 'It's not . . .'

'All you've done for this girl and she thinks you're nothing. Just another man that doesn't live up to her expectations. Can you see it now? Can you see what we're doing? We're fixing this. One person at a time. Natasha wouldn't care if you lived or died . . .'

'I don't care if you live or die, I don't care if you live or die, I DON'T CARE IF YOU LIVE OR DIE.'

Mark tried to shut out the screams coming from Natasha, but instead they filled his head. He struggled against what he wanted to do. To say. To walk away and never look back. To let it happen.

He breathed in deeply and the feeling evaporated.

'That's what she really thinks of you. Do you see it now? This is what they *are*. They're liars and cheats. I can get rid of her, just like the rest. I can send her to the other place, so she'll suffer for what she's done. She hates you. She hates us all.'

'I don't care,' Mark replied, but he could hear the anger in his tone. He knew John could hear it too. 'That's not why I tried to save her.'

'You really need to work on your lying skills. Maybe I can help you there. You couldn't see my lies earlier and you're used to dealing with liars. I've got so good at it over time. No one knows a thing I do now. My family have no idea what I've been doing for the past year. Just constantly complaining that I spend too much time on my computer – then moaning when I disappear for a few days to do what I've been doing. They've never suspected a thing. I killed a man while he was eating fast food at a service station. Came back and it was like it never happened. They didn't even wonder where the hoodie I'd been wearing had gone. It was covered in his blood. Do you know how that feels? Do you know what real power is? You should try it now. Take the power back.'

'I don't need to.'

'Think about it, Mark ... can I call you Mark? I feel like I know you now. I can see how much it hurts you to be rejected by her. It's there, written all over your face. There's so many of us out there, just like you.' He shone the light across the faces of the men standing close by, each of them wearing faces of what Mark could only describe as barely constrained glee. They were enjoying this. All of them. Enjoying the feeling of power they had.

'Only, we've found a different path,' John continued, his chest puffing out. 'A different way. Sure, I bet you could forget about her within a few days. Find some other slut to warm your bed. But you won't want that, will you? You were willing to do so much for her and she just ... she just doesn't care. That's not right.'

'It doesn't matter to me,' Mark said, but even still, he could feel the lies. The shame, if Natasha had been lying to him. He looked over at Natasha, seeing the way she was shuffling on the spot. A wave of anger coursed through him. He tried to ignore it. 'I just want her to be safe.'

'Leave me alone, Mark,' Natasha said, a glint in her eye that disappeared as the light shifted. 'Go. I don't want you.'

'She hates you, Mark,' John said, turning to one of the men nearby and nodding. 'We're always told we have to wish them well and send them on their way, but why should we? They wronged us, so why shouldn't we strike back against that. I'm giving you the chance to do that. Here and now. No one knows you're here, I'm guessing? No one will know you were too late. You can punish her for what she's done to you. Watch her suffer and become no more, for all of it.'

'No ...'

'You tried to give your life for this woman and this is how she repays you? She thinks nothing of you. You repulse her, just like Holly was repulsed by me. Even after I treated her like a fucking queen. I gave everything to her and she just ignored all of it. Well, that's not how we do things now. We show them who runs the world. Let Natasha experience the same. I'm giving you the opportunity to take something back. She tried to steal your life, now you can take hers.'

'Watch her play the final game. I'll do the rest,' John said, lowering his head and staring towards Mark. 'It'll look like suicide. No one will ever know. I'll be gone. You can live your life.'

Mark couldn't speak, watching it happen in front of him. John was still, then started nodding.

'I understand,' John said, then whispered in Natasha's ear. She flinched at the closeness of him.

'One . . . two . . .'

Mark watched her move backwards and forwards, moving her feet at John's instruction, as he pointed the phone – it was a phone, he could see that now – in her direction. She counted out her steps, moving them in increasingly bizarre ways.

'This isn't happening,' Mark said, beginning to move, as he watched it unfold. His feet finally obeyed him. He moved towards them, charging, before a flash of light exploded in front of him and he realised he was looking at the sky.

Standing over him, one of the men who had been standing with John. The one he'd nodded towards. In his hand, he could see something, dull and extended. Then, there was a glint of something which shone across his vision and then disappeared.

There was pain growing inside him as he tried to breathe. His hands were clutching his side, but he didn't know why. When he took them away, they were sticky.

Muffled shouts came from a world away. A scream. Then someone's hands on him, pulling at his shoulders.

'I'm sorry, I'm so sorry.'

He turned his head, trying to locate where the voice was coming from, but all he could see was a body on the floor. The light from a phone, shining into his face.

John, his head turned in his direction, a smile across his face.

Then the world shifted again and darkness crept in.

AFTER

Fifty-Six

She wasn't a survivor.

That's why she was there, talking to a group of teenagers. A politically driven course of meetings, which would supposedly stop what happened to her and Emily, and Joanna, and Holly, and so many others, from happening again.

She wasn't a victim.

She didn't know what she was.

It would take a while to get used to seeing her photograph in the paper. Her story of what had happened that night.

Not that she remembered much of it.

Parts of it were vivid, stark, horrifying. Other parts were blurred and malformed. She was remembering more of it day by day, but wished she wasn't.

Ignorance can be bliss.

The end was a memory that was one she actually remembered well.

She remembered the feeling of the rope around her neck. The burn of it, the weight of it.

The end had been there. Waiting for her.

She remembered Mark. The hurt and anger on his face, as she'd lied.

The feeling of the rope and tightening around the leader's throat, before she'd realised what had happened to Mark.

She had visited him while he was in hospital. The blood loss was a worry, but they always knew he'd come through it.

The fear in those other men's faces, as they had been joined by the other detective working the case. The voices soon growing in number, as arrests were made and the boys – because that was what they were – suddenly realised how serious it all was.

She remembered a young lad, a couple of years younger than her, lying bloodied and beaten on the ground.

She knew she had done that. Lashing out in a blurred haze of violence. Fighting for her life.

She hadn't seen Mark Flynn since he'd been released from hospital. She'd see him soon, she imagined, at the trial. She didn't know if she wanted to be in the same room as him. He was considered a hero by all. He had stopped the lad from killing her, after all. That's what everyone was saying.

She had a different memory of him from that night. Of him not acting quick enough.

Perhaps, one day, she thought, she would remember it all as vividly as the feeling of the rope cutting into her neck.

John Redwood. What a ridiculously normal name.

It had been in the media for months now. How an eighteen-year-old boy had managed to kill so many people without being caught. In the space of ten months, he had managed to not only set himself up a network of people willing to suggest women to kill, but also evade capture.

Pretending it was about blackmail, when it was simply a case of male violence. The forum had disappeared from where it had been. Police from a few different countries were trying to investigate, but were struggling.

All started by one young teenage boy. Countless newspaper headlines screamed the same question.

How does this happen?

Natasha knew how.

She suspected every woman in the room – in every room – knew as well. All of the victims – no, *survivors* – in their own way.

The detective's voice droned on, Natasha listened, as he explained to the young people in the room what could happen online. How no one was really safe, even if they thought they were anonymous.

She'd asked for this, but didn't know if it would actually make a difference. She had to do something and she thought someone close to the case that was now so infamous might make a difference. That's where it had all started, after all.

Online. Where the real world always feels far away.

She could feel the odd glance her way. Hear a few whispers. They would all know her face. The image of the story. The star of the show.

Maybe she should just move on.

Maybe she should ignore what was happening around her, hidden away. All these young minds being groomed into believing something that wasn't true, that they were owed something.

Maybe there was no future.

Maybe she should at least try.

*

Mark was moving more freely now, but it had taken time. After that night, it had felt as if every movement was cutting him in half. The pain had been more than he felt able to handle at first, but it was getting better.

Being stabbed at least six times will do that to you. Multiple surgeries to repair the damage. Months of physiotherapy. Counselling thrown in from his employer.

He was lauded as a hero, but he didn't feel like one. He had waited too long and paid the price.

'You sure you want to do this?'

Mark turned to DS Cavanagh, who was sitting in the driving seat and waiting for an answer. 'I think it's only right. This is the end of it, right?'

'Until the trial. Or trials, I should say.'

This was the first time he'd seen the DS outside of the hospital, but Mark knew that it was only the beginning now. 'If you hadn't been there that night ...'

'She's alive because of you,' DS Cavanagh cut in, before he had a chance to finish. 'They would have killed her if you hadn't shown up. I was just there to tidy up. And she was doing a fine job of making sure that even though you'd been taken down, that she was going to survive.'

'I'm just glad you tracked me down.'

'ANPR,' DS Cavanagh said, grinning to himself. 'Never thought I'd be putting a fellow copper's number plate in the system, but I had to do something.'

'Thank you all the same.'

DS Cavanagh waved it away, like it wasn't needed or warranted, and maybe it wasn't.

'Come on, it's time.'

Mark followed him up the path to the Burns's house. It had been a couple of weeks since that night. Since the family had been told who was behind the death of their daughter and sister.

And niece.

Big ol' Uncle Rich had been released from custody, when it was finally accepted that Mark had been right all along.

His life hadn't been over.

Five men had been in the park that night. Four had been arrested, including John Redwood. Each one had broken down in interview. Given details of the online forum, where plans had been made. They swore up and down that they weren't there to hurt anyone, much less kill, but Cavanagh had broken them eventually.

The DS had told him this on one of his daily visits to the hospital. Investigations around the other deaths in Leeds and Newcastle were ongoing. Mark guessed that John Redwood may not have been present for those who died there, but that didn't make him any less responsible. He started this. The Game was his creation.

DS Cavanagh knocked on Burns's door. It swung open, a uniformed officer standing at the entrance. They followed them through to the living room, Mark standing back and waiting.

The Burns family.

Mark could see Uncle Rich, heading the pack, head and shoulders above everyone else there. He was standing at the mantelpiece, the same position he'd been in when Mark had first arrived at the house a couple of months earlier. Julie Burns was on the sofa next to him, looking even older than when he'd seen her last. Stephanie next to her, arm around her mother, still holding her up.

Charlie, the youngest member of the family, wasn't to be seen.

Julie spotted Mark first, pushing past Rich to get to him.

He hadn't seen her since that night at the police station, but news of what had happened must have reached her. Another who thought him heroic. He accepted her gratitude, the rubs to his arm. The thanks and promises to do anything he needed. Rich then did the same. He imagined his offers of 'help any time you need it. You need anything, you tell me,' were probably more likely to happen than Julie's. Less legal, also.

And they wouldn't be remembered for very long, after what was about to happen.

Mark continued to wait then, as planned, with DS Cavanagh talking things over with the family, he slipped upstairs. He could hear the uniform behind him.

Charlie Burns was in his bedroom, the same young lad with the weight of the world on his shoulders. He looked a little paler, dark rings under his eyes.

'Charlie, how have you been?' Mark said. 'Getting on with things okay?'

'Yeah, suppose,' Charlie replied, looking behind him quickly, then at the floor. 'Bit hard with all this going on, like.'

'I bet,' Mark said, crouching down a little to Charlie's level. 'Listen, I wanted to talk to you about something. Think it's important we have a little chat.'

'What about?'

'I think you know.'

Charlie shook his head slowly. 'Haven't got the first idea.'

'I know what you did.' Mark waited for some kind of reaction, but Charlie was a blank slate. 'We don't know who suggested Emily to him. Who told him to target her, but I know. They've managed to work them all out, except for her.'

'I didn't do nothing ...'

'Stop, Charlie,' Mark said, placing a hand on his shoulder. He gripped a little tighter, ignoring the shooting pain up his side. 'It was you. I don't know why, or what you thought was going to happen, but I know it was you. That letter that I found in the attic – you wrote it to put the blame on Stephanie. We found all the people in that park that night, except for one. Then, I remembered the logo I saw on the back of a jacket. The band I've not heard of or seen before. CCTV tracks everyone in this city, without them even realising. You were there, but managed to get away.'

'I don't know what you're talking about ...'

'Yes, you do. You hated your sister and wanted to punish her. It was all you. I don't know why and maybe you'll never tell us, but want to know my guess? Jealousy. That's it. I remember everything you said to me, the last time I was stood in this room. I remember you talking about The Game. I remember the way you talked about your sister. The way you kept trying to say your uncle had something to hide. John told me that the victims were all left in places he was asked to leave them. When she fought back, you needed a cover story. Now, I don't like coincidences, but there was one here. Your uncle's yard wasn't that far away. You helped take her there because John needed your help when it all went wrong. You knew your uncle would be the one who would go down for her murder.'

'You don't know anything ...'

'You're wrong about that,' Mark said, his face now only a few centimetres from the young lad's. 'You probably think we'll never find any evidence on that computer, but you'll be wrong about that too. I promise. Your family are going to know what you've done and you'll have to live with that forever. Charlie Burns, this officer has some things to say to you now.'

Mark stood aside and allowed the uniform to take over. Watched Charlie's young face begin to comprehend what was happening.

There was a moment of struggle, as Charlie began to shout and plead for his mum. Tried to shout his innocence, but it was too late.

His life as he knew it was over.

'Everything okay, Mark,' DS Cavanagh said, joining him upstairs, once Charlie had been taken away. 'Did he say anything?'

'Nothing we weren't expecting.'

'Hopefully we have enough. At least to prove he was there that night. And everything before that. I'm betting you're right about this as well, though. You haven't been wrong yet.'

Mark nodded, then allowed himself to be led away. Now, it was over. There would be more to come, but he felt as if it were really over finally. That all the pieces had been discovered and now someone else could stand back and work out what the full picture was.

Every now and again, he remembered that brief moment of anger back in the park. That still kept him awake at night. The idea that he could have ended up just like all those other men and boys out there. All those who had been prepared to watch someone they professed to care for be killed by John. To revel in their deaths, as if they deserved it.

It didn't matter that he had been able to ignore it. To know that John was wrong. To know that it wasn't the truth. That Natasha didn't mean anything she said.

For the briefest of moments, Mark had been no better than them.

The nervous feeling continued to build, trying to work out what he would say if John's solicitor asked him about his thoughts that night.

What lies he would tell.

That's all he had left.

Lies to allow him to sleep at night.

Acknowledgements

This book is in your hands thanks to the work and support of many, many people. My deepest appreciation to the following ...

Steve Cavanagh, Craig Robertson and David Jackson, for all the friendship and support. Bethan Jones, my editor, who was instrumental to getting this novel right – no easy task! Thanks for the brilliant notes and believing in the idea. Also Jess Barratt, who is still the most amazing publicist. A huge thank you to the whole team at Simon & Schuster, who stuck with me for five books and turned me into a full-time writer back in 2014. You made a dream come true. Although this is the last book we'll work on together, I will forever appreciate what you've done for me and will miss you all. For Jo Dickinson, who worked on this book all too briefly, but greatly influenced it. To Agent Phil Patterson, who continues to be an absolute rock. For all the readers, who continue to come back to read what's happening in Scouseland. Thank you so much. To Liverpool F.C. for breaking that thirty year duck. It was our year. Finally to Mike Hale, Jemma Hale, Daniel Veste, Laura Veste, for being more than just family. Also, the rest of the Veste, Woodland, Hale, Kirkham, Brisk and Smith clan.

And the best for last, as always, Emma, Abigail and Megan. My whole life.

DON'T MISS THE OTHER CHILLING, COMPULSIVE NOVELS FROM ACCLAIMED THRILLER AUTHOR LUCA VESTE

THE MURPHY AND ROSSI SERIES

'Luca Veste's Murphy and Rossi series hits the very pinnacle of modern crime fiction. Totally compelling' **Steve Cavanagh**

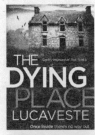

'This is a twisty, psychological crime debut in a gritty setting: a new favourite for police procedural lovers' **Clare Mackintosh**

STANDALONES

'Tense, chilling and HUGELY scary' **Mark Billingham**

SIMON &
SCHUSTER